Praise for *A New Leash on Love*

"Sexy and fun… Wounded souls of all shapes and sizes, human and animal alike, tug at the heartstrings and evoke the right blend of tears as well as laughter."

—*RT Book Reviews* Top Pick, 4.5 Stars

"Auspicious…a warm, cuddly tale full of dogs, cats, kids, and genuinely likable adults. This heartstring-tugger is certain to win fans."

—*Publishers Weekly* Starred Review

"The head might lead you in one direction, but what's in the heart will always win in the end… I really enjoyed this warm, wonderful story."

—*Romance Junkies*

"Pet lovers will adore all the animals introduced in Burns's sweet romance."

—*Booklist Reviews*

"A ragtag cast of supporting characters, human and otherwise, shines… Which is sweeter: reading to find out if heated disagreements will turn to hot romance, or a shelter full of animals all waiting for their forever homes? It's a toss-up, but both are pretty darn sweet."

—*Foreword Reviews*, 5 Stars

Also by Debbie Burns

RESCUE ME
A New Leash on Love
Sit, Stay, Love

MY FOREVER HOME

❤ A RESCUE ME NOVEL ❤

DEBBIE BURNS

sourcebooks
casablanca

Published by Sourcebooks Casablanca, an imprint of Sourcebooks, Inc.
P.O. Box 4410, Naperville, Illinois 60567-4410
(630) 961-3900
Fax: (630) 961-2168
sourcebooks.com

Printed and bound in Canada.
MBP 10 9 8 7 6 5 4 3 2 1

For Cathy,

a dog lover and Cards fan
who left St. Louis but kept it close at heart.

Chapter 1

AFTER SPENDING FOURTEEN MONTHS IN EUROPE, TESS Grasso had racked up a healthy list of once-in-a-lifetime experiences. Especially for a twenty-six-year-old who'd never been out of her home state before then. Tess had been back in her hometown of St. Louis for a month, and even though she was no longer seeing famous works of architecture or artwork or meeting people from all corners of the planet every day, the list was still growing.

For instance, before this morning, she'd never been crammed into the confining back seat of a 1969 Mustang alongside a 103-pound Saint Bernard. An oversize, invasive, drooly Saint Bernard.

Not that Tess minded. She'd been a die-hard dog lover for as long as she could remember. She wasn't much for classic cars or confining back seats, but snuggling up alongside Fannie, the senior-aged Saint Bernard who belonged to the High Grove Animal Shelter until she was adopted, was almost fun. And since Tess had yet to renew her driver's license after coming home, it was either catch a ride with a friend or ride her old Schwinn ten-speed.

And since today was Halloween and the last half of Tess's day was cram-packed, it was either miss seeing the High Grove Animal Shelter's Halloween Pet-A-Palooza or catch a ride. She'd been hearing about the event nonstop for the last week and was excited to experience it firsthand.

Ever since she'd returned home, Tess had been volunteering at the shelter's only off-site location, an old
mansion where thirty-eight dogs that had been part of
an illegal fighting ring were being rehabilitated so that
they could come to the shelter to be adopted out. Even
though Tess was trying to get her own career off the
ground, she dedicated a part of every day to working
with the sweet-natured dogs who were starting to shine
after being given a second chance at life.

Earlier this morning, Fannie, her back-seat companion, had been brought from the shelter to the private
estate for what was being called phase two of the former
fighting dogs' resocialization. After several weeks of
work, many of the rehab dogs were being rewarded with
greater degrees of canine socialization. The dogs Fannie
had been introduced to this morning had already com-
pleted a few successful visits with Orzo, the shelter's
laid-back corgi, who was also up for adoption.

Due to Fannie's massive size, she was considered a
next-level dog. As with Orzo, nothing seemed to faze
Fannie, and she got along great with other dogs. But
dogs that had been mistreated the way those at the estate
had been were likely to be especially uneasy around
dogs Fannie's size, and the rehab team was in the process of rebuilding their trust in other canines.

As suspected, Fannie had done great with the project
dogs this morning. And nearly all the dogs who'd been
introduced to her had also done fabulously.

As they neared the shelter, Fannie leaned further into
Tess with every turn. Tess's leg was going a touch numb
under the dog's weight, so she did her best to wiggle
closer to the door. Doing so drew Fannie's attention

away from the strip of front windshield visible between the front bucket seats and toward Tess. She gave Tess's long, wavy brown hair a determined sniff and left behind a rather unpleasant string of drool.

Tess lifted the lock of slimed hair so the drool wouldn't soak into her jacket. "Any napkins up there by chance, Kelsey?" Tess raised her voice over the loud purr of the Mustang's engine.

In the Mustang's front passenger seat was Kelsey, the shelter's lead adoption coordinator. She was leading the rehab effort at the private estate, along with the driver, Tess's longtime friend Kurt. He was a former military dog handler and the lead dog trainer at the estate. Tess thought it was just about perfect how Kurt and Kelsey had gotten together while working at the remote estate with the dogs.

At Tess's request, Kelsey fished through Kurt's glove box. "Aha." Craning to reach around the deep bucket seat, Kelsey passed a few napkins Tess's way. "Oh, Tess, there's more space on Fannie's other side than on yours. Can you nudge her over?"

Tess took the napkin and squeezed her damp lock of hair dry. Whenever she worked around dogs, she made a habit of showering at night instead of in the morning. Tonight would be no exception. "I tried, but she only leans harder. It's a good thing I'm a sucker for a cuddly Saint Bernard."

Three months ago, Fannie had been found tied to a post in front of the shelter without so much as a note. This was baffling to Tess. Fannie's bad habits were minimal to none. She was potty-trained, dog friendly, nondestructive, and gentle. And judging by the condition of her coat, her weight, and her trusting temperament, she'd been well cared for. If she hadn't already been a senior dog, she'd have been adopted several times over. Tess's fingers were crossed that Fannie would go to a great home.

As they neared the shelter, Kurt had to park nearly two blocks away. The street was lined with cars on both sides, and the parking lot had been roped off hours ago for the afternoon activities.

The Halloween Pet-A-Palooza was the shelter's second biggest event of the year. Previous adopters were encouraged to return with their pets for a variety of games and a pet costume contest that was becoming more elaborate every year. Pet-A-Palooza was also an adoption event, and Tess had heard that the popular festival often resulted in one of the biggest adoption times of the year, the first typically being the week before Christmas, and the other the week after the city's annual spring parade day.

Once they were parked, Tess clambered out of the back seat and out the passenger side door. If the classic Mustang wasn't her friend's pride and joy, Tess would have commented that cars had come a long way in terms of everyday conveniences, like providing a way to get in and out with ease.

Fannie surprised them all with her agile hop over the folded-forward front seat. Free of the confines of the car, she gave a whole-body shake and wagged her bushy tail.

"Oh, hang on," Kelsey said. "Let's get Fannie's costume on here." From a purse that was big enough to double as an overnight bag, Kelsey pulled out a Saint Bernard–sized whiskey barrel attached to a thick leather collar.

Fannie didn't seem to mind it being buckled around her neck.

"Simple, but perfect, don't you think?" Kelsey asked. "It was in our costume collection. I grabbed it this morning. She's our only Saint Bernard right now, so she had clear dibs."

"Good thinking." Tess rubbed Fannie atop her forehead. "I'd say she looks ready to help Swiss monks search for stranded travelers along the Great Saint Bernard Pass."

Kurt chuckled. "Tess, the dog trivia you've amassed over the years never fails to amaze me."

Tess squinched her nose. "Just remember you want me at your table if the shelter ever hosts a dog-themed trivia night."

Even from where they'd parked, Tess could hear the beat of "I Want Candy" as it pulsed through the beautiful but brisk fall air.

"I'm so glad you guys get to see how cool this is," Kelsey said as they headed toward the shelter. "It's my favorite event of the year, and the only one where I can walk a dog and win a cupcake at the same time."

Kurt shot her a skeptical look. "Are you telling me there's a cakewalk here for dogs?"

"Yep. And don't knock it till you see it. It's the Pupcake Walk. Every year, I play with one of the dogs till I win. There are killer cupcakes for adults and specialty pupcakes for the dogs. And that's not all. There's a dog-and-owner agility course that's made its fair share of appearances on YouTube and several activities just for the dogs, like dog-bobbing for miniature wienies, a sandbox skeleton yard, and the ever-popular game-scented straw maze."

"By game, do you mean, like, pheasant and duck?" Tess asked.

Kelsey nodded. "It's amazing what you can find at hunting goods stores. And you'll see how crazy the dogs go in the maze. It's not funny how much scent marking those straw bales get before the day is over."

Tess laughed. "You guys think of it all."

"It's because we've got a good group, and we've been able to perfect it over the years."

"And you're sure it's okay that I take some of the dogs through the activities?"

"Oh, no question." Kelsey pulled her in for a hug as they neared the shelter, reminding Tess just how much taller her new friend was. Tess had topped out just below a petite-framed five four. Kelsey, an earthy blond, was a good five inches taller. "Just because you're helping at an off-site location doesn't mean you aren't a shelter volunteer."

"And in case she didn't tell you, Kelsey's been singing your praises around here," Kurt added. "We couldn't train at the pace we've been keeping without the skilled help you give every day."

Tess let the compliment roll over her, remembering that the best thing to do with a compliment was to accept it graciously. Whether it was any one person's fault or a random sampling of genetics, she'd reached adulthood feeling a touch inadequate in just about every way except for her work with dogs.

Thanks to those transformative months in Europe, Tess had found peace and satisfaction with herself she hadn't known she'd been missing. And she'd come home ready to make a success of the healthy-pet canine-consulting business she was hoping to get off the ground.

Tess switched the leash into her other hand as the

shelter came into view behind the surrounding trees that were in full fall color. Fannie let out a woof and wagged her tail.

The unassuming redbrick building was decorated with an array of pumpkins, life-size dog and cat scarecrows, straw bales, and spiderwebs. The front parking lot was already a buzz of activity, even though the event didn't officially start for another twenty minutes.

In addition to the activity stations, a food booth sold snacks for both people and pets, a silent auction, and a booth where one of the shelter volunteers would be drawing caricature sketches.

The shelter was small enough that it only employed a handful of people, and Tess knew each of them. The parking lot was filled with dozens of unfamiliar faces that she figured were a combination of volunteers, past adopters, and the public.

Many of the leashed dogs in the parking lot were in costume. Tess spotted a black Lab who'd had an impressively anatomically correct dog skeleton painted onto his coat, a wiener dog in a banana suit, a three-headed dog whose two papier-mâché heads matched its real one, and a Lhasa apso dressed as an Ewok. Tess's favorite was a mixed-breed white dog that had been painted so realistically with zebra stripes that she had to do a double take.

With an uncharacteristic burst of energy, Fannie leaped forward, dragging Tess along behind her. It took rebalancing her weight in the opposite direction from Fannie's pull and locking her feet on the ground for Tess to keep Fannie from diving into the throngs of the crowd.

Kurt chuckled. "Want a hand? I wouldn't be surprised if she outweighs you."

"No thanks. I've got this." Tess pulled a treat from her jeans pocket and asked the excited dog to sit at attention. "I do, however, know which dog I'd like to start with." Fannie gobbled up the treat, leaving a moist spot on Tess's palm. "So, big girl, what do you say we get some of that energy out in the agility course first?"

"I think that's a smart idea," Kelsey agreed. "It's set up around back, along with the game-scented straw maze. That should tucker her out. You too, by the way. That agility course is a cardio burst for people too."

As if in understanding, Fannie tugged Tess onward. "Grab a dog, guys, and we'll see who's buying lunch later," Tess called over her shoulder. "And no, I didn't forget one of you is a former marine."

Then she let Fannie lead her away, but not before hearing a duet of chuckles and agreement following her.

———

The penetrating flash from the photographer's camera made Mason wince. He didn't need to count back the days since the accident to know the effects of the concussion were lingering.

"A few more will do it." The photographer, a middle-aged guy who'd recognized Mason in the crowd and asked for a few quick shots, was barely audible over the din from the crowd gathered at Ballpark Village in downtown St. Louis for the city's biggest late-into-the-night Halloween party.

The leopard-bikini-clad chick at Mason's side, the one whose name he hadn't paid any attention to, moved closer to him, implying a connection they didn't share. This season, Mason's strongest yet, had left it all but impossible for him to go anywhere without being asked to pose for a picture. He hadn't minded at first. And he didn't mind it now, but in the days since the accident, he was becoming more conscious of the image each snapshot portrayed.

This chick had approached him after he'd left Thomas for a trip to the bathroom. She'd been coming on to him, holding nothing back, when the photographer spotted him. Mason's left arm was bound in a sling, so she was drawn in close at his right side. He closed his hand loosely atop her shoulder, keeping his body straight and not leaning in toward her, advice he'd been given by his publicist to help ward off the party-guy image a dozen or so wild nights this last year had created.

She had her hand pressed flat against his stomach, her pinkie resting above the rim of the wool kilt that was currently itching the hell out of him. She was clad only in the leopard-spotted faux-fur bikini—long tail, pointy ears, and all—and had the body to pull it off.

Only Mason wasn't interested, however clear her signals were.

It was Halloween night and he was here, working the crowd and signing autographs and locking his smile in place, for one reason only. He'd shown up tonight to keep a promise to a buddy even though it conflicted with a stronger promise he'd made himself.

The season was over, and winter was coming. Mason was craving the quiet the way he craved water after a strenuous workout. The insanity that the most successful season of his career had brought would taper down. It had been a marathon year, and he was ready for the finish line.

The fame he'd acquired still felt oddly surreal, sort of like the Ford Escape he'd been in had when it had careened across the highway and tumbled into an embankment. Maybe there were some things you were never ready for. Not the things that changed your life in ways you'd never seen coming or even the ones your father warned you about.

The photographer snapped another few shots, then Mason stepped back, reclaiming an inadequate bubble of space around him. Leopard Girl's smile faltered. "Oh, come on. I can't let a man who looks this good in a kilt out of my arms without a fight. How about I buy you a drink and we find a spot in the corner to enjoy it?"

Mason read what she was saying with her eyes as clearly as he heard what she was saying with her lips. A year ago, he'd have brought her back to his place and let her rock his world. Hell, who was he kidding? A month or two ago even.

"I appreciate the offer. Maybe another time."

"You sure about that? I bet I could come up with something you'd like just fine. I'm full of ideas."

Mason didn't doubt she was. He'd met his share of women with agendas like hers. Said yes to enough of them too.

He thanked her again, but let the finality seep into his tone. The din of the crowd was starting to hurt his head, just as the bright lights were. He'd had enough tonight. The world—lights, sounds, commotion—was still stark, harsh when he overdid it.

Twenty-six nights ago, he'd lain in the ER, disoriented from a concussion and trying to lie still for a CT scan of his left shoulder and collarbone. He'd sworn then and there he was done with the sporadic partying and racy nightlife that had landed him in the back seat of that Ford Escape.

He scanned the crowds, searching for Thomas. When Mason had left for the bathroom, they'd been talking to a small group of die-hard Red Birds fans. Now, Mason found his buddy and teammate encircled by a small crowd of women who seemed more excited by Thomas's Conan the Barbarian costume—supposedly worn by Arnold Schwarzenegger—than his career stats.

Compared to Thomas's dressed-up loincloth, the green-and-black tartan kilt and black silk vest Mason had been cajoled into wearing weren't so bad. Mason didn't know where his buddy had gotten them, but Thomas had acquired his share of authentic outfits. He even had an aboriginal headdress that took up a full shelf in one closet and a stovepipe hat supposedly worn by a member of Lincoln's Cabinet.

Mason came up behind Thomas, tapped his shoulder, and offered the very real excuse of a headache as his reason for taking off early. Thomas was disappointed but didn't press.

All it took was heading outside into the night and feeling the cool air wash over him for Mason's release to be palpable. He loved the pulse of the city, loved living in his converted warehouse loft so close to the stadium, but lately he'd felt an unmistakable stirring in his chest to head home.

When he'd left the serene but stiflingly quiet rolling farmland near Dubuque, Iowa, for college, he'd never imagined longing for the solitude he'd lost in leaving it. Back then, he'd craved city living, replete with all the culture and chaos that came with it nearly as much as he'd wanted to be a pro ballplayer. He'd been fortunate to get both wishes, though St. Louis was a smaller city than he'd imagined settling in when he'd left for college.

Now, a little over ten years later, he was struck with a wave of nostalgia for the Halloween night he was missing back home. A quieter, simpler Halloween full of people who thought they knew everything there was to know about you—and who were largely right.

A glance at the out-of-character Movado watch he'd forgotten to take off showed it was ten thirty. The only Halloween tradition he'd experienced until he was eighteen would be winding down. His extended family and a handful of friends always made for his parents' farm on Halloween night, showing up an hour or so before dark. If the weather was good, as it was here, there'd be a roaring bonfire outside, and at the side of the yard nearest the house, there'd be a few folding tables covered with his mom's worn linens. They'd be loaded with all the Halloween regulars, like his aunt's jack-o'-lantern stuffed peppers, his cousin's zombie meat loaf, his mom's pumpkin-turkey chili, and his dad's home-crafted hard cider from apples harvested on their farm.

Dinner would be long finished, and the assortment of homemade pies would be picked over. His uncle Ron would be dozing in his reclining folding chair after having enjoyed one too many hard ciders. His mom and aunts would be wrapping up leftovers while the younger kids and grandkids played the inevitable game of chase after finishing the skeleton hunt his dad set up year after year in the woods beyond the east field.

As Mason walked to his loft, it occurred to him that

nothing was keeping him here. He could head home for a few weeks. The season was over. He contemplated the logistics—the physical therapy appointments he'd have to move, the follow-up with his surgeon regarding the shattered collarbone that would hopefully be well healed before spring training rolled around—as he walked away from the stadium and through empty streets toward his place.

Three blocks from his building, he caught a glimpse of movement down a narrow side street. Something was there, just out of reach of the streetlights, watching him in the darkness. He stopped, his muscles tensing automatically as he scanned the cave-like hole created by the century-old brick warehouses on either side.

He was wearing a kilt and hadn't tucked anything except a single credit card into the leather sporran around his waist. And even had he not been dressed as he was, Halloween night wasn't the best time to investigate darkened alleys. But Mason had high hopes for what lingered in the darkness just out of eyesight. He strode into the dark toward it, his night vision kicking in as he left the glow of the streetlights.

The moon wasn't yet out, and the city lights always dimmed the stars. He stopped a hundred feet in, not wanting to scare off the interloper he felt ahead of him in the darkness.

Odds were it was a homeless person setting up camp for the night. Or tonight, Halloween night, it could also be a couple pranksters having mostly innocent fun.

It wasn't though. Mason finally spotted the four long, white legs and the white fur under the dog's chin in the darkness. The animal was fifty feet away, facing him.

The rest of the dog's body, the parts covered with black fur, was invisible.

Mason sank onto his heels, doing his best to ignore the raging itch from the wool kilt as it pressed against his legs, and whistled low and soft. *Maybe tonight's the night.*

The dog made a sound that Mason guessed was half yawn, half whine, but didn't move.

"I didn't bring you anything, boy, but if you'd just let go of that stubborn streak and follow me home, I'd cook you up something great."

To Mason's surprise, the dog burst into a trot straight toward him. Mason waited, holding his breath. The animal stopped as abruptly as he'd started, leaving a mere fifteen feet between them. This close, Mason could make out the white patches just above the dog's eyes in the thick, black fur of his face, giving him an intelligent, inquisitive look.

"It's not the safest of nights to be a stray dog in the city anyway," he added into the silence. "What do say you hang up your hat and call it a day?"

The dog's tail, black with a white tip, stuck out behind his body, neither relaxed nor stiff. He gave it a single flick in answer, then turned abruptly and trotted down the alley into the darkness.

Mason stayed in place, watching the spectacular animal retreat until the last visible patch of white, the tip of his tail, disappeared into the night.

"I get it, John Ronald, I get it. You don't answer to anyone. But if you ever change your mind, you're definitely the dog for me."

Chapter 2

BEFORE MOUNTING HER OLD SCHWINN VARSITY ROAD bike the following Monday afternoon, Tess glanced at her watch. She was forty-five minutes behind schedule. She'd been with Kurt and Kelsey at her volunteer job all morning and had lost track of time. The hours she spent working with the dynamic group of rehab dogs at the private estate were often the best hours of Tess's week.

Since she was also determined to get her healthy-pet consulting business off the ground, she'd made a personal commitment to spend the second half of every day focused on it. And while she wouldn't trade the forty-five minutes she'd overspent with the dogs for being on schedule now, Tess needed to get moving.

She had a meeting this afternoon with the owner of Pouches and Pooches, a popular and expanding local chain of high-end stores that catered to savvy pet owners by selling upscale pet products, scarves, and purses. Not only had the owner been open to meeting with Tess when she'd spoken on the phone with him last week, but he'd sounded excited about the services she hoped to offer.

A win today would give Tess a much-needed boost of confidence in her business model. From sales calls to drop-in visits at dozens of area stores, she hadn't received the best of receptions. And Tess's only paying client to date had resulted in a loss after she'd factored in her expenses.

In hopes of making up for lost time, Tess pedaled hard in between stoplights and having to yield to traffic. One of these days, she needed to force herself to get to the DMV to renew her expired license. She'd not driven since before she left for Europe. Even though biking and taking public transportation were tedious at times, she experienced tiny waves of panic whenever she gave serious consideration to getting behind the wheel of a car. She'd never been in a car accident, so she wasn't entirely sure why the thought of driving had become intimidating during her months away, even if she'd never been crazy about it.

She suspected her hesitation had something to do with not fully getting over her dad forcing her to learn to drive using a stick, coupled with coaxing her into turning down a busy street at rush hour her second time behind the wheel. She still remembered the angry looks on some of the other drivers' faces as she stalled the car time and again.

Tess's dad was a good-hearted man but also a very black and white one. He was the kind of father who'd scoffed at training wheels and tossed her into the pool before she was a confident swimmer. Maybe this was why Tess had chosen to stay with her grandma since she'd gotten back from Europe a month ago. Her parents had worked so much when she was growing up that her grandparents had all but raised her. Tess's other siblings, one brother and one sister, were twelve and thirteen years older than her and had left home when she was little.

Another reason Tess hadn't moved in with her parents after Europe was that, a year after Tess's high school graduation, they had moved away from the Hill, the Italian American St. Louis neighborhood that was as much a tourist attraction as it was a hub for the wealth of independently owned Italian restaurants packed within its single square-mile. The Hill was where Tess had lived all her life until she'd left for college. Tess's parents now lived, as Nonna put it, a "difficult" twenty-minute drive away in South County.

At her parents' new house, Tess had a bedroom that she'd never spent enough time in for it to feel like hers. Still, it was replete with a newer, more comfortable bed than the worn-out spring mattress at Nonna's, as well as a full-size closet that could be just for her.

But Tess suspected that even if her father had been a more nurturing man, she'd still live with Nonna. If she added up all the weekends and holidays and summers she'd slept over at Nonna's, it was no wonder the thousand-square-foot, century-old house felt like the natural place to be. Her grandfather not being around anymore was still taking some getting used to though. He was the reason she'd come home as abruptly as she did.

Just a month ago, back in early October, Tess had been harvesting grapes in exchange for room and board on a small farm in Switzerland. She'd had a dwindling stash of euros and a slew of new memories from a month spent on the rural farm overlooking Lake Geneva and the Alps in the distance.

Before she'd gotten the call about Nonno's heart attack, she'd been making plans to backpack into Belgium before the last of her money ran out. A friend, a Spanish girl she'd traveled with earlier in the year, had promised that a visit to one of the most picturesque towns in the world, Bruges, Belgium, would be worth the investment. One of Europe's best-preserved medieval towns, Bruges was one of the most remarkable places to take in Christmastime splendor.

As she cycled into the outskirts of the Hill, Tess remembered back to a few hours before she got the news about her grandpa. Nonno had been in critical condition but was awake and alert. It was time to get home, her dad had said. After draining the last of the money in her bank account to move up her plane ticket home, Tess packed her belongings and flew out of Geneva International Airport on the first open flight. Nonno died when she was somewhere over the Atlantic.

Her dad met her at the airport in St. Louis, smelling of cigarette smoke and looking thinner and older than her fourteen months away warranted.

"He was glad you were coming home," her dad had said.

Now that Tess was home to stay, she was determined to make a success of the business she'd dropped out of vet school for two years ago. Tess didn't need to become a skilled surgeon to help animals the way she wanted to. Holistic animal therapy was an emerging and exciting field. From therapeutic massage to essential oils to natural foods and products, Tess had become a believer in natural healing for pets. Not finishing vet school didn't make her a failure.

If only her track record for not sticking with things wasn't so long. Or something her big, loud, and vivacious extended family had a knack of reminding her about. Like the fact that she'd quit ballet in preschool or gymnastics in kindergarten. Soccer was a second-grade failure. Scouting, a fourth-grade one. She'd dropped out of yearbook in the tenth grade. She ended it with her first serious—too serious—boyfriend in eleventh grade and her second one in her senior year of high school. She'd left the Catholic church while an undergrad. Tess was pretty sure grumblings over that one had been heard in Argentina, even though she'd promised to return when women could talk openly in the church about birth control. Most recently, Tess had walked out of vet school in her second year of grad school.

That had been the breaking point. Shortly after that, she'd quit the biggest, most important thing of all—her family—and took off for Europe.

Sure, the last time was different. She'd applied for and been accepted into an internship on a sustainable farm in Tuscany. But just because she'd found an enticing reason to leave didn't mean her family hadn't been the driving force behind why she'd so desperately wanted to get away. And also a giant part of the reason why, when the internship was over, she'd applied for a long-term-stay visa and chosen to backpack throughout Europe, drawing out her dwindling savings the best she could.

Narrowly missing the overturned trash can as she pedaled into Nonna's driveway, Tess reminded herself that what she was doing now was different from all those other activities.

She was good with dogs. Dog training was the one thing she'd been introduced to as a kid that had stuck with her. And she'd been more than good at it. Her mentor, Rob Bornello, had told her so often enough.

Tess had been ten when she'd been allowed to shadow him for a day—several years younger than Rob was comfortable taking on, but he'd made an exception when he'd heard how dog crazy she was. According to her mom, Tess's first word after *mum* had been *daw* for dog, and her first animal sound had been *ruff*.

Over several years of shadowing Rob whenever she could and trying out what she'd learned on her extended family's pets, Tess had become a skilled trainer. She'd learned how to read most dogs simply by studying them. It was a language that was hard to put into words, but she picked up on their movements, their body stance, the energy in their eyes and in their bodies, the position of their tails, and the way they were holding their heads and ears. It all melted together into a dynamic picture that she could read, and she was usually good at communicating back.

The suitcase Tess took on the business calls she'd been making the last couple of weeks had a binder full of her training success stories: dogs who'd been hardcore counter surfers and dogs who'd all but refused to be housebroken until Tess had figured out how to reach them. These sorts of training behaviors tended to be relatively easy successes for her.

Figuring out why dogs were scratching off the hair behind their ears, why they didn't sleep comfortably through the night, or why they were biting incessantly at their feet were harder questions to answer but didn't always require the costly services associated with vet visits. And deciphering these sorts of problems had become Tess's passion.

Remembering a few of the amazing dogs she'd worked with over the years helped Tess's doubts about her business model slip away. She parked her bike and hung up her helmet, ready to head back out soon, catch the bus, and make a success of her biggest business opportunity to date.

—◦◦◦—

Two and a half hours later, Tess stepped out of the in-renovation redbrick warehouse a couple blocks from the Red Birds' stadium in downtown St. Louis and tugged her jacket closed. The thick, dark blanket of clouds overhead was growing more ominous by the minute. She had several blocks of walking to reach the bus stop with the most direct route back to the Hill. She was thoroughly exhausted and hoped the rain would hold off a bit longer.

There was no hurrying either. Not when she was lugging her loaded-down spinner suitcase. She'd also brought along her old, heavy laptop and was carrying it in her backpack. With any luck, she'd make it on the bus before the rain started falling.

To Tess's disappointment, her meeting with the owner of Pouches and Pooches had been nothing less than chaotic and full of interruptions. They'd met in what was to be the company's newest location in downtown St. Louis, just blocks from Ballpark Village and in view of St. Louis's best-known landmark, the Arch. What was sure to soon be a trendy and popular shop in a bustling downtown area was still a chaotic fifteen-hundred-foot construction zone. The owner's attention had been divided between Tess's presentation and nonstop flooring and wiring questions by the construction crew.

She made it through her still-being-fine-tuned spiel and was attempting to show him some of her products and demonstrate their effectiveness with real-life success stories when he'd held up a hand, stopping her. He was sold. He'd recommend her services to the customers on his mailing list. And he had twelve thousand customers on it.

She'd been ecstatic before finding out that he wanted a thirty-five percent cut of the gross income from any business she earned from his referrals. Considering Tess had planned to only earn about that much on gross income herself, this seemed all but impossible.

Tess was debating how to counter his offer and wishing she had more business savvy when a bigger emergency called him to one of his other stores. He gave her his card and told her to contact him once she'd had time to think about it. She'd headed out feeling more than a touch disappointed.

A familiar wave of insecurity rocked her as she headed toward the bus stop. She'd visited almost every independent pet store in St. Louis and several veterinarians too. Why was the concept of truly healthy dogs and cats such a hard sell?

Noticing that the sidewalk ahead was torn up in several places and that she was about to be forced onto the street, she hoisted her suitcase off the ground. It felt fifty pounds heavier than it had at the beginning of the afternoon. The fat, cold raindrops that began to pelt down from the dark-gray clouds didn't help it feel any lighter.

As raindrops dampened her clothes, Tess became uncharacteristically disheartened. Back when she'd left vet school two years ago, she'd had a vision. Maybe getting her idea off the ground would be easier if she'd taken business classes while getting her undergrad degree. Only back then, she'd been dead set on becoming a vet and figured the business end of it would come later.

As Tess neared Market Street and her bus stop, she saw she'd almost reached the end of the sidewalk construction. The muscles in her arm and shoulder were exhausted from carrying her heavy suitcase, and walking on the edge of the city street wasn't the safest of actions. Just as she'd reached the spot where the sidewalk was no longer blocked off, a truck passed by, splashing a wave of old, filthy water onto her leather boots and cotton leggings. And with the rain picking up, she was starting to full-body shiver. She couldn't reach the shelter of the bus stop quickly enough. Or her grandma's small, cozy home where, after a hot shower, she'd slip into comfy clothes and sip a mug of hot tea.

Three people were crowded under the small bus-stop shelter, two seated and one standing. The standing one, a lanky man in a dark suit, stepped over to make room under the cover. He gave her drenched clothes a sympathetic glance before becoming absorbed in his phone again.

Tess thanked him and attempted to tuck both her body and her suitcase under the thin slip of remaining roof and out of the rain. Her laptop was dry, at least. Not only was it in a water-resistant case, but her long-used backpack still had waterproofing sealer on it.

The other two people crowded in the small space made no acknowledgment of her arrival. A woman took up most of the space on the bench, or at least her bags did. On the fraction of the bench that was left was an older man with a newspaper open on his lap. Rather than reading it, he was staring across the five-lane street and mumbling in disappointment about the Red Birds,

St. Louis's much-loved major league baseball team, and their disappointing end to what had apparently been their best season in nearly a decade. Not that Tess had any idea. To her baseball-crazy family's disapproval, she'd mostly stopped following the sport in college, then entirely when she'd left for Europe.

The intensity of the man's stare had Tess following his gaze. On the opposite side of the street was Citygarden, the small but picturesque three-acre fountain and sculpture park that opened to a view of the old courthouse and the Arch. In the wind and rain, the popular park was all but deserted this afternoon. The only person visible, not far from the giant sculpture of Pinocchio, was a guy with an arm sling who was balling up an empty leash and kicking at the grass in frustration.

When there's smoke, Tess thought. She searched for a sign of an escaped dog. She spotted it dashing through the bushes and sculptures at the edge of the park. The dog was small, stocky, and white. From this far away, her best guess was a Westie. She flinched as the yapping animal dashed into the street, causing an approaching sedan to slam on its brakes. The dog wheeled to face it, barking as ferociously at the grill as its small stature allowed. After completing a round of rapid-fire barking that stopped traffic in all lanes, it dashed back into the grassy park.

Once again, it was watching the guy who was trying to catch it and making sure to keep well clear of him. The man's attempts to make it stay put were only causing it to retreat farther.

Barely conscious of the fact that she'd made the decision to do so, Tess hoisted her suitcase and dove back into the cold rain. The park was on the other side of

Market Street. She had to dodge traffic and jog across five lanes to get there. Her suitcase thumped against one calf as she ran, likely creating a few bruises she'd discover later.

Once she closed the distance to a bit less than twenty feet, Tess heard the guy curse as he headed into the western edge of the park in pursuit of the dog.

"Hey, you!" She was determined to stop him before his frustration drove the dog into the street again. "Stop! Just stop, will you?"

It still wasn't all-out pouring, but the fat, cold drops were soaking into her thin jacket. Thankfully, the guy, whose left arm was immobilized, had heard her and was turning around to see who'd called out to him. As soon as he stopped walking, the Westie, thirty feet ahead of him, stopped and cocked its head curiously toward Tess.

"Stop, please! Just stop moving! You're too imposing!" Tess dropped her suitcase and backpack under a bush that had lost most of its leaves but still offered a bit of protection from the rain. She double-checked the small pocket of her jacket to make sure she had a few of the treats left that she carried with her for emergencies like this one. "You'll never get him back this way."

As she drew closer, Tess noticed that the man was tall and had a defined, athletic build. Having topped out at five-four, she often thought of people over six feet tall as ones who swam in a different gene pool. This guy was well over that mark and broad shouldered enough that some innate part of her that was perceivably connected to her reproductive system responded by emitting a spurt of adrenaline. "Way too imposing," she repeated under her breath as she closed the distance between them.

He was also sans dog, she reminded herself, which was why she'd left the cover of the bus stop.

"Just stay here, okay? If you stop trying to close in on him, I think he'll stop moving away from you. What's his name?"

"Hers," he said, taking in Tess's puddle-splashed boots and clothes. "It's Millie. And please, give it your best shot. She goes berserk off leash. She's my neighbor's and she doesn't like me on a good day, but even less in the rain. She slipped her collar."

He offered the leash in her direction, but Tess shook her head. A sudden gust of wind blew the chilling drops sideways, causing her to shiver. "Thanks, but she's watching. Do me a favor and act like your attention isn't on her for a minute. I'll head down the park next to the street to keep her from heading back out there. Once I'm far enough away from you, I'll see if I can get her to come to me."

"Yeah, sure. And thanks," he called after her as she hurried toward the edge of the park.

Tess kept watch on the little Westie in her peripheral vision. She headed west along the curb at the edge of the park until she was parallel to the animal. Millie had stopped advancing west and was alternately dashing in crazy circles and stopping to bark in the guy's direction.

Maybe it was because Tess was better with dogs than the imposing guy with the sling was. Maybe it was because frightened and overexcited dogs often found women more approachable than men. Whatever it was, Tess found the little Westie much more accommodating than the guy had.

As Tess moved toward the dog, she kept her gaze

averted, approached at a slow, even pace, and offered calm and continuous praise. She stopped walking when she was still a good four or five feet away. She knelt in a squat and offered a treat in her outstretched hand. Millie zoomed over, stopping a foot and a half in front of Tess's hand. The little dog sniffed the air and wagged her tail, then trotted over easy-peasy. The Westie was quick but gentle at taking the treat. Once Millie had munched it down, Tess dropped another one onto her open palm, but didn't extend her hand as far.

As Millie munched the second treat, she let Tess rub one warm but wet ear. When Millie leaned into the scratch, Tess worked her way lower, then locked her hand around Millie's side and drew her close. Once Tess had her, she nodded to the guy who was watching intently fifty or sixty feet away.

"I'll take that leash and collar now," she called as the soft glow of success filled her. *At least one thing has gone right today.*

A bus had come and gone while she was over here. Tess suspected it was the line she was supposed to be on and that she'd be waiting another half hour for a new one. It didn't matter though. Catching the cute little Westie and keeping her safe was more important than getting home and warming up.

When the stout little dog showed no resistance or fear, Tess scooped her into her arms and stood.

"Hey, well done!" the guy called as he jogged over, brushing rain from his forehead. It was beading up on his thin, fitted long-sleeved shirt.

"Thanks. I've had practice." It hit her a second time what a physical anomaly this guy was, too fit and all-American to blend into any crowd. His hair was a wavy light brown, and his eyes were a striking blue-green. He had a smile that belonged on a poster, white teeth, and a deep dimple in his right cheek that was visible even with a few weeks of stubble on his cheeks and chin.

"I owe you big time. If anything would've happened to her, I'm pretty sure I'd have been murdered in my sleep…not that I'd have been able to sleep," he said, grinning. "She's a master at slipping her collar. Usually I'm one step ahead of her, just not today."

Tess laughed as Millie both growled and wagged her tail at the guy. "She seems not to be quite sure what to think of you."

"You can say that again. My neighbor had knee surgery and I've been taking her out when I'm home, sometimes three times a day. Just when I think we're good to go, she goes all Mr. Hyde on me."

"Does she bite?"

"No. Just barks and runs about like a Ping-Pong ball."

"It kind of seemed like she was playing. Maybe that's what she needs. A good bout of play at a dog park." Tess nodded toward the collar. "Do you mind snapping that back on while I hold her? I don't want to risk setting her down first. Or can't you in that sling?"

"My hand's fine. It's my shoulder." He stepped in closer than Tess was expecting, and she was showered in his scent. She didn't know guys' colognes, but his smell reminded her of a walk through the woods with maybe a hint of sandalwood and lemon. Whatever it was, the rain likely accented it, and Tess would've liked to wrap herself up in it.

He also had really good hands, she noticed as he

clipped on Millie's dark-pink collar. Tess tested the collar with her free hand and wasn't surprised when she could slip more than the suggested two fingers underneath.

"I can tighten it," he offered, voicing her thoughts.

"That'd be good. They tend to work themselves loose over time from pulling and all." He stepped in even closer as he whirled Millie's collar around and worked at pulling the extra material through the tri-glide slide. This close up, all that stubble was a beacon drawing Tess's attention to his lips and white teeth.

She couldn't help but notice that he wasn't wearing a ring. *Odds are a zillion to one that he's got a girlfriend, Grasso. And he's not even your type.*

Only, Tess wondered, if you had to remind yourself someone wasn't your type, how could you be sure they weren't? *He's sporty. You like bookish. Besides, getting lost in those arms would be like hugging a tree trunk.*

He finished and stepped back, and Tess had to blink herself back into reality. "I'll, uh, put her down now. You could maybe suggest a martingale collar or a body harness to your friend. Westies are notorious for slipping their collars with those stout necks of theirs."

"I will. Listen, I'd like to thank you, but I'm not sure how. Not only did you catch her, but you've gotten soaked in the process."

Tess shrugged as she stood upright from setting Millie on the ground. The little Westie sniffed her wet boots, seeming as calm and content as if she'd never gotten worked up at all. Her tail wagged with the constancy of a reliable clock. "It's all in day's work, and I was pretty soaked when I got over here." She glanced at the clouds. "I thought it was going to let up, but now it seems like it might get worse. I'd better grab my things and run. Thanks though."

She held out a hand, hoping to look more confident and self-assured than she felt around him. It didn't help that she was shivering. She didn't need to look in the mirror to know that her lips had become an unattractive shade of blue. All the while, Mr. Sporty wasn't in a jacket, and the raindrops were still beading up and rolling down his water-resistant shirt.

"Oh, come on." He closed his hand around hers but didn't shake it, which caught her off guard. "Are you parked close? Let me walk you to your car. I didn't even get your name."

"I'm, uh, busing it, actually." *Busing it? Is that even a word?* She needed to pull her hand away, but he wasn't letting go. His skin was warm, and his grip was inviting and strong. And her knees were practically melting into her shins.

She glanced down the sidewalk at the spot where she'd stashed her suitcase and backpack and blinked unexpectedly. The slightest hint of panic nudged in. She scanned the landscaping for a sign of them, but there wasn't any.

"You're busing it?" he was saying. "Where are you going? I'll give you a ride."

He must have moved them behind one of the evergreen bushes. Surely that was it. Only he'd been at least ten feet from them, and she'd almost swear he'd never moved until he'd walked in her direction. But would she have known if he had? She'd been zeroed in on Millie. Aside from a woman with a poodle at the opposite end, the park was deserted. But had it always been?

"Did you see my stuff?" Panic was flooding in so quickly that it was as if a dam had broken. "My suitcase and backpack. Do you know where they went?"

Tess pulled her hand away and hurried down the sidewalk toward the middle of the park where she'd come in. He followed, having no trouble coaxing Millie along. The little dog trotted willingly beside Tess.

By the time Tess reached the bush where she'd set her things, she was in a jog. Her suitcase was filled with her success stories. All of them. And all those dollars' worth of thoughtful purchases. And then there was the laptop in her backpack. The one with all her research. And every treasured photograph she'd downloaded from her trip to Europe. Dear God, why hadn't she gotten around to backing her stuff up on the cloud? Her cell phone too. And the cell numbers of dozens of amazing people she'd met while away. All of it. Vanished.

Gone.

A sharp, chill gust blew so hard she had to adjust her footing. Rain, in smaller droplets but quadrupled intensity, pummeled sideways into her, stinging her face and neck. Not liking the increased ferocity of the afternoon storm, Millie began to whine at her feet.

Somehow, impossibly, all of it was gone on a wind Tess had never seen coming.

Chapter 3

MASON BECAME COMPLETELY SURE OF ONE THING AS the girl bent forward, gripping her knees as if she'd just taken a bat to the stomach. Whoever had taken her things had better watch out. Anyone who picked on a rescuer in the middle of rescuing had it coming.

He'd hardly been paying attention to her at first and had paid none to the fact that she'd dumped her things. With the craziness of late, he'd been bombarded nearly every time he'd stepped out of his building. It had been a great season for the team, and he'd had his strongest year yet, so maybe some of it was to be expected.

But ever since the accident, his face had been plastered over the news more than it had during his best weeks of the season. It was hard to go anywhere, especially wearing the sling, without being noticed.

Those first few seconds, he'd had no reason to think she was anything other than a fan who was coming over hoping for an autograph or, worse, someone coming to flirt. But she didn't seem to have a clue who he was. She was only interested in talking about the dog.

She was also soaked to the bone and shivering. He was rapidly getting that way too.

He scanned the park, looking for a glimpse of someone hurrying off with her luggage. A woman was jogging away from the park, leading a long-legged poodle, but she wasn't carrying anything. A few businesspeople were darting in and out of the buildings on the other side of Chestnut Street. Some had umbrellas and briefcases, others didn't. He scanned the shrubbery for someone hiding behind the dense brush and caught a glimpse of motion at the southeast edge of the park.

"Hey, take the leash, will you?" Mason pressed the leash into her hand and dashed off before she could ask why. Millie, inconsistent as always, barked after him as if she hated for him to leave.

At the far corner of the sculpture park was a popular hollow metal sculpture of a giant head lying sideways. Mason had caught a glimpse of someone stepping into its hollow neck, though his view had been partially blocked by tree limbs.

He was nearly there before he realized he couldn't identify the girl's stuff. If the guy had something suspicious, he'd drag him back to her. But when he reached the open neck end of the statue, swiping raindrops off his forehead and out of his eyes, he stopped. Someone had gone in out of the rain. A homeless guy. He'd been hauling a ratty, military-grade duffel. He seemed oblivious to Mason's arrival as he pulled off a jacket he'd been wearing. He wore layers of dirt like clothing, and Mason would put him in his late forties. His clothes were worn out and soiled, and his shoes, an old pair of Converses, were falling apart.

"Hey," Mason said, leaning his head inside the neck, but not crawling in. "I'm with a girl on the other side of the park. Someone just stole her stuff. Did you see anyone with a suitcase and a backpack?"

The guy stopped undressing to look at Mason, then cleared his throat loudly. "Think this is an airport? You gotta watch your own stuff around here. It's them Iraqis you gotta watch for. Got three tours notched in my belt, and by God, I swear you can't trust an Iraqi."

The guy had a far-off look in his eyes. Mason suspected he was only half-aware of the world around him. He reached into his pants' pocket for his wallet but remembered he didn't have it. "Hey, want to tell me what size shoes you wear, guy?"

Mason didn't get an answer this time. The man was too busy filling the air with all the reasons he wouldn't trust an Iraqi, and none of them were reasons Mason wanted to hear.

"Hey." Mason knocked on the metal to get the man's attention. The knock reverberated through the hollow head and circled back. "Stick around here a little while. I'll come back. I'll bring you some shoes, got that?"

Whether or not the guy would, Mason didn't know. He jogged back through the rain and cutting wind until he reached Millie and the girl. She was walking the dog in his direction, her shoulders hunched from the wind. Beside her, Millie's tail was tucked, and she looked thoroughly ready for the cozy warmth of the plush bed waiting in his friend's loft.

"Dead end. Homeless guy."

The girl nodded, swiping a soaked strand of dark-brown hair back from her face. She was shivering hard and clearly on the verge of crying. Mason had to hold back from touching her in reassurance. She was petite in her leggings and tall, soaked leather boots. Her heart-shaped face was pale from the cold, but her lips were full and enticing.

"I'll go with you, if you want to report it. There's a police station a couple blocks from here."

"I don't…I don't know that it'd do any good." Her lower jaw was starting to quiver. "I should go." She offered the leash his way and glanced across Market Street in the direction she'd come. "Oh…"

Her face fell even lower, and Mason was pretty sure he knew the direction of her thoughts. "Is your wallet gone?"

She pressed her lips together and swallowed. Not wanting to upset her any further, Mason did the talking instead.

"Look, my place isn't far. I'll grab my truck and give you a ride home, but first we'll circle the side streets and alleys around here. Pickpockets are notorious for dumping extra weight as fast as possible. Maybe we can recover some of your stuff."

She folded her arms tightly across her chest and looked around, as if searching for a second option. "Thanks, but I don't want to put you out."

Mason turned his right palm skyward as if he was trying to catch the drops. The rain had slowed to become an even, steady drizzle, but the cloud blanket further west was ominous. "Putting me out would be to ask me to hang around here to see if the rain will soak into our last still-dry crevices. Come on. It's this way."

He took off toward the northeast corner of the park. After a few seconds of hesitation, she followed. If his left arm weren't immobilized, he'd have had to work hard not to drape it over her back. She was devastated but holding it together admirably, causing Mason to want to help her even more.

Rather than press her into conversation, he listened to the peaceful, lulling drone of the now-steady rain and the patter of Millie's soaked paws as she scurried along in front of them, leading the way with the confidence of a dog who knew her home range well.

Mason wasn't one to get cold easily, but he could feel the chill setting in. Beside him, the girl was walking with her arms still folded over her chest, and her fingertips were turning blue.

"Just another two blocks."

"Thanks," she said, "for helping me."

"You were doing a favor for me, and someone stole your stuff. If I left you out in this rain to fend for yourself, that would group me with the worst of the worst."

"Would you mind if I used your phone to call someone?"

"Not at all. But it's up there. I'm on the top floor. So is Millie's owner, Georges." He pointed to the sixth and top floor of the redbrick building that used to belong to a high-end fountain pen company that went out of business in the early eighties. The building had been used off and on for storage until a real estate developer purchased it in 2005. That company had gone out of business in 2009, a year after the twice-postponed construction of twelve upscale lofts was supposed to begin. A new developer had bought it after it had sat empty for several years.

Mason had been the second person to buy into the twelve-unit development, just after Georges. Then he and Georges had bought the rest of the undeveloped units and become co-owners of the building. Despite Georges's many eccentricities and their many differences, they were also good friends.

They reached the entrance none too soon. When his fingerprint proved too wet to be read by the scanner that unlocked the lobby door, Mason entered the six-digit backup code. The red light over the panel switched to green, and the magnet that held the door locked released.

Switching Millie's leash to the hand of his slinged arm, he pulled the door open and nodded for the young woman to go in.

She stepped back a foot. "Thanks, but I'll stay out here."

The concrete awning overhead was part of the swell underneath the second-story windows. It kept most of the rain out of the building entryway but not all, and she was clearly freezing.

"In the rain? I get you've got no reason to trust me, but at least come in where it's warm." He motioned toward the furnished lobby that often felt like a waste of space. The twelve-unit building was too small for a doorman, and most of the residents came and went through the building's basement garage. Aside from when one of the tenants was waiting for a ride to show up or a guest to arrive, hardly anyone used the lobby.

She bit at her lower lip and looked inside the lobby, then back at him. "I'm not trying to be rude. It's just… You could be anybody and"—she shrugged helplessly—"I don't even know your name."

Her words resounded through his mind. He could be anybody. To her. Not the story, *the sensation*, he'd become. *Anybody*.

And somehow, that mattered to him more than anything had in months.

He worked to keep his tone light. "I'm glad you brought it up. I was just thinking the same thing about you."

She gave a light shake of her head, her eyebrows furrowing in confusion.

"I hear you," he added. "You can't be too careful nowadays. I mean, it's possible this whole thing could be a ruse to get me to bring you upstairs where you plan to overpower me and plunder my loft and do who knows what else."

A small laugh bubbled out of her. "Me? Overpower you?"

He shrugged with his good shoulder. "You look little but mighty."

Her small laugh rolled into a larger one. "Okay. I'll wait in the lobby." She stepped in ahead of him, wiping her soaked boots on the mat and keeping her arms closed over her chest. "I'm Tess."

"Tess, huh? Nice name." He stepped in behind her and Millie. The heat was on, and the lobby felt particularly inviting, thanks to that and the glowing lamps on the side tables on either side of the couch.

Mason let the door fall closed after them. When the automatic lock snapped in place, her hesitant smile fell.

"Is it just Tess, or is that short for Theresa?"

"Contessa." The single word seemed to be swallowed up by the empty room. "My family's Italian."

"Contessa," he repeated, but this time the big, quiet room didn't seem to swallow it. "But you prefer Tess."

"Wouldn't you?" She stepped tentatively off the rug and onto the marble floor left over from the old showroom that dated back to the late eighteen-nineties. The lobby had been renovated using as many of the showroom's original features as possible. The rest of the building—the parts that hadn't been seen by customers—was considerably less ornate.

"Oh, I don't know," he answered. "My name's

Mason, and it's not short for anything except maybe mason jar. I come from a family of several generations of farmers, and they're a little bit of everything except Italian." He motioned toward the couch. "Make yourself comfortable. Only you're soaked, so I don't know how that's possible."

She thanked him and headed for one of the two leather chairs.

"I'll be back in a few minutes. I'll bring you a towel and a dry jacket." He coaxed Millie onto the elevator. The finicky dog was more willing to jump over the metal floor trim some days than others. Today, she bounded over the divide with no persuasion.

As the doors closed and Mason lost sight of the girl—of Tess—he found himself strongly hoping she didn't give in to the fear and indecision so clearly riding under her surface and take off. Despite the less-than-perfect circumstances of the moment, his desire to have more time with her was surprisingly strong.

—◇◇—

Tess could hardly feel her toes, and her soaked thighs and numb fingers began to sting as the heat of the lobby warmed them.

The reality of what had happened at the park and its likely aftereffects was too much to process. The guy had been more than kind. Funny too. But what would Nonna or her parents say if she got in a car with him? He hadn't pushed when she'd chosen not to follow him upstairs to his loft. This made him seem safer somehow. Yet he had a fading black eye and was wearing a sling, and she'd no idea how he'd gotten them. For all she knew, he could have a ferocious temper. It certainly didn't seem like it, but she couldn't know with any certainty.

In Europe, she'd backpacked and hitched rides from one small town to the next. She'd made friends with fellow travelers, often joining up with backpackers she'd just met and traveling with them for a town or two before parting ways. It was crazy, but all of that had felt so much safer than following a guy into the lobby of his hotel in her home city.

Maybe it was an omen. Maybe she should take off and head back to Pooches and Purses. The owner would be gone, but surely the workers would let her use a phone and hang there until whomever she decided to call came and got her.

The idea of calling her family made her stomach begin a new set of somersaults. Comments they'd not even yet made—and maybe never would—circled through her mind.

What was wrong with her that she didn't think they'd be supportive or sympathetic? And why did her thoughts have to circle so quickly to what they'd say or think? Why did she have to assume the loss of her luggage would be another marked failure in their eyes?

She'd lost so much. The treats, dog food, lotions, and oils were replaceable. The stories, not so much. She could contact some of her old clients and ask them for a second round of quotes and pictures. There was the cost of replacing her laptop. The cell phone in her backpack had been the one she'd left in a drawer when she left for Europe. It was outdated by at least three models and had had more than its fair share of quirks. She'd been more than overdue for a new one. She'd get the money for all of that somehow. The files on her computer and the photos and cell numbers were what couldn't be replaced.

Photos flashed through her mind of the hole-in-the-wall bookstores and antique markets and mom-and-pop bakeries, and of the castles and villages she'd visited. So did the phone numbers of the friends she met along the way. Some of the best moments of her life, so irretrievably gone.

In the quiet but cozy room, Tess doubled over, burying her head between her knees, and finally gave release to the tears that had been piling up underneath the surface.

Chapter 4

"SO, PICK YOUR PASSION FOR A COLD, RAINY afternoon. Coffee, tea, or hot chocolate?" Mason asked as he circled his red Dodge Ram pickup truck up the ramp and out of the basement garage.

It was a good thing he couldn't drive with his left hand, or he'd have had to work hard at not letting his right one close over Tess's knee in reassurance. She looked close to irresistible in the big, leather bucket seat on the other side of the console, wearing the several-sizes-too-large hoodie he'd lent her.

"Um, hot chocolate, I guess, though there are compelling arguments for all three."

"Unless you need a jolt of caffeine, I can promise you won't be disappointed with their hot chocolate. It's a coffee shop just up the road. I'll run in. You can wait here out of the rain. I know you've got to be in a hurry to look for your stuff. It shouldn't take more than a couple of minutes."

"Thanks. You don't have to, but if you're going for you as well, a hot chocolate would be nice."

Mason left his truck idling because he could see she was still shivering and he didn't want to kill the heat. He dropped a few coins in the meter and jogged inside. By the time he came back with a giant hot chocolate for her and a coffee for him, she looked a lot further from tears than she had when he'd returned to the lobby from his loft. He'd sensed that she'd only pulled herself together at the ding of the elevator.

He opened his door and placed the drinks in the console cup holders before gripping the steering wheel to climb into the high seat, a move he'd perfected in the time his left arm and shoulder had been immobilized. He couldn't say for sure how he used to get into his cab. It had been second nature.

"Is it hard driving one-handed?" she asked.

"So far, so good. It's my collarbone and shoulder, not my arm. I'm counting the days until I get this sling off."

He was glad when she didn't follow her question with a second one about how he'd been injured. He worried that telling her he'd been in a car wreck might cause her to make a connection he was hoping she wouldn't make. Not today. Today, he wanted to be generic Mason from a generic farming family in Iowa. He didn't want to be the single, pro baseball player just about every social-media gossip column had tagged in one sensationalized story or another this summer. He didn't want to be a player on the field or off. He just wanted to be a guy helping a girl recover her stuff.

She lifted her paper cup in both hands and took a cautious sip. "You weren't kidding. This is the real stuff. Thanks. Thanks for everything."

"By everything, do you mean *not* watching your stuff while you were saving the dog I was supposed to be taking care of?"

He drove toward the side streets and alleys that surrounded Citygarden. With any luck, they'd find her suitcase or backpack tossed on the ground or in a Dumpster.

"I didn't ask you to watch my things. The park

seemed empty. I figured it was safe, and I was focused on Millie."

He shook his head and turned down the first alley north of the park. "It seemed empty, didn't it? Do you want to describe your stuff so we both know what we're looking for?"

"I had an aqua-colored backpack. The suitcase is a hard-shelled spinner. It was rose pink, a gift. They weren't exactly color-coordinated. But you know what they say… You start from where you are, right?"

Memory rushed over Mason. *You start from where you are.* He'd heard that line once before and had never forgotten it. Twice in his twenty-nine years, he'd felt so on top of his game that he'd almost believed nothing could bring him down. Twice he'd been wrong.

Most recently, he'd been proven wrong just four weeks ago. The Red Birds had made it to the playoffs, and he'd had a phenomenal second season with them. An old college buddy had been in town, and what had seemed like a well-deserved night of partying had led to the two of them piling into that Escape, his buddy in the front, Mason in the back. The chicks who'd picked them up were hot, but even before the crash, Mason hadn't been feeling it. Leaving the bar to go to one of the girls' places had been for his buddy's sake. He'd been dumped recently and was craving the diversion.

As fate had it, less than a mile after entering the highway, the just-under-the-legal-limit driver who'd looked away from the road a second or two too long had nearly driven into another car. She'd corrected too hard and lost control, causing the SUV to careen across two lanes, flipping twice before coming to rest on the side of an embankment. Thanks to nearly a dozen airbags, the two women had only minor cuts and bruises. His buddy had suffered a small fracture to a lower-neck vertebra and needed surgery before he could return home. Mason's nose was broken, and his left collarbone was crushed, preventing his participation in his first-ever playoff season. The fact that the driver was married and had removed her ring for the night was something Mason learned in the chaotic aftermath.

The other time Mason had been knocked down, he'd had a much harder time getting back up. He'd just finished his junior year of college and had gotten word that he was being considered for that year's MLB draft. He'd gone home to his family's farm in Iowa thinking he was infallible. Then one fateful talk with his dad had left him angry and rebellious. That afternoon, Mason had lingered outside when the game of catch he'd been playing with his cousin was cut short by a thunderstorm barreling their way.

He'd stood in the field too long watching the clouds race in and trying to lose the leftover fear lingering in him from his conversation with his dad to the power of the storm. He still remembered feeling the electricity that had been building in the air, causing the hairs on his arms and the back of his neck to stand on end, and thinking what an unstoppable force nature could be.

That was the last thing he remembered. He woke up five days later to learn he'd been struck by lightning and that he owed his life to the CPR his cousin had given him until the ambulance arrived. The strike had blown out his left eardrum and left him with a ringing in his ears that lasted a year. He'd also barely been able to move the left side of his body. His arm had been worse than his leg. Moving it was not only excruciating, but also nearly impossible. And no one would say for sure how much, if any, movement would return or if, like the hearing he'd lost, it was gone forever. He'd had to deal with fatigue, disorientation, headaches, and irritability too.

The partial paralysis of his left side had been as terrifying as it was enraging. Mason had wanted to be a pro baseball player ever since he could remember wanting anything, and reaching that dream had been so close he'd almost been able to touch it.

He'd acted like a caged bear during those first several sessions of physical therapy, lashing out at a string of therapists who wouldn't give him the answers he wanted to hear. He'd finally been passed along to a bad-tempered woman on the verge of retiring who wouldn't take his shit.

"You want to play ball tomorrow, then move that arm like I say today. You were handed a plate of crap, and now you can quit, or you can work your ass off and set your mind to getting your body back under your control. It's the best choice anyone's ever given, isn't it? Starting right from where you are."

Mason did as the woman instructed, and the path to full recovery was long—several years long—and chock-full of bumps and ruts and washouts. By twenty-five, he was finally back to playing close to how he'd played when he'd been struck at twenty-one. The Orioles picked him up for his first season when he was twenty-six. He'd been a mediocre player for them and a slightly better one for the Brewers before getting transferred to the Red Birds two years ago.

What kind of coincidence was it that he was hearing

those exact words again now, after he'd had a second brush with the chaos and uncertainty that had the potential to derail a career in a fraction of a second? And after a season of riding high on top of his game and feeling once again like he had the world under his feet. His friend Georges thought that Mason's subconscious was sending him a message after the wreck, a loud, clear one that he needed to figure out quickly.

And here was this girl, not recognizing him from anywhere but reminding him so strongly of the connection of life. What message had he not gotten after the lightning strike? What message was he not getting now?

You start from where you are.

"So, were you heading out of town or are you just getting back?" he asked, wanting to change the direction of thoughts he didn't have an answer to.

Her eyebrows knotted momentarily, then her face relaxed in understanding. "That's a good question considering what we're on the hunt for. Neither, really. I got back from Europe about a month ago, and I'm staying put in St. Louis for a bit."

Mason parked the truck at a row of three Dumpsters, two trash and one recycling. "Europe, huh? I've never been, but I'm taking my parents in January." He slipped the truck into Park and switched his wipers to low. "You can stay here if you'd like. I'll call you out if I see anything."

Tess unbuckled her seat belt. "Thanks, but they're my bags. I'll Dumpster dive."

They headed out into the drizzling rain together. As Mason peeked behind the Dumpsters, a cat dashed out from underneath and ran down the street.

"Poor kitty." The way Tess looked after it was further proof of the kindness in her heart that she'd shown with Millie.

"Feral cats are pretty good at taking care of themselves. It's the dogs you see around here that get to me." Mason picked what seemed like a clean spot on the closest Dumpster's lid and lifted it. It was cleaner inside than he'd imagined and a quarter full of tied bags of trash, a computer monitor, and a silk plant that showed more dust than green foliage.

"True," Tess said, moving to the adjacent Dumpster with him. She stepped close enough to him as she peeked inside that he caught a whiff of her scent—soft, sweet, and subtle. It mixed with the stink of the Dumpsters, confusing his nostrils.

When the third Dumpster, the recycling bin, proved empty as well, they climbed back into the truck and Mason continued cruising through the streets and alleys around the park. On the fifth stop, they surprised a dog who'd been hanging out behind a Dumpster that was out of the rain under a roof overhang. Mason was only a bit surprised to see that it was John Ronald.

The magnificent animal dashed away to about the distance between home plate and second base, then turned and stood in the rain, watching them with pricked-at-attention ears. Mason whistled loudly. The dog, which Mason guessed was mostly husky mixed with something big and long-legged, responded with a single wag of his tail.

"*That*," Mason said, "is my dog. He just doesn't know it yet. Or maybe he does, and he's still trying to deny it."

Tess looked from Mason to the dog, and back to

Mason. "He's watching you like he knows you, that's for sure."

Mason wished he'd thought to bring some treats in the likely event they'd run into John Ronald on this Dumpster prowl. He'd been in a hurry to get back to Tess and had only been thinking of the guy in the statue head. He'd grabbed a pair of running shoes he didn't often wear and a couple of muscle drinks, all he had in his near-empty refrigerator, and would drop them by when he and Tess circled near the park.

Mason whistled again. After a few seconds, probably determining that Mason was empty-handed today, the dog turned and trotted away, his long legs making fast tracks. Mason would put him at seventy-or-so pounds, eighty if he wasn't so overly lean.

"Not today, huh, John Ronald," Mason said under his breath.

Tess was suddenly studying him harder than she had since she'd told him to lay off on his attempts to catch Millie, since she'd called him imposing.

"What did you mean, 'your dog'?"

He shrugged. "He's a stray who hangs out near my building. We've had a few moments, but I haven't been able to get close enough to catch him. If I ever do, I intend to keep him."

Her mouth opened a fraction of an inch, calling Mason's attention to the fullness of her lips a second time. Even though the rain had slowed to a dull drizzle, it was still cold and wet, but she didn't seem to notice any longer.

"And why John Ronald?"

Judging by the incredulous look that had spread

across her face, Mason's best guess was he'd done something either impossibly wrong or impossibly right. He just didn't know which.

Hoping it was the second, he opted for the truth, letting it fall out in a display of rare vulnerability.

"The first night I saw him, I was up in my loft. It was six or seven months ago—early spring, I guess—and the moon was full. I told you, I'm on the sixth floor. I have a decent view of the street below my loft. After I spotted him, I stepped out on my balcony to watch him. The white patches on his body and above his eyes stood out in the moonlight, and I could have sworn that he was looking up at me even before he stopped walking. I was afraid if I went downstairs and outside, I'd scare him off, so I dropped him hot dogs from my balcony, and he ate them. He even caught a few before they hit the ground.

"When I ran out of them, I headed downstairs and outside as fast as I could. I think he knew I was coming. He was already at the end of the block, but he was looking my way like he was waiting for me but needed the distance to feel safe. He watched me for a while, but then he turned and left like he did just now."

Mason shrugged, thinking of all the interactions he and the dog had had since that first night. He'd been doing his best to catch the stray, but hadn't had any luck. "I leave him food on the street under my balcony. Sometimes he leaves me things too. Odd things. A dead crow once, but also trash. I know it's him, because one time I spotted him carrying a hat. By the time I got downstairs, he was gone. The hat was waiting for me by the building door."

Fresh tears blossomed out of nowhere, brimming on

Tess's lower lids. She blinked them away without shedding them. "But why John Ronald?"

"Because calling him Tolkien didn't feel right."

She dropped his gaze so quickly that Mason knew she'd gotten the confirmation she'd been looking for. "'Not all those who wander are lost.'" It was such a quiet whisper on her lips that Mason almost wasn't sure he'd heard it. It was said so softly that he suspected it wasn't even meant for his ears.

She shook her head as if she'd just heard something she didn't quite believe. He was about to ask for clarification when she turned away from him and stalked abruptly over to the Dumpster to check behind and in it for her stuff. When this one proved to be a wash like the first four stops had been, she returned to the truck without a glance in his direction.

Mason climbed into the truck after her, wondering if perhaps the universe had just shifted for him a third time, only this time much less painfully so.

─────

Tess knew that it was on her to talk, to explain her odd line of questioning, but she couldn't. She'd been completely waylaid. It had started with his kindness to her and to the homeless guy he'd encountered in the park.

Those were remarkable but ordinary things. Things you remembered about a stranger long after you parted ways. Things that changed the course of your day and sent you to bed mulling over a small but profound connection.

But the Tolkien quote, the one from the poem she'd carried in her backpack across Europe, the backpack she'd lost meeting him, was too much to process. That single line of poetry meant more to her than any verse she'd heard.

Those words meant something giant to him too. They had to. She hadn't clarified he'd named a stray dog with wanderlust John Ronald because of the same line that had given her meaning in the darkest moments of her life. But after the story he'd shared, she didn't have to. She wanted to know what this connection meant. Wanted answers from a universe that either she didn't know how to listen to or that wasn't in the habit of talking to her.

The final thirty minutes of Dumpster searching were quiet, wet, smelly, and unproductive. The only thing that came from them was that she'd never look at trash the same way again. Wherever her things were, they hadn't been thrown into one of the Dumpsters in the side streets or alleys surrounding Citygarden.

Somehow, Tess knew after running across remarkable-looking John Ronald that her stuff was gone for good. She just didn't know how to explain that to Mason. She was too raw and exposed after all that had happened for that level of honesty with a total stranger.

Finally, when Mason admitted they'd combed as much of the area as he knew of, he asked if she wanted to go to the police station. Tess thanked him but asked him to take her home instead.

She gave him directions to Nonna's small, brick, portico-style shotgun home on the Hill. Fifteen minutes later, when they entered the Hill's single square-mile border and she directed him toward Nonna's, she saw the neighborhood from a stranger's eyes.

Italian-colored flags flanked the main street entrances to the Hill, just as they did the popular street corners within it. Tess couldn't remember how old she was when she realized that while the fire hydrants in her neighborhood were painted red, white, and green, and topped with bright-yellow caps, elsewhere in the world, they were starkly yellow.

Yards here tended to be infinitesimally small compared to most in other St. Louis neighborhoods, and Tess wondered if there were more Virgin Mary concrete statues in the carefully pruned yards of the row houses they were passing or flags on street corners. And just a few days past Halloween, pumpkins, gourds, scarecrows, straw bales, ghosts, and skeletons still lined many of the porches of the modest frame or brick homes.

Mason drove past an old man with stooped shoulders who was sweeping cobwebs from the corners of his covered porch. Tess remembered trick-or-treating at his home nearly two decades ago. He and his wife had passed out cannoli instead of candy, and the pastries had been better than even Nonna's.

When they reached Nonna's, Mason parked in a rare open spot along the sidewalk out front, and Tess was struck by how his truck was nearly as long as her grandmother's yard was wide.

He slipped the truck into Park and slowed the wipers to a rhythmic pulse. The soft rain fell around the pickup, wrapping it in droplets like a snug blanket. His gaze combed the house, the chipping paint of the double swing on the covered porch, and the concrete statue of the Virgin Mary, her hands spread open in welcome, that was nearly lost in a crowd of browning-out mums along the walkway. The Red Birds flag still hung on the garden's wrought-iron flag post.

The thousand-square-foot house her grandparents lived in their entire marriage wasn't much to look at, but it was one of Tess's favorite places in the world. Looking at it now, it struck her for the first time how little decorating Nonna had done for Halloween this year. She wondered if Thanksgiving and Christmas would be different. Not that Tess would blame her if they weren't. Nonna had been married to Tess's grandpa for over sixty years.

Tess started to unzip the cozy Vineyard Vines hoodie Mason had lent her, but he held up his hand. "Keep it. It could never look that good on me."

Tess's cheeks grew warm, but she didn't argue away the offer. The hoodie was warm and cozy, and she didn't ever want to take it off.

She caught a glimpse of movement in the darkened dining-room window. Nonna was always looking out her window to inspect the tourists who parked in front of her house on their way to one of several thriving Italian restaurants up the street. Would her grandma notice she was inside the cab? Whether or not she did, Tess needed to get moving.

But needing to go and wanting to leave weren't the same thing.

"I'm sorry," she said. *Sorry for what? For taking up his time? For using up his gas? For not sharing what his story about John Ronald had meant to her?* "Thanks for helping me look for my stuff." Saying that was easier than offering an explanation.

"You never told me what you were doing out there today. Where you were going."

Tess considered her answer in the quiet that hung

between them. The radio, tuned to a popular country station, was turned low, somehow drawing Tess's attention to the music more than if it had been turned up. "I'm trying to start a business. I was lugging a bunch of stuff around. That's why I needed the suitcase."

"What sort of business?"

Even in the darkened afternoon, his eyes were a beautiful mixture of blue and green. And his hair was just wet enough that it called to her to brush her fingertips through it. She balled her fingers into fists and rested her hands in her lap. The warm cab and renewed blanket of rain invited her to linger.

All those months in Europe, she'd had a hundred opportunities for one-night stands that she'd never pursued. Maybe her heart wouldn't be beating as hard right now if she had.

She shook her head at his question, not able to reveal her business dreams to him, or the driving passion behind them that was her desire to make a difference in animals' lives. Not now. If there was one less barrier between them, she was pretty certain they'd both be leaning in until their lips met in the middle over the wide console.

So instead, she said the first thing that popped into her head. It came out before she actually contemplated it. "So, um, you probably feel as gross from those Dumpsters as I do. You can come in and wash up if you'd like. But if you do, you should know my grandma will force food on you. Lots of it. You won't be able to say no. No one ever can. She's a good cook though, so it's not so bad."

He looked from her to the house and back to her. He

seemed about to say yes when his expression darkened. "I would if I could. Another day." He mentioned the future with such easy, assured conviction that Tess felt with rare certainty that there would be another day in store for them, and maybe not just one. "Will you tell me what all you lost at least," he added, "in addition to your cell?"

She took a breath in hopes it would turn important objects into mere words. "A laptop. Pictures. Testimonials. That sort of thing."

He nodded and leaned over the console, flipping open the glove box. Inside were a baseball glove, a truck manual, napkins, and a few pens.

He grabbed a pen, flipped the glove-box door closed, and lifted her empty cup into the air. He transferred it to his left hand and held it as he wrote a phone number that started with an area code she didn't know. No name though. The familiarity of the gesture made Tess's heart thump harder. Then he pressed the paper cup into her hand. Their fingers brushed. His touch was even more inviting than when she'd first felt it in the park. A strong buzzing began behind her ears.

"Since I can't call you," was all he said.

Tess locked her fingers around the empty cup. The sugar from the hot chocolate still coated her lips. "I hope…I hope one day he lets you catch him."

She grabbed her still-soaked jacket and hopped out without saying anything else, knowing if she did, she'd end up leaning in and letting their lips brush together in a kiss she'd swear he was asking for with his eyes with the same urgency she was feeling inside.

After climbing the slanted-from-settling steps two at time until she reached the cover of the porch, she turned and looked his way. It didn't surprise her to find he was still watching her as intently as when she'd been inside the cab.

A part of her was full of silent admonitions for getting out of the truck, for leaving that cozy space filled by their warm bodies. Another part, the part that needed to be alone to process an impossibly momentous afternoon, thanked her.

Then Nonna pulled open the sticking wooden door, determining Tess's next move for her. With a small wave in Mason's direction, Tess turned and headed inside.

Chapter 5

COLDER TEMPERATURES HAD BLOWN IN ON THE HEELS of yesterday's rain. Tess could feel the brisk air seeping through the thin glass panes of the windows in Nonna's spare bedroom. Tess had taken to sleeping on the twin bed farthest from the windows. Not only was it a touch warmer, but it also had the better of the two mattresses, and that wasn't saying much. She tugged up the worn, flower quilt after pressing Snooze on the loud alarm clock. It was officially the time of year to make sure the ancient radiators were on and dialed up before going to bed.

Attempting to hold off the racing thoughts of what today would bring for a few minutes longer, Tess snuggled deeper into the blankets. She also hoped to linger in the last few beautiful strands of the dream she'd been having about her and Mason when the ancient clock had buzzed her awake. She mused over the quickly fading details, some of the more peculiar ones strikingly odd now that she was fully awake.

In the dream, she and Mason had been in a truck, but he'd been sitting in the passenger seat and she'd been snuggled on his lap, facing toward the door. She'd been letting her lips savor the smooth skin of his neck and the short, stiff stubble along his chin and cheek.

She'd had unlimited legroom even though her legs were stretched out in the direction of the passenger door, which would be impossible in real life. Also odd was the fact that she'd been perfectly comfortable exploring his neck and face with her lips, but at the same time highly disappointed and impatient that he wasn't kissing her in return. He was *supposed* to be kissing her, but he was holding back, and she didn't know why.

Weird. Weird, completely fictional dream, Tess.

The alarm blared a second time. Tess gathered courage similar to what she would need to dive into a deep pool of chilly water, then threw off her blankets and shut off the alarm. Since she'd be biking this morning, it was too cold for a shower. Thankfully, she'd savored a long bath last night. She slipped into a worn pair of jeans, a cami, and a cozy cardigan.

She needed hot coffee, but not the nearly tasteless stuff from Nonna's three-pound plastic container of Folgers or the stale, powdered milk creamer that were pantry staples here. In Tess's opinion, coffee was one of Nonna's few food-and-beverage fails. Tess craved a brisk espresso like she'd enjoyed in Florence or a creamy café au lait like the ones she'd savored in Normandy.

She suspected her strong cravings this morning for the coffees she'd had in Europe were likely made worse by the stress of the decisions she needed to make today. She was going to need a new phone and a laptop. She was going to need to start over. And to do that, she was going to have to make money.

When Tess had bought her plane ticket to Europe, she'd started out with close to nine thousand dollars in her account. By deferring her student loans, living frugally, and working odd jobs for room and board when she could, Tess had stretched the money out much longer than she would have imagined possible. She used the last of it on her plane ticket home for her grandpa's funeral and to replenish her business supplies.

Now she was broke and needing to start over. From scratch.

And as much as she wasn't looking forward to going back to work there, a job was always waiting for her at her aunt and uncle's popular sandwich shop. She'd worked there from the summer after she turned fourteen until she left for college and every summer and holiday that she came home. She'd been told more than once that she was the reliable sort of worker her aunt and uncle would always take back, even had she not been family.

It wouldn't be as if she was begging for a special favor to go back one more time. *Still*. She couldn't escape the feeling that it was the same as admitting that her business hopes after dropping out of vet school were just another in a long line of failures.

Oh well. Waiting won't make things any simpler.

After getting dressed, she freshened up and headed into the kitchen for a mug of subpar coffee from the automatic pot that had brewed a twelve-cup batch some time before her alarm went off. She helped herself to two of Nonna's dollar-sized lemon ricotta pancakes left over from yesterday's breakfast and popped them into the microwave for a few seconds. Even day-old and warmed up in a microwave, they were still delicious.

Before heading out, she scribbled a note for Nonna, who was sleeping in later than usual. Afterward, Tess opened the small, packed coat closet opposite the front door. Mason's hoodie was in there, crammed off to the side among twenty or so other coats and jackets. It was several sizes too big. It made no sense to wear it. Instead,

Tess pulled out the buckeye she'd discovered in one of the pockets. She ran her thumb atop the smooth, shiny nut and felt a flash of longing wash over her. She wanted to see him again, wanted it more than she should have.

Nonna had spotted her with the buckeye last night and told her that the peculiar-looking nuts brought good luck when they were carried in your pocket. Had it brought Mason any luck? Tess hoped so. She slipped it into her jeans. After yesterday's losses, she needed all the help she could get, even unlikely as it might be.

After pulling on a pair of gloves and her all-weather North Face jacket, she headed out back for her bike. It was just over six miles to the dog rehab at the High Grove Animal Shelter's private house in South City, and it was certain to be a cold one.

Her old friend Kurt, the one leading the retraining, had offered several times to pick her up. Kelsey, his girl-friend and coworker, had offered too. Most days, Tess found the bike ride relaxing and a good way to organize her thoughts and plan out her next business steps.

But the closer winter got, the less appealing the ride would be. *Good thing you're going to have to dramatically cut your volunteer hours to make room for a near-minimum-wage job that's just down the street.*

Tess biked toward Angelo's Sandwich Stop. It would already be bustling inside as the staff baked their ever-popular bread and prepped for the heavy lunch crowd. She might as well get it over with and let them know she'd be coming back. She could smell the bread in the ovens from several buildings down, and her mouth watered automatically. There were good things about working there.

But what if they needed her today? After the crazy mess of yesterday, Tess desperately wanted one more day to savor doing something she loved. And her volunteer work with the dog rehab at the Sabrina Raven estate was near the top of that list.

As if tugged on by the same force of self-preservation that had carried her to Europe, Tess biked off unnoticed. She'd do it this afternoon. The shop closed for the day at four. She would make sure to be back by then.

The ride to the Sabrina Raven estate, the private South City mansion that had been willed to the High Grove Animal Shelter, was mostly a flat, easy one. If she didn't have to be on the same roads as some early-morning commuters who weren't ecstatic about sharing the road with cyclists, it would be a peaceful but chilly way to start the morning.

She knew any lingering stress over yesterday would fall away when she got there. Tess loved everything about the rehab. The old mansion was incredible, for one thing. Even though it needed a lot of updates, it was warm and inviting and reminded Tess of the villa where she'd spent a few weeks last summer at a winery, participating in the harvest.

She also enjoyed working with Kurt and Kelsey. Even though they were newly dating, they still made her feel welcome.

What she liked the most, what brought her there day in and day out when she had a long list of other things that needed to be done, were the dogs. She loved each one. Frankie, a scarred blue-nosed pit bull, was close to being her favorite, but each dog had a unique personality, and they all had their merits. She couldn't wait until the dogs were ready to head over to the High Grove Animal Shelter where they'd be up for adoption and on the road to finding forever homes.

The bike ride to the South City mansion was typically thirty minutes, with stopping at lights and intersections, and it proved no different today. Tess neared the quiet residential street where she turned off for the estate, wondering if one day the stark difference between this section of the city and the Hill wouldn't stand out to her as much.

The homes here were on average twenty or thirty years older, most spanning back well over a century, but to Tess, that was the least of their differences. These homes quadrupled the average house square footage on the Hill, and there was room to breathe between them.

Tess had grown up playing with friends in the streets or down at Berra Park, or curled up in the window seat in her family room, reading a book and ignoring whatever was being watched on TV.

But here there was room to garden, or put up a tree house or swing set, or play a game of chase in the grass. Maybe the yards weren't as massive as out in the sprawling suburbs, but they were spacious for city yards. The Sabrina Raven estate had been built on a double lot at the end of a quiet street and stood out to Tess as a haven nestled away from the pulse of the city.

As she was turning down the street that led to the mansion, her attention was caught by the familiar silhouette of a jogger and a big-boned white dog heading her way from the opposite direction. She squeezed her brakes and came to a stop, balancing on the pavement with the tips of her shoes as she waited for them.

It was Kurt. He was out jogging with Zeus, an

Argentine mastiff who would be one of the first dogs to head for the shelter. As far as any of them could tell, Zeus was blessed not to have been in any fighting rings before he was confiscated, even though he had been housed with several other dogs who'd not been as lucky. Zeus was young and playful and didn't mind being around other dogs.

"Morning," Kurt called out. "Do me a favor and ride closely by him, will you?"

Tess didn't have to ask why. Kurt had been putting Zeus through test after test, making sure the playful dog didn't have any unpredictable stress triggers. A man who lived nearby was eager to adopt the mastiff as soon as the injunction was lifted.

So far, Zeus didn't like firework-level booms, but few dogs did. When exposed to them, he tucked his tail and whined. Nothing else had fazed him.

Trusting Kurt to act in Zeus's best interest, Tess sped closer by the jogging pair than she would have under normal circumstances. Without losing the pace Kurt had set, Zeus yipped and wagged his tail hopefully as she zoomed past.

Tess circled back, slowing to ride alongside them as they jogged back. "Good boy, Zeus!" she praised. "He's ready, Kurt."

"It seems so."

Tess understood Kurt's need to be certain that every dog he sent on to the shelter was healed and ready.

As she pedaled along next to him, Tess felt a touch overdressed in her thick jacket and gloves. Even though the temperature was still in the forties, the sun was shining brightly as it rose in the sky, promising a pleasant day ahead. Kurt was wearing only sweatpants and a tight-fitting T-shirt that drew attention to his toned arms. And he was sweating even though she could see his steamy breath.

He reached over and gave the ponytail sticking out from underneath her helmet a gentle tug. "If you're dressing like that now, I can't wait to see what you bike here in come January."

"Come January, I hope that either you or Kelsey is going to be picking me up."

She'd known Kurt since shortly after she began training with Rob Bornello when she and Kurt were teens. He was a couple years older, which back then had felt like a bigger age difference than it did now. They'd had a love of dogs in common and had bonded over it, though it had taken multiple efforts on Tess's part to break through Kurt's barriers and get to know him. He'd not been much for conversation even before he spent eight years in the military. They'd hung around each other often enough over the years that he'd come to feel more like a sibling than a friend, more even than her decade-plus older brother and sister did.

"How'd the sales pitch go yesterday? Any luck?"

"Only if you count bad luck." *Aside from meeting Mason*, she thought. Her thoughts went to the coffee cup she'd left on her dresser. Would she have the nerve to call him later? What would she talk about if she did?

As they headed along the empty road, Tess relayed the story of how she'd lost her things. When she got to the part about how Mason had driven her around to search the Dumpsters near the park, Kurt shot her a disapproving glance but didn't interrupt. She left out the weird parts, like how she had Mason's buckeye in her jeans pocket and his phone number on the cup. And how she'd found him delectably attractive even though he had a sporty look, and so far, she'd always been a bookworms-over-jocks sort of girl.

Kurt was sorry to hear all that she'd lost. Even Zeus seemed to catch the tension in her voice and whined up at her without losing a beat of his stride.

"I was wondering why you didn't answer Kelsey's texts yesterday afternoon," he added.

Tess continued to pedal alongside him as they neared the circular driveway of the estate and Kurt slowed to a walk. He was hardly winded.

"What texts? I hope it wasn't not to come today, because I could really use one more day of this before donning my sandwich-maker cap tomorrow."

Kurt's forehead knotted into a V as he leaned over to give Zeus a hearty pat on the shoulder. "You're going back to Angelo's? Are they short on help?"

"No, I'm short on cash, and I have to replace my stuff somehow."

The front door of the house pulled open, and Kelsey stepped out onto the porch. "Hey, *chica*," she called, then waggled her eyebrows at Kurt. "I hope you're about to tell me you talked her into it." The earthy blond directed her attention Tess's way, folding her hands in prayer below her chin. "Pretty please? You're perfect for this. Trust me."

Tess dismounted her bike and looked back and forth between them. Maybe they hadn't been dating long, but they already seemed to be speaking a language of their own. "Guys, talked me into *what*?"

Chapter 6

For all Mason's ease in attracting women of late, he was surprised by the hesitation clinging to him like a coat of dust from stacking hay. He suspected that every step with Tess mattered, and he didn't want to falter on any of them.

Just before she'd slid down from his cab yesterday afternoon, he'd wanted to sweep her still-damp hair back from her face and run his fingertips along the smooth skin of her temple and cheek. He'd wanted to experience the taste and feel of her lips. He'd wanted to know every reason she was holding back, all the things she wasn't saying.

And he wanted to see her again.

He also wondered if she was a Mac or PC sort of girl.

A gift card was a safer bet, he knew. But dropping off a gift card felt about as impersonal as sending one to her via Amazon. He browsed the aisles at Best Buy, debating his choices. The techie sales guy assisting him knew his stuff, but his questions weren't helping Mason feel any more at ease.

Mason didn't know what sort of business Tess was in or whether she'd used her laptop for design, basic word processing, or a bit of both. He didn't know how much RAM or how many gigabytes of storage she'd need either.

After being assured she could exchange it if it didn't

suit her needs, he ended up choosing a top-of-the-line MacBook Pro. He drove straight to her grandmother's on the Hill where the row houses all looked pretty much the same. Fortunately, navigating back there was easier than he'd feared. Not having been one hundred percent sure she'd call, he'd committed the address and first major intersection to memory before driving off yesterday.

Reaching the house, he parked three doors away on the opposite side of the street. Regardless of how much he'd like to see her, he'd made the decision to deliver the laptop without knocking. He hoped to leave it on the porch without being noticed.

Although he hadn't done anything to lie about or hide his identity yesterday, sooner or later she'd make the connection. But her *not* discovering it for another meeting or two couldn't hurt. And someone in that house was a Red Birds fan. If Mason had any say in the matter, his second meeting with Tess would be as private as their first had been.

Using the yellow notepad tucked between his seat and console, he scribbled a note and dropped it in the bag.

> *It was a 50/50 toss-up whether you like Mac or*
> *PC. Feel free to exchange it if I chose wrong.*
> *Thanks again for yesterday.*

It was a pathetic thank-you. He felt like a kid in middle school sitting at the kitchen table, his mom hovering behind his shoulder, reminding him that adjectives and adverbs were brightly colored crayons on paper.

Folding the note in half, he dropped it inside the bag

and scanned the darkened windows of the matchbox house. The brick needed a bit of tuck-pointing, but the house was otherwise clean and well cared for.

As he pushed open the driver-side door, he had an urge to forget his plans and knock. He wanted to see Tess, and he wanted to meet her family.

But what if that caused her to see only Mason Redding, Red Birds third baseman? Or, even worse, the Mason Redding who had been chosen one of the city's most eligible bachelors in a number of polls this year, thanks in part to the partying he'd tried but failed to keep on the down low?

No, he needed to find a way to see her again without any of that stigma coming into play. He jogged up the steps and rested the bag against the doorframe. He was halfway down when he caught sight of an older woman walking up the sidewalk from the opposite direction.

She was short and wearing a simple dress, a faded purple cardigan, and flats, her head cocked sideways as she looked him over. She walked with the hint of a limp, but he guessed she was in her mid-eighties, so maybe that wasn't an anomaly. She was carrying a paper grocery bag in her arms.

He was about to cross the road to his truck when she spoke to him.

"She won't be home for a few hours."

Tess's grandma. It had to be. *Of all the luck.*

"I noticed your truck from down the block," she continued as she closed the distance between them. "You'd best come in. I'll fix you something to eat."

Mason was searching for a polite refusal when she held out her grocery bag.

"I'll let you carry it up the steps." It wasn't a question. "Did she tell you how we lost her grandfather last month? He went to the market for me every day after he retired. I made a habit of forgetting to put something on the list about once a week so I'd have the excuse to go myself."

When she kept walking and didn't stop talking long enough to let Mason get a word in, it seemed like he had no choice but to follow her.

"It's the simple routines I miss the most. Like how he carried his plate to the counter and set it on the same spot after every meal for sixty-three years, and the way he'd search his shirt pocket for his reading glasses before feeling for them on the top of his head, no matter how many times he found them there."

There'd been no introduction, no real greeting. And she wanted him, a total stranger, to follow her into her home.

"You're young enough that if I hadn't read about what you've gone through, I'd guess you wouldn't understand," she added, sending a wave of shock through Mason. "But I suspect you know how it feels when you have to adjust to a new routine that isn't as simple as the one you're used to."

She'd made it to the porch steps and was reaching for the bannister. She glanced his way long enough for him to notice that her eyes were bright and sharp. As she took the first step, she chuckled at his obvious surprise.

"So, me knowing you is more surprising than her *not* knowing you? As much attention as you get, I'd have guessed otherwise."

Mason shook his head. "Both are a surprise, if you want the truth."

She waved him up behind her. "Come on. The longer we stay out here, the more likely it is we'll have the whole block descending on us."

Not knowing what to say, he followed her up.

"It's heavy enough, whatever this is." She lifted the bag holding Tess's computer out of the doorway.

Mason shifted the shopping bag to his slinged arm and took the Best Buy bag from her. She pressed the wooden door open with some effort. "Did she tell you what happened yesterday?" he asked.

"About meeting you or losing her things?"

He shrugged. This entire situation was surreal enough to have his thoughts whirling in a thousand directions. "Both, I guess."

"Tess's things getting stolen knocked the wind out of her. And she's hard enough on herself when things are good." Mason followed her across a cluttered but cozy family room and into the galley kitchen. The single long counter was crowded with jars marked for flour and sugar, ceramic mixing bowls, a coffeepot, and a few plates of home-baked goods. There were only a few inches of open space. She pointed toward the less-crowded table, making it clear he was to set the bags there, without pausing her talk. "Harder on herself than any of us ever were on her. Set on proving herself too, with this dog business."

"Dog business?"

She pulled a bundle of fresh, dark-green herbs and a block of butter from the bag after he set it down and was reaching back in for something else when she stopped, inspecting him with renewed interest. "She didn't tell you? That's a surprise. When I saw you two in your truck, I thought you were having a moment, but how can you have a moment when you hardly know anything about each other?"

Once again, Mason was at a loss for what to say.

"It's no surprise she didn't recognize you. I never could get her to sit still to watch more than a few minutes of anything on the television. Either her nose was in a book or she was outside. And she was away for over a year. Me, I don't think I missed more than three games this summer. When I saw you from the window yesterday, I knew I'd seen you before, but it was dark and hard to see inside your cab. Just now when I saw you jogging away from that truck toward the porch, I knew instantly. I'd have gotten it yesterday if I'd seen the sling."

Mason raised his arm, causing a sharp pain to race across his shoulder. "I wouldn't say it's helped me slide into anonymity." He wanted to ask more about the dog business she'd been referring to, but decided to ask Tess in person.

"And my granddaughter didn't recognize you, so you're back for more."

Mason swallowed in the suddenly quiet room. When he had nothing to say in response, she pulled a box of Twinkies from the bag. He found himself blinking over how out of place they felt in this Italian American kitchen.

"They're my one vice," she said in explanation. She folded the empty bag and smoothed it flat against her stomach.

"Are you going to tell her who I am?"

"Should I?"

He took a risk. "I'd like to see her again first."

"You think she won't give you the time of day once she learns who you are?"

Not only was this old woman easy to open up to, she seemed to know how to slice through the layers to get right at the source. "That's what I fear more than what I think. You know her. What do you think?"

"I think," she said, "that my granddaughter is a meal to be appreciated, to be savored, not a drive-through snack."

His jaw fell open an inch. "No, ma'am. I, uh, didn't think she was."

"I follow baseball. My granddaughters follow the gossip columns. If I were to believe half of what I've heard, I'd say you have an appetite for fast food."

Mason cleared his throat to stifle his surprise. *What do you say to that?* He drummed his fingers on the table.

"But fortunately for you, I'm old enough to take everything with a pinch of salt. And what I think is that maybe you're ready for some home cooking." She gave a swift nod and motioned toward the couch. "Have a seat. Have you eaten lunch?"

Mason was almost certain she'd switched from talking about how she didn't want him thinking of her granddaughter as a one-night stand to actual food. "Ah, yes, ma'am."

"*Ma'am.* I like a young man who knows his manners. I'll make you a cup of coffee and plate you a slice of cream cake. It was better yesterday when it was just a day old. At two days old, it's lost some of its moisture."

Mason crossed the room and sank onto the worn and frayed cloth couch. There was a funeral program on the side table. It was resting against one of the framed photos, and Mason felt a rush of sympathy for the woman. He suspected that no matter someone's age, it would never be easy to let go of someone you loved.

"I met Stan Musial once," Tess's grandma said. From where he was sitting, he could see about half of her body as she poured a cup of coffee and placed it in the microwave. "I have his autograph in a drawer somewhere. He was considerably smaller than you, and he was no small man. I guess it takes bigger and bigger athletes to keep breaking those records."

He lost sight of her for a second, but then she came back into view, a serving knife and a plate in hand. "I listen to most games on the radio. When they're televised, I'll watch but keep the volume down. I've heard a lot of talk of how you struggled to come back."

Struggled to come back. She could only mean from one thing. And it was the one thing he'd thought about—almost nonstop—since the car accident last month.

Being a lightning strike survivor was the sort of thing that was talked about. A lot. Quotes from the interviews he'd done—ones in which he'd confessed how long and exhausting the recovery road had been—were mentioned time and again on air when he was up at bat. Both the physical and mental aspects of his recovery.

Mason had no doubt this had added to his fame. It was the strongest irony he knew—how the thing that had nearly kept him from his dreams later became the thing that made him bigger than life to many. It separated him from his teammates, from players striving hard in their own ways to be great at the game.

"How do you take your coffee?" she asked when he didn't respond to her comment.

"Black is fine. Thanks."

"What is it you brought her?" she asked as she carried over the cake on a delicate plate and the coffee in a daintier cup than Mason could remember ever drinking out of.

"A laptop. She probably told you that she was helping me catch an escaped dog yesterday when her stuff was stolen."

"She did." She handed him the plate and set the coffee on the side table. "What a laugh it will be when I tell my granddaughters I served cream cake to Mason Redding. Whenever it is that I tell them." She gave a wave of her hand as if in dismissal, and Mason wasn't sure what that meant.

"The cake is delicious. Really good." He could taste the cream cheese, ample powdered sugar, and finely diced nuts. Who needed Twinkies when they had this?

Her answering smile was small, but she seemed pleased. She closed the fingers of her right hand around the gold band on her left ring finger. "She's run before. I don't want her running again. My gut tells me if you tell her who you are, she'll shut you out. She's struggling with…things."

Mason nodded, hoping she'd offer more.

"My granddaughter is not a stepping-stone. I'll give you a few weeks unless I start to think you are using her as one. She can't see it, but I can. The life she's meant for is just a beat or two ahead of her. She needs a bridge, and from what I've heard, you do too."

Mason wasn't entirely sure what had just happened, but he heard himself answering in agreement. If he was right, she'd just given him permission to keep his identity from Tess.

Chapter 7

FOR ALL TESS'S EXPERIENCE WITH DOGS, THE realization that she'd spent very little time in animal shelters felt a bit like an epiphany. It went without saying that she was a huge proponent of rescue and adoption, but ever since her early training with Rob Bornello, dogs had had a way of finding her. Only a few months had gone by when she wasn't helping to find a home for one misplaced dog or another. She'd even saved a few from the throes of sterile, city-run pounds. She'd just never done any of it through the auspices of a shelter.

Tess stepped into the High Grove Animal Shelter a little under an hour after leaving Kurt and Kelsey. It was her third visit here, and she was no less moved by the shelter's charm than when she'd first toured it a few weeks ago. Since then, she'd not stopped thinking about the difference it was making in so many lives—animal and human.

The shelter was about as far from an impersonal pound as possible. In fact, the main room had a homey feel. There was a colorful gift shop filled with dozens of things she wanted to buy, a training area and small stage, an adoption area, even a coffee, tea, and snack bar. On one wall of the front room was a ten-foot-wide, floor-to-ceiling photo mosaic featuring many of the happy animal-and-people love connections that had been made during the shelter's nearly twenty-five years in operation.

And that was just the beginning. An area for the felines called Kitty Country encircled the far end of the front portion of the building. Twenty-four kennels, some single and some double, housed a lively variety of beautiful felines. Each kennel was big enough for a small litter box, a play area, a regular bed, and specially made kitty slings. The slings were plush-lined durable nylon that hung from the top of the kennels and were popular napping spots.

There was also a brand-new floor-to-ceiling kitty play area called the Cat-a-Climb, named in honor of one of the shelter's donors, a mountain climber and architect who'd designed some of the revisions that were still under way in the rear of the building. The Cat-a-Climb was enclosed with a tear-proof mesh screen that the cats could climb. The screen was held in place by rough-hewn timber. The play area was only about six feet in diameter, but it was chock-full of tunnels, ramps, hideaway boxes, and toy birds and butterflies dangling on strings from the ceiling.

Healthy, vaccinated cats and kittens got to enjoy time out of their kennels each day as employees rotated a handful at a time into the play area. Tess had lost track of time watching cats of all ages play together. Their antics were not only charming, but also contagious. One high-energy cat after another drew others into its games.

Even before she had seen what was on the other side of the double doors separating off the back half of the building, Tess knew the shelter was a special place. Her tour of the back half had cemented this belief.

While louder than the front of the building, the dog kennels were also a giant step up from the cold, sterile rows of chain-metal cages and concrete floors of most of the shelters she'd seen. Here, each kennel was divided into three sections. The back portion was concrete floor, while the front was part artificial grass and part raised bed. And inside each kennel was a combination of tennis balls hung on ropes from the ceiling, treat-dispensing dog puzzles, well-worn stuffed animals, and cozy blankets.

The kennels along the sidewall of the building had pet doors that led outside to separated, enclosed runs, enabling the dogs to get fresh air and stretch their legs. Tess had been told that the dogs who'd been at the shelter the longest were housed in these kennels.

The back wall of the building was closed off by a tarp due to an expansion project that would be finished in a few months. Behind the building, a small dog park was under construction as well. Megan, the shelter director, had promised to invite Tess to the big unveiling party that was being planned for after the start of the next year.

Today, Tess's third time here, left her no less moved by the unique shelter than her first two visits. The only difference was that today she'd been asked here for a reason.

A remarkable and slightly terrifying one.

While waiting a few minutes for Megan to finish with a customer, Tess busied herself by examining the gift-shop goodies and trying not to let her nerves get the best of her. Megan finished with her customer and was diving into details so quickly that Tess could hardly process it all.

"I think the best spot to film you would be here," Megan said. She was heavily pregnant and had a radiant glow about her. They'd made their way to the back of the main room, and Megan was motioning to the

Cat-a-Climb. "Assuming we can make the lighting work. Patrick is working on that. It would be cute to film in the back with the dogs, but let's face it: it's frequently loud enough back there to hamper filming."

Tess's belly flipped as if it were in its own gymnastic competition. Lighting. Cameras. A designated filming location. This was *so* not her. *Wasn't it?*

Kurt and Kelsey had recommended Tess to spearhead a YouTube series the shelter wanted to embark on. The most incredible part was that Tess was being asked to help spread the word about natural behavior training and holistic pet care to a potentially bigger audience than she'd ever meet distributing brochures through local pet companies.

Considering the shelter's large social-media following, it was a better opportunity than Tess could've even imagined.

Assuming you wouldn't bomb it by rambling on incoherently like you did in your college speech class. She swallowed back her hesitance about performing and focused on what Megan was saying.

"I understand if you want to think it over. But from what Kurt has shared, you really know your stuff." Megan gave Tess a hopeful look. "We've been wanting forever to do more than host biweekly classes here. Education is a big part of our mission, but when we're short-staffed or underfunded, it doesn't always make our priority list. And with this baby coming and Kelsey so wrapped up at the Sabrina Raven estate helping to retrain the dogs, it was looking like we might have to put this on the back burner awhile longer. Then at yesterday's staff meeting, Kelsey thought of you. She thinks you'd be great on camera. And honestly, online video tips and tutorials seem like they might be the best way to help our clients when they need it most."

Tess's thoughts flashed back to seventh grade and the social studies project she'd been so excited to tape. She'd written the script and practiced it a dozen times in front of the bathroom mirror. She'd been full of confidence till she stood in front of the video camera and tried not to focus on the blinking red light.

Tess Grasso, you're twenty-six and a world traveler. You can do this in your sleep.

"So, um, Kelsey said you've got a list of priority topics you'd like addressed?" Tess asked.

"Yep. Ideally, we'd like to focus the first ten or so online videos on the biggest pet-adoption trouble areas we tend to see. But you'd be writing the dialogue. I know you're starting up your own business, and as long as there are no selling attempts on camera, we'd be fine with you advertising your services to anyone who reaches out to you with questions."

It was almost too good to believe. A couple hours of prep work a week, combined with a bit of confidence, and she'd get to be the host of the *Healthy Pet, Happy Pet* online video series.

Someone pinch me, please.

"Yeah, of course. I'm in. Absolutely." She bit her lip, but it didn't stop the excited grin from spreading across her face. "One hundred percent in. Only, before we hammer out the details, I have a proposition of my own I'd like to throw out."

Megan shrugged one shoulder. "Sure."

"When I came in, I noticed you had a job posting on

your bulletin board for a full-time worker. I asked Fidel, and he said you haven't hired anyone yet." Hoping for a yes more than she probably should, Tess plunged ahead. "I'd like to apply for the position. If I were hired, you could save the money you've offered to pay me to write the scripts and film the video clips. I'd be happy to do that after work on my own time."

Megan's face lit with surprise. "Wow. Are you kidding? I never considered that you might be interested in taking a full-time position here. I have to warn you though, the only thing we have available right now is a basic starting position. From what Kurt shared, you're a master-level trainer and partway through a vet degree. There's a lot of grunt work in this position, and it only pays a couple dollars an hour over minimum wage. I'd love to tell you otherwise, but it's all we've got right now. It's mostly scrubbing kennels, walking dogs, moving cats around, that sort of thing." Megan raised one eyebrow hopefully. "If you're interested in that, I'll help you fill out the application right now."

After the hard news of yesterday—*Could all that only have happened yesterday?*—this turn of events was almost too good to believe. "I'd be honored to be considered for the position."

"You have no idea how happy you've just made me," Megan said, squeezing Tess's hand. "I've been worried about going into labor early and leaving this place short-staffed. With you on board, Tess, we'd be ready for anything."

Tess had to refrain from bouncing up and down. "If you hire me, I'll give you my absolute best. You won't regret it."

"You don't have to tell me that twice. Kelsey and Kurt have been singing your praises all month."

Tess felt like an enormous weight had been lifted. "To be honest, the business I was hoping to start isn't going anywhere quickly. I was close to taking a full-time job elsewhere, but working here would make me the happiest person in St. Louis. I'm not even kidding."

Megan pulled her in for a hug. "Have a seat, and I'll grab you an application. And I'll call Kelsey and Kurt to tell them the good news."

Even though the bike ride from the shelter to Nonna's had Tess battling more traffic congestion and aggressive drivers than she was used to, she was still riding a wave of happy adrenaline when she got home. Not only did she not have to go back to sandwich-making, but she was going to work with animals *and* get to offer the help and advice she'd been hoping to relay, potentially reaching a wider audience than she'd ever imagined.

All this made losing her things not hurt nearly as badly as it had just hours ago.

After parking her bike in front of the shed behind the house, Tess headed in through the rarely locked back door. She paused in the doorway to unroll a jeans leg at the calf. Whenever she biked in jeans, she rolled up the right leg to keep it from getting caught in the spokes.

Nonna was in her favorite chair, legs elevated on a footstool, stitching a loose seam in what Tess assumed was a pair of her grandpa's old dress pants.

The sight sent a ripple of nostalgia through Tess. Her grandparents had lived comfortably together for sixty-three years. She'd heard them bicker and gripe at each other every so often, but now that she was older, she understood they'd grown used to each other like a comfortable, well-worn pair of shoes. She could barely fathom what it would be like for her grandma to adjust to life without him.

"Hey, Nonna," she said, planting a kiss on the sprayed-stiff hair atop Nonna's head before going into the kitchen for a drink. She'd biked nearly eighteen miles today, and the muscles in her legs felt rubbery. She'd be sore tomorrow for sure. "How was your day?" Figuring that once she relayed her job news, it would consume the conversation, Tess decided to hold off to see how her grandma was faring. She'd been unusually quiet yesterday evening.

"Not as quiet as some. I thought I'd better get your grandfather's clothes in shape to take to Goodwill. Jesus knows they won't do any good filling up the closet here."

"If you want me to go with you when you take them in, I can." Tess returned to the family room with a tall glass of water. "Did you go to the store?" she asked, passing a large Best Buy bag on the kitchen table.

"Only the market. On the way home, I spotted your gentleman's truck in the street. He was dropping that bag at the door."

Tess blinked. She was standing next to her grandma again. She looked at the bag on the table with renewed interest. It *couldn't* be from him. That didn't make any sense. "Mason's truck? Are you sure? Did you actually see him?"

"If you count inviting him in for cake seeing him, then yes."

Tess could've picked her jaw up off the floor. Mason had been here. In this house.

Her stomach did a soft roll, and what was likely a goofy-looking smile tugged at her lips. "How long ago did he leave?" She headed for the table and set her glass down with a clunk. Instead of a gentle roll, her stomach started to prance and buck as she peeked inside the bag. There was a sleek box with the Apple symbol on the top. She lifted it out, reading the words *MacBook Air* on the long side.

Mason had brought her a brand-new MacBook Air.

"No fricking way," she mumbled to herself. Twelve feet away, Nonna cleared her throat. She'd never tolerated cursing of any sort.

"Nonna, this is crazy. Did he say anything about this?"

"Should he have? He didn't. But there's a note at the bottom, if you missed it. And yes, I looked. If it was meant to be private, he wouldn't have delivered it in an open bag."

Tess fished inside for the note. She pulled it out along with a gift receipt. She read it twice, searching for words and confirmation it didn't contain. He hadn't even signed his name for what she suspected was a thousand-plus-dollar gift.

A MacBook Air.

She'd never owned anything this nice. The laptop that had been stolen was a hand-me-down from her uncle. Over the four years she'd owned it, she'd paid the price of a decent new laptop in piecemeal chunks to defibrillate it over and over again.

"You can't just give someone a MacBook Air."

"Can't?" Nonna asked. "Show me 'can't.' He did, didn't he?"

Tess opened the box and stared at the sleek, shiny laptop and still-wrapped-in-plastic accessories. She couldn't accept this.

Could she?

"Nonna," she said, abandoning the laptop and returning to the family room. "How did he explain this?"

Her grandma glanced up from her sewing, looking at Tess over the top rim of her bifocals. "I told you. He didn't. He liked the cream cake though. He said his mother bakes a good deal, but he'd never had a cream cake before."

Tess would've been surprised if anyone ever admitted to not liking one of her grandma's Italian cream cakes. They were her specialty. But that was beside the point. "That laptop probably cost more than a thousand dollars."

Her grandmother gave a *hmph* as she tied a knot in the thread. "I wouldn't be surprised if he spent close to that in gas getting here in the truck he's driving."

"Nonna, what do you think I should do?"

"Me? I say enjoy your new computer."

Tess made for the spare bedroom she'd claimed as her own since returning to the States and scanned the top of the crowded dresser. Tess would've loved to unpack and really make the room feel like her own, but there wasn't an inch in a drawer or closet in Nonna's small house that wasn't already taken up by something or other.

As Tess searched for sight of the cup, an alarm began to go off inside her. She'd set the cup in the far-right corner between Nonna's jewelry box and a stack of magazines that needed upcycling. Only it wasn't there any longer. Tucking her fingers tightly against her palms, Tess surveyed the room. It wasn't on the night-stand or the old chest of drawers either.

"Hey, Nonna, I left a paper cup on the dresser, and now I can't find it. Did you move it?"

Nonna had the pants folded on her lap and was clos-ing her sewing kit when Tess rejoined her. "That empty paper cup? Yes, I tossed it."

Panic was setting in heavily. Of all the things sitting around in this house, Nonna had gone for her cup. "In which trash can?"

"The kitchen, I think."

Tess hurried into the kitchen. The can was empty. "Did you take the trash out?"

"Of course. It was trash day."

Tess braced herself as she headed outside. She wasn't surprised to find the trash can empty, aside from a bunch of goo in the bottom. A few unexpected tears stung her eyes. What would Mason think when she didn't even call to offer her thanks?

No. That wasn't going to happen. She knew where he lived. Sort of.

She glanced at her watch. She had about an hour of light left. If she hurried, she could bike to his building and leave a note of thanks taped next to the entry. Or better yet, she could enter the basement garage and leave a note on his windshield wiper if he was home.

She could wait for tomorrow, but she was starting work at the shelter and had promised to be there first thing. And with full-time hours, she'd be lucky to be able to get home tomorrow on her bike before dark. This reminded her that she hadn't told her grandma the good news yet. However, if she was biking downtown, she was pushing it on the amount of daylight left. Her news was going to need to wait until she got back.

"Nonna, I'm running a quick errand," she said as she stepped back into the house, letting the screen door bang shut behind her a second time. "I'll be back to help with dinner in an hour."

"I'll be here. Though I feel like I should remind you there's no lit fuse connected to your bottom."

"I know, Nonna. I'll explain it all when I get back." Tess composed a quick note of thanks on one of her grandma's violet-patterned thank-you cards and included a line of explanation about the cup, then scribbled her grandma's landline number at the bottom. Afterward, she slathered on a second round of deodorant and ran a brush through her hair, even though another thirty minutes in the helmet would make the effort pointless. She grabbed a forkful of cream cake for energy, then headed out.

Maybe it was silly to bike thirty minutes to thank Mason for a computer she'd not yet turned on, but it was the sort of silly she couldn't suppress.

———~~~———

Mason stepped out of the shower and stared at his reflection in the partially fogged mirror, scanning his left shoulder and arm for the inevitable muscle loss that had been sure to hit while his arm was in a sling.

Why his left side?

Again.

The accident had rekindled old fears. He'd woken

up too early the last four mornings in a row, his sheets damp from the sweat of nightmares. It took shaking out of the last shards of sleep to remember that this recent brush with immobility carried no threat of permanence. Collarbones healed. He'd survived worse; that was for certain. By the time spring training rolled around, these few months of rest and recuperation would be long behind him.

It was a strange feeling, not knowing what to do with himself most of the day. Including spring training and postseason playoffs, this season had stretched over eight jam-packed months, and Mason had played in about 150 of the 162 regular season games. From mid-February till he got in the accident in early October, days had greeted him with a blur of never-ending activity.

Now, he seemed to have nothing but long stretches of time between sporadic appointments. In the promise he'd made himself to get control of a life that had been feeling too unconstrained, he'd curtailed his nights out to nearly zero. He had a few postseason interviews lined up, but most were over the phone. His workouts were scaled down and most often solitary. Half the team was scattered, spending the winter in their home states or away on vacation. Most of his teammates who lived in St. Louis had families and were hunkering down now that the season had ended, making appearances here and there and savoring the quiet, short as it was sure to be.

Mason had planned a month-long trip to Maui with a buddy to surf and unwind, but he'd had to back out after the accident. A month in Maui without being able to surf or scuba dive would've been torture. On top of that were the demands of his physical therapy schedule and follow-up appointments with the surgeon who'd repaired his shattered clavicle.

He ran the ring and index finger of his right hand along the ridge of his clavicle, over the fresh eight-inch scar that railroad tracked along it. He should give serious thought to going home to his family for a month or two. He could find a physical therapist to continue with there.

What about Tess?

Mason huffed as the thought raced across his mind. What about her? It had been one meeting. One chance encounter. How could he expect it to mean anything? It would be crazy to stick around here in practical isolation in hopes it might.

But the thought of leaving—of *not* seeing if something could come of their chance encounter—felt like he'd just tried on a teammate's glove.

After the trip to Tess's grandmother's and before his physical therapy, he'd spent a half hour at Georges's, talking to his four-decades-older friend about the way he'd been moved by Tess. Not just moved, but shaken off an axis.

"Everyone needs to grow up some time," Georges had said. "Some of us put it off longer than others. Now is as good a time as any for it to happen to you."

Mason had been a tad pissed by the comment, but he understood what his friend meant. Georges was nearing seventy and had spent a good deal of his life before he'd met Richard, his late partner, finding himself and wandering from city to city across Europe and Asia. Georges was in his early forties when he met Richard and claimed it wasn't until after they'd fallen in love that he'd picked up his first paintbrush. It was only then, he insisted, that he'd been ready to let all that he'd seen and experienced find form on canvas.

Georges had left his home in Paris and followed Richard to America, first New York, then to St. Louis for Richard's job transfer. Richard had died almost three years ago, half a year before Mason met Georges. Georges had considered moving back to New York or to his hometown just outside Paris, but he said he wouldn't until he grew tired of painting the St. Louis skyline, and even though it was a moderately small city, he hadn't yet.

Georges had never taken a single art class but had become locally famous. His giant, acrylic skyline portraits of the city typically sold for forty or fifty grand. Shortly after Georges and Mason cosigned on the building and officially created a business together, Georges had gifted one of his paintings to Mason. It was a skyline view of the stadium and surrounding old redbrick buildings mixed with shiny, new skyscrapers. The sky changed from stormy and dark on one side to clear and bright on the other. The sun, well hidden behind purple-gray clouds, created—perhaps impossibly—striking reflections on some of the skyscrapers.

Georges was also a lifelong Lord of the Rings fan. He'd been intrigued to hear about Tess's skill with dogs, and he'd been particularly impressed to learn of Tess's reaction to the name Mason had given the stray. Before Mason had headed out for this therapy session, Georges had shoved his leather-bound fiftieth edition of *The Fellowship of the Ring* at him, insisting he needed to read it again after Mason had confided that he hadn't read it since the summer before eighth grade.

To stave off the emptiness he was feeling, Mason

could order in tonight—he hadn't ordered from the authentic Vietnamese place that delivered in a while—and read it again.

He finished drying off, hung his favorite chambray linen towel on the hook, left the steamy warmth and heated tile floor of his bathroom, and headed into his bedroom. Downstairs, the majority of his 2,200-square-foot loft was open and had a spacious air due in part to the eighteen-foot ceiling throughout most of it and the ample windows. His bedroom and attached bathroom were above the only section of the loft that was divided into two floors—the kitchen and guest bedroom—and accessible only by a winding iron staircase. The street-facing wall of the bedroom was lined with floor-to-ceiling windows that faced toward the stadium and the Arch, but the loft was high up enough that he never worried about privacy.

Before heading into his walk-in closet, he lifted his phone off his bed. Two missed calls from Georges and one voicemail. Mason had just left him two hours ago. Chances were Millie needed to go out and Georges wasn't feeling up to it. Georges's pain levels still crescendoed over the course of the day and were worst in the evening.

Mason dropped the phone back on the bed and was in the closet pulling on a pair of boxer briefs when he heard a knock and Georges's distinct French accent rising from downstairs.

"Where's the fire? Hang on a minute," he called down, even though he doubted Georges, who was continuing to knock impatiently, could hear him.

Mason grabbed a T-shirt and his favorite Fog Linen

lounge pants, tossed them over his shoulder, and jogged down the winding stairs to the main floor. His bare feet had just landed on the reclaimed hundred-and-fifty-year-old Baltic pine floors that covered the main level when he remembered he'd left his sling upstairs on the bathroom door handle.

It seemed his friend had forgotten Mason's code again. Half the time, Georges walked in without an invitation. The other half, he typed in wrong numbers until the door locked up. Rather than leave Georges waiting and most likely disturbing everyone on the fifth floor below them, Mason jogged over and threw open the door.

"Give me a sec, won't you, you ingrate," he said playfully.

He was half turned toward the stairs when he caught a glimpse in his peripheral vision of a second figure standing next to his buddy.

Mason stopped short, locking eyes with Tess for a solid second before she turned away, flushing deep red and turning her attention to Millie, who was in the doorway, wagging her tail and growling up at Mason as if he were a stranger.

That was when it hit him that the only thing he had on was a pair of underwear. "Shit. Georges, really? Shit."

Georges, who was leaning on his cane, stepped forward and grabbed the door handle. "Don't get those god-awful undies in a pinch," he said as he pulled the door mostly closed. "Put some clothes on, and join us at my place."

Then the door was closed, and Mason could hear Georges chuckling on the other side, confessing that he himself had never been a fan of underwear at all, so it was a good thing Tess hadn't just knocked on his door after he'd gotten out of the shower, and nothing about the night felt quiet or lonely after all.

Tess was here. Tess was *here*, and Mason hoped to God that Georges—who was a fan of painting in the nude and letting the world know about it—would remember to show just a bit of discretion until Mason could get dressed and get over there.

Chapter 8

TESS WAS DOING HER DARNEDEST TO ACT AS IF SEEING Mason in his underwear wasn't that big a deal. Trying to act as if she was still paying attention as Georges motioned her into his loft after him.

Tess had biked up to the front of the building and was dismounting when she'd noticed Millie and Georges fifty feet away in a small patch of unpaved earth encircling a tree. Millie had been noticing her too. The little Westie had been barking and pouncing and wagging her tail in all-out excitement. She'd also been tugging hard on her leash, and her cane-wielding owner was wincing. Remembering that Mason's friend had recently undergone surgery, Tess had hurried over and rewarded Millie with a friendly rubdown to put an end to the leash pulling.

Georges had clearly heard how Tess had helped rescue his loose pet yesterday. As soon as she stood up again and began to introduce herself, he'd pulled her in for a hug.

They'd talked for several minutes, and Tess had gotten the distinct feeling that Mason had shared quite a bit about her. This made her stomach do a pancake flip. Georges had known about the computer, and that Mason had spent time with her grandma this afternoon.

She'd tried to give Georges the note she'd written for Mason, but he wouldn't hear of her leaving without coming up and giving it to Mason herself. So she'd stashed her bike in the lobby and followed Georges and Millie onto the elevator. When Mason hadn't answered his phone and they'd reached the sixth floor, one that needed an elevator key or code to access, Tess wasn't sure if she hoped Mason wasn't home or just wasn't near his phone. The thought of seeing him had caused her blood to pulse like when she was climbing a never-ending hill on her bike.

And that was before he'd answered the door in his underwear.

That...that had been surreal. Tess was pretty sure she'd felt a similar sense of awe in Florence standing in front of Michelangelo's statue of David.

People didn't look like that. None she'd ever met, anyway. He was muscle and strength and beauty of form.

Tess pulled her thoughts together as she looked around Georges's open loft. One wall was exposed red brick, the ceilings were impressively high, and the furniture and accessories gave the loft a modern air like Tess had seen in certain hotels and hostels in Switzerland and Germany and other modern European hot spots. A giant canvas painting of the St. Louis skyline on a rainy day hung on a muted-gray wall.

"What a beautiful painting," Tess said before registering that Georges had just asked her something. She replayed the words and realized that he was asking her to unhook Millie's leash from her collar since bending was difficult.

"Of course." She freed the eager Westie and gave her a rub across the top of her haunches. Millie thumped her leg to the rhythm, then raced around the spacious loft like a lit firework before hopping up onto the back of the couch and staring out the window as if she was ready to take over sixth-floor guard duty.

"He told you I'm a painter?" Georges was saying.

"Mason? No. Are you telling me you painted this?" Tess headed over, her lingering insecurity from having seen Mason in his underwear draining away as she became absorbed in the giant painting. It was a remarkable city skyline with hues of St. Louis's trademark red brick blended with ample amounts of silver, gray, and a wider array of rich, deep purples than Tess would've imagined possible. "Wow. It's beautiful. And peaceful."

"Peaceful, you say?"

Tess shrugged. "I don't know much about art, but that's how it makes me feel."

"I agree. I think that's why this is the one skyline I've painted that I kept. It's here in St. Louis that I finally connected with my peace, something I owe Richard. God rest his soul."

Tess was still admiring the painting when she heard the front door pushing open. Millie dove off the couch and zoomed across the loft as Mason stepped inside.

Feeling a bit like she was about to make a dive herself, Tess turned toward the door, her breath locking in her lungs. Mason was dressed in jeans and a long-sleeved shirt and wearing his sling, but his wavy brown hair was still wet enough to give him the just-got-out-of-the-shower look.

And he was staring at her as though she were the only one in the room. Staring at her as though she wasn't standing next to his friend, and Millie wasn't lunging around him in closer and closer circles, barking ferociously and occasionally wagging her tail.

"I didn't think he'd have someone with him. Sorry about that."

Tess had been ready with an apology of her own and wasn't sure how to answer. Thankfully, Georges didn't give her much of an opportunity.

"Young lady, if Mason startled you, then you should consider yourself lucky it wasn't the two of you knocking on my door while I was creating one of my skylines."

"Yeah, Georges, let's not scare her off any worse."

Tess looked back and forth between them. "I'm not sure I want to know."

"Since he started it… Georges paints in the nude." Mason closed the door and headed over to join them. "At least when it's not midwinter. When I think he might be painting something, I've gotten in the habit of reminding him to put on a robe whenever I knock."

It was impossible to suppress a giggle. Tess looked at Georges for clarification.

"It's true." Georges threw up one hand as if in defeat. "When I paint, I don't like to feel confined. And when I'm creating something, I don't want to be troubled with nuances like clothes."

Tess tried to lock her imagination down. Georges was practically bald, most likely in his early seventies, small, and frail, and she didn't need an image of a naked version of him rolling around in her imagination. "Whatever works, right?"

A smile tugged at Georges's thin lips. "Right. We artists must stick together."

"Oh, I'm no artist. To be honest, I never progressed much past stick people." Tess wondered why he made the assumption.

"Perhaps you aren't a painter, but Mason says you are gifted with dogs, and your quick thinking likely saved my Millie's life. You are an artist using a different medium."

Tess wasn't so certain she agreed, but she thanked him anyway. "She's a really sweet dog," she added. Millie had given up trying to ward Mason off and had plopped sideways on the floor in the middle of their group. She was panting and thumping her tail rhythmically as they talked.

"She is. She belonged to my partner, Richard. He passed away a few years ago. Now it is just Millie and me." Before Tess could offer any condolences, he continued. "I am being an inconsiderate host. Can I offer you coffee or tea?"

"Thanks, but no. I have to get going. It'll be dark soon, and I'm biking." Before she lost her nerve, Tess tugged the thank-you card from her jacket pocket and offered it toward Mason. "I just wanted to thank you for the laptop. You really didn't—you don't—have to do that. At all."

Mason took the card, and the tips of their fingers brushed, sending a hot, fiery shiver down Tess's hand and along her arm.

"Considering the circumstances, it was the least I could do." Mason's brows pinched together. "You biked here from the Hill?"

Tess shrugged. "I pretty much bike everywhere. Just not after dark."

"I'll give you a ride. We can throw your bike in the back of my truck. Though there's no hurry."

Tess's legs were beyond rubbery from the extra

biking she'd done today, and it was going to be hard to make it home before dark. And riding in the dark was an activity she didn't enjoy. Still, the thought of being alone with Mason after having just seen ninety percent of his body threatened to create an outbreak of hives across *her* body. "Uh, thanks, but I promised my grandmother I'd be back for dinner."

"Then I'll take you back now." Mason shrugged as if it wasn't a matter for debate, and Tess realized there was no getting out of it without a good deal of arguing.

She heard herself agreeing before turning toward Georges. "It was great meeting you. I hope you heal quickly from your surgery."

Georges nodded. "Come again. Please. There's much we can discuss."

Tess could feel her palms starting to sweat even before Georges's door was shut. To make things worse, the hallway between his and Mason's lofts seemed to magnify every sound. Thankfully, as soon as Mason pressed the down button on the elevator, he left her to grab his keys, so she had a minute by herself to gather her composure.

As he jogged off, she racked her brain for things to talk about that wouldn't lead back to seeing him in his underwear.

While waiting, she scoped out the hallway. It was sparsely decorated but had rich taupe walls and beautiful hardwood floors. *That's it, Tess. Talk about how pretty the barren hallway is. That'll show you aren't nervous.*

Mason stepped out of his place, sliding a wallet into his pants and jangling a set of keys. He'd taken the time to put on a fitted leather jacket that made his shoulders look even broader.

"So, uh, I'm just going to come out and say it." He nodded toward her lower legs. "The fact that you biked here explains why you've got your right pant leg rolled up to the calf and not your left." His face lit in an easy grin. "I was wondering if it was a fashion statement."

If Tess could melt between the floorboards, she would have. In the commotion of greeting Georges and Millie, she'd forgotten to roll down the right side of her jeans. She could feel the blush spreading color all the way down her neck. She took her time unrolling her jeans in hopes the blush would dissipate.

"That's just like me." Feeling more blood draining to her face the longer she took, she stood up. "It's so my jeans don't get caught in the spokes, but I guess you realized that or you wouldn't have made the connection."

The elevator dinged as it opened. Mason nudged her elbow with his as they stepped onto it. "Kidding. I knew what it was right away. I used to ride everywhere. Once when I was in college, I made it all the way through my second class before I realized I'd done the same thing, only my calves don't hold a candle to yours."

Tess suppressed a deeper wave of panic as the elevator door closed. His compliment didn't help her blush dissipate either. If it lingered much longer, it was going to look painted on. "My bike's in the lobby, by the way," she said when he pressed the button for the garage, one level below the lobby.

He pressed the lobby one as well. "I'll drop you there, then I'll drive up and meet you out front."

"Thanks."

Tess was relieved the elevator wasn't one of those

slow, grinding ones. She practically lunged out when the doors opened.

As she glanced back, Mason grinned. One side of his mouth drew up higher than the other, calling her attention to his deep dimple. "See you in a minute."

Instead of grabbing her bike after the doors closed, Tess headed over to an adequately reflective piece of framed artwork. She did her best to finger comb through her hair and make sure the mascara she'd applied hadn't smudged during the windy bike ride. When she was through, she took one deep, calming breath and headed outside with her bike. Her helmet, hung by the buckle on the handlebar, swung rhythmically against the side of her wrist. By the time the automatically locking door clicked shut behind her, Mason's truck was rolling up the nearby ramp.

He said your calves are nice. There was no denying it. Tess was crushing hard. Only, she usually went for the bookish sort, the kind of guy with an ambling stride who was as likely to trip over the crack in the sidewalk as she was.

It stood to reason that her year and a half without a date had her hormones craving a testosterone fix.

Mason hopped out of the truck and dropped the tailgate. He hoisted her bike into the air effortlessly with one arm. When he had it parallel with the truck bed, he frowned. "I'm still figuring out what I can't do with one arm in a sling. How about popping up there to help lay it down?"

"Sure." Tess was agile enough, but some things were easier agreed to than done. The gate was higher than her belly button, and the hard metal was uninviting.

"The easiest way is to step up on the back tire and then swing your leg over."

"I did an internship on a sustainable farm in Italy through a connection a friend of mine had. And I have to say, the flatbed trucks over there are much lower to the ground." She did as he instructed, grabbing the top of the truck bed for support as she stepped up on the tire. She was swinging her leg over when she realized he'd set her bike back down and was wrapping his hand firmly around her elbow.

"Pretty much everything over here's bigger, isn't it?" he replied.

He was right behind her, and his proximity made her afraid she'd slip and smack her face on the top of the truck bed.

"What'd you do to your shoulder?" she spat out, desperate to take attention off her *not* answering his question. His tone didn't carry any implied suggestion, so Tess's racing thoughts of some things that were likely bigger than she was accustomed to were hers and hers alone.

"Wrong place at the wrong time. You know how it goes. I should be getting the sling off later this week, and that won't come a day too soon."

Tess's feet landed in the bed, and she stood up. It was lined with a black spray liner, and she was more worried about the damage her bike might do to the truck bed than what it might do to her bike.

Once more, Mason hoisted her bike, lifting it to the height of the bed as if it were a handheld five-pound weight, not a gangly ten-speed. Tess didn't know why she was surprised. She'd just had a good glimpse upstairs at why it was so easy for him.

"Just lay it down anywhere?" she asked, rolling the bike to the opposite edge.

"Yeah, it won't matter."

He waited by the open tailgate and raised a hand to help her down after she was finished. Even though she could've gotten down fine without it, Tess let her hand close around his. She felt the jolt spider-web up into her collarbones and down past her pelvis. The skin of his palm was thick and tough without being calloused, and Tess could imagine the contentment that would come from taking a long walk with him and never letting that hand go. Like when she was little and on a field trip with her class to the zoo. It had started raining, and they'd abandoned the zoo for the nearby art museum. Tess remembered worrying that she'd lose her way and be lost, but her teacher was considerably taller. Tess had been comforted by the knowledge that all she needed to do was keep sight of her teacher, and everything would be fine.

Immediately after her feet smacked the pavement, Tess dropped Mason's hand, only to have it close even more firmly over her shoulder. She tensed before realizing his attention was no longer on her.

"Look," he said, nodding toward something down the street.

Tess turned to spy the stray dog—John Ronald—several hundred feet away, watching them intently. The gorgeous black-and-white husky or malamute mix had his head cocked inquisitively, and he was carrying what Tess thought was a very worn shoe in his mouth.

For the longest time, none of the three of them moved. It was clear to Tess that she and Mason were the sole focus of the stray dog's attention. A car with a booming, obnoxious bass passed on the street in front of the building, and the dog didn't even seem to notice.

"All the stuff you've been doing to get his attention… It's working," Tess said.

Mason let go of Tess's shoulder and took three or four slow but deliberate strides toward the dog before dropping into a squat. He called to the stray in a low, calm, but strong voice and clicked his tongue. He rubbed the fingers of his right hand quickly back and forth along his thumb, calling the dog to him a second way.

John Ronald noticed and gave a few pumps of his tail. Abruptly, the dog dropped the shoe on the ground in front of Mason and gave his giant body a shake, his long legs sprawling apart a few inches as he did.

Tess's heart sank as the magnificent animal turned and trotted away. It was ridiculous to think the dog would just trot over and follow Mason inside, but she'd been hoping it anyway.

Feeling a touch of Mason's disappointment, she climbed into the passenger side of the enormous truck.

The drive to her grandma's house was filled mostly with talk of dogs, first John Ronald, but then they branched out. Tess confessed what Nonna had clearly already hinted to him, that she was trying to start her own healthy-dog consulting business but not having much luck.

When Tess told him about taking a job at the shelter, he smiled, shaking his head. "I know that place. It's awesome. Congratulations. You'll love it. A buddy of mine is the architect who designed some of their renovations—and all the lofts in my building—but that's a story for another time. Do you know much about the dogs they rescued from that fighting ring? It made the news back in September, but I've not heard anything lately."

Tess shook her head in disbelief. "I don't know why it surprises me when I'm reminded how connected everything is. Yeah, I have. Ever since I came back from Europe, I've been volunteering at the old house where the dogs are being kept until the court case is over and they're ready to be adopted out. I was trained by the guy who's organizing the rehab effort across several agencies."

"No kidding? What a small world indeed."

"It's just hitting me that I won't be able to see those dogs as much now. Hopefully the case will be settled soon, and they'll start coming into the shelter for adoption. I can't wait to see them be adopted into loving homes after all they've been through. Each one of them is sweet and remarkable, kind of like your John Ronald."

Mason pulled up in front of her grandmother's house without having asked for a single direction. The idea that he knew the way here so easily made Tess's heart thump. Inside the house, a lamp on the table in the family room shone an inviting yellow. Outside, the last lingering light of the sun was clinging in the air, and night was swelling from the shadows. The lights from Mason's truck shone atop the Prius parked alongside the curb twenty feet ahead.

"I'm sure they are," Mason answered.

It was time to get out, but Tess didn't want to leave. She unbuckled her seat belt but didn't move. "So, the laptop. I don't know that I can accept it."

A single crease lined Mason's forehead. "You lost yours helping me. I wanted to do it. And I don't want you to worry that buying it put me out, because it didn't."

After recognizing that her tension was palpable, Tess relaxed. She'd had her lips pressed tightly together. "If I keep it, I'd like the chance to make it up to you."

The lopsided smile that made her heart wallop reappeared. "What're you thinking?"

"John Ronald. I want to help you catch him."

His smile fell as quickly as it had popped up, and he studied her face in the glow from the dashboard instruments. Tess wanted to know what he was thinking and could only hope he'd open up to her. She didn't know him well enough to guess.

It was too dark to see the color of his eyes, but Tess was hungry to. She'd already memorized what a perfect mixture of blue and green they were. She'd seen him wear blue and knew that his eyes reflected it brilliantly, and she suspected the same thing happened when he wore green.

"He may not be lost," she continued before the last bit of her nerve slipped underneath the seat, "but I'm not entirely sure that means he's found. When I saw him tonight, I got the feeling that he wants to come to you, but he's afraid. He's a stray, and it's terrible the way some people treat them. You're probably hoping he'll come to you on his own or he'll let you catch him, but that's a jump he might not know how to make until it's too late. Life is hard for strays. Really hard. And if animal control catches him, God only knows what kind of chance he'd have."

Mason thumped the side of his thumb against the top of the console as he seemed to consider her words. "I'd like that," he said finally. "And your offer takes the pressure off me to figure out the best way to tell you that I want to see you again."

It had been on the tip of her tongue to add that she'd had some experience catching strays, but words fled. Tess bit her lower lip to keep her jaw from dropping to the floor.

"So, yes, I'll take your help. Gladly," Mason said. "And I'm going to try really hard to stay true to form and act like you offering this and not something less personal didn't just hit home deeper than you could know."

Tess shook her head. What could he possibly expect her to say in return?

"So instead," he continued, his smile reappearing, "I'll admit that while I've never gone on a real stray-dog hunt, I suspect that it'll work up an appetite even in someone as petite as you, and I'll offer to make dinner."

"I'm a vegetarian." *That's your answer? That's the best you can do?*

His smile widened. "That rules out the three meals I claim to have mastered at the most basic of levels, but I'm up for a challenge. What night's good for you?"

Tess pressed down her delight. He wanted to make her dinner. "It's Tuesday. I work the next several days, but I'm off at five. I think we could have as much luck in the evening as during the day. We'll just need flashlights. And any night's good for me, as long as it isn't raining. He'd likely be hunkered down in the rain, and it's unlikely we'd find him in the same spot as yesterday."

"How about Thursday? I'll pick you up. Is six thirty all right?"

Tess heard herself agreeing. Instead of dinner and a movie, it was dinner and dog catching. So much for a cute pair of boots and a skirt to undo the image of the dorky pants-rolling that was probably burned into his brain.

"I wrote this in the card, but my grandma threw away the cup with your number on it. I should've said so earlier, but that's why I rode to your place. I didn't want you thinking I wasn't appreciative about the laptop. It'll probably be a few days before I get a new phone, but my grandma's number is in the card if you need it."

"Thanks. I'm glad you came over, but I'm pretty sure my number is on a slip of paper on your grandma's fridge. She asked earlier if you had my number. When I told her that I'd written it on a cup, she said cups were no place for phone numbers and had me write mine on a piece of paper. She said it wouldn't get thrown away if she stuck it to the fridge."

Tess clicked her tongue. "She knew I was looking for a cup after I found the laptop. You'd think she'd have told me that before I dashed out."

"If you ask me, it worked out pretty well that she didn't." For a split second, Tess got the feeling that he was about to lean in to kiss her, but then he shifted farther away and pushed open his door. "Speaking of bike rides, I nearly forgot your bike was in back."

Denying that the wave washing over her was disappointment, Tess hopped out and met him around back. Once the bike was down, he handed it off to her and swung the tailgate shut. Tess pressed her palm against the buckle of her helmet strap hanging off a handlebar.

"Good luck tomorrow," he said, hooking his thumb into his jeans pocket.

Tess thanked him. She remembered a flash of the dream she'd awoken to, the one in which she'd been kissing him and he'd been holding back. Had that only been this morning? It felt like a week ago.

It hardly seemed possible that she'd only met him yesterday. If he was holding back, it was the right thing to do. How off the wall was it that if he had kissed her, she'd have kissed him right back? It struck her how very out of character that would be for her.

Her last real boyfriend—they'd broken it off nearly two years ago now—had been someone she'd connected with mentally and emotionally, but not physically. They'd been dating for nearly a month when Tess had realized that every time he leaned in to kiss her, she had to keep herself from pulling away.

She couldn't imagine wanting to pull away from Mason. Not unless she learned something dark and ugly about his personality.

What was she doing? *Get it together, Tess.*

She looked toward the house. "My grandma's probably waiting. I'll see you Thursday?" She forced a step toward the driveway; it just didn't turn out to be very large one.

"Six thirty," he repeated. "And never fear. I'll have takeout cued up on my phone in case dinner sucks."

Tess laughed. "Can I bring something? Dessert?"

"Just your sweet self."

Her mouth went dry. She didn't think in all her life she'd ever wanted to be kissed as much as she did now. The urge was ridiculous but impossible to suppress. Then she remembered the taut, enticing muscles in his arms, chest, and shoulders and took off toward the driveway. "Thanks again for the ride."

"Anytime, Tess Grasso." Then he was getting back in his truck, and as she headed up the driveway, Tess was left to contemplate how Nonna must have told him her last name. And he'd remembered it.

Chapter 9

THE DOG HAD WATCHED THE MAN FROM A SAFE DISTANCE. After deciding that it wasn't safe to approach any closer, the dog had dropped the enticing shoe that he'd found on the far side of his territory. He'd carried it here in his mouth as a reward for the man who had become a reliable source of food. The dog found something most nights on the ground near the building that carried the man's scent. The man ate like an alpha of alphas.

This wasn't the first time the dog had seen the man in the company of a woman, but it was the first time the dog had seen him orient his body around a woman the way he'd done with this one, as if he noticed nothing but her. The dog knew enough about humans to understand the importance of the man's movements. He wanted her as his mate.

Of all the humans that shared the dog's territory, and the others who moved through his streets into occupied buildings, this man held the dog's interest the most. It wasn't only because the food left by the man was so tasty that it made the dog salivate even when he dreamed of it. Other humans tossed him bits of their meals at times too. But the dog's interest in this man sprouted from the man's interest in him.

The dog had seen similar affection given by other humans to the well-cared-for animals they brought into the buildings throughout the dog's streets. The man wanted to bring the dog into his human world, to share his living space and his food. The man wanted to form the quiet trust with him, the one that kept humans and dogs together even when the humans didn't have ropes tied around their dogs' necks.

The dog knew this before today when the man sank low to ground, making sounds that encouraged the dog to move closer. After watching the man long enough, the dog had turned and trotted off toward the river. Carrying the shoe had made him thirsty. And the dog would not heed the man's call today.

This wasn't the first human who had wanted to form the quiet trust with him. The first time a human had wanted to do that, the dog had been a young pup living with his mother and his perpetually limping sister far, far from here. Although leaving there had meant the dog had never again seen his mother or his sister—the last of his littermates not to have been taken away by a human—the dog was content to live here where the sun was less harsh and there was always water in the river except on the coldest days of winter when it was locked underneath a blanket of cold, frozen earth.

The dog could scarcely remember his first home. It had been a scorched, dry one where the barren earth glowed the same color as the last rays of the sun before it sank below the horizon. The only time that home had been tolerable was when the sky was dark and the sun was hiding.

The family of humans who had taken him from it had carried the scents of many different lands on them. Inside the smelly, confining metal thing that the dog had since come to know as a car, the space was packed tight with their things. The dog had not enjoyed being crammed inside; it made his stomach pitch and roll.

He'd since learned to avoid cars whenever possible. They were dangerous things that carried humans from place to place but sometimes sent animals who didn't move out of their paths quickly enough into the great sleep.

The car that had carried the dog away with the four humans and their belongings was the first and only time he'd been inside one. The alpha man reeked of the burning trash that he lifted to his lips and sucked on, making him cough and wheeze. His alpha man's mate was quiet and had hardly paid a moment of attention to the dog.

It was their two children, a small boy and a larger girl, who had wanted to form the quiet trust with the dog. The girl was better at it than the boy. Her hands were gentle and loving as they moved from his ears along his body to his tail and even down to the pads of his feet. It was a strange delight to be petted by her. From her, the dog learned that, unlike his mother whose affection came from her mouth and tongue, humans gave affection with their hands. The boy petted him too, but in addition to the pleasure the boy's touch gave, there was sometimes pain as the boy's small hands knotted into fists and pinched the dog's fur.

The three of them traveled together in the rear of the car while the alpha man and his mate traveled in front on the opposite side of a padded wall. When they weren't giving the dog affection, the boy and girl were either squirming or wrestling each other or sleeping as the car took them farther and farther from the dog's first home.

The longer they traveled, the angrier the alpha man became, and he communicated with his family through human growls instead of soft-spoken words. When salty drops of water fell from the girl's eyes and mucus dripped from her nose, the dog had wanted to please her. He found he couldn't get close enough, so he contented himself by balancing atop her small, thin legs as he licked the drops away. This made a bubbling sound erupt from her chest and stopped the salty drips from flowing down her cheeks.

The sun left the sky, and the car still took them farther and farther away. The girl slept again. In her sleep, she released her bladder, bathing their seat in her urine. The dog, whose own bladder had been painfully full, released his urine on the seat as well. His belly had long been cramping from hunger, and his mouth ached where budding teeth pierced his gums. He longed to chew on a stick or piece of debris. Finally, he contented himself by chewing on a part of the seat that stuck up above the rest. It was metal and bitter but cool and hard enough to ease the pain in the dog's mouth.

He was still chewing on it sometime later when the man began growling again, this time louder than ever before. The stale air in the car vanished as a wild, whipping wind began to blow about. The fresh smells that had filled the air first delighted the dog.

If the dog had known he'd never be with the girl again, he'd have licked her awake. Very soon after the fresh air began to whip about, the man had reached over the divide and grabbed the dog on the back of his neck, lifting him in one easy swoop over the divide and up into the part of the car where the man and his mate were sitting.

The dog's feet had never even touched the seat. Instead, the dog was heaved out of the car. For the wildest moment, he'd felt as if he was suspended in the air as the wind seemed to carry him above the earth.

The dog landed on the street with the hardest smack of his life. One back leg buckled underneath him and then refused to move like the other three. A piercing, unbearable pain shot up his leg and through his body. It was difficult to breathe, and cuts and scrapes covered his body.

The dog had lain still, panting and terrified, until he'd spotted car after car barreling toward him, their bright lights beaming at him, blinding him. Full of a fear he'd never experienced, he dashed for cover, running on his three good legs until his body would no longer carry him, and the cars and their blinding lights were far enough away that he no longer cowered in terror.

He passed the night licking his wounds, full of a more painful hunger than he'd yet known. In the distance, he could smell the life-giving water of the river that had helped sustain him ever since. Full of a weakness that threatened to overtake him, and with one back leg dragging behind, the dog made for the river at first light.

He drank and drank and drank. Afterward, he crawled to a group of bushes and hid under their green leaves. There, he slept the day away.

He passed the next few days like that, eating scraps that had been abandoned on the street by humans and drinking from the river, holding his back leg up as he moved when he had the strength and letting it drag behind him when he didn't.

He grew weaker and less interested in the world as the days passed, and he knew he was the closest he'd ever been to the great sleep that one of his littermates had fallen into not many days after they had been born.

Thought of the great sleep had begun to comfort him the way the girl's hands had comforted him as they moved over his body.

The dog had stopped paying attention to the world when the second and last—until now—human who had cared to form the quiet trust with him entered his world. The first time he took notice of this human, she was leaning over him, using her fingers to wipe a salty, rich grease across the top of his tongue.

Unlike the girl, she was not young. Her hands and fingers were bent and stiff, but she used them without complaint, dipping one finger into a can of something rich and greasy and swiping it across his tongue again and again until the great sleep retreated out of his reach.

In the many days that followed, she taught him that she was Donna, and when she wanted his attention, she would say the word she reserved for him alone, Blue. As time passed, the ferocious hunger left, and his leg healed enough to work like the other three, even though it throbbed and pulsed for many, many days afterward.

Donna never once tied a rope around his neck, but he remained with her anyway. Unlike the alpha man who had thrown him from the car, Donna's words never came out in a growl. And, as with the girl, her touch was enticingly soft and caring. The dog liked the comfort of her hands and the warmth of her body at night. Donna slept in warm nooks and crevices made by the city's buildings and, when the sun grew too weak to warm the earth, inside abandoned ones.

Occasionally Donna slept near other humans, but they were seldom ones that the dog trusted. Mostly, it was just Donna and the dog.

The dog's body changed as time passed. His legs stretched long, and every part of him became stronger. Bigger, sharper teeth grew, enabling him to crunch through bones and sticks, though he was careful to never let his mouth clamp shut when Donna pressed a bit of food onto the top of his tongue.

The dog learned much about humans during the two full changes of the seasons that he lived with Donna. He learned to understand bits and pieces of their language. He learned that some humans were kind and loving, others were detached, and still others, like the first alpha man he'd encountered, were cruel. He learned not to approach the humans who gifted Donna food but to watch from a wary distance. He'd nearly been pulled into a car by one once. Had Donna not fought the man off, the dog wouldn't have gotten free.

In addition to getting food from humans, Donna had her own scavenging grounds. She knew where delicious food was dumped behind buildings. Inside these buildings, vast numbers of humans came to gorge themselves until their bellies hurt and needed to be rubbed, and then they left, making for their cars.

Unlike the dog, Donna never drank from the river, though she often walked him there. Instead, she used her bent fingers to twist open pipes connected to buildings and drank from those.

When humans gave her paper or small circles of metal, she often disappeared for a short time into a building and came out with a foul-smelling drink that the dog had no interest in. When she drank it, salty drops would run from her eyes the way they had the girl's, and then she'd sleep.

Donna loved to use human language when they were alone. It never once left her lips in a growl. The dog watched her movements and met her gaze, watching and learning. He picked up on human words like *food* and *water* and *drink* and *stay* and many others. He enjoyed it when the words Donna spoke came out in gentle, rambling melody that reverberated in her chest and carried through the wind across many buildings.

The dog had been content with Donna. They had passed many days hungry or wet or cold—and some days a mixture of all these things—but none had ever been as painful or empty as that first day before she'd filled his mouth with grease and pulled him from the shadows of the great sleep.

More than half a cycle of seasons ago, back when the sun was least able to warm the earth and rain only fell as cold, frozen powder, Donna had sunk into the great sleep. The night she'd fallen into it, it had been impossible for the dog to keep warm, even with his thick fur and inside the abandoned building where they'd taken shelter.

Donna's body remained there for many days. The dog had first hoped that she'd wake from the great sleep. He licked her and whined and tried to draw humans toward the building where she lay, but none listened.

The dog continued to sleep beside her night after night until the smell rolling off her had warded him away. One day, when the first buds were popping open and releasing their enticing scents, humans found her and took her away. It was harder to enter the building after that because the door was no longer ajar, but the dog climbed a rickety set of metal stairs to an open window and entered that way. He kept going inside until the spot where she had lain no longer carried her scent, then he never went in again.

He missed the feel of her hands and the sound of her voice, missed the melody of it on the wind. He'd found that food was harder to acquire without her. The big metal boxes that she'd pulled delicious meals from were impossible for him to open, so he expanded his range as he scavenged. Great hunger returned, enough to make him weak at times, but never enough to call him into the great sleep.

He shared his range with other dogs, and he marked over their scents daily. He'd scuffled with other males and mated with two females. One female was now gone, he didn't know where, and the other was heavy with pups. He'd like to have kept her as his mate, but after they'd coupled together, she'd fought him, snapping and growling until he went his own way. He ran across her sometimes as her belly grew fuller. He left scraps of food in corners of the city that were heaviest with her scent.

One of her paws was turned in at an angle from an injury that had long ago healed. Since she moved slower than other dogs, her range was smaller, and it was easy for him to locate her every day. She snarled when she saw him, like she snarled at other dogs.

She wanted to keep to herself and raise her pups.

As the dog trotted toward the river on the narrow, less-traveled streets he'd once shared with Donna, a whine passed across his throat. Perhaps some time he'd trust the man that had been leaving him food enough to follow him inside his building. He thought of the man and imagined being enticed by him enough to crawl onto his lap and lick his face as he'd done with the girl when he was a pup, or enough to lay as close as possible beside him at night as he'd done with Donna.

Then his thoughts flashed to the man who'd tossed him from the car, and the dog determined that today the only thing to do was to return to the river and lap up a bellyful of water.

Chapter 10

TESS COULD ONLY REMEMBER ONCE BEFORE EXPERIENCING the soft, bubbly rightness that was percolating from her chest all the way down to her toes. That first time she'd felt she was exactly where she was supposed to be, she'd stumbled upon a town in a popular spot in Italy in which she'd only been planning to stay an hour. She'd been backpacking with a friend, an Egyptian girl she'd met in Greece whose number she'd lost when she lost her phone. They were headed into Florence for a gelato festival because going from Monaco along the coast and into Florence to sample some of the best gelato in the world seemed like it would be worth the trek.

Because of that bubbly rightness she'd experienced, Tess didn't make it to Florence for the gelato festival. Instead, she arrived a full month later than planned. Tess's hour-long scheduled stop in Vernazza, a quaint Italian town that was part of Italy's Cinque Terre, had fated her for something else entirely.

It was mid-May, and the town had a sleepy air, even though the late-spring sun warmed her skin. The countless tourists of July and August were still a promise on the sea-salt wind. Tess and her friend arrived in Vernazza on a Tuesday morning. The locals were busy purchasing from the open-air market that brought everything from fresh flowers, jewelry, and artwork to clothes and food to the locals once a week.

Tess had been in Europe nearly a year then. After the three-month-long internship that had brought her there had ended, she had made the decision to stick around and backpack through as many countries as she could before her money ran out. In Italy, using the creative advice of fellow backpackers, Tess applied for and eventually received a long-term-stay visa, allowing her to stay another full year if she lived frugally and could afford it.

By the time she arrived in Vernazza, she'd seen more world wonders than she could tick off on her fingers and toes. But none of the towns, cities, museums, or gardens she'd visited had made her feel the way she felt in Vernazza. The bubbly, happy sensation that took over was from more than the bright, stalwart buildings sandwiched between the sapphire-blue sea and the steep, green terraced hills they were built into. The town was not only welcoming, it was healing.

The month Tess spent there enabled her to let go of the last lingering stress she'd been carrying from the drama that had driven her out of St. Louis and away from her family. It was there that she'd let go of her anger, hurt, and resentment, and remembered how much she loved the dynamic and at times overbearing group of people who'd raised her. In Vernazza, Tess met fresh-faced versions of her stubborn, set-in-their-ways parents, aunts, and uncles and began to feel a deep appreciation that had previously evaded her. She also fell in love with the town's charismatic older generation. To Tess, they colored Vernazza with an array of calming purples similar to those that she'd appreciated in Georges's landscape of St. Louis.

In addition to the people, there was the town itself.

A multitude of cacti and flowering grapevines and olive trees blanketed the towering, terraced hills, filling the air with a natural perfume that Tess wanted to drink. It didn't matter that her Italian was broken and her accent was American; Tess had belonged. She rented a room the size of a closet from an old woman who sold flowers for a living and ended up running deliveries for her in exchange for meals. She would have stayed longer, but the months on her extended-stay visa were rapidly ticking away, and Tess wanted to take in as much as she could while she was there.

The second time Tess had experienced the sensation was moments ago, her second day of work at the High Grove Animal Shelter. She'd become immersed in the chores and activities filling the morning, and a glance at the clock showed two hours had passed, two hours that felt like a mere matter of minutes.

This happy, chaotic place fit her—the friendly staff, wide array of animal-loving volunteers, and ninety-two remarkable animals. It was going to be a week or two before she learned all their names and deciphered their individual personalities, but Tess had already gotten an introduction to many of them, and she was certain she'd fall in love with every dog, cat, rabbit, and guinea pig in the place. *And* she was going to get to host an online well-pet video series.

The realization of how perfect it was had happiness warming her all the way into her fingers and toes.

Too late, she realized her reverie had caught Patrick's attention. Even though Patrick spent most of his time at the shelter, he often went to the Sabrina Raven estate in the afternoons, so she knew him pretty well.

"Are you thinking of a good joke?" Patrick asked, cocking his head at her.

Patrick was about her age, midtwenties, with rusty-brown hair and brown eyes, and Tess had never seen him out of a pair of cargo pants. Even before Megan had commented during Tess's orientation yesterday that Patrick put seven slices of salami on his sandwich each day, Tess had known he was a stickler for routine. She'd also suspected he had high-functioning autism well before anyone mentioned it. One afternoon, while working with him at the Sabrina Raven estate, he'd listed every animal that had been given a name with some form of *Tess* in it since he'd begun working there six years ago, including a dog who'd been given the name Testimony a few years ago in an online contest.

Although she'd heard that he wasn't always great at connecting with people, Patrick was a natural with animals and knew how to relate to them on many different levels, and Tess was going to enjoy working with him.

"No," she said, answering his question. "Just really happy to be here."

"I have a joke."

"I'd love to hear it." Tess had just stepped out of the Cat-a-Climb. She'd been sweeping out the loose hair inside before bringing in the next round of playmates, and her nose was itchy.

"Why did the leopard refuse to take a bath?"

"Because it hates water?"

"Because it didn't want to come out spotless."

Tess chuckled. "That's funny."

"Your answer is more realistic."

"Yeah, well, I'm pretty sure it's okay to forego realism when it comes to jokes, don't you think?"

"If you're interested in finding out, why don't you follow me out back when you're finished bringing in the next group of cats?"

Tess had no clue what he was referring to, but she was open to finding out. "Sure."

The next three cats in line for some playtime in the Cat-a-Climb were wild-born siblings that had been using an older couple's basement crawl space as a home base before being caught and brought in. The cats, two females and one male, were now about four months old. They were still underweight and recovering from a bad case of fleas but otherwise healthy. No one knew what had happened to their mother, but she'd stopped coming around and taking care of them before they were old enough to be successful on their own.

The young cats had been spayed and neutered, had their shots and were free of fleas, and were ready for adoption. One female was a calico, and the other male and female were orange tabbies. Tess had heard that Ms. Sherman, a woman who currently owned nine cats but liked to keep an even ten, was considering adopting the male and would be in to see him next Monday, if he was still available. Tess had heard about Ms. Sherman from Kelsey and was eager to finally meet her.

After the cats were in and creating a mini cyclone as they chased each other around all levels of the Cat-a-Climb, Tess headed into the dog kennels in search of Patrick. When he was nowhere to be found, she asked Fidel, a long-time employee who was hosing down one of the kennels.

"He's outside, waiting on the Savannah cat."

Tess wanted to ask for clarification but decided to wait. Patrick was standing in the parking lot between the building and the Island of Many Smells, a small gravel area where they encouraged the dogs to relieve themselves before taking them on short walks.

Patrick was watching the back entrance and glancing at his watch. "Roger's driving in from downtown near Broadway and Olive. If he hasn't encountered traffic, he should be pulling up any second."

"Who's Roger?"

"A volunteer who works with a feral-cat rescue group downtown, Nine More Lives. Do you know it?"

"No, but to be honest, I've mostly moved in the dog world till now." Tess's attention was drawn to a thick wad of yellow rubber gloves in one of Patrick's hands. She couldn't tell how many he had, but it was more than a single pair, and she wondered what they were for.

"They trap wild cats and vaccinate and spay or neuter them. Most of the cats are rereleased, but when we have space, we take some in to adopt out."

"I think I read about that group awhile back. How do they decide which ones to keep and which ones to rerelease?"

Patrick made a *That's easy* face. "The cats who want to claw you to pieces when you try to handle them are released faster than the ones that will stand a bit of petting. They also take age into consideration. Breed demand too, which is why we're about to get the Savannah cat."

Patrick seemed to note Tess's surprise even before she spoke. "They trapped a Savannah cat? Downtown?"

Tess had read about the cats when she was learning about the exotic animal trade in vet school. Although she'd never seen one in person, she'd always wanted to. They were a mix of domestic cats and servals, which were African wild cats.

"Yes, they did." Patrick gave a half wave to the steel-gray pickup pulling into the back lot. "Here he is."

Tess shoved down a dozen questions as the driver parked and shut off the ignition.

"Roger and Tess, you should meet one another," Patrick said in what Tess thought was the most unusual introduction she'd ever had.

Tess reached to shake Roger's hand after he stepped out of his pickup, but he shook his head, smiling. "Trust me. I'm doing you a favor. Once you get a whiff, you aren't going to want to touch these digits. It seems our Savannah got sprayed by the skunk the church was trying to trap before getting trapped in the cage himself."

"Aww."

"Yeah. Even smelling like he does, the hungry guy couldn't resist the hot dogs that were inside. And as for my hands, I could barely take the smell coming off my fingers the whole way over, and all I did was lift the cage into the back of my truck. He's a beaut, but he smells god-awful. I hope you've got a bath ready for him, Patrick."

"I do. And I've prepared a triple batch of de-skunking shampoo."

Roger wiggled his fingers in the air. "I'll think I'll give my hands a good scrubbing before I head back. I'll help you get him inside first." He had a shiny bald patch on top of his head and wore a kind expression.

"I can smell him from here." Tess had caught a strong whiff of the pungent, earthy smell from a solid ten feet away. The poor cat had to be as miserable as he was terrified. Not only had he been caught in a trap, but he'd been sprayed by a skunk too. At least Tess knew now why Patrick had the gloves.

He tossed one of the pairs to Roger. "There's no reason to make it worse."

"You can say that again."

Using the tip she'd learned from Mason, Tess hopped up on the back wheel for a peek as the two guys tugged on gloves.

Even with his unusually long ears pressed flat against his head and hunkered low in the cage, the trapped cat was strikingly beautiful. Like Patrick had said, his markings were right off the African savannah; irregular black-brown spots dotted his back and legs, much like a cheetah. His eyes were a striking amber gold.

"Wow. He's exquisite."

He was also big for a cat. Really big. His legs were tucked underneath him, but that didn't hide the cat's obvious lankiness. Tess would put him at upwards of twenty pounds, and he was clearly underweight. She could make out his ribs with no effort.

She cooed a string of soft-spoken words. His ears flicked toward her for a split second, then he hissed. That was followed by a deep-throated growl that Tess would have no problem respecting.

"Poor, sweet kitty."

Tess hopped down and trailed after Patrick and Roger as they carried the cage into the back of the building. The brand-new wash station was in the far corner of the dog kennels and had a door that enabled it to be closed off from the rest of the area. For the most part, only the dogs were given baths, but Tess figured there were exceptions every now and then.

"Keep me posted on this guy, Patrick," Roger said.

"I will."

"And it was nice to meet you, Tess. Welcome to the family."

"Thanks. I'm excited to be here."

After Roger headed out, Patrick shook a bottle that was full of a bubbling, foamy white substance. After glimpsing the bottles sitting next to it, Tess assumed it was a mixture of baking soda, hydrogen peroxide, and dish soap.

"I've heard apple-cider vinegar works pretty good too," Tess said.

"We may need to try that next. This should do a better job of cutting through the oil. To rid him of the smell completely, he's most likely going to need two or three baths. Are you okay helping to bathe him? With Megan due in January and Fidel having a skunk sensitivity, my options are limited, or I wouldn't have asked you. Not on your second day."

"I'm game. I've never bathed a skunked cat—or any skunked animal—and I'm big on not knocking something till I've tried it. But wow, he reeks, doesn't he? My eyes are starting to water." She could also feel her gag reflex kicking in, but she willed herself to suppress it.

Patrick flicked on the overhead exhaust fan. "Thank you for the reminder. It looks as if most of the spray is on the front of his chest and underneath his chin."

Tess had worked with Patrick enough at the Sabrina

Raven estate to know to watch and listen for his cues when he became absorbed in a task. It seemed as if words fled him when he was focused on a task at hand, but Tess didn't mind. She'd grown up around a father who was the quiet type too. When he was mid-project, Tess's mom could seldom get more than a grunt out of him.

As Patrick adjusted the temperature of the water coming out of the spray hose, Tess tightened her ponytail, locking away lost strands of hair. Then she followed Patrick's lead and slipped into one of the bulky but waterproof nylon aprons and a pair of thick rubber gloves. Both items were several sizes too big, but Tess was happier to be swimming in them than smelling like skunk for the next week.

"Don't forget goggles," Patrick said, passing her a pair.

"Poor kitty didn't get such luxuries before being doused." She aimed her words at the unhappy cat as she strapped the goggles into place. It felt a bit as if she were getting ready for one of her grad school labs.

"It's my experience that the faster we can be, the better," Patrick said. After reconfirming that the water was a good temperature, he didn't hesitate the slightest when it came to pulling the formidably sized unhappy kitty from the cage. Wrapping one hand around the scruff, Patrick was able to slide the cat out and transfer him without complaint into the waist-level bath station. "You hose; I'll hold."

"He'll never forgive me," Tess said as she aimed a gentle shower of water at the cat. She started at his feet and moved upward. The smell radiating off him was so strong that Tess's nausea grew. Even breathing through her mouth didn't help. She could taste the sulfur coating her tongue, reminding her of a chemistry experiment gone drastically wrong.

"The breed isn't averse to water like many cats. Some even enjoy baths," Patrick offered.

With the two of them working as a better team than Tess might have expected, given how quiet Patrick became as they worked, they had the gangly, much-perturbed cat marinating in a hefty amount of Patrick's foamy concoction within minutes. The only bit of the cat that wasn't covered in sudsy white foam was his face. The unhappy feline spent the entire time growling a deep, low growl but didn't try to escape, which Tess figured was due to a combination of Patrick's secure hold and the surrounding three steep sides of the stainless-steel washing station.

"I have a feeling this awful smell is soaking into my pores," Tess said. The comment set off an alarm inside her. It was already midafternoon, and she had a date—if that's what it was called—with Mason mere hours from now.

And she was going to go into it reeking of skunk.

"It shouldn't, since we aren't getting it on our skin."

She desperately hoped not. Smelling like a skunk tonight wouldn't do much for her track record. The first time she and Mason had met, Tess had lost her most valuable possessions. The second time, she'd impulsively biked across the city at dusk to deliver a thank-you note, and he'd felt it necessary to give her a ride home. She wasn't even going to think about the pants leg incident. The expression *Third time's the charm* swam through her head. Tess wasn't entirely convinced she wanted to come across as *datable* to Mason, but she also wasn't certain she didn't.

However her muddled feelings played out, *not* sending him running for the hills tonight would be a good thing. Mason might not be her norm, but she wasn't going to deny that her heart beat three times faster when she was around him. And a big part of her wanted to know where that might lead.

As she and Patrick watched the clock tick away the ten excruciatingly long minutes that were necessary to neutralize the odor, Tess wasn't sure if she was growing numb to it, or if the room was growing less and less pungent.

Megan popped in at minute seven and peered over their shoulders at the cat. "Poor, stinky thing. He's gorgeous; there's no denying that. I've got a spot set up in quarantine with his dinner inside when he's finished. We'll feed him lightly tonight to make sure he keeps it down. I don't want him gorging and throwing up, and he's likely nauseated from the spraying. Tomorrow we can start with his vaccines, a deworming, and upping his caloric intake after Dr. Washington sees him."

Tess couldn't contain her curiosity. "Is it already decided to keep him and adopt him out rather than rerelease him? Or is that something you decide later?"

"Since he's a Savannah cat, and they're so rare, it's next to impossible that he was feral-born," Megan said, placing her hands on the small of her back and arching backward in a stretch. Tess could only imagine how exhausted Megan had to be, heavily pregnant and working long, cram-packed days as she did. "Which means he either escaped or he was dumped. By the looks of him, he's been roaming awhile. We'll check lost-and-found ads on Craigslist and some popular pet blogs to see if someone has been searching for him. Assuming they're not, we'll adopt him out, but we'll vet his new owner pretty heavily. Sometimes these guys make great pets, but sometimes they don't and they're turned out on the street. Yet when they aren't wild-born and taught by their mothers to hunt, they often starve to death. We'll want to make sure someone isn't just adopting him for his looks but is ready to accept the whole package, whatever that turns out to be."

"That makes sense." Tess's eyes were starting to sting and tear even underneath her goggles. Using her less-than-dexterous gloved fingers, she carefully lifted them up and wiped the top of her shirt over her eyes.

"I'm really sorry, Tess," Megan said. "Your second day, and you've been roped into one of the stinkiest jobs there is."

"Hosing out the poop Dumpster is worse." Patrick's comment was very matter-of-fact, and Tess figured she wouldn't argue.

"I don't mind. I'm just hoping the little guy forgives me."

Megan gave her a soft smile as she reached for the doorknob. "He will. It never fails to amaze me how easy it is for these guys to forgive."

Patrick nodded toward the clock on the wall. "Tess, you're good to rinse, but test the water again first."

In no time, the Savannah cat was rinsed and dried and carried to his kennel in quarantine. The shelter's quarantine room was a small but well-ventilated room for new arrivals and had a limited number of cages spaced several feet apart for cats and dogs alike. In here, the lights were kept low and soft, meditative music was piped in through the speakers. It was also off-limits to the public.

In quarantine, animals that exhibited high levels of stress, like the Savannah cat, were left to decompress, sleep, and eat until they were deemed healthy enough to join the adoptable animals up front. There was also a strict decontamination procedure when it came to working in the room, and Tess hadn't yet been shown how to clean inside it.

Today, only two other animals were in quarantine, both small breeds of dogs. One was a senior beagle-pug mix that had been found tied to a trash can in front of a nearby pet store. The other was a Chihuahua with a bad case of gingivitis who had come in yesterday.

Once the cat was shut in his kennel, Tess and Patrick hung back to watch his next move. He hovered in the corner for a few minutes, his golden eyes flicking between them and his new surroundings, then slunk to the food dish and began to eat, darting nervous glances their way.

"Do you think we should leave him alone?" Tess asked. She'd removed her sweaty gloves and goggles before coming in but couldn't wait to shed the bulky nylon apron too.

"Yes. He'll relax and get used to his new surroundings tonight. Tomorrow, you can feed him and give him some treats. He should feel considerably better by then."

After washing her hands and face with some of the leftover solution, Tess returned to the front room to finish out her day. She had a headache pressing into the top of her skull and her stomach remained queasy, side effects of the skunk spray, but she wouldn't have missed the experience for the world.

Chapter 11

STARING AT THE LARGE BOWL OF GOOEY MUSH IN front of him, a seldom-experienced sensation swirled through Mason's torso, one that he could only attribute to a lack of confidence.

He wasn't a cook. He knew how to make three dinners—favorite meals his mom had made time and again when he was growing up. He'd learned to make them by hanging out in the kitchen, helping out and watching in eager anticipation of the meal that was coming, rather than having learned the real basics of cooking.

His mother was a fantastic cook and made everything from memory. She owned a single cookbook, a *General Foods Kitchens Cookbook* from the 1950s that his late grandmother had passed along to her at one point or another. It sat on the far end of the counter, propped up by an antique ceramic rooster, although he'd never seen her use it. She also kept a small recipe tin with old family recipes on tattered and food-stained recipe cards. She almost never needed to reference those either.

His mom was the real thing. She made things from scratch and added pinches and dashes rather than measured spoonfuls into her recipes. Like Georges, she was an artist, with food her medium.

So why Mason had believed her when she'd told him that it would be easy to make a vegetarian meat loaf instead of the traditional one he'd learned to replicate, he didn't know. The bowl of slop in front of him didn't look like it could ever turn into a tasty meat loaf.

He'd been committed to making Tess dinner after learning she was a vegetarian, even though it meant stepping out of his comfort zone. Sometime before leaving for college, he'd become pretty damn efficient at cooking his favorite meals: pot roast, meat loaf, and fried catfish.

His mom knew his skills in the kitchen better than anyone, and he trusted her to tell him if he was getting in over his head. Yesterday, when he'd called to check in, he'd attempted to ask her advice as casually as possible so as not to start her asking a hundred questions about Tess that he couldn't or didn't want to answer. True to form, she'd jumped at the opportunity to help. She'd been trying to eat healthier since his father had been diagnosed with exorbitantly high cholesterol levels and, as she put it, had been learning to use "the Google" for healthier meal ideas and to learn a new heart-healthy way to cook.

This morning, Mason had awakened to an emailed recipe that she'd thrown together for his dad last night. Mason wasn't sure if it was because his mom didn't know how to copy a link or because she'd modified it with a few helpful directions of her own, but she'd typed it into the email.

At the bottom, she'd written that she hadn't told his dad it was vegetarian until after he'd finished eating *and* after he'd commented that he wouldn't mind having it again. This made Mason chuckle every time he read it. His dad was a fourth-generation farmer and about as set in his ways as anyone Mason had ever met. Eating vegetarian wasn't something that would settle easily with him.

Mason's family owned six hundred acres in one of Iowa's most fertile valleys. More than one commercial farm had tried to buy his dad out over the years. He was getting older and claimed it was getting harder and harder to make a profit every year. Still, his dad refused to give up land that had been in the family for so long. Close to fifteen years ago, he'd sold off a couple hundred acres to make ends meet. If it killed him, his dad was fond of saying, he wouldn't chop away any more.

Mason was making enough now to support his parents as long as they needed it, but as of yet, his dad had refused to take a penny from him.

Staring at the bowl of unappetizing goo in front of him, Mason reminded himself that stubbornness ran in his veins, and of his personal commitment to acknowledge it when he was in over his head.

Pulling out his phone, Mason placed a much-needed call. "Hey, what're you doing, sleeping?"

It was four o'clock, but Georges sounded like it was the middle of the night.

"I may have dozed. Your timing remains impeccable."

"I'm going to pretend I don't hear the sarcasm in that forced French accent of yours. Can you get out of that lounge chair and hobble over for a second? I need your help."

Chuckling at having goaded his friend into releasing a string of French curses his way, Mason hung up. He was still rereading his mom's directions in case he'd missed something when he heard Georges at the door, pressing the electronic code to let himself in, something he hadn't done with Tess, which should have served as a clue to Mason that he'd had company.

"In the kitchen," he yelled when the door pushed open. An off-leash Millie burst into the loft, barking up a storm as she raced in circles.

"My help comes with a price. She should have a potty trip soon, and I'm not moving well today."

Mason glanced over at his friend. "You okay?"

Georges waved a hand in the air as he shuffled into the kitchen using his cane for support. "Tell me what 'okay' is, and I'll give you an answer. I'm alive, and I am going to recover. That's all I know. So, what is the emergency?"

"Tess is coming over. I'm cooking dinner, but I don't think it's turning out right."

"Because I can see the tension in your face, I'm going to hold my tongue until your disaster is righted. Which of your three dinners are you making?"

"The meat loaf, sort of. She's a vegetarian. My mom emailed me a recipe, but it's nothing like what I usually make."

Georges scanned the messy countertop. Cleaning was Mason's least favorite part of cooking, and he typically tackled it after dinner. Tonight, he needed to get this finished so he could clean up the mess before heading out to pick up Tess.

"You bought a food processor?" Georges's gaze landed on the packaging from the processor adding to the mess of dishes on the counter. "You could've borrowed mine."

"It was a gift a few Christmases ago. I just haven't had a use for it until today."

"So, why is it you called me over?"

"It's this." Mason jiggled the bowl of slop he was supposed to pour into the meat-loaf pan.

"It looks like pig slop."

"Tell me about it."

Georges lifted the recipe Mason had printed out and, after holding it up and out for a better look without his glasses, surveyed the counter once more. "How many lentils did you use?"

"A cup, like it says."

"Cooked or dry?"

"Cooked."

"That's your problem. It's the comma's fault. It should be a cup of lentils, cooked, not a cup of cooked lentils."

Mason lifted the lid from the saucepan that still sat on the stove. There were plenty of lentils left over. "I wasn't sure how many dry lentils would make a cup of cooked lentils, so I measured a dry cup first, then cooked them according to the directions on the bag."

"Well, there you have it. Drain and mash those, and your veggie loaf will thicken up fine." Georges pointed toward the barstools on the other side of the counter. "Bring me one of those, and I'll sit awhile and watch you cook your vegetables."

Mason wasn't entirely sure that lentils were considered vegetables, but Georges didn't look like he was feeling well enough to argue. Once he was resting on the stool, Millie made her way into the kitchen and plopped on the cool floors, panting contentedly.

"Two years I've known you, and I've not seen this side of you. She is a cute girl; I'll give you that. But tell me the truth. If she knew who you are, would you still be cooking for her?"

Mason could feel the touch of a scowl forming on his face as he transferred the drained lentils into a mixing bowl to mash them. "I like that I'm not a sensation to her. I like that when she looks at me, she sees me."

"Are you forgetting that the baseball player who played well enough this season to have been in the running for MVP is also you?"

Mason released a slow, controlled breath. "I know it is—I know I am—but it's been my experience of late that people don't see both the guy and the baseball player anymore."

Georges picked up a slice of mushroom that lay abandoned on the counter and pressed it between his thumb and forefinger. After most of it fell back to the counter, mashed and abandoned, Georges ran his thumb along the gray-brown smear it left behind on his forefinger. Mason knew his friend well enough to know that a part of him was lost in the color of it. Georges lived in colors.

"How long are you going to wait to tell her, young man?"

"A week, maybe. I don't know."

"I suspect if you sleep with her before you tell her, you'll lose her."

"I'm not… I wouldn't. Hell, I promised myself I won't even kiss her until I tell her."

Georges gave him a sharp look, one unkempt brow knotting into a peak and creating a wave of deep creases across his forehead. "It's quite serious, then, isn't it?"

Mason wasn't sure what to say, which he figured was most likely answer enough.

~~~

As the first few billows of steam began to fill up the small, confining bathroom, Tess frowned at her reflection. Her belly was brewing with lingering nausea from bathing the cat, and her cheeks were bright red from the bike ride home. Not only was it chilly, but she'd pushed herself so she'd have more time in the shower, hoping to wash off the lingering skunk odor.

She couldn't remember sparing more than a glance at her naked body since before she left for Europe. She'd always been on the thin side. Even in college when her friends were stressing over the freshman fifteen, she hadn't gained more than a pound or two. As a kid, annual physicals had left her mom determined to put more weight on her in the coming year.

Skinny and weak—scrawny—was how she'd imagined herself most of her life.

For the first time, it hit home what her time in Europe had done for her self-image. There, she'd eaten and worked and laughed and played and not given her body a single thought. She'd not worried about being weak or skinny or inadequate.

Most likely, she'd always be envious of curvy, vivacious women, but for the first time, the woman staring back at her in the mirror didn't feel *less than*.

Maybe it was the often-strenuous backpacking or the bike riding since coming home. Maybe it was because she'd figured out how to let a lot of the crap go that had been weighing her down. Whatever the case, the twenty-six-year-old staring back at her in the rapidly fogging mirror wasn't embarrassed about her body. She was toned in places she'd never been before, like her thighs and triceps, and maybe her boobs weren't anything to post about on Instagram, but they fit her body and that was enough.

Remembering how small Nonna's hot-water tank was, Tess snatched up the bottle of freshly made de-skunking mix she'd brought home from the shelter. As she crossed over to the shower, she stepped on her dirty jeans that were discarded on the floor.

"Ouch!"

Her left heel had landed squarely on the buckeye she'd found in Mason's hoodie the other day. She hadn't quite decided if it was because her grandma had told her buck-eyes brought good luck when carried with you, or if it was because it had belonged to Mason, or both, but she'd been dropping the shiny thing into her pocket each morning since. During rare moments of quiet introspection, she'd slip her hand around its smooth, irregular surface and appreciate the hopeful peace that moved over her.

Not wanting to lose it in the laundry, she pulled it from the pocket and left it on the crowded counter near the sink, then hopped in the shower. If the buckeye was bringing her luck, hopefully the shampoo would work wonders and keep her from smelling like skunk tonight.

She was mostly worried about the smell clinging to her hair, and she wanted a full ten minutes to let it soak.

Knowing she'd run out of hot water well before the required ten-minute soak was up, Tess shut off the water after lathering on the shampoo, twisted her hair up in a foamy knot, and wrapped her torso in a towel. Shoving the heavy vinyl shower curtain out of the way, she sat on the edge of the tub, counting out the available minutes till Mason was due to be here.

For your date.

Her stomach flipped. *You're hunting for a stray dog, Tess. This is not exactly a date.*

Maybe that was true, but he was also making her dinner. Tess had only had a guy cook dinner for her once. That had been in college, and he'd used a microwave and an electric skillet to heat up packaged food in his dorm after they'd been dating for a month. Still, she'd been pretty swept away by how romantic it seemed at the time.

But she wasn't in college anymore. She was an adult. And she was incredibly attracted to the guy who was making her dinner.

She ran her palm along her shin, testing for stubble. What was she doing? She would most likely still smell like skunk after doing her best to get rid of it. There was no way she'd let Mason get close enough to determine that she reeked.

She held out another few minutes until she was so chilled she was starting to shiver all over, then started the shower again. With any luck, Mason would be a few minutes late. To get herself put together, she was going to need every minute she could get.

Chapter 12

"So, I've never actually done this before. I keep telling myself I've got permission, but this still feels a bit like breaking and entry." Tess's key slid effortlessly into the lock. Still, she was almost surprised when the lock clicked open without objection. At the very least, she'd expected it to stick and to have to work to open it.

It took a second or two to realize that Mason was grinning. "I think you mean breaking and entering."

Tess wrinkled her nose. "Now that you say it, it felt a little weird coming out of my mouth."

Mason's hand closed over her shoulder in a reassuring squeeze as Tess pulled the front door of the shelter open. "So, there's no night shift on duty?"

"Not unless one is needed, and right now it isn't. Typically, the animals are on their own from when the last person leaves at six or so until the first one arrives at seven in the morning. My shift's eight to four thirty, and it occurred to me today that I really need to renew my license, or my bike ride home will end in the dark after the time changes next week."

"You mean you're biking here too? From the Hill?"

"Yeah, I kind of have an aversion to driving again. It's never been a form of recreation for me, and I've been out of practice for almost a year and a half. Every time I think about getting behind the wheel again, it gets a little hard to breathe." Tess bit her lip at how silly it sounded as she flicked on a few lights.

"I'll take you out to practice."

Tess shook her head emphatically. "Thanks for the offer, but I don't think there are roads wide enough and empty enough for a hundred miles for me to practice in that monster of a truck."

"I actually know the perfect place. No traffic. No pressure. Just fun."

Tess heard herself agreeing, even though she was silently kicking herself for bringing it up in the first place. The last thing this whatever-it-was between them needed was for Mason to witness her having a full-fledged panic attack, which was quite possibly going to happen.

Although they had just been swinging by the shelter to grab a catch pole in case their search for John Ronald was fruitful and ended up with them having need of one, not taking a few minutes to introduce Mason to some of her favorites felt wrong. "So, it's dusk and probably the best time all day to find John Ronald on the move, but would you like a quick tour? I know you said you've been here, but I'm not sure how long it's been. I could introduce you to some guys that'll melt your heart and put it together again."

"I'd love a tour. And I suspect waiting until dark won't hurt. Most of my sightings of John Ronald have been well after dark, some were even really late at night."

"That makes sense. Strays get pretty good at modifying their schedules to encounter the least number of people." Tess let the front door fall shut behind them and tapped her foot as she looked around. "There's so much to show you. The renovations under way are something to see, but the animals make the place. And not just the dogs. I wouldn't have labeled myself a cat person because I've only worked with dogs, but there are some real sweeties here."

Tess led him toward the cat kennels. Most were dozing, but a few cats were awake and ready to play. Trina, the shelter's resident cream-and-silver three-legged cat, was hanging out on the counter in front of the kennels. "This is Trina." Even though Trina was dozing, Tess knew the affectionate cat was always up for a good scratch, and rubbed her under the chin. "She's a permanent resident and getting up there in age now. She was found in New Orleans in the aftermath of Hurricane Katrina on a piece of driftwood with her mom and a few other kittens. Her leg was already missing, and there's a bunch of theories of what might have happened, but no one knows for sure. She's one of my favorite cats because she's just so chill. She's a behavior model for the other cats too. When new ones come in and see her hanging out in front of their kennels all calm and relaxed, it helps them not be afraid."

"That makes sense. Does she mind being held?"

Trina was now fully awake and rubbing her cheeks along Mason's knuckles. "No, she'll let you carry her around, if you want to. Our other resident animal is a blind cairn terrier. He's up there in age as well, and I think he's dozing on his bed in the gift shop."

Mason surprised Tess with the confident way he settled Trina over the length of his forearm—upright and not cradled, with her legs hanging free between his arm and his side.

"So, you like cats?"

Mason shrugged. "I grew up on a farm. We always had a couple cats around. I like their independence. Once we catch John Ronald, if he needs a companion, I'll get him a cat."

"I don't know why, but that surprises me."

He grinned. "Kind of the way it surprised me that you don't drive?"

"Good point." She laughed. "We're one for one then."

Keeping in mind that they had a time crunch if they wanted to search for John Ronald before dark, Tess refrained from taking any cats out of the kennels, though she pointed out ones with more remarkable stories, including a few pulled from nearly flooded storm drains, ones discovered cohabitating in unsuspecting homeowners' houses, and two pulled from summer floodwaters.

As Tess finished with the cats, Mason pointed to the empty Cat-a-Climb.

"I told you my buddy is the architect who designed some of your recent renovations. I saw a 2-D version of this on his computer months ago."

"That's cool. And I can't believe you actually know someone who summited Mount Everest."

"Yeah, I know. It was his second attempt. The first was a couple of years ago, but a storm cut his window too short. I guess you could say that he's driven. Driven but cool. He's a remarkable architect too. He's the one who drew up renovations for my building. That's how we met. He does a lot of work downtown. Though you'd never know any of this if you didn't hear it from someone else first. He's not one to brag. Or talk at all, really, until you get to know him."

"I know people like that. And I have to say, it still throws me that considering we met under such different circumstances, you saw the Cat-a-Climb before it was even built. You'd think I'd be used to how small the world is by now. In Europe, I met more than a few people who'd eaten at my uncle's sandwich shop on the Hill, and I got to help harvest grapes in Switzerland with someone whose parents went to my high school years ago."

"That's cool, Tess."

She next led him back to the dog kennels. Many of the dogs were sleeping off their recent dinners, though most perked their ears and half opened their eyes as Tess and Mason passed through. To keep them from getting too excited, Tess kept the lights dim and her voice down.

It was funny to her, but she could remember struggling for nights on end to memorize things in school, like the order and names of the presidents, but after being introduced to the majority of the dogs and hearing their individual stories a single time, she'd committed most to memory. She didn't even have to spare a glance at the charts as she pointed several out to Mason.

She took the time to point out the perpetually happy-faced tan-and-white corgi that had been at the shelter for eight months. "Orzo here has been helping with the rehab of the confiscated fighting dogs that we talked about. I've been working with him for a month, while the rest of these dogs are new to me. He's great at the rehab. When it comes to reading cues and getting along with other dogs, Orzo's perfect. And his story is sweet in a very literal sense. He's an owner surrender. When he came to us, he was drastically overweight. From what I heard, he mostly ate leftovers from his old owner's bakeshop. His recent blood work shows an amazing change for the better. He lost several pounds, and he loves to go on walks now. When they first got him in, he'd drop to the ground in a heavy pant every ten feet or so when they tried to take him anywhere."

"Wow." Mason balanced on his heels in front of Orzo's kennel and let his fingers get a strong licking.

When he was finished, she introduced him to a few others that had captured her heart and wouldn't let go, including Clara Bee, a friendly and eager-to-please four-year-old yellow Lab who had been rescued from the throes of a puppy mill.

"Of all the dogs here, my heart goes out to her the most." Clara Bee was in one of the largest kennels the shelter had. After the eager Lab had a good sniff of Mason and was wagging her tail so heavily that the entire back half of her body wagged along in anticipation, Tess opened the door and motioned Mason to join her.

Clara Bee didn't mind sharing her spacious kennel one bit. The sweet girl circled around them, nuzzling their hands and leaning heavily against Tess's leg. Tess stroked a silky ear as Clara Bee pumped her tail. "One of our volunteers was turkey hunting a couple hours south of here and got lost. He stumbled onto private property and found five adult dogs and a few unsold pups living in unhealthy conditions. He worked with authorities to get the place shut down immediately, and he even got most of the dogs taken straight into foster care.

"Clara Bee's living conditions were the worst of the bunch. She barely had space to move, and her hips were a mess. No one knows how many litters she had, but it was too many, too soon. She wasn't in shape to go into a private home, so she came here. She's had two surgeries, and she's doing great. She spends a lot of the day standing of her own will, and her daily walks are getting longer and longer." Mindful of her surgery scars, Tess gently patted Clara Bee's right hip. "This foot still drags when she gets tired, but I've seen a huge difference since I first met her nearly a month ago."

"Wow." Mason shook his head. "It's not right that someone could do that."

"It isn't, but thankfully, she and all the Labs who lived with her will get to finish out their lives in loving families. And it was touching to see how many people came forward to donate money for her surgeries. The real miracle is how tame and loving she's gotten in just a few months. Considering the tiny space she was allotted and its condition, it's unlikely she had any positive contact with people before she was rescued. She was extremely timid at first, but she's really begun to bond with the staff and volunteers. She will even play with people in the play yard. I'm not going to lie: every time I see that, I tear up."

Mason sank to a squat and let Clara Bee lick his nose and chin. When her purple tongue swiped across the stubble covering his chin, Tess repressed an urge to reach out and brush her fingertips across it as well.

"Was Clara Bee her name when she came here?"

"No, she didn't have a name that we know of. Everyone who donated money for her first surgery got to suggest a name. Then, on the day of her surgery, her name was chosen by Facebook vote. Clara Bee is short for Clara Barton, who—in case you don't remember— started the Red Cross and was active in the women's suffrage movement. The name won by a landslide. I think people felt like it was a way to give our sweet girl back some of her power."

When Mason didn't respond but kept quiet, stroking Clara Bee's neck and scruff, Tess suspected he needed a bit of quiet to recover. After a full minute passed, Mason patted the happy dog on the side and stood up.

Tess stepped out first and was searching for a less-heavy shelter story when she thought of the Savannah cat.

"Oh, do you still want to see the Savannah cat?" Before she'd gotten in Mason's truck, she'd warned him how she'd had a close encounter with a skunked cat and could smell nothing aside from the skunk scent circulating through her nostrils. She made him promise to let her know if the smell was still hanging out on her body as well. When she'd tried to describe the unusual breed of cat that had caused this afternoon's commotion, Mason had admitted he'd never heard of it.

As soon as Tess opened the door to quarantine, Mason arched backward, fanning his nose. Tess had clearly become desensitized because the room didn't seem to smell any different from every other breath she'd taken since bathing the cat.

Judging by Mason's reaction, it seemed the poor kitty was going to need another bath or two before he was fully rid of the smell. "You weren't kidding." He whistled softly. "You're brave to have tackled bathing him."

"I'm pretty sure I won't be able to smell anything for a week at least. But I feel confident saying that if your eyes don't begin to water and you don't grow nauseated and develop a splitting headache in the next few minutes, he smelled worse when he came in."

Mason shook his head, chuckling. He scanned the mostly empty crates, and his eyebrows arched when he spotted the Savannah cat. "Wow."

"He's remarkable, isn't he?"

Even though the cat was cowering in a far corner, his large size and cheetah-like markings were striking. "Yes, he is. I'm not sure what I'd think if I'd spotted him on the street."

Noticing that the cat's ears were flat and his tail tucked, Tess stayed several feet from the cages. Neither of the two dogs in quarantine was happy to see the visitors either. Not yet, at least. Tess was confident the kind and loving treatment they were given would soon warm all three of their timid spirits.

"Hopefully, by the time he's out of quarantine, he won't smell. I can give you a proper introduction then."

As soon as the words were out, a wave of vulnerability slid over Tess. It was a big assumption to declare so openly that she'd be seeing Mason again.

"I'd love that." His fingertips brushed over the small of her back as he followed her out.

The rush it gave her swept all the way into her toes.

"So, like I said, I could spend all night talking to you about these guys, but they're safe and on the road to healthy, happy lives. I'll grab that catch pole, and we'll focus on finding someone who probably needs us more than he knows."

Chapter 13

FOR THE BETTER PART OF AN HOUR, MASON DROVE THE backstreets and alleys within a few miles of his house. Their search scared three cats out of different Dumpsters but didn't turn up John Ronald or any dogs at all.

The dashboard clock on Mason's truck read a quarter to eight. "So, I know you can't smell anything but skunk, but if you're getting hungry, we can take a break, eat, and try again afterward."

"Sure. I'm starving. And I can't wait to see what you made."

She'd asked earlier, and he'd said it was a surprise.

The conversation had flowed easily all night, which Mason couldn't say was an experience he'd shared with a girl in a while. He was doing his best not to bring up anything that would have him skirting the truth about his career, so instead he volunteered a lot about his family— his parents, siblings, cousins, grandparents, and aunts and uncles—and his life growing up on a working farm.

After declaring that she'd never lived on more than a tenth of an acre of ground until she'd participated in an internship program on a sustainable farm in Europe, Tess had seemed fascinated to learn that he'd been trusted to drive a tractor at age eight and a truck on farm property at age ten. After she joked about how she'd grown up in a single square-mile town that had seemed like an entire world to her, he'd commented that his father's six-hundred-acre farm and the Hill were about the same size.

"You had no neighbors at all for a square mile?" she'd asked, sounding as if that was difficult to believe.

"No neighbors for much farther than that. My dad's farm was closer to nine hundred acres when I was a kid, and the surrounding farms were all just as big or bigger."

After listening intently to some of his experiences, Tess had offered several of her own from her internship in Europe harvesting grapes and olives. When Mason mentioned again that he was taking his parents in January, she'd reached over the console and pressed a flattened hand against his shoulder, insisting that he'd love it.

She listed a dozen experiences and sights that competed as her favorites, and Mason felt a wistfulness in his chest. *Next off-season, you're taking her, not your parents.*

Granted, it was an extreme thought considering this was a first date, if that's what they were calling it. The truth was, it didn't really feel like a date. None that he'd been on anyway. It felt more like what happened when two people who were raised in very different circumstances began coming together just as they were supposed to.

He knew not to declare that aloud. She'd probably hop out of his truck and run for the hills. But he'd bet a hundred points on next season's batting average that she was feeling it too.

Having reached his building, Mason drove down the ramp into the basement garage. He'd flipped off the ignition and was stepping out when he spotted Dana Felton walking toward her car. For a split second, his feet locked to the concrete floor in indecision. She was the one resident in the building who had a hard time seeing him as ordinary Mason and not Mason Redding, Red Birds third basemen, and worse, she could almost never refrain from making comments on what she'd read about him on one social media site or another. She didn't seem to care that Mason didn't want to hear the latest gossip. And she was the last person who lived in his building that he wanted to run into while with Tess.

Figuring that not acknowledging her would be worse, he nodded Dana's way, then hurried around to meet Tess. As soon as Tess shut her door, he clicked the lock twice in hopes the beep would help fill the quiet pocked only by footsteps on smooth concrete.

"So nice to see you without that brace," Dana called out, sending a fresh wave of tension through his limbs. "How's that arm feeling?"

"Good, thanks." Then, hoping it would stop her from saying any more, he added, "Have a nice evening, Ms. Felton."

Mason closed his hand over Tess's back as they waited for the elevator to reopen, and Dana reluctantly got in her car.

An unexpected panic slid over him as the doors jangled open. Even though he wasn't one to hang pictures of himself on the walls, he'd had a few special moments captured and framed, and they normally dotted his bookshelf. He'd remembered at the last minute to take them down and shove them into the back of a drawer. But had he forgotten anything else?

It was ironic, but the more Tess grew to mean to him, the less excited he was to tell her the whole truth.

And he wasn't sure if it was his imagination, but

she seemed to stiffen against his hand on her back. He dropped his hand as they stepped on and the door closed.

A glance in her direction showed that sudden tension lined her face.

"Hey, everything okay? If something's worrying you, I'd like to know."

When Tess clamped a hand over her stomach, Mason couldn't *not* notice how inviting her body seemed underneath the thick sweater she had on.

Rather than replying, she shook her head, triggering his attention in a new way. Something wasn't right. He was about to ask when she grimaced.

"I don't know if it's backlash from the skunk or I'm a bit carsick, or maybe both, but I'm not feeling very good all of a sudden."

He'd just pulled out a key and turned it in the elevator lock, enabling him to trigger the sixth-floor button. "You still okay going upstairs?"

She gave a quick nod. Under the fluorescent panels of the elevator, her smooth olive skin had taken on a distinctive pale-yellow appearance. He'd seen that look from time to time on some of his buddies after they'd pushed a workout entirely too hard. Even if it wasn't fun, throwing up might be the quickest way for her to feel better.

He led her out of the elevator and into his apartment without talking. Once inside, he flipped on a few lights but kept them relatively dim. "Bathroom?"

She nodded, lifting her hand off her stomach and locking it over her mouth.

The upstairs master bathroom was bigger and nicer, spa-worthy almost, but required climbing ten feet up the winding metal staircase, and Mason figured she wasn't in the space for that. He led her across the loft into the Jack-and-Jill guest bathroom that connected the two main-floor guest rooms on the far side.

A half bath was closer, but it was a tight, confined room, having been built inside an old dumbwaiter shaft to allow for as much openness as possible on the main floor.

"What can I get you?" He flipped on the bathroom light, sliding the dimmer down halfway. "Ice chips? Damp washcloth? I can never remember if it's hot or cold that's best."

"I'm fine for now. Thanks."

Mason stepped out and shut the door. He hadn't even made it to the kitchen when he heard her muffled retching. Switching destinations, he jogged upstairs, feeling a sharp pain run down his arm without the support of the brace. He'd been given the all clear yesterday morning to try going without it.

He pocketed the fear of the effects of the injury hanging around, affecting him next season. There was nothing he could do but follow the advice of the doctor and therapists who were committed to having him on the field before the season began.

From his master bathroom, he grabbed a washcloth, wet it, and headed back down. He listened outside the guest bathroom door. When it was determinedly quiet, he knocked. "Would you prefer space or a washcloth? I can give you either."

Her voice was low and muffled through the closed door. "A washcloth would be nice. Thanks."

He opened the door to find her sitting on the floor on the fuzzy bath mat, her back against the tiled tub.

Her knees were tucked up, and her face was buried between them.

He sat on the edge of the tub and gathered her long, dark hair together in one hand, then laid the washcloth on the back of her neck.

A soft moan escaped her. "That feels heavenly. Thanks."

"I'm sorry."

"Why? You aren't the one who just threw up in the prettiest bathroom you've ever been in." Mason laughed, but Tess shook her head. "I'm still too nauseated to be humiliated, but I know it's coming. And for the record, this bathroom could be in a magazine. The exposed red-brick wall really makes it."

He smoothed his hand over her back, savoring the feel of her. Slender and succumbing. It took reminding himself that he was not—definitely not—allowed any sort of move until he told her everything to pull his thoughts from where they wanted to go.

"Thank you, but don't be embarrassed. This bathroom has seen much worse than you could ever give it. While I wouldn't have complained if you hadn't, you made it to the toilet and you flushed. That's much better than a buddy of mine did a few months ago. And if you're wondering, it's an entirely new rug that you're sitting on."

A small laugh bubbled up. Even through her sweater, he felt it resonate across the back of her ribs. She sat fully upright, pulling the washcloth off the back of her neck and dragging it over her face. "I feel much better. Thanks."

"Think you're feeling good enough to move to the couch? I could make you some hot tea."

"That sounds terrific. Thanks." She stood up cautiously, not seeming to mind his hand closing over her elbow as she did.

She headed for the closest of the double sinks. Her jaw dropped when she spotted her reflection in the mirror. "Oh my God. My hair. It's like Medusa hair. I guess it was that de-skunking shampoo. Why didn't you say anything?"

Mason didn't mean to laugh, but he couldn't suppress it. He'd thought it was cute and didn't mind that her hair was quite a bit fuller than the other times he'd seen her. De-skunking shampoo or not, she was a remarkable brunette with long, sexy hair. And more than once, he'd imagined losing his hands in it. "Tess, you're too hard on yourself. You're beautiful and your hair is a turn-on, even when it's a little…well…bigger than usual."

Her lips parted as their eyes met in the mirror. Even in the half-dimmed light, Mason could pick up on her blush.

He shrugged, unable to suppress a smile. "Just saying it like it is."

"I, uh… Thanks. I'll be out in a minute. I'm just going to wash up."

Mason nodded. "I'll start the tea."

He stepped from the room, closing the door to give her privacy. As he headed for the kitchen, he reminded himself that absolutely, under no circumstances whatsoever, was he allowed to so much as kiss her tonight.

Chapter 14

As the sun began to sink low in the sky, the distinctive scent penetrating the air from the broken windows of the building told the dog what he would find inside it. This troubled him but didn't stop him from wanting to get in.

It had been two days since the dog had caught a fresh scent of the female he'd mated with, the one whose belly had thickened and whose already-troubled walk had slowed considerably the last few days. The only food she seemed to have been eating was the food he'd been leaving for her.

Having trailed her scent across her territory, the dog knew that the night before she'd entered this building, she'd slept behind a Dumpster. The ground where she'd slept that night still smelled of something ripe and unfamiliar. It was different from the way she'd smelled when she'd allowed him to mate with her. This new scent didn't fill him with a renewed ache to mate, but had heightened his curiosity to find her. It was a blend of blood and mucus and something else he'd never smelled.

Yesterday, he'd followed her trail to this building but couldn't find how she'd gotten in. Today, before coming here, he'd trotted throughout her usual range and discovered no fresh whiffs of her scent. So he'd returned here.

Today, the smell of her wafted out of the building,

confirming his thoughts. Still, he wouldn't rest until he found his way inside. The entries to the building were shut, doors and windows alike, but somehow she'd gotten in.

One side of the building was blocked by a fence. The dog traveled alongside the fence until he reached a section where the fence was mangled and broken just above the ground. He could smell her faded scent here and understood this was how he could get to her.

After finding that he was too large to crawl under the mangled fence, he dug and dug at the earth below it. While he was digging, a car passed close enough to catch his notice. He looked up and saw that it was filled with several men, including one who beckoned him from an open window. The dog stopped and sniffed. He could smell the sickly scent of Donna's stringent drink emanating from their pores and their breath. The dog bolted off, running far out of their sight, returning only when he could no longer hear or see the car.

After a lot more digging and a struggle, he was finally able to crawl underneath. The sharp fence scratched his sides through his thick fur. Once inside the fence, he stood up and shook himself off. Then, he followed his mate's scent straight to a heavily rotted door. Using a paw, he was able to tug the heavy door open enough to slip inside.

The smell inside the building was stale and choking, reminding him of some of the buildings where he'd spent dark, cold nights with Donna, nights that he'd passed eagerly waiting for the sun to rise and Donna to be on the move again.

Nose to the ground, the dog hopped over the discarded

human things inside the long-empty building. Far down one hallway, the dog heard several tiny cries and trotted toward them. A whine slipped from his throat before he entered the room. As he'd known from outside, his mate had followed Donna into the great sleep, but not before giving birth to her pups.

He sniffed each one and nudged them with his nose. They were males and females of different colors and sizes. They were helpless and immobile, cuddled together into a giant, wriggling ball at her side. He could smell from their breath that most of them had been able to drink their mother's milk before she grew still, but they couldn't drink it now. They huddled and whined and slept and waited.

Smelling the fading milk on their breath, the dog was reminded of his own days as a small pup, reminded of being content and warm and safe against his mother. He remembered the feel of her tongue—warm, wet, and healing—and the delicious smell of her fur.

The dog sank to his haunches, then to the floor beside them, licking them and warming them, but unable to provide them with the nourishment they needed. They sniffed and nuzzled him as he warmed them. Beside them, their mother lay still, her eyes closed in the great sleep.

The dog barked and howled, hoping to entice a human into the building. If Donna were with him, she'd wrap them in blankets and care for them. But Donna was gone. And there were no other humans the dog trusted.

He lay close beside the pups to keep them warm and finally dozed himself. When he awoke, it was dark, and the pups were noticeably more still. The dog understood that giving them warmth wouldn't be enough to keep them from following their mother into the great sleep.

Parting from the pups, the dog left the building and struggled underneath the fence, determined to take action though unsure of what action to take.

He barked loudly at the first several cars that passed. Most passed by without acknowledging him. One car made a terrifying, blaring noise that sent the dog running. Another car stopped, and a human called to him from inside it. He approached cautiously, barking and yipping as he wagged his tail, hoping the small group of humans inside would understand his signals.

Instead, the dog was surprised to have something thrown at him. It smashed hard against his hip after he'd spotted it being hurled toward him and had dodged to the side. The object was long and wooden and clanked to the ground, rolling away. The dog limped off in the opposite direction of the car, filled with fear and desperation.

He traveled in the direction of the man who had been leaving piles of food for him, though it was too far away to entice the man toward the building with the waiting pups. When he reached the man's building, he found a small pile of crunchy food waiting for him. He gobbled a few bites and then barked, looking up toward where the man had once stood and thrown him delicious food. He barked and barked, but the man didn't appear.

Not knowing what else to do, the dog scooped up a mouthful of the crunchy food, holding it between his tongue and the roof of his mouth. He headed back toward the pups, hoping it would be a replacement for the milk they were craving.

Chapter 15

SOFT, INVITING MUSIC — A CELLO, SHE THOUGHT — FILLED the air, and Tess was deliciously cozy. Cozier than she could remember being in a long time. A faraway but deep baritone barking seemed to pulse an irregular beat to the music.

Tess was snuggling deeper into the world's softest blanket when consciousness flooded in. She blinked her eyes open. She was in Mason's loft, curled into the corner of his giant couch. She'd fallen asleep waiting for a mug of tea. Now, it was on the coffee table, waiting for her.

She'd been dreaming they'd caught John Ronald, thinking she was burying her fingers deep into his gorgeous fur and that he was trusting her enough to do it. While, realistically, she'd been snuggling deeper into Mason's cozy blanket.

If only John Ronald would let them catch him. If he'd come with them willingly when they found him. Life was immeasurably hard for stray dogs. Tess's hunch was that John Ronald hadn't been feral born. His distinctive markings were too closely related to a purebred husky or malamute for that to be likely. And from the two quick sightings she'd had, he didn't look feral, just wary of humans. Tess could only assume he'd been abandoned or lost and hadn't had enough positive experiences with humans to seek them out for help. That was the case with many strays.

As Tess's foggy sleep thoughts cleared and wakeful-ness kicked in, so did embarrassment. She'd thrown up in Mason's bathroom. Knowing she'd have to face the music sooner or later, and not one to procrastinate, she tossed off the blanket and looked around.

Mason was in the kitchen, his back to her, attentively slicing something on a cutting board. Even from thirty feet away, Tess was able to appreciate his physique. Broad shoulders. Lean, strong legs. A remarkable butt.

"Hey." She cleared her throat and stood up, refolding the blanket. "How long was I asleep?"

Mason looked over his shoulder and smiled. "Thirty or forty minutes, tops. How's your headache? And your stomach?"

"The headache is gone, thankfully, and my stomach is rumbling in a good way. I think I just needed to shut down for a bit. And it coincided almost too perfectly with sinking into this couch and getting covered with that blanket."

"I hear you. I like my bed, but whenever I can't sleep, I head to the couch, and that always does it."

Tess lifted her now-cool mug of tea and carried it into the kitchen and away from the wall of windows and the remarkable St. Louis night skyline. If this were her place, she'd get nothing done in the evenings as she cuddled against that couch, sipping tea and gazing at the beautiful downtown lights.

"I had no idea a veggie meat loaf could smell so amazing. I'm so hungry, I could eat... Wait, I don't think you can say you could eat a bear when you're vegetarian, can you?"

Mason laughed and told her she could say whatever

she wanted. He was slicing through a cucumber with a gleaming chef knife. The gas oven was on warm. Tess hoped the meat loaf hadn't been ready too long.

"After I reheat this tea and we eat, I'll be good to get back out there again. If you're up for it, that is."

Using the tip of his chef knife, Mason pointed to the microwave. "Make yourself at home. I'm game for trying again. I've been standing here thinking what it could be like if we succeed. I want him. No question. And I know he'll have a better life. A much better life. But I can't help but wonder if he'll *want* to be here."

With the tea heating, Tess joined Mason at the opposite counter. "He will. I'm sure he will." Her hand closed reflexively over his forearm in reassurance, and she had to refrain from jerking it away. Seeing his strength was one thing. Feeling it underneath her hand was another.

What would he do if she slid between him and the countertop and allowed her lips to land where they wanted?

Um, hello, Tess. You just puked in his toilet a half hour ago. You probably have vomit breath.

She stepped back, dropping his arm. "Do you have honey?" she asked as the microwave dinged and shut off.

"Yeah. In the pantry." He jerked his head toward the far end of the kitchen. "I'll let you grab it. My hands are a mess."

Tess used the opportunity to assess his pantry. It was relatively uncluttered, and she spotted the honey right away. But she couldn't resist checking out the additional pantry contents. Nonna, who made nearly everything from scratch aside from her abiding sin of Twinkies, had said that a pantry revealed more about a person than a set of dresser drawers. Other than two big jugs of protein

powder, one chocolate and one vanilla, and a seem-
ingly unopened jar of protein-enhanced peanut butter,
Mason's pantry was stocked with a variety of everyday
foods. Among other things, it held a large container of
instant oatmeal, regular peanut butter, ramen noodles,
cans of chili, and several boxes of macaroni and cheese.
There were two six-packs of Schlafly bottled beer and a
bottle of bourbon on the bottom shelf. For John Ronald,
there were a box of treats, a half-empty bag of kibble,
and several cans of wet food.

On the top shelf of the pantry, a family-sized box of
Cocoa Puffs made Tess smile.

"What?" he asked as she headed back. He pulled
open a drawer and handed her a spoon. "Are you grinning at my juvenile selection of pantry foods?"

"That's a big box of Cocoa Puffs."

"Aren't they a kitchen-pantry requirement?"

"I certainly wished that growing up, but not in my
house. At least not unless it was a special occasion. My
parents both worked full-time when I was growing up,
and I went over to my grandparents' house every day
before school. My grandma's idea of a quick breakfast
is a bread roll with butter and jam or day-old biscotti to
dip in her coffee."

"Somehow that doesn't make you sound deprived, if
that's what you were aiming for."

Tess laughed as she squeezed a bit of honey into her
mug. As she stirred, she noticed his countertops for the
first time. They were several inches thick and she was
betting handcrafted, judging by how much they looked
like artwork. Her guess was that they were custom concrete, but she didn't ask.

This made her think of his comment about being in sports sales as he was driving her home the other day. She'd meant to ask more about it, but the conversation had taken a turn elsewhere. She thought about bringing it up now, but didn't. Whatever "sport sales" meant, he was clearly good at what he did, but drawing attention to their two very different income levels might be a downer to the easy flow of conversation.

Just outside the narrow galley kitchen was a remarkable hardwood dining table long enough to bring to mind *Beauty and the Beast*. Mason had set two places, one at an end, the other in the seat adjacent to it. Tess's heart beat at the intimacy of it.

This was so much better than dinner in a dorm room.

"How can I help?" Tess asked and took a sip of tea. It cradled her belly wonderfully, so she took another.

"I'm almost done, thanks. I have a red on the counter and a white in the fridge, if you're up for wine. I understand if you aren't."

A glance at the bottle of red caused Tess to do a double take. It was a Barolo, a wine produced in Piedmont, a part of Italy that sat at the foot of the Alps a few hours' jaunt from where she'd traveled in Switzerland. She'd backpacked through Piedmont twice and had splurged on a glass of Barolo at a local restaurant.

She lifted the bottle off the counter to inspect it more closely. It was surreal, thinking she'd passed the winery where this bottle had been corked. It made her feel oddly connected to a life she'd left behind. It was the second time around Mason that the world felt small and accessible.

Earlier, Mason had mentioned taking his parents

to Europe. Standing beside him, barely knowing him, Tess had the craziest desire to take him there. To have him experience life the way she had. Even if it was for a short time. Living small and quietly, learning from locals where to get the best deals to stretch the dollars she had, taking on odd jobs for room and board when the opportunity arose.

But she barely knew him. And would someone who clearly had the kind of money he did even be interested in that?

"I'd like to try this, if you're up for red."

"Sure." He pulled a corkscrew from one of the top drawers. "How about you open it while I finish up?"

Mason had a beautiful salad prepared, and a small pot of gravy was warming on the stove. When he opened the oven, she spotted a ceramic bowl of mashed potatoes, another of green beans, and the veggie meat loaf.

As Tess opened the wine, she thought of her grandma. Nonna had taught her never to belittle someone's effort in the kitchen by equating their work to trouble, or Tess would've been tempted to comment on how he hadn't needed to go to so much trouble to prepare dinner for her.

"Wow," she said instead. "Everything looks great. I can't wait to try it."

"Thanks. My, uh, slow season is in winter. Cooking is a hobby I've wanted to take up for a while. Like I said, before tonight, I'd only ever made three different main dishes."

"You said that, but you didn't tell me what they are, aside from meat loaf, that is."

"Want to guess?" Mason grinned as he carried over the salad bowl.

"Absolutely. Let's see. You grew up on a farm in rural Iowa, and your family is not Italian, so I'm guessing one of them is not lasagna."

"You would be correct."

Tess drummed her fingers on the counter. "What's farmy to cook? I'm trying to picture the Cracker Barrel menu in my head. And before you ask, I only got to eat there when I went to Florida with my cousin's family on vacation. We got to stop once each way. Okay, let's see. Chicken and dumplings?"

Mason chuckled. "Nope, though that's one of my mom's go-to winter meals."

"Country-fried steak?"

"If we were playing hangman, you'd have a head and body."

"Chicken pot pie?"

"And there's a leg, or is it the arm next?"

Tess clicked her tongue as Mason took a seat next to her at the table. "Pot roast?" she said, taking a seat.

"Well done."

"Really?" Tess waggled her eyebrows at him. "Pot roast and meat loaf. Two very hearty meals. Impressive."

"I bet you hang before you guess the third."

Tess pierced a bit of salad with her fork. She silently counted off the meals she'd guessed.

"Barbecue ribs?"

"Add the second leg. I can barbecue as well as the next guy, but I wasn't counting it. Slathering a rack of ribs with some sauce and enjoying a beer while it sizzles over the coals isn't the same as preparing a meal from scratch."

"True, I guess. Though I've never barbecued anything except a couple of precooked hot dogs over a fire." She pointed her fork his way. "Don't tell me. I'm going to get this." She took another bite of salad and was halfway through chewing it when it came to her. She smacked her palm against the table and hurriedly swallowed. "OMG, I've got it. I've totally got it. I know your third meal, Mason..." Tess paused. "I know your third meal, but I don't know your last name. How weird is that?"

Mason sat back in his chair and took a sip of wine, appraising her, his mouth pulled up in the crooked smile that she adored. "With that reaction, this is the all-or-nothing round. Get it right, you win. Get it wrong, that's the arms, feet, hands, everything, and you're hanged."

"I'm okay with that, only what are we playing for?"

"I don't know. I haven't thought about that. Something bigger than who does the dishes, that's for sure."

Tess agreed with him. "How about winner calls it?"

His gaze dropped to her mouth for two solid seconds before returning to her eyes. "Yes, definitely."

She was drawing in a big breath for effect when she heard the abrupt, distinctive barking for the second time. The first time, she'd thought it had been a dream. Only it hadn't been. And this wasn't the rapid-fire territorial barking of a dog who'd spotted another dog walking past and was claiming its territory. This was sharp and punctuated. Attention-getting. And it seemed to be coming from outside.

She squeezed Mason's hand a second, then stood up and headed for the wall of windows. "Can we go out on your balcony? That barking. Something's not right."

"Sure. Over here."

As soon as the door was open, the barking was so

sharp and pronounced that Tess became certain something was off. She followed Mason onto the balcony.

Mason sucked in a breath as he looked down. "Holy shit. It's him."

Tess grabbed the railing and peered down into the darkness. It was John Ronald, and he was looking directly up at them. From the pale-yellow gleam of the streetlight, Tess could just make out that the dark fur on the back of his neck was ruffled and his tail was stuck straight behind him as if in alarm.

"Something's wrong," Tess repeated. Without taking the time to explain, she dashed back inside, first to Mason's pantry to grab the dog treats she'd spotted, then to the door. She grabbed her boots as she passed but didn't take time to put them on.

She was in the hallway, repeatedly pressing the elevator button, when Mason stepped out and shook his head. "The stairs are faster. And in case I ask you later, I moved the meat loaf to the warming drawer and the oven's off." He threw open the fire-escape door. "This way."

Mason took the concrete steps two at a time. Barefoot, Tess raced down after him a single stair at a time. He reached the bottom a flight before she did but waited for her, holding the fire-escape door that opened directly to the lobby. "Let's take it slowly, so we don't scare him away."

Breathless, Tess nodded. Mason hardly seemed winded. She scolded herself for what an inappropriate time it was to wonder what kind of cardio routine he had.

They crossed the lobby together and reached the door at the same time. Although the dog was around the corner on the side street that Mason's loft faced, Tess could still hear him barking. She tugged on her boots and followed Mason out the door. He wrapped his hand around hers as they headed toward the corner.

Tess kept telling herself it was dark, and she'd been seeing things. Whatever it was she'd spotted from the sixth floor was probably just another present the dog had brought for Mason.

But it wasn't. Somehow, she knew it wasn't. They rounded the corner together, and Tess squeezed Mason's hand. "Do you think it's dead?"

"What's dead?"

He hadn't spotted it.

"There's a puppy at his feet. It's not moving. It might be dead."

John Ronald pivoted to face them and backed up several feet, leaving the puppy where it lay. He barked several times and wagged his tail, looking from the puppy to them.

Not wanting to scare him off, Tess headed toward the puppy slowly but confidently. John Ronald stopped barking and watched attentively.

Tears of relief flooded her eyes as she scooped the helpless creature into her hands. It was alive—barely, but alive. She pulled it to her chest, warming it in her hands. "Mason, he carried it here. It's full of slobber."

Mason shook his head. "You think he was trying to save it?"

Tess stroked the puppy, stimulating it with her thumb, as she watched the dog. His gaze was fixed on Mason before he trotted ten feet farther away, then turned toward him again, wagging his tail and letting out a single bark.

Tess didn't need to see the black-and-white markings of the puppy to know why a stray male dog had such a keen interest in it. "Mason, I think he's trying to save a whole litter."

Chapter 16

EVERY TIME MASON FELT CERTAIN HE'D LOST SIGHT OF
the dog as the tenacious animal seemed to be swallowed
up by the night, he'd catch a glimpse of a now-familiar
pattern of black and white in the darkness ahead. The
dog seemed to sense when, with his quicker stride, he'd
pressed too far ahead. He'd turn and wait in the darkness, watching but rarely barking.

John Ronald was leading Mason deeper into a section of the city that was riddled with long-abandoned
warehouses. It was an area most people did their
damnedest to avoid while in cars in full daylight. The
only inhabitants of this dilapidated burrow were either
homeless or meth heads or troubled youth hoping to stir
up even more trouble. Thank God he hadn't allowed
Tess to convince him to send her in pursuit of the dog
instead of him.

Mason had been sending Tess back upstairs for some
blankets, jackets, and the keys to his truck when John
Ronald had begun to trot off. The dog had paused a few
hundred feet away, barking and prancing in a zigzagged
circle, as if beckoning them to follow.

"We're going to lose him, Tess," he'd said. Rushing
out as they did, Mason hadn't even thought about grabbing his keys. And with the puppy in the shape it was
in, it needed immediate care. "I'll follow John Ronald
on foot. You can get that puppy warmed up and use my

truck to catch up with us. The keys are on the counter. Call me. I'll pin you my location."

"Mason, I can't drive your truck. It's a tank. And I don't have a phone, remember?"

They'd gone back and forth a full minute before Mason had closed his hands over her shoulders. "Tess, you can do this. You *need* to do this. You're more capable of helping the puppy anyway."

His words having sunk in, Tess had reluctantly agreed. To get her back upstairs, Mason rang Georges on the video intercom. "Hey, let Tess up, will you? And she needs to borrow your phone. Meet her in the hall, and you'll see why."

Fearing he'd lose sight of John Ronald if he let him get any farther ahead, Mason had taken off after him. Tess's "Good luck" just reached his ears.

The farther away from the familiar downtown sights they drew, the harder it was to tell, but Mason suspected he'd been following the dog at a brisk jog for nearly two miles. After trailing John Ronald blindly for a few minutes down a deserted street with no streetlights and only the moon and stars for light, Mason stopped to catch his breath. He'd lost sight of John Ronald completely. He was closed in by two abandoned redbrick warehouses that spanned a full block on each side of the street. In the darkness, they seemed heavily boarded up, but Mason still felt the hairs on the back of his neck stand on end. It'd likely be safer to walk through the Alaskan wilderness at night than to pass through here.

In the building to his right, Mason could swear he heard a single, muffled cough. He headed on at a walk, listening for the sound of barking as well as a glimpse of the evasive dog. He was beginning to fear he'd lost him completely and could only hope the dog would reappear. Then suddenly, off to his left, there was a burst of movement that had Mason throwing up his fists. It was John Ronald. He'd been waiting in a shadow all along, and Mason hadn't been able to see him. Now, the gangly dog was only a body length away. He stared at Mason in the darkness for a full three seconds before heading on. Rather than continuing along the street, John Ronald darted around the corner of the building, beckoning Mason with a wave of his tail.

Just as the dog began to trot the length of a rusted metal security fence that enclosed the back of the building, Mason's phone blared into the night, startling both him and the dog. Mason jumped, and John Ronald whirled to face him, growling.

"It's okay, buddy," Mason said, pulling out his phone. It was Tess.

"I'm driving. It's totally crazy, but I'm driving this giant thing. I'm out of the garage and following the pin. Did you get in someone's car? The GPS reads that you're just over two miles away. I should be there in eight minutes, according to this."

"I'm still on foot. We've been moving fast. Heads-up that we're not exactly in a place that's bustling with activity. Keep the doors locked and the windows rolled up. And stay on the phone."

"Okay, but I can't hold it and drive this tank. I'm putting you on speaker."

Since he'd been driving Georges places after his surgery, Mason had connected Georges's phone to his truck's Bluetooth, but Mason would first have to walk

Tess through how to disconnect his phone, and right now he didn't want to give her anything else to stress about. "That's fine."

"Has he taken you to the rest of the litter?"

"I think we're getting close." John Ronald was trotting alongside the fence again, and now that Mason wasn't shut in by a second looming building, moonlight gleamed on the gravel alongside the fence. He could see how the ground was dug up twenty feet ahead of the dog. "How's the puppy?" he asked Tess.

"Warming up. Georges gave me a couple boxes and towels, so I didn't have to search for yours. It's not ideal, but I force-fed her some butter and a few drops of water. It's better than nothing till we get her to the shelter."

Mason waited as John Ronald hunkered low into a crouch and squirmed with considerable effort under the torn-up section of fence. Once on the other side, the gangly dog trotted halfway to the warehouse, then stopped and turned to wait for Mason.

"That's quick thinking. Nicely done, Tess. Hey, I'm about to squeeze under a fence and go into a building. I'm going to put my phone away but stay on the line."

He put his phone on speaker and slipped it into his jeans pocket. He heard a thin version of her voice agreeing and telling him to be safe as he sank to the cold ground and onto his back. He shoved his arms through the hole, ignoring the piercing pain in his left shoulder, reminding him of the long road ahead to be ready for next season.

Shrugging off the pain, he grabbed the torn fence and pulled himself through the hole. It was a tight, muddy, and uncomfortable squeeze, and a sharp pain shot through his shoulder and arm. It was hardly wide enough for his shoulders to fit through. He heard his shirt ripping and felt a piece of broken chain link scraping into his side.

"You really had to want to get in here to make it through that, didn't you, guy?" Mason pushed the rest of the way through and stood up, trying to ward off a wave of unease at the idea of heading into that dilapidated building with nothing more than the light from his phone. As soon as he was on his feet, John Ronald trotted inside through a rotten, partially hinged door that had been wedged open.

The smell of mold and refuse and God knew what else smacked Mason in the face before he'd stepped inside. Using his phone's flashlight, he shone it around the darkened, cave-like interior awaiting him. Large sections of ceiling tile had fallen to the floor in places. In others, it hung down from the ceiling, still partially connected to the cross supports. Insulation—he was betting asbestos—hung from the ceiling in clumps like thick spiderwebs. Somewhere above it, water was dripping. The thin, high *plunk* resonated through the vast, empty room, reminding him of a tomb.

The floor below Mason's feet was riddled with debris. From plastic office chairs and a shattered coffeepot to the clumps of ceiling tile and sections of ripped-up flooring, it was a garbage dump, and Mason was following John Ronald through it down a hallway into God knew where.

He did a double take when the beam of his flashlight landed on a plush chair tucked against one wall, facing into the cavernous room. Resting on the torn seat was a man's cloth hat partially covered by dust and debris. On the floor beside the chair was an overturned bourbon glass. Mason had sympathy for whoever had once sat in that chair, greeting the end of an empire. Like the changing seasons, dreams swelled and peaked and waned. It was likely that whoever had sat there had experienced all three.

Ahead in the darkness, John Ronald let out a single bark, beckoning Mason deeper into the building.

—∿—

If John Ronald had found them during rush hour, Tess's anxiety over getting behind the wheel again—and in a two-and-a-half-ton truck, no less—might have gotten the best of her. At nine o'clock on a weeknight, however, the streets were practically deserted. The farther she followed Mason's pin-marked location into the old warehouse district, the emptier they became.

After the first mile and lots of meandering through one-way streets and obeying stop signs, she got the feel of how much force to apply to the brake and pedal. And even though she was driving deeper into a more isolated and unwelcoming area, her confidence grew as she neared Mason's pin.

Her excitement swelled as Georges's phone announced she had arrived. She'd swallowed her reservations and driven. *A truck no less.*

She shifted into Park but kept the truck idling. "I'm here," she called out, knowing she was still on speaker. She placed the palm of her hand over the puppy who was cradled in a cozy towel in one corner of a box she'd gotten from Georges. If Tess was perfectly still, she could just make out the rise and fall of the pup's lungs. She could only hope the little girl's siblings were fighters too.

"I can hear you." Mason's voice resonated up from the phone and through the truck interior. "Just park out front. I'll find you a better way in than the way I came."

Tess agreed and hung up. She debated what to grab to take inside with her. The puppy was in a large enough box that several siblings could fit inside with her. And snuggling together wrapped in a warm blanket would be the best way to get them to the shelter. She dropped several towels into the box, mindful not to disturb the puppy, then the box of hard-to-resist treats and one of the slipknot leashes she'd brought along from the shelter. The catch pole was in the truck bed, but hopefully they wouldn't need it.

She stepped out the driver-side door and looked around. Now that she was no longer locked safely inside the truck, it hit home how dark and run-down an area they'd followed the dog into. Tess wasn't sure she'd have been as brave as Mason to follow the stray down this deserted street all alone. It was a good thing she'd trusted Mason's confidence in her and driven.

She had just picked up the cumbersome box and was shutting the driver-side door with her backside when, fifteen feet away, a door of the warehouse exploded outward with tornado-like force, shattering into pieces and sending debris skittering across the pavement in front of it.

Tess screamed reflexively even as her brain registered that it was Mason stepping across the threshold and into the night. "Mason, that scared me half to death!"

"Sorry about that. It was bolted shut. I didn't expect it to disintegrate like that when I kicked it."

He met her halfway and closed a hand over her elbow, and they headed toward the building together. His towering, athletic frame flanking her side as they neared the looming warehouse was a comfort.

"Later, we'll celebrate you driving my truck under that kind of pressure. That took courage, Tess. And even though I knew you could do it, that doesn't mean I don't appreciate your willingness to jump in." Mason's hand moved from her elbow to land between her shoulder blades. "Want me to carry that?"

"I'm fine, and thanks. All's well that ends well, right? So, did you find them?"

"Yeah."

Tess froze midstep. There was something in his tone. "What's wrong?"

"They're alive. I'd just found them when you got here. There are six or seven more; I didn't get to look at them too closely. It's just…they weren't abandoned. Their mother is with them. There's no way around this; she didn't make it. I'm guessing she's been dead a day or two."

The weight of Mason's words washed over her. Tess knew this was going to be the hardest part of working at the shelter. She'd never stop wanting to save them all.

"Oh, Mason." She wanted to say more, but her throat locked tight. He stepped through the busted-open doorway and into a dark, dank room. She followed, hardly able to see but somehow still able to feel the dilapidation all around her.

"Look, why don't you stay here where I can hear

if you yell, but I'll take the box and bring the puppies to you."

"Thanks, but I'd like to have a look at the mom. If I can discern what killed her, we'll have a better time treating the puppies."

Even in the darkness and in spite of his stubble, Tess could see that this made Mason frown. At first, it seemed as if he was going to object, but after a second or two of silence, he led the way, lighting a narrow path with his phone's flashlight.

And even though she was keeping an eye open for the dog, Tess almost jumped out of her skin when she spotted John Ronald not far ahead in the darkness, waiting for them. She and Mason had moved from the small room where they'd entered into a long, narrow hall.

"I hear you. This place beats any haunted house I've been in," Mason said when Tess flinched. "The puppies aren't far ahead. Just a couple doors down on the left."

"Were these offices?" Tess peered into a small, square room as they passed. It was dimly lit by a stream of moonlight pouring through a window.

"I think so. I entered through the back of the building where whatever was made here must have been manufactured. It was considerably bigger and had the feel of a mausoleum."

Tess stepped closer to Mason. "So, uh, feel free to avoid using words like 'mausoleum' until we get out of here." She was all about not needing a guy to feel whole or protected, but there were exceptions to every rule.

After shooting Tess and Mason a backward glance, John Ronald dashed into a room ten feet ahead.

"We're here."

Tess strained to hear the puppies whimpering but could hear nothing other than her and Mason's footsteps. John Ronald didn't so much as make a sound as he moved over the refuse covering the floor.

Mason pulled Tess to a stop in the doorway. "Let's give him a minute." John Ronald had made it to the far side of the room. After a thorough sniff, the long-legged dog began to lick what Tess could only assume were the puppies.

"Did he show any signs of stress when you approached them?"

"Not too much. He growled once but backed into the opposite corner and let me look them over."

Tess offered the box Mason's way. "What if you hold the puppy back here while I check them out?"

"Yeah, sure. I'm sure you know this better than me. Just take it slow."

As soon as Tess took a single step into the room, John Ronald stopped licking the pups to watch her warily. Not caring too much about what she said, she started up an easy, quiet diatribe, hoping the dog would be able to hear the reassurance in her tone. She lifted two towels from the side of the box and a few of the treats, then crossed slowly but purposely toward the pups, who after John Ronald's licking, were making a few soft whimpers.

Tess's eyes were adjusting to the dim light, and she could now make out their silhouettes. They were snuggled tightly against one another and their eerily still mother.

John Ronald let out a long, low growl as she closed in on them. Tess paused her step but continued with a string of soft, easy words. John Ronald backed up several feet, eyeing her warily. "It's okay, big guy. It's okay."

Near the doorway, Mason sank down, setting the box on the floor. He unwrapped the towel and lifted the pup in his hands, holding her out John Ronald's way. It worked to pull the watchful dog's attention off Tess long enough for her kneel at the floor in front of the other pups.

Several pieces of soggy, uneaten kibble lay scattered next to the pups. A rush of emotion flooded Tess. It seemed John Ronald had brought them some of the food Mason had left out for him. But there was no possibility of them being able to eat it, as young and undoubtedly weak and helpless as they were.

John Ronald sank onto his haunches catty-corner to them and released something between a whine and a growl as he returned his attention to Tess.

This close, the smell rolling off their mother made Tess's stomach lurch reflexively. And she'd thought she was immune to smells tonight.

Tess ran her fingertips over the puppies. Mason was right. Their body temps were lower than they should be, but each one was still breathing. As carefully as she could, she placed each one on the towel and wrapped them up together. Including the pup that John Ronald had carried to them, there were seven altogether, and they seemed to be a motley crew of mixed breeds.

It was hard to make out much about the mother without Mason's flashlight, aside from the fact that she'd had a short, dark coat and had been stocky, most likely a pit-bull mix. Tess wished for the flashlight for a closer look, but she worried if Mason left the doorway, John Ronald would take off.

"Can you shine the light this way? But keep the door

blocked. Something tells me John Ronald isn't planning on accompanying us out of here."

"I was thinking the same thing."

After a bit of shuffling, the deceased mother dog was bathed in the light—dim and bright at the same time—from Mason's phone. Tears welled instantly in Tess's eyes. The dog had been a beautiful brindled American Staffordshire terrier mix. She'd also been riddled with an array of scars. From what Tess could see, they were heaviest in the neck and shoulder area. *Someone probably fought her and then dumped her*.

Reminding herself that she'd once been a vet student examining animal cadavers to discern cause of death, Tess attempted to lock her feelings away as she studied the dog. She took in the terrier's pronounced ribs and swollen back leg. But her eyes filled too heavily with tears, and she couldn't see anything at all. In school, in a lab, she'd found it difficult to distance herself from the animal in front of her. Here, it was impossible. This poor dog had come into this wretched building to give birth and had died curled protectively around her litter.

Tess sniffed and dragged her sleeve over her face, not caring that the mascara she'd applied for her date that wasn't a date was likely running down her cheeks.

"What can I do?" Mason's tone was filled with a tenderness Tess had never before heard from him.

"I'm okay." Her voice sounded nasal, but she cleared her throat and forced herself to think about the puppies. "I'm going to bring you a few pups at a time, I guess. I thought I could carry them in the towel, but I'm worried one could fall out. And if you leave that door, John

Ronald's gone. I'm sure of it. He's nervous and swallowing a lot. I'm kicking myself for not grabbing that catch pole from the truck bed."

Mason slipped the phone back into his jeans pocket, and the room was dimly filled with silvery moonlight once again. "I agree. And I think we're better off not relying on the flashlight to catch him. Or we'll be blinded whenever he's out of the beam of light. Once we get the puppies in the box, we'll switch places and you can block the door."

Tess carried them over, two at a time. They were each small enough to fit comfortably in one hand. Cradling them against her skin, it was disturbing how much cooler they were compared to her. It was also likely that they'd been undernourished coming into the world.

They're going to survive. Each one of them. That's all there is to it.

John Ronald rose to all fours again, though he remained backed into the far corner. He released a blended array of whining and growling as Tess carried the puppies across the room to Mason, who had a space ready for them in the box.

After Tess's third trip, Mason tucked in the two remaining puppies, wrapped them up, and nodded at Tess. "Stand here a moment, will you? I'm going to lift that door and try to use it as a barrier. Otherwise, when I get close to him, I wouldn't be surprised if he bolted right past you."

Tess stepped to the side as Mason lifted a busted-up door from the corner of the room and leaned it haphazardly against one side of the frame.

John Ronald's growls reached a new crescendo as his

escape was blocked. Even in the dim light, Tess noticed the hair on his scruff fluff up to stand on end.

"Mason, be careful."

"I will."

It took clamping her top teeth over her lower lip to refrain from saying more. Her shoulders flinched as Mason approached, leash and treats in hand. It was his turn to talk softly and easily. When he was six feet from the dog, he dropped to a squat and opened his palm, calling the dog to him.

John Ronald remained on all fours as he surveyed the room. Mason tossed the anxious dog one of Tess's moist, savory liver treats that even well-fed dogs found hard to resist.

"Easy, boy," Mason chanted. "I know you're hungry. If you'll let me take you home, I can promise an array of bison or salmon or raw food…or whatever we're supposed to feed dogs now. You won't be hungry anymore, and no one will mistreat you."

Fresh tears stung Tess's eyes, but for an entirely new reason. When John Ronald cautiously lowered his head and inhaled the thrown treat with a split-second flick of the tongue, they spilled down her cheeks. The tension in the room seemed to war against time, and Tess wasn't sure if it was minutes or seconds before John Ronald took two steps closer to Mason for a second treat.

He seemed to know not to stare the dog in the eyes. He kept his gaze locked on the treats in his palm and cajoled the dog closer and closer with tossed treats until he was only a foot away. Then Mason divided the treats between his hands and raised one in John Ronald's direction.

A hesitant, almost deflated growl filled the room. Licking his lips, John Ronald lowered himself until he was in a crouch, then army-crawled close enough to swipe the treats off Mason's palm with his quick tongue. When they were gone, Tess waited with bated breath as Mason slowly, deliberately reached out to touch the dog.

Tess knew not to utter a sound, but every part of her wanted to tell Mason what a great job he was doing, to offer encouragement that he was reading the dog correctly. A tear settled in the hollow of her neck as Mason's fingertips sank into the thick fur at John Ronald's cheek.

In the dim light, it was impossible to tell for sure, but after a bit, it seemed as if John Ronald was even leaning into the scratch.

"Good, good boy," Mason was saying in a voice that Tess could fall asleep to every night for the rest of her life. "I bet you're hungry for more, huh? I've got a few more in my other hand, but before I give them to you, I'd like to slip a leash over that thick, scruffy neck of yours."

Then Mason shifted, and the next several seconds were blocked from Tess's view. She knew he was reaching for the leash when John Ronald raised his head warily.

"Come on, boy, let's do this."

And then, craning to see over Mason's shoulder, Tess watched the dog move in for the rest of the treats but not before Mason draped the slipknot leash over his face and behind his ears.

"Good, good boy." Mason let John Ronald lick his empty palm. "Let's get you home, and we'll get you something else to fill that belly."

At Tess's feet, one of the puppies began to whimper with renewed energy.

"Tess, think you can slide that door over?"

The door was rotted, but it was also solid wood and heavier than Tess might've expected, but she was able to slide it to the adjacent wall. Afterward, she lifted the box, creating as little disturbance as possible, both for the puppies' sakes and for John Ronald's.

It took ten minutes and a lot of coaxing on Mason's part to get John Ronald to walk beside him and not tug backward with every step, but they made it to the truck. Tess headed around and opened the passenger-side extended cab door. She slid the box onto the seat and buckled it in, then closed the door.

Mason had the driver-side extended cab door open and was frowning down at John Ronald. Tess headed around to join them but hung back.

"Think he'll devour me if I try to lift him?" Mason asked.

Tess opened her mouth to answer but paused as John Ronald let out a single whine, tucked in his haunches, and leapt onto the back seat. Realizing at the last second what the dog was doing, Mason let go of the leash just in time. Once in, John Ronald kept standing and dug his nose down through the top of the box, sniffing the puppies.

"I didn't see that coming." Mason shook his head, amazed, and closed the door. He pressed it shut gently enough that he had to give it a push to get it to close properly.

As soon as he'd turned around, Tess dove into his arms without so much as contemplating it. She pressed her forehead against his chest and locked her arms around his torso. He'd ripped his shirt somehow. She'd not noticed inside, but she noticed now.

She didn't think it was all her, but their bodies locked together enough to chase the cold night air away. Tess had grown chilled to the bone over the last twenty minutes. Neither of them had a jacket. She'd been shivering and was pocked with goose bumps but hadn't realized it because she'd been so focused on the puppies and John Ronald.

"This either, really." Mason locked his strong arms around her and pressed a kiss on top of her head.

Something between a laugh and a cry escaped Tess's throat. What felt like a month ago rather than a mere four days, she had suspected that hugging him would be no different from hugging a tree. Now, she wasn't sure if she'd ever been more wrong. Mason was delectably warm and inviting.

"You were great in there," she mumbled into his chest.

"You weren't so bad yourself."

He ran his hand the length of Tess's hair. She kept still, savoring it. Gradually realizing that the longer she remained in his arms, the harder it was going to be to pull away, Tess forced her legs to take a single step back that they didn't want to take. But her arms wouldn't let go, and it seemed neither would his.

She looked through the back window at John Ronald, whose head was craned in their direction, though his scruff was no longer standing on end. "I think the hardest part with him is over, Mason. The anticipation of getting caught is usually the worst part when it comes to catching strays. Now that he's with you, I think he's going to do just fine. Just keep doing what you did inside. It was perfect."

Mason shook his head ever so slightly. One corner of his mouth pulled back in a small smile. The visible sliver of his teeth gleamed white in the moonlight, calling her attention to his mouth.

"That's nice to hear."

For a split second, Tess readied herself for the kiss she was certain was coming. She'd never been looked at like this before and *not* been kissed. She remembered toiling away under the hot Tuscan sun and getting into a conversation about love and life with an old olive farmer while taking a break under a narrow pergola. It was the human hunger for connection that brought young lovers together, he'd said.

Then Mason's expression changed as quickly as a set of curtains being drawn shut. He stepped back a foot and released her before turning away to fumble for something in the front of the cab. John Ronald, who'd returned his attention to the puppies, jerked his head out of the box and let out a startled woof, clearly unnerved by a human intruding into the quiet interior of the truck. "We should probably get moving while he's relatively calm."

Tess released a breath she didn't know she'd been holding and heard herself agreeing.

Maybe she hadn't been looking for Mason—hadn't been looking for anyone—but here he was. She was dangerously close to being hooked. But why did it feel as if that dream she'd had about her kissing him and him holding back had been more foreshadowing than fiction?

Chapter 17

AS MASON STRUGGLED TO COME OUT OF A HEAVY slumber, a sharp pain shot through the side of his neck. He clamped a hand over it and winced. It seemed he'd fallen asleep with his neck at a near-ninety-degree angle.

He blinked in the dim light, more disoriented than he'd been in a long time. A very long-legged dog loomed over him in the darkness.

"What the...?" Mason bolted to a sitting position, his muscles tensing. He jerked at the baritone woof that pierced his ears.

He'd fallen asleep on his couch. And now John Ronald was standing on top of his coffee table just twelve inches away, staring him down.

"Hey, boy, it's okay." He cleared his throat and swiped sleep from the corners of his eyes.

John Ronald was still staring him down. And panting. On top of his coffee table.

"What's the matter? Can't sleep in here?"

Mason wanted to reach forward and pet him but remembered he needed to pace himself. The dog had come with him almost willingly, but there was a long road of trust building ahead of them.

After dropping Tess and the puppies at the shelter and loading up with a bagful of the supplies for sale in the shelter's gift shop, he'd brought the dog home. Mason had wanted to stay at the shelter and help Tess with the puppies, but she'd been adamant about not bringing John Ronald into the building.

Since the dog was a stray, shelter policy would require him to go straight into quarantine like the pups. However, Mason was set on keeping him. There was no reason to lock him in a kennel for who knew how long before bringing him home. Instead, Mason had taken him home and would get him to a vet first thing in the morning. The dog didn't look sick, but he was going to need a series of shots, deworming, and who knew what else, along with adequate nutrition as he recovered from the life of a stray dog. But he'd have a comfortable, caring home as he did.

After that remarkable rescue, which hopefully would save those puppies' lives, Mason had felt terrible separating the brave dog from the pups. But there was no other good option. They were going to need around-the-clock specialty care to have an optimal chance of survival.

As soon as Mason stood up, he was hit with a sickening smell circulating through his loft. It could only mean one thing.

"I think I might know why you're staring me down, guy."

Tess had warned him not to feed John Ronald too much, no matter how hungry the dog seemed. She had said she suspected that no matter how little he ate, his system was likely going to be shocked as he transitioned to a regular, healthy diet.

Stopping at the amount of food she'd recommended hadn't been easy, but he'd listened and not given John Ronald a second helping. Not even when John Ronald had looked from the bag of food to Mason and back to the bag.

After flipping on the light, Mason spotted the inevitable pile of poop. It was on the hardwood floor near the front door. "System shocked, I'd say. Well, at least we've got that stool sample covered now. And kudos for missing the rug."

Mason headed for the dining room table where he'd hung the leash over a chair. John Ronald hopped off the coffee table and trailed a few feet behind. Before Mason had left the shelter, Tess had buckled a bright-blue collar around John Ronald's neck, saying that it would match the dog's striking eyes.

"Come on, guy. Let's go outside." Mason grabbed a handful of treats and the leash, then stepped into the open foyer. If he could help it, he never wanted John Ronald to feel trapped around him again. After sinking to a nonthreatening squat and remaining patient a few minutes, Mason was rewarded with John Ronald stepping in close. The hungry dog swiped the treats from Mason's palm with a flick of his warm, moist tongue. He didn't even flinch when Mason clipped the leash to his collar.

"Good boy," Mason said, giving him a slow, easy pat on the shoulder.

A glance at the clock showed it was 4:00 a.m. It had been well after one when Mason had drifted off, so no wonder it still felt as if he were moving in a thick fog. He wished he could shoot off a text to Tess to check on her, but she'd insisted he return Georges's cell phone to him. He wasn't about to call the shelter or her grandma's at this time of night either.

With any luck, she was sound asleep in bed. She'd promised to call one of the employees to help her with the puppies if she needed it. And rather than asking

Mason to drag John Ronald into the truck again tonight or leave the overwhelmed dog alone in his loft, Tess had insisted she'd have her dad bring her back to her grandma's when she was ready to head home.

Abandoning her at her place of work without a car or a cell phone wasn't the best way to end a first date, but under the circumstances, they'd both been doing their best.

He'd make it up to her. Actually, it was going to be a struggle to wait for the next opportunity. When she'd dived into his arms, it had thrown him completely off guard. He'd been overwhelmed by a desire to pull her closer and not let go. And rather than admitting it, he'd made a joke. But there was nothing he could do about it now.

He knew he needed to come clean and tell her everything. However, there was a nagging rumbling up from his chest telling him not yet.

It wasn't that he wasn't sure about her. He couldn't believe how sure he'd become and how quickly. Everything about her intrigued and enticed him. He wasn't one to believe in soul mates or kindred spirits or any of the early-relationship talk that people seemed to grow to regret. But he also wasn't going to deny that he'd felt a connection with her right from their first couple of minutes together. And it was only getting stronger.

And all of that left him more anxious about telling her the truth than all the times put together that he'd been at bat last season with the bases loaded.

Mason pushed out a deep breath. There was nothing he could do about any of this tonight.

John Ronald followed Mason willingly out of the loft and down five flights of stairs. Even though the narrow brick-and-concrete stairwell was confining, Mason didn't want to stress the dog out with the elevator yet.

Outside, it was cold enough to see their breath, and the sky was a clear, dark blue-black. The stars that weren't diluted by city lights—a fraction compared to the ones he'd grown up seeing—shone overhead.

Mason led John Ronald to the nearest sizable patch of earth sandwiched between the street and the neighboring building. After a quick sniff, John Ronald pulled in his haunches and started to poop. This time, it was considerably less formed. Mason determined to wait till morning before picking that one up.

"So, for the record, thanks for waking me up. I'd rather do this anytime."

John Ronald cocked his head, the pointy peaks of his ears nearly touching on top of his head. Mason liked that the dog seemed to have an interest in his words. Rather than heading back inside, Mason led him down the empty street a block or two, letting John Ronald sniff and get familiar with his new surroundings. He seemed to grow accustomed to the confines of the leash quickly, giving Mason confidence that John Ronald would soon think joining Mason's household was a good thing.

In the quiet, still night, John Ronald stopped sniffing the ground and licked his lips, then let out a soft, almost inaudible sigh.

"Feeling better, guy?"

John Ronald looked up and studied him, his expression more curious than afraid. Then his mouth fell open in an easy, comfortable pant that Mason's dad had told him was as close to a smile as a dog could get.

Mason reached down and scratched him between

the shoulder blades. "Just so you know, if that's all the thanks I ever get from you, it'll be enough."

For a second, it seemed as if the clock was broken, but it was digital, and Tess figured that was unlikely. It had been just after ten when Mason had dropped her at the shelter. She'd woken her grandma up with a phone call then, letting her know what had happened and that it would be a long time before she was home.

The fact that it was now ten minutes after four seemed impossible. Six hours had flown by in the space of what felt like a jumble of minutes.

After Mason left, Tess had slipped into priority mode. Thankfully, the shelter was set up with the supplies she needed. Her first step had been to move the puppies into quarantine and get them cuddled in a kennel under a blanket next to a hot-water bottle for extra warmth.

The two dogs on the opposite side of the room hardly paid Tess any attention, but the Savannah cat watched her warily, his long ears flattened against his head. Perhaps it was because the smell was still lingering in her sinuses and she'd grown immune to it, but she could hardly detect the skunky odor that had so clearly pervaded the room six hours ago.

She wanted to offer the thin cat a treat, but thought it was best not to go near his kennel. Since she couldn't know for certain what had killed the puppies' mother, it was important to respect the fact that the puppies could be carrying disease. And while she wasn't entirely familiar with the shelter's specific quarantine regulations, Tess sanitized her hands every step of the way to ensure she wasn't contaminating any door handles or supply cabinets or, God forbid, any of the other animals in the room.

Early in the night, Tess had spotted a binder of quarantine regulations on one of the shelves between the top cabinets, although she waited to thumb through it until after she'd given the puppies their first and much-needed round of nourishment.

Seeing how the first pup was acting more alert after the swallow of butter at Mason's, Tess gave each puppy a few drops of corn syrup in a medicine dropper while waiting for them to warm up enough to suckle a bottle. As cold, lethargic, and undernourished as they were, it was likely they were dangerously hypoglycemic.

She had suspected the corn syrup would help right their systems enough to enable them to nurse, and she'd been right. By the time Tess had gotten seven syringes sterilized and filled with four cc's each of formula, the other six pups had also been showing clear signs of revival. However, as weak as they were, Tess suspected they wouldn't be able to nurse from a newborn bottle until they'd recovered some strength.

Before syringing them, Tess took their temperatures to ensure they were warmed up enough. If they were colder than 94 degrees, there was a risk that their digestive systems wouldn't properly digest the formula. All pups except one had warmed up above 95 degrees. That pup, a girl who looked most like John Ronald except she was a lighter gray in places where his fur was black, was hovering just under 94 degrees. Tess waited to feed her until last. By the time Tess got to her, the pup's temperature was 94.2 degrees, and Tess said a quick prayer that the little girl would continue to warm up with a bit of nourishment in her.

Tess also had gotten their base weights recorded in a journal. She'd identified the seven puppies by gender, coat length, and coat color. In addition to the girl who looked most like her father in body type and markings, there were four other girls and two boys. Two of the girl pups were all black, though one had a longer coat than the other. One boy pup had longer fur and black-and-white markings like John Ronald but had the stocky build of a pit-bull puppy rather than the longer legs of a husky. The last three, two girls and the other boy, were a gray-brown brindled mix like their mom had been, but the boy had longer fur than his two sisters.

In addition to giving them the formula—which they'd need every two hours—Tess used warm, moist cotton balls to stimulate and clean their bottoms. At only a few days old at most, they couldn't go to the bathroom on their own. With Tess's help, all but one—the smallest pup whose temperature was lower than the rest—urinated a minuscule amount onto the cotton balls. And one of them, the brindled male, even defecated a tiny but encouraging sliver.

Tess recorded how many cc's of formula each one took and what they did bathroom-wise. By the time she had finished feeding and caring for them, sterilized the syringes, and reviewed the shelter's quarantine rules—thankfully none of which she'd broken—it was time to start over again.

It had been a little after midnight then, and she'd taken the time to turn on one of the computers and email the news to Megan and Patrick before starting on a second round of weighing, feeding, and stimulating their little rumps. And that was how she'd passed the rest of the night.

Now, just after four o'clock, as she readied the syringes for the puppies' fourth feeding, she could feel the fatigue setting in heavily in her lower back and legs and tiredness clouding her thoughts. She needed caffeine—and lots of it—if she was going to get through till sunrise. Thankfully, the shelter's break room was stocked with a coffeepot and the works to make a decent cup of coffee.

Before stepping out of the room, she hovered near the puppies' kennel door and listened. She was comforted by the sounds of their breathing. A few were even softly grunting in their sleep. This was an extraordinary improvement compared to their inaudible, shallow breathing when she and Mason had followed John Ronald into the warehouse.

She slipped her hand into her pocket and squeezed the buckeye tight for a second or two. *They're going to be just fine. All of them.*

Before leaving to grab a cup of coffee, Tess shot a glance at the Savannah cat. He was resting curled against the corner of his kennel, his head leaning against the sidewall, one eye half open, watching her as he dozed. "Sweet kitty," she whispered and was rewarded by spying a single twitch of the tip of the cat's long tail in response. She knew enough about cats to know a twitch of a cat's tail wasn't the same as the wag of a dog's tail, but at least it was a response.

She headed for the break room and brewed a pot of coffee. As she waited for the pot to fill, she eyed the small, worn couch with hungry exhaustion. It would be heavenly to rest her exhausted body even for a few minutes, but if she did, she could quite possibly drift off on the spot.

She remained standing and did a few stretches instead. She was pouring the freshly brewed coffee into a faded "Who rescued who?" mug, new ones of which were sold in the gift shop, when she heard the bells hung from the front doorknob jingling.

She would have sworn she'd locked the door after Mason left, but she tensed until she heard Megan's voice calling out a hello.

"Back here!" Tess fisted her mug of steaming coffee and headed around the corner. Megan had flipped on the front lights and was locking the front door behind her. She was in a cozy pair of sweats and a light-green maternity shirt that hugged her belly.

"So, I'm guessing you got my email." Tess added, "You didn't have to come in, but I'm really glad you're here."

"Are you kidding? I'm just sorry I didn't check my email when I got up at one o'clock to pee." Megan made a wave of dismissal with her hand. "I can't sleep more than half the night now anyway. What a story, Tess! How are they?"

Tess crossed two fingers on each hand. "Better, I think. They're warming up and moving more. And they're more responsive now. At least, I feel like they are. I've been recording everything. Come on back. I'll show you."

Tess took a few sips of coffee but set the mug down before they headed into the quarantine room and scrubbed up.

"Journal or puppies first?" Tess asked, drying her hands.

"*Puppies!*"

Tess felt some of the tension that had been lining her shoulders ebb away. It was an enormous relief to have another experienced body on hand. She opened the puppies' kennel and lifted the blanket that was covering them. "Your timing is perfect. I was just getting ready to feed them again. I'm trying to stick to three or four cc's every two hours."

The seven siblings were snuggled so tightly together against the edge of the water bottle that they looked physically entwined.

"Oh my goodness. They're perfect." Megan clamped a hand over her mouth as she leaned in close to inspect them. "What a miracle this whole thing is, Tess. And I'm not even going to pretend my tearing up is all the pregnancy hormones flowing through me right now. I go all gooey inside whenever I see puppies this tiny. They're just *so* perfect, aren't they?"

Megan's words struck a chord. Everything had been so chaotic and precarious at first, and Tess had felt like she'd been battling the clock to keep them alive. She hadn't yet allowed herself to take in what precious creatures they actually were. At least not until now. As she looked at them, all Tess could see were perfectly shaped noses and silky fur and scrawny bodies with round bellies.

She'd made it through the night in emergency mode. All those facts and figures from her vet school courses had been floating through her head. Stats about optimal body temperature for properly functioning organs and the survival rates of abandoned puppies compared to how long they'd gone without nursing had played over and over in her mind.

For the first time since she'd come upon the first little girl in the street in front of Mason's house, Tess allowed herself to connect with the emotion coursing through her body and to see the perfection of each individual one. They were soft and inviting. Seven small miracles. And no two looked the same. A few were larger bodied or longer legged, and each one had markings that would distinguish it from the rest.

"It's hard to believe these guys wouldn't have had a chance if it wasn't for a stray dog," Megan added, reaching into the kennel to carefully stroke the dark-gray-and-white one's smooth forehead with the side of her thumb.

"I know. He's a beautiful dog. Wait till you meet him. The guy I told you about has been trying to catch him for several months, but tonight the dog came to him. And the funny thing is, we'd been combing the streets that the dog usually frequents earlier in the night. If we had found him and caught him, I'm not sure he'd have been able to save these guys."

Megan clicked her tongue. "Unbelievable. Watch and see, Patrick will get our social media sites buzzing with this story."

"I've heard he's become a post guru."

"He really has." Megan's expression brightened even more. "Oh, Tess, it just hit me. In Patrick's posts about the puppies, we can mention your video series. There's no better publicity than when it's spread naturally."

This afternoon before the Savannah cat came in, Tess had created an outline for the first video. Patrick wanted to keep the clips between three and five minutes long. The first one would be filmed on Wednesday afternoon. The video's focus was going to be on budget-friendly

ways to help keep the family dog satisfied and enter-
tained in the face of overly packed family schedules.
From arranging free playdate exchanges with friends'
pets to easy-to-make treat-dispensing puzzles, TV time,
aromatherapy, and more, Tess had come up with twelve
inexpensive and hopefully effective ways to bust at-
home dog boredom during busy times of the year.

Even as exhausted as Tess was, she noted the happy
disbelief washing over her. Just a couple of days ago,
when her stuff had been stolen, she'd felt as if she'd lost
everything. Now, instead of working at her uncle's sandwich shop, she'd taken a job at one of the coolest places
she knew. She'd gone on a date with a guy she was completely head-over-heels crazy about. If there'd been any
doubt at all, watching him with John Ronald had sealed
the deal. And now, thanks to a spectacular dog, seven
miraculous puppies had a fighting chance at life.

It was almost too good to be true.

—⁘—

It'd been ten years since Mason had had a dog he'd
called his own. Growing up on a farm, he couldn't
remember a time there hadn't been a dog or two around.
After reading *Shiloh* for a summer reading project when
he was ten, Mason had saved up his allowance and
bought a beagle pup of his own from a man who was
selling them at the county fair. Mason had loved that
pup like he loved his sister. Not quite two years later,
the pup disappeared during hunting season. Living on
as many acres as the Reddings did, none of Mason's
family's pets—aside from the horses—were leashed or
confined to a fence.

Every so often, one of their neighbors shared a story of one of their dogs or cats disappearing, so it wasn't unheard of, and Mason's dad did his best at the time to help Mason understand that it hadn't been anything he'd done wrong. "Some dogs just have the wanderlust, Son," he'd said time and again until Mason had finally stopped blaming himself.

After waiting over half a year in hopes his dog might return, Mason had dipped into the truck fund he'd begun and bought Nacho, one of the neighbor's yellow Lab pups, because he'd heard Labs were less likely to wander off than beagles.

When Mason left for college, he'd left Nacho, who was nearing seven, at home with his parents and his dad's loyal cattle dog. By the time Mason had a place of his own, Nacho was too geriatric and settled into an old dog's routine to handle a big life change, so he'd remained on his parents' farm. Three years ago, Mason had been playing for the Orioles, his first season in the major leagues, and was winding up a three-game series with the Red Sox when he'd gotten the call that Nacho was passing on.

"He'll be gone before you can get here," his dad had said. "Don't you worry yourself about it, Son. You gave him a good life, and now he's moving on."

Not heeding his dad's advice, Mason had headed for the airport with nothing more than the sweats he'd changed into after the game and taken the first in a series of flights to get to Cedar Rapids, Iowa, which was just over an hour drive to his parents'. He ended up getting home in time to say goodbye and even had his hand on Nacho's shoulder when the dog took his final breath a few hours later.

Now, even though it still felt a touch surreal, here was John Ronald. For the two years since he'd bought his loft, Mason had considered adopting from one of several rescue organizations working in and around the city. But every time he came close, he started thinking about how much of the year was spent traveling and talked himself out of it.

Then, several months ago, when he'd spotted John Ronald for the first time, Mason had felt a connection that he hadn't felt with an animal in years. He told himself that if he could catch him, he'd find a way to work through the logistics of what to do with a dog when he was out of town.

And now here he was, standing in a vet's office, trying not to feel like an ogre when John Ronald looked his way after getting poked with a few necessary shots and having a vial of blood drawn for a heartworm test—and for a DNA test while they were at it. The stool sample Mason had brought in had shown John Ronald wasn't a carrier of parvo, which was a relief. The dog was fifteen pounds underweight and had worms, but those were easy enough fixes.

It was the vet's next question that threw Mason for a loop.

"I assume you'll want to neuter him?"

Mason swallowed. Did he? It wasn't that he wanted to breed him. Now that he was an adult, Mason knew that more animals than he cared to think about wound up in shelters or pounds or were put to sleep every year.

But keeping an animal with wanderlust captive *and* cutting off his balls felt like a bit too much.

"There's a long list of health and behavior benefits. If

you're unsure, I can give you a brochure. It's not something you'll need to decide today. He needs to recover and put on weight first. And since it will mean going under anesthesia, it'll mean no food or water after midnight, that sort of thing."

"Yeah, sure. I'll take the brochure home and read it."

The vet looked at him over the top of a pair of rectangular glasses. "It would be in his best interest. Especially since he's been a stray for God knows how long. It could help take his edge off."

Mason assured the vet that he'd give it serious consideration. Nacho had been neutered. All his dad's dogs had been, which wasn't the case on a lot of farms. Puppies underfoot were too distracting from the work at hand, his dad had said.

Although Mason knew he should go ahead and commit to it now, he hoped he'd feel less guilty by the time John Ronald was in good enough shape to handle it. With any luck, maybe it would be clear the dog *wanted* to stay with him by then.

One can dream, can't they?

Mason had paid and was coaxing John Ronald into the back seat of his truck when a familiar meeting notification chime rang out from Mason's phone. He pulled it out of his pocket and glanced at the screen.

"Shit." In the chaos of last night and getting John Ronald to the vet this morning, he'd forgotten about a photo shoot at a marketing company in Chesterfield for Nuts Up, a new-to-market whey-protein-enhanced peanut butter that Mason was endorsing. The photo shoot was out in the county, and he was due there in fifteen minutes.

He was tempted to call his agent and have him reschedule the appointment, but the photo shoot had been pushed back twice due to the car accident. A sling and a black eye weren't exactly the power-athlete images Nuts Up wanted in their ads. Now, he was bruise and sling free. And since his uniform had been couriered over separately from the Red Birds management office, Mason didn't need to do anything aside from show up.

After John Ronald was settled, Mason offered him a few of the treats left in his pocket. "You were a good boy in there, buddy."

Once in the driver's seat, Mason shot off a text to his agent, letting him know he'd be a few minutes late to the appointment and that he was bringing along a dog. His agent, who managed Mason's career from Philadelphia, replied in seconds like always, no matter the time of day or night.

> Late, dog-bearing Mason is better than no Mason.

Mason tapped the steering wheel with his thumb as he glanced back at John Ronald in the rearview mirror. "Sorry, guy. One hopefully quick pit stop, then we're going home."

To Mason's surprise, John Ronald leaned through the wide gap between the front bucket seats and shoved his cool, wet nose into Mason's ear before settling down across the back bench seat, his long, gangly legs draping over the edge. Not sure if it was a show of affection or just a sniff, Mason decided he was happy with either.

Chapter 18

To say Tess's internal clock was messed up was an understatement. She wanted coffee, toast, and scrambled eggs, not the heaping bowl of steaming pasta marinara Nonna had just placed in front of her.

"Elbows off the table, Contessa." Nonna pulled a wedge of Parmigiano-Reggiano from the fridge and unwrapped it from the butcher paper. Tess was still rubbing sleep out of her eyes when Nonna slid the wedge across a grater over Tess's pasta bowl.

"Thanks, Nonna. That's enough cheese." Considering that Nonna was finally accepting that Tess's vegetarianism didn't include meat-based pasta sauce and had begun serving her delicious marinara instead, Tess wasn't about to complain that it seemed like 7:00 a.m., not three in the afternoon. "How was your night, Nonna? And your day, I guess."

"The same as most other days. Did you hear that your cousin Anthony's wife is going to have another baby?"

"Nuh-uh. Wait, won't that make four kids under, like, six or something?"

Nonna pursed her lips. "And they've been barely getting by this year as it is."

"Well, hopefully it'll work out. Things usually do."

As Tess wound a mouthful of pasta around her fork, Nonna took a seat in the chair catty-corner from her rather than tinkering with the dishes on the counter as usual, which Tess took to mean her grandmother wanted to talk. And for some reason, Tess didn't think it was about her cousin.

"Everything okay, Nonna?"

Nonna stretched a cloth napkin flat across the table in front of her and began to fold it as Tess ate.

As soon as she swallowed the first bite, Tess realized she was famished. She'd been so exhausted this morning when she'd gotten home that she'd fallen asleep without breakfast. And now that she was eating, it hit her that she hadn't eaten a full meal since lunch yesterday.

"Your friend called earlier. I told him you were asleep."

"Kurt?" She'd been meaning to check in and see how things at the Sabrina Raven estate were going. She missed working with the group of sweet dogs there and looked forward to working with them when they came over to the shelter to be adopted out.

"Not Kurt. Your other friend."

Nonna had a look about her that belied her attempt to make this appear to be a casual conversation. "Do you mean Mason?"

"Yes, Mason."

Tess's heart did a skitter, then a double thump. "What'd he say?"

"He wanted to drop off a meat loaf. I told him you were still sleeping since you're working again tonight. He's going to stop by with it at the shelter later tonight."

Tess sipped from her glass of lukewarm water as she processed her grandma's statement. Nonna never added ice because of some old wives' tale about it weakening the immune system. When she was younger, Tess had always gotten up and added her own. But after her stint in Europe, she had grown accustomed to room-temperature water.

"In case he didn't explain, he cooked for me last night." Tess allowed what felt like a silly grin to tug up the corners of her mouth. "I didn't get to eat it though, because of the chaos over the puppies. Last night, he said he'd drop some by today so that I could try it."

"It's not every day that a man will cook for a woman."

Tess debated telling her grandma that times were changing, and it probably wasn't as unusual as her grandma thought, but opted not to pursue it.

"I know that you're a woman of the world now. You were gone for over a year, and a dozen men could have cooked you dinner. I know that. But you're under my roof now, so I get to say it."

The way Nonna said it, Tess got a feeling she wasn't talking about dinner at all. She dropped her fork and knotted her fingers in the base of her hair. "Oh my God, Nonna, can you please not be about to talk to me about sex? I'm twenty-six years old. You had, like, three kids at twenty-six. And I'm *not* having it right now, even though I don't have to tell you that."

"I was pregnant with your uncle Tito at twenty-six, yes, but I also had a husband to support me and this very roof over my head."

After stabbing a heaping forkful of pasta with sudden vigor, Tess shoved in a mouthful and spoke through it. "Nonna, there's this thing nowadays called getting to know each other. That's *all* we're doing."

"Over meat loaf."

There was something about the way her grandma said it that made Tess snort with her mouth full of pasta.

This reminded her of being a kid and watching her older cousins pull spaghetti noodles out of their noses on Friday nights at her aunt's house.

Catching the look that grew even more pointed on her eighty-four-year-old grandma's face as the term *meat loaf* seemed to reverberate through the dining room, Tess was suddenly choking back laughter, and tears were stinging her eyes. "Over meat loaf," she repeated as she caught her breath.

"Get to know him better, Contessa. That's all I've got to say. No matter how good his meat loaf is, I suspect it's worth waiting for."

Tess buried her face in her hands in laughter, and this time Nonna joined her.

"Nonna, if I agree, can we *not* talk about this anymore?"

Tess looked over to see that Nonna had folded the napkin into a small, thick square. "Yes, so long as you know that I enjoyed a good meat loaf in my day, and I suspect you will too. And maybe with that very young man. Just use the good head that God blessed you with, and everything will work out fine."

Tess was agreeing when they were interrupted by a knock at the door.

"It's probably your cousin Anthony. I'm babysitting the kids so they can go shopping for bunk beds for the oldest two."

"I'll get it." Tess hopped up and swiped the palm of her hand over her mouth. Spotting the lone guy on the other side of the stoop through the family-room window, Tess nearly stopped in her tracks. It wasn't her cousin—or anyone she might have remotely expected to see there.

It was Patrick, and he was wearing what for him was an uncharacteristic scowl.

"Hey," Tess said as she pulled open Nonna's heavy and sticky door. The old wood had swelled to the point that it was never going to open easily. "How's it going, Patrick?"

"I looked up your address in the paperwork you filled out on your first day."

"Oh. Well, that makes sense. Do you want to come in?"

There was a breeze making a mess of Patrick's fine brown hair. "No."

Tess hung there a minute, wondering if he had any clue how awkward this felt to her.

Please, oh please God, don't let him be about to ask me out. It would lead to a great degree of awkwardness she wasn't ready to face. Even if Mason hadn't been in the picture. Patrick was about her age, an animal lover, and cute enough, but she couldn't handle dating someone who functioned in an immaculate world of routine as he did, even down to the time of day that he stopped for a break, 10:42 a.m. Whether it was at the shelter or the Sabrina Raven estate, that was the time of day—because he didn't like odd numbers—when he stopped to enjoy an Orange Crush, the sugary drink that carried him through until lunch and his salami sandwich. Every day.

"I'd have called," he added, "but you don't have a cell phone."

"Oh. I'm, uh, planning on getting one soon."

"You should. They're convenient, and they save lives."

Tess felt her eyebrows rising into peaks but tried to call them down. When she first started working with Patrick at the estate, Kelsey had pulled her aside and let her know that sometimes to figure him out, Kelsey had found she'd need to guide the conversation along.

"So, uh, is there something specific you wanted?"

"Yes." Patrick's scowl returned. "I thought you should be prepared before you come in tonight. It's looking like we are going to lose one. It's possible we have already."

Tears flooded Tess's eyes faster than she could blink them away. "The girl with the lower body temperature?"

"Yes. The one who you said has markings like the husky who found them."

"I've been worried about her." Tess brushed tears from her cheeks. "What's going on?"

"Megan talked with Dr. Washington. He's calling it 'fading puppy syndrome.' He suspects she didn't get enough colostrum either because she was born last or because other complications arose. Without enough colostrum, it's difficult to keep infections in check."

"How are the others?"

"Progressing as healthy puppies should. Good body temps, increasing suckling strength. All have defecated today. Based on their latest weights, they've gained two ounces over last night when you brought them in."

"That's great." Tess swiped at the few stray tears that had slipped down her cheeks. She tried to keep her mind from going into overdrive, but it did anyway. Could she have warmed the puppy faster or slower? Should she have waited longer to give her the first few cc's of formula? Had she needed more electrolytes first?

"Megan said you would be upset. She said to tell you that six puppies are thriving because of your effort last night. With a litter that has suffered the neglect they have, those odds are higher than expected."

"Thanks, Patrick. Do you know what's being done for the little girl? Is she still with her siblings?"

"Yes, Megan thought keeping them together was the best thing for her."

Tess shot a hesitant glance toward the dining room table. Nonna had gotten up and gone into the kitchen. She'd likely prefer Tess to stay home and help her second cousins, but Tess couldn't hang here and wait for the inevitable. "Did you hear if they are running any new tests on her?"

"Megan deferred to Dr. Washington. He didn't feel any more tests were necessary. Even in healthy litters, it isn't uncommon to lose some of the pups."

"I swear, this more than anything is why I dropped out of vet school. I never figured out how to disassociate from the individual enough to work with a level head around sick and injured dogs."

"That's lucky for High Grove."

"Thanks. And I appreciate you coming here to tell me, Patrick."

"I assumed you'd want to know." He jutted a thumb toward his truck. "And it was only six minutes out of my way. I'm bringing Fannie back to the shelter. She's been with me at the Sabrina Raven estate this afternoon."

"Oh." Tess wasn't sure how to reply. What she was sure of was that if she stayed here, she'd be little to no company to her second cousins. Her mind would be on the puppy. That sweet little creature with the perfectly shaped nose and silky, dark-gray-and-white fur. "Hey, would you mind if I caught a ride in with you?"

Patrick's head dipped sideways a bit. "If you leave

with me now, that would put you arriving over four hours early for your night shift."

"I won't clock in." Tess shrugged as her throat threatened to lock up. "I just need to be there."

Patrick's brows knitted together, putting a crease in his normally smooth forehead. Tess counted out a few beats as she waited, knowing that he needed extra time when it came to disseminating emotions. "Okay," he said, then looked toward his truck and added, "I have a clipboard on the passenger seat. I can move it."

"That'd be great. I'll just run in and tell my grandma I'm leaving."

Tess made quick work of explaining to her grandma why she needed to leave so early, then hurried to her room to throw on a pair of jeans and a comfy Henley and hoodie. While heading out, she called over her shoulder, promising her grandma she'd check in later.

As she neared the truck, Fannie shoved her giant head and chest between the Tacoma's bucket seats to watch Tess approach from the other side of the front passenger window. Tess opened the door and hopped in, surprised at how much smaller the cab was compared to Mason's Ram.

Fannie greeted her with an eager lick across Tess's ear. Tess swiveled to face her, making sure to give a double-handed rubdown of Fannie's silky ears. "Were you showing those dogs how a sweet girl like you can behave?"

Fannie panted happily as Patrick responded. "She's doing well with them. And they're improving. When you're back on the day shift, you can ride over with me one afternoon."

"I'd like that. I miss those guys. And what about

Fannie? I take it there were no interested parties today before you two left?"

"Not today."

"I know she's a senior dog, but I'm really hoping someone gives her a chance, and soon. She's so well behaved—and trained, for that matter. She's housebroken. She sits at attention, lays down, and stays. And she's great on a leash. All that stuff takes time and dedication. That's what I don't get. Who treats a sweet girl like her so well, then ties her to a post without so much as a note?"

Patrick cocked his head. "If we knew, she'd be an owner surrender, not an unknown."

"True that." After giving Fannie a final pat, Tess faced front and buckled her seat belt as Patrick slipped the truck into first gear. "*C'est la vie. C'est. La. Vie.*"

Chapter 19

IT WASN'T THAT TESS QUESTIONED DR. WASHINGTON. He was a seasoned vet, and she remembered the facts she'd learned in school even before taking a few minutes when she first arrived to read up on fading puppy syndrome. But knowing and accepting litter survivability rates didn't change the way she felt about that little pup. Or help Tess feel any less responsible for her.

She'd been the first one to treat her. She'd decided when the little creature's temperature was warm enough to proceed with formula. Unless she did everything in her power to give the little girl the best fighting chance, Tess would be an emotional mess.

Sometime after Patrick had left for the Sabrina Raven estate with Fannie, the little pup had been pulled from the rest of the litter. It had become apparent that her temperature was remaining a degree or two lower than the rest of her siblings. There was a hope that wrapping her in a towel in a box and placing a heating pad underneath might help her temperature stabilize.

Since Tess wasn't officially working until 8:00 p.m., she was able to focus her full attention on caring for the little pup. She'd been alarmed to find how the pup's reflexes were considerably slower than when she'd left this morning.

While the rest of the litter had progressed to nursing out of newborn bottles and no longer needed to be force-fed drops from a syringe, this wasn't the case with her. In fact, Tess was troubled to read in the puppies' care journal that the runt's most recent feeding had been abandoned when she seemed to be gagging on the formula rather than swallowing as she'd done previously.

Reading this had caused Tess's eyes to fill with tears, but she blinked them away and headed over to the nearest available computer, where she pulled up an online vet student forum that had become a trusted source of information for her. After a bit of researching, a spark of hope ignited.

With tedious care, some pups were able to recover from fading puppy syndrome.

This was all the encouragement she needed. First, she prepared hydrating fluids for the little pup by dissolving measured amounts of salt, sugar, and honey in boiling water. Then, every five minutes for the next several hours—hours that seemed to go by in a blink—Tess slipped a few drops of the cooled fluid between the pup's gums and onto her tongue. She hoped it wasn't her imagination, but after establishing this new routine, Tess would swear the pup was intentionally swallowing the fluids. Tess also rubbed a bit of undiluted honey on the weak puppy's gums.

It was after six when Megan finished with her last feeding of the other six puppies and joined Tess in the newly remodeled break room before heading home for the night. Megan, it turned out, had been at the shelter ever since she'd come in at four that morning. Tess could imagine how tired she must be. She'd not fully caught up on sleep yet either.

When Megan joined her, Tess was cross-legged on

the comfy new sofa, and the puppy was in a box on her lap with the heating pad underneath. Megan sank next to her with obvious care, which, considering the size of her belly, was likely necessary.

Tess had one hand cupped around the puppy's body and was using a corner of the towel to dry her mouth after giving her a few drops from the eyedropper.

"Look at that," Megan said. "I just saw her swallow. And it seemed to have more strength to it."

"That's what I've been thinking. I keep telling myself not to get excited, but I'd swear her movements aren't as lethargic."

"Have you taken her temperature lately?"

"Not for an hour almost. If you'll hold her, I'll grab the thermometer and take it now."

After passing Megan the puppy—box, heating pad, and all—Tess headed to the supply room for a sterile thermometer. When she returned and took the pup's temperature, she was ecstatic to find it was 96.3, over half a degree warmer than it had been when Tess had started that afternoon.

Megan clicked her tongue as Tess read the temperature aloud. "Tess, you've only been here a couple days and you keep outdoing yourself. I'm still counting my blessings that you're working with us."

"Thanks, but honestly, I've been sitting here doing the same thing. This is right where I need to be and, no surprise, it's so much better than dressing sandwiches." Tess sank against the couch, reminding herself it was too early to let her guard down. "I know there's going to be a naming contest for these guys, but for tonight, I've been calling her little Zoe. It's Greek and means 'life,' and it just feels right to call her that. At least right now."

Tears welled instantly in Megan's eyes, and she fanned her face, a small smile lighting her lips. "It's these pregnancy hormones. I swear I tear up at everything anymore. But that—that's the perfect name, Tess." She brushed her thumb over the dark-gray-and-white fur on the little pup's forehead. "Zoe. It's perfect. Absolutely perfect."

———

A few minutes after 8:00 p.m. didn't feel like the ideal time to brew a pot of coffee, but Tess was going to need it to get through a second long night. Thankfully, Zoe was doing well enough that Tess didn't have to offer her drops of saline fluid every several minutes. Zoe was sleeping in her box on the counter in the quarantine room as Tess readied the bottles for the other six puppies' next feeding. Zoe had progressed to getting a few cc's of formula in a syringe but still didn't have the strength to suckle from a newborn bottle.

The original tests that had been run on the puppies had all come back. They didn't have parvo or heartworms or the raised white blood cells that indicated they were fighting strong infections. Not even Zoe.

Not quite twenty-four hours ago, when she'd seen the lifeless mom curled around her pups, Tess's biggest fear had been that they could lose the whole litter to a devastating bout of parvo. Strays were often carriers, living in weakened conditions as they were.

Although Patrick had assured her that the rest of the puppies were doing well, Tess hadn't let herself fully believe it until she saw them for herself. Patrick had been right. Their strength was visibly more pronounced compared to last night. They grunted and squirmed and sneezed and whined. Less than twenty-four hours ago, they'd hardly moved even when nudged. Tonight, cuddled against one another, they were a warm, cozy blend of dark gray and white, black and white, brindled browns, and brown and white, reminding Tess of a wintry quilt.

Soaking in the sight of them as she readied their first feeding of her shift, Tess didn't mind that her eyes filled with tears for the second time that day.

If she was going to tear up over the sad things, she might as well do so over the beautiful ones too.

She was lingering in front of their kennel, relishing the sweet grunts and snorts that escaped as they dozed, when several of the dogs in the main kennels began to vigorously bark. At this time of night, they were typically quiet as they dozed off their dinners and the commotion of the day. Tess cracked the quarantine door and strained to hear what had caught their attention. After a second or two, she heard a spurt of soft but persistent knocking from the front of the building.

Mason. It had to be.

Tess headed out of quarantine and through the dog kennels toward the thick glass doors separating off the kennels.

She wasn't disappointed. A few hundred feet away, she spotted Mason at the front door in a pool of light. He wore a black button-down shirt tucked into a crisp pair of jeans and a light-gray jacket that was unzipped, and all Tess wanted to do was stare. Her pulse began a sprint as she headed into the main building to unlock the door. Thankfully, the brown-handled bag he held gave her something else to focus on.

"Hey there," she said after pushing open the door. "Nonna said you were coming. And that you were bringing that beautiful meat loaf we didn't get to taste."

"Yeah, about that." Mason grinned as he followed her into the quiet main room, his free hand closing around her arm for a stride or two. "When I took it out of the fridge, it looked like a brick. So, I tried it, and it tasted a bit like cardboard. I think it was in the warming drawer a few hours longer than it should've been. I'd like to think it would've been better last night, and I'll ask for a redo when things settle down." He held up the bag. "Either way, I didn't want you going hungry, so I ordered take-out from Tree House. I wasn't sure what you might be in the mood for, so I got you a couple of things."

Mason handed off the bag, and Tess giggled as she took on the weight of it. If it was an ounce less than five pounds, she'd have been shocked. "That's sweet, Mason. Really sweet. I can't tell you how touched I am that you ordered from an all-vegetarian restaurant. And you're staying to eat, right? Because this feels like enough food to feed the whole staff, and I'm the only one here."

He jutted his thumb in the direction of his truck, parked perpendicular to the building. "I've got John Ronald. It's been a long day for him. But like I said, as soon as things settle down, I'd like a redo on that dinner."

The emotions that swirled through Tess were much like a slice of cinnamon-raisin bread looked. He wasn't staying. But he wanted to cook for her again. And he was here now at least. "I'd like that. A lot." The thought of waiting an indeterminate length of time until things settled down to have more than a minute or two with him seemed like small-scale torture, though Tess tried not to let it show in her face. She'd never been the kind of person who needed to see the guy she was dating every day. And this crazy-weird thing between them hadn't even officially been defined as dating. "But you don't have to cook for me. I can help, or we can eat out or whatever."

"I *want* to cook for you." For the first time, Tess noticed his gaze abandon her face and slide to her body. It lingered, and Tess felt his hunger before he blinked and glanced over toward the cat kennels. "And even though today didn't feel like it, it's my slow season at work. Cooking will give me something constructive to do."

"Constructive is good. My grandma always says so anyway." She forced the lightness to stay in her tone. "The second that any of her grandkids turns on the TV or pulls out a device."

Mason laughed. "Your grandma's the real thing. Hey, so how are the puppies?"

Tess took a breath. "Six are doing really well. Gaining ounces and getting stronger. The seventh—we're calling her Zoe—has been touch and go this afternoon. The vet labeled the weakness she's been displaying as fading puppy syndrome. As the name suggests, it isn't the best prognosis, but I don't think I'm just being optimistic when I tell you she seems to be doing better."

He nodded, searching her eyes. "You know your stuff, Tess. Trust your instincts. Just remember, whatever happens, you're doing your best. If you want the truth, they were all so cold and lethargic last night, I've been more worried about how you'd take it if none of them could be saved."

"I was worried about that too. But you should see their progress for yourself. Zoe's with them in quarantine, if you have a minute or two."

"Yeah, absolutely." He shot a glance at his truck. "John Ronald should be good for a bit."

Tess placed the bag of food on the counter, figuring Trina wouldn't bother it, and led Mason through the dog kennels into the quarantine room. The lights were kept at half strength there to encourage rest and recuperation, and for the first time, Tess felt the intimacy of it.

She motioned Mason toward the deep, stainless-steel sink and kept her voice low. "If you don't mind washing your hands first, that'd be great. I'm pretty sure mine might permanently prune from as much washing as they've had in the last two days."

Mason stepped next to her, and Tess's legs threatened to turn to jelly. Her heart pounded at his nearness and with their hands so close together in the running water.

Why hasn't he tried to make out yet?

Impossibly close to instigating a session herself, she finished up and headed over to Zoe. Tess lifted the top of the blanket to find the tiny pup burrowed in a warm, cozy mound at the side of her box. To Tess's surprise, Zoe actually made a soft whimper when Tess brushed her thumb over her forehead.

The delight that washed over her at Zoe's progress cooled her racing blood. At least, it did until Mason joined her, stepping close so he could see, and Tess was bathed in his intoxicating scent. She wanted to lean in and sniff, and maybe, just maybe do a little tasting while she was at it.

"We're only picking them up at feeding time right now, but you can pet her."

Mason brushed a thumb over Zoe's small, silky body. He smiled, and his teeth gleamed in the dim light. Tess wasn't sure if she'd ever actually *yearned* to kiss anyone before. In fact, she was sure she hadn't. She was also sure this was what yearning felt like. Her mouth salivated as it did before a first bite of something scrumptious, and she felt heat fan out from her chest and down into her underwear.

Just last night, she'd been the one to step in and hug him, and she loved how her face had met up with his chest.

"Look at that," Mason said, his mouth pulling into a crooked grin as he slowly brushed his thumb over Zoe's body. "Last night...I don't know what she looked like, but tonight, it's easy to see what a perfect little creature she is." His voice was low and quiet, and the intimacy of it made Tess weak in the knees. He stepped back and closed his other hand over Tess's arm. "Whatever it is you've been doing, it's working."

Tess gave a one-shoulder shrug. "Thanks, but if there's anyone who deserves more praise than we can give him, it's John Ronald."

"If you'd like to give him some, follow me out after I take a look at the others. If I leave him out there too long, he's likely to chew the interior up."

After showing Mason the other six and washing up a second time, Tess and Mason headed back through the building.

She got a whiff of deliciousness as they passed the bag of food on the counter. Trina had come out from wherever she was sleeping and was lying on the counter next to it. Chance had finally gotten off his plush dog bed and was planted on the floor just below it, proving his sniffer still worked just fine. "Here are two guys who would like to share this great-smelling dinner."

Mason chuckled and stopped to give Chance a scratch. "Chance, right? You said he's blind, if I remember, though he doesn't look it."

"Or act it, but yeah, he's blind."

Tess trailed out the front door after Mason, letting it jangle shut behind her. Night had fully set in. Billowy, silver-white clouds raced across the moonlit sky. The clouds were thin enough that the three-quarter moon shone through them, lighting up the night.

She debated running back in for her jacket but opted not to. Cold air seeped through the thin Henley she was wearing and she suppressed a shiver.

Ten feet away, from inside Mason's truck, John Ronald lifted his head at their approach and let out a single woof. His long body was stretched between the back seat and the front passenger seat. He'd been sniffing the console over the glove box.

"I ordered something from Tree House as well. Some kind of faux-chicken cutlet, which I guess proves there's a first time for everything. I'll let you know what I think."

Tess giggled. "If you don't like it, I think I know who'll eat your leftovers."

As they neared, John Ronald backed up until he was seated on his haunches in the back seat of the cab. Through the tinted back windows, the white patches on his face and chest glowed in the dim light, but the rest of him was lost to shadow.

"I meant to ask. How was his vet visit?"

"He did great. They're waiting on some blood work, but even though he's thin, he's got good muscle tone. I don't know how long he was a stray, but he's hung on better than most on his own."

"Does it feel real that he's yours?"

Something close to a scowl flashed across Mason's face as they reached the truck and watched him from outside the back of the cab. "If you want the truth, sometimes I feel like I'm keeping him captive."

Tess closed a hand over the back of his arm. The taut muscle of his triceps made her struggle to keep her train of thought. "Just give it time, Mason. He's going to have to build up trust."

"I know. And that trust thing goes both ways. Every time I fall asleep, I wake up a few hours later to find him staring at me. Once he was on top of my coffee table. The second time he was standing on my bed. It feels a bit like he's deciding whether he wants to eat me and not my leftovers."

Tess giggled as Mason popped open the back door and clipped on John Ronald's leash that had been tucked in the pocket of the door. The dog leaned his head out but remained standing on the seat as he looked around. After half a minute passed, he hopped to the asphalt with a solid thump.

Two feet away, Tess sank to squat and turned her palms face up for him to sniff. John Ronald stepped forward cautiously, his cool, moist nose tickling her skin. "You gorgeous dog, you. Next time I see you, I'll bring you one of the puppies' blankets to sniff. And once your shots kick in and they're out of quarantine, Mason and I will arrange a playdate. At least a few of them are yours, but I'm not entirely convinced about the others."

It was Mason's turn to laugh.

After a thorough sniff, John Ronald swiped his tongue across her palm, then turned his attention to their surroundings. The warm wetness of his tongue and the brisk chill of the air blanketing her combined to create a deep shiver in Tess as she stood up. Mason noticed. Still holding John Ronald's leash, he switched it from hand to hand as he slipped off his jacket and offered it to her.

Thoughts of the warmth from Mason's body that was likely trapped inside made the jacket impossible to refuse. Even though she was swimming in it, Tess slipped it on and tried not to make it obvious that she was savoring the woodsy scent of his cologne. "Thanks."

John Ronald looked around the parking lot and at the building as if he was assessing the place. Then he trotted closer to Mason's truck and lifted his leg to urinate on the tire.

"I've discovered he likes to scent mark. *A lot*."

"Outside only, I hope?"

Mason made a face, shaking his head. "No, but I think he's getting it. Trying to stop him midstream and get him outside is the only disadvantage I've found to living on the sixth floor."

"Yikes. Well, you know what they say. Patience is a virtue."

Tess's attention was drawn to the belt wrapped around jacketless Mason's hips; it acted like an exclamation point underneath that fabulously fit torso. It was a continual challenge to keep her focus, so she dove forward with what she knew best. Dogs.

"I don't know what you're using, but I've got some remedies I could mix up and bring over to help break down any scent that's been left behind where he's marked. Otherwise, he might keep marking the same place. But I'm guessing I'll be on the night shift another few days. When the pups are a few days stronger, we're going to let some of the volunteers rotate in at night. For now, it's either me or Megan. Fidel has an evening job, and Patrick doesn't handle routine changes easily. And as for Megan, she's about to have a baby. Her schedule's going to be messed up soon enough. *So*…if you'd like, I could swing them by tomorrow afternoon before work. Or if not, some other time."

"That'd be nice. But if you're thinking about biking over, call me. I can pick you up. It's only going to be in the thirties tomorrow."

"Thirties, huh? Okay, you can pick me up. I'm really going to have to take that driver's test sooner or later."

"Do you have a car?"

"No, I sold it to my cousin before leaving for Europe. Though my grandma hardly drives anymore. I can borrow her car."

"Your days off are Thursday and Friday, right?"

Tess nodded.

"Do me a favor, will you, and don't make any plans."

Tess felt her mouth fall open a touch. She waited, but he didn't continue. "Okay, but are you going to say why?"

"No." He smiled and shook his head.

His smile was growing even wider when he turned and coaxed John Ronald to hop into the back seat again. To Tess's surprise, John Ronald hopped in with very little persuading. Once inside, he tucked his tail and sank onto his haunches. His mouth gapped open in an easy pant. Tess thought he was adorable.

"Oh, I meant to tell you I let the vet draw his blood for a DNA test while we were there this morning. I should get the results in a few days."

"Did you? Cool. I can't wait to see what else is in those genes of his besides husky." Even though she didn't want to part with it, Tess slipped out of Mason's jacket and offered it his way after he closed the back door. Mason took it and held it without putting it on. His fingers brushed over hers, warming her in a different way.

"I don't know how much help I'd be, but call me tonight if you run into any problems with those little guys."

"Okay, and thanks. For everything."

Tess dug her fingernails into the palms of her hands as a bold thought popped into her head. *What's there to lose? Just do it.*

"So, ah, remember last night, right before we heard John Ronald barking outside your loft? I told you I knew what number your meal number three was."

Mason smiled. "Yeah, we never got back to that."

"Is it still all or nothing? Winner calls it?"

His smile fell, and his gaze locked on her lips as if he could read her thoughts, almost making her lose her nerve.

"Yes."

"Your third meal is fried chicken. And don't tell me it isn't, because I know I'm right."

"What is it you're calling?" The way he was staring at her, it was clear he knew already.

She had to rise to her tiptoes to reach him, but she brushed her lips over his. His hands tightened reflexively around her hips, and he pulled her against him just long enough for her pulse to burst into a sprint. She was opening her mouth to take in more of his when he abruptly let go and stepped back, nearly backing into his truck.

"Sorry."

Sorry. She'd kissed him, and he was sorry. *He's sorry?* It didn't seem possible that she could be reading it wrong, but he actually looked embarrassed *for* her.

"Oh crap. I get it." She covered her face and spoke into her hands. "Wow. I'm such an idiot. You're totally not into me that way."

One of Mason's hands locked around her wrists, pulling her hands away from her face and into his chest. "I promised myself I wouldn't do this. Not yet."

Tess looked up to find Mason moving toward her. He paused with his lips an inch from hers, a smile crinkling the corners of his eyes. "And for the record, you're wrong. It is fried, but it's catfish, not chicken." Then his warm mouth locked over hers.

Mason's kiss was neither hesitant nor pleading; it was paced to go nowhere and everywhere at the same time. His lips were firm and moist, and his stubble tickled her chin and the sides of her mouth. She opened her mouth and let her tongue explore the rim of his top teeth, then his bottom, then the tip of his tongue. She could taste mint from something strong, like an Altoid.

Blood pounded in Tess's ears, making her wonder if eardrums ever burst from excitement. She wanted more, and she wanted him to offer it to her.

As if he was magnetic north to her south, her body sought an impenetrable closeness against him. She slipped her wrists free and let her hands close on either side of his face. As if his kiss provided her oxygen, she pressed harder against his mouth.

A deep, low groan escaped him. Then his hands clamped over her shoulders and their bodies were shoved apart. Tess felt as if she were a tight-fitting lid that had just been wrenched off a bottle.

"Holy shit, Tess." Mason dragged a hand through his hair and turned to pace the empty parking lot. Inside the cab, John Ronald let out a single woof.

Holy shit? No one had ever said that to her after a kiss. *You've also never gone batshit kiss crazy before, Tess Grasso.*

The skin of her lips felt like it was on fire, and she was out of breath. When they'd first come outside, she'd had the shivers. Now she was practically sweating.

She was debating whether to apologize when Mason returned, dragging his hand through his hair a second time. "You failed to mention that you went to kissing school."

But Tess wasn't in the space for small talk. Not any longer. "What did you mean *not yet*?"

He drew in a long breath. "I made a promise to myself to take it slow with you."

"Because you think I'm frail or something?"

A flash of a smile passed across his face. "You're anything but frail. I knew that before we kissed. I know it doubly well now."

A smile tugged at her lips, but she was determined not to give him an out. She needed an answer like she needed oxygen. "Are you going to tell me why?"

"Yes." He stepped forward and brushed his thumb down the length of her temple. "Thursday. I'll tell you everything. Unless you can switch shifts with someone and get off work sooner."

Tess shook her head. "I don't think there's anyone who'd be able to do that right now. What is it you want to show me?"

"If I tell you ahead of time, it won't be the same."

His thumb slipped to her neck. The skin underneath it seemed to burst into life, which made her wonder what it would be like to have those hands explore her. Everywhere.

She folded her arms across her chest. "Okay."

"Tess, don't be mad." He leaned down and pressed his forehead against hers. Their lips were impossibly close, but Tess wasn't going to initiate a second kiss. "If you knew how hard it's been to hold back…"

"Then don't." She closed her eyes, soaking in the feel of the smooth skin of his forehead against hers.

His thumb circled the hollow between her neck and collarbone. "Give me until Thursday. I'll make it up to you. With these hands. With this mouth. I promise. I'll make it up to you in a way that'll make you glad we waited."

Tess's breath abandoned her body. She opened her eyes and stepped back, breaking their connection. "I-I think I'll be good with that." She rolled her shoulders, hoping to dissipate some of the energy coursing through her. "For the record, my knees just about gave out a second ago." She swallowed hard. "So, I think maybe it's in both our best interests that I don't come over until after Thursday. If you need help with John Ronald's scent marking before then, you can grab a bottle of Nature's Miracle. And I'm going to stay really busy thinking about *not* you."

Mason laughed. "I'll be counting the hours. All thirty-three of them."

She smiled, letting the tension slide from her body. "You're good on the fly."

"Yeah, well, being good on the fly is one of my talents."

She took a step back. "I'd better check on those puppies."

"Thursday then. Call if you need anything before that."

"So I don't have to do the math, what time Thursday?" she asked as he headed around to his driver-side door.

"I was hoping five o'clock. If that's okay?"

Tess shrugged. "Sure."

She was jogging back toward the shelter when he called after her. "Just so we're on the same page, that's a.m., all right?"

"A.m.?"

With a smile, Mason slid into the driver's seat and shut the door. The big engine revved to life, and the headlights flipped on. The wink he offered in her direction was barely discernable in the dimly lit night.

After sucking in a determined breath, Tess headed inside and locked the door behind her.

Thirty-three hours.

Chapter 20

THE MOON ROSE HIGHER INTO THE SKY, SENDING A stream of glowing white beams of light across the floor. The dog paced the length of the man's sleeping area after waking from a doze and startling from the strange new smells that danced across his nose. From atop the soft mound where the man slept, the man twitched and jerked in a distressed sleep before turning and resuming the quiet, still sleep in which he'd passed the earlier part of the long night.

Restless and eager for a deeper stretch of his legs, the dog left the room and paused to stare down into the lower part of the man's territory. After studying the empty, dark room, the dog made the awkward climb down the steep, tightly wound stairs into the larger area below. He gazed out the wall of glass into the night and sniffed the air, but the thick pane muted all scent except what flowed in through thin seams in the corners.

Forming the bond with the man was different from how it had been with Donna. Donna had never used a rope to keep him with her, but the dog had rarely left her side except to scavenge for food or to drink from the river. Whenever he'd been gone from her, his longing for her had been stronger than the freedom he'd felt trotting farther and faster than her labored walk allowed.

The dog liked the man's quick step and confident

touch, just as he liked the scent of the man's hands and skin. When the man patted him and rubbed his ears, the dog felt a sense of belonging he hadn't felt since before Donna entered the great sleep.

The man also gave him food, more food than Donna had ever been able to offer him, and the dog's stomach swelled pleasurably. He enjoyed watching the man prepare food, and he savored the smells that filled the air inside the man's territory, sending a rush of saliva over the dog's tongue and causing a pleasurable anticipation in his belly.

The dog didn't like that the man kept his living territory closed off from the outside world or that he couldn't get to the river to drink. Instead, the man kept a large dish filled with water from a faucet that smelled like the faucets Donna had drank from. The water quenched his thirst but left a strange taste on the dog's tongue.

The dog also didn't like the war of scents of other dogs and people that drifted through the vents or the barrage of dimmed sounds that pressed through the walls. The dog wanted to explore this new territory and leave his scent in more places than here in the man's living area and outside the building.

Abandoning the window, the dog headed over to the door through which the man left and entered. He sniffed the air seeping through the seam and caught the scent of a female dog who wasn't in heat but whose frequent bark communicated a general, constant excitement to which the dog didn't relate.

Smelling that the female had passed not far outside the door and had done so recently, the dog lifted his leg and scent marked on the door. Afterward, he headed over to a rug that covered the floor and scratched and scratched until he'd left an adequate scent on it too.

Afterward, he sank to the floor and gnawed on the wooden leg of a chair that the man had sat on tonight to eat his food. The dog chewed and gnawed until the tension finally fled from his teeth, tongue, and mouth. Then, when his eyes grew heavy and sleep beckoned him, the dog clambered up the tight, winding stairs again and hopped up to the soft mound on which the man slept.

After watching him in his easy sleep, the dog circled over and over until the cozy bedding underneath felt right, and then he curled up and drifted off to sleep alongside the man.

Chapter 21

IF TESS HAD ANY QUESTION ABOUT HOW SHE WAS DOING, the skeptical look on Patrick's face answered it for her. What had ever made anyone think she'd be good on camera, she didn't know. It was her third attempt, and try as she might, Tess couldn't unfreeze her stiff Barbie arms while talking to the camera and motioning toward the boredom-busting samples she'd readied for the first video segment. These included an empty but sealed water bottle pierced with a few holes and stuffed with essential-oil-scented cotton balls, an activity puzzle she'd made from cardboard, rope, and PVC pipe, and a jumbo-sized ice tray for homemade doggie Popsicles. She was also under no illusion that, whenever she turned, her spine and neck were moving any less stiffly than a mannequin body.

She stopped midsentence and collapsed her forehead onto the counter underneath her. "I didn't think I'd be *this* bad." When she looked up, she gave Patrick a hopeful glance. "Hey, what if I write the script and get everything ready, but someone *else* does the video part? Because, let's face it: I'm pretty sure this is going to bomb if we use me in these videos."

Patrick shut off the GoPro that was mounted to a tripod in the middle of the room. He had been filming at a slight angle in front of the cat kennels so he could catch activity in the Cat-a-Climb and Tess would still have a counter to stand behind.

Rather than answering, Patrick paced the room, mumbling inaudibly as he worked through something.

It was Wednesday evening, and they'd waited until the shelter closed for the day to start filming. Aside from a volunteer who'd come in to work a late-evening shift with the puppies now that they were doing better, the place was empty. The volunteer, Mia, was in back, and Tess and Patrick were alone in the main front room.

"Imagine how bad I'd suck in front of a real audience," Tess mumbled more to herself than to Patrick.

"I believe we'll find the opposite is true." Without offering further explanation, Patrick disappeared into the dog kennels, leaving Tess alone to avoid looking directly at the GoPro. As she waited, she pulled her script from underneath the counter.

After a quick squeeze of the buckeye she was still keeping in her pocket, she practiced the first few paragraphs—the ones that felt the stiffest—in which she introduced herself and the shelter and talked about the main goals of the short video as she tried motioning clearly but also naturally toward the products on the counter. Only it was so much harder than it seemed. Kudos to all the people featured in television commercials.

She was shaking her neck and arms loose like Jell-O when Patrick stepped back in through the kennel doors. He was leading Orzo, the sweet corgi who was one of Tess's unofficial favorites.

Patrick was followed by Mia, who was leading Fannie, the good-natured Saint Bernard Tess had been enjoying taking on walks whenever she had a few minutes of downtime.

Tess swallowed. So much for not having an audience.

Rather than offering explanation, Patrick passed Orzo's leash to Tess, then grabbed a nearby chair that he set in the middle of the floor. Afterward, he moved and lowered the tripod, aiming it several feet lower and in front of the open floor along the north wall.

"The background isn't as appealing, but I'll zoom in on Orzo and on you."

Mia sank into the chair in the middle of the floor and made a kissing sound to draw Fannie's attention to her. After sitting for a good scratch, Fannie sank to the floor alongside Mia and splayed flat, her legs sticking out in four directions.

"Tess, have you met Mia?"

Tess nodded, thinking how Patrick had been in the room fiddling with the GoPro twenty minutes ago when the two of them had met for the first time and talked for several minutes, which further solidified Tess's belief that Patrick only paid attention to what he wanted to.

Though Tess's best guess was that Mia was only a couple of years older, she was a mom of a seven-year-old and the shelter's resident artist. She had chestnut-brown hair that she wore in a long, loose pixie cut. The cut was cute enough that Tess would have given serious thought to copying it if she thought it might complement her face the way it did Mia's. Pixie envy, she'd heard it called.

"You have confidence issues and stiffness in front of a camera that you don't have in person," Patrick said, tilting his head as he looked from her to the supplies on the counter.

From the chair, Mia pressed her lips together to stifle a laugh, and perhaps oddly, Tess felt a bit of her unease slip away. Tess smiled too. "Um, thanks?"

"I think the dogs will help. And so will Mia."

Although Tess didn't quite get what Patrick had in mind, she suspected he might be right. Having two dogs she connected well with in the room was already helping, and Mia seemed kind and understanding, more relatable than Patrick.

"Can you sit on the floor with your feet tucked under you for ten minutes or so? It will look better on camera than cross-legged," Patrick said.

Tess shrugged. "Sure." She was in jeans and had a long-sleeved thin, white shirt underneath one of the shelter's purple logo T-shirts. She'd left her hair in a low ponytail so that it wouldn't spill all over the place as she demonstrated the products. She'd even applied a light coat of makeup when Patrick had suggested it could be helpful on camera.

"What is it you have in mind?"

"You're comfortable with customers, and you're a natural with animals. That is what we need to show on video. But you look like you are starring in a low-budget infomercial. You need to let the audience see how you relate to dogs."

Rather than hurting her feelings, this touched Tess's funny bone. She felt even better when Mia joined in the laughing.

Patrick didn't crack a hint of a smile, but he didn't seem fazed by their laughter either. "And instead of looking at the camera like you are afraid of it, you need to think of Mia and Fannie as your audience. Think of the woman who came in earlier today with questions about her dog and how you answered her. You're doing the same thing; you're just talking to people while they are at home."

What he said made sense. She should have thought of this before.

"And I'll film next to Mia, but look at the camera if you can."

Tucking her feet under her butt, Tess settled into position on the floor in front of the wall full of pictures of adopted animals and their new owners. No sooner had she settled than Orzo half climbed onto her lap in an attempt to douse her face and neck in licks.

"Mind if I straighten a few things?" After wrapping Fannie's leash around one chair leg, Mia walked over and knelt in front of her, offering a soothing smile. "Don't mind me. Not only do I have a seven-year-old, but before I draw animals, I get them to pose for a few dozen pictures. When it comes to snapping photos and shooting video, I've gotten pretty good at spotting what you notice later and wish you'd corrected."

Up close, Mia's eyes were a startling shade of blue-gray, and they exactly matched an exotic-looking pair of dangly earrings she was wearing. Tess sat still as Mia fiddled with her T-shirt collar and freed a lock of her hair that had found its way underneath it. "You look great. And your clothes are perfect. You come across as friendly, approachable, and inviting. I'd give your video a shot if I saw it pop up on my Facebook feed or wherever you guys are sending this."

"YouTube, but linking to it with our Facebook account," Patrick said.

Mia gave Orzo a scratch on one ear and headed back to her seat. Fannie, who'd been watching contentedly, gave Mia a determined sniff. "Tess, maybe this will help. Picture me as Fannie's new owner, which I'd probably be for real if one of my family members wasn't allergic to dogs. But for the sake of this, let's pretend I'm here with my giant Saint Bernard Fannie who hates her crate so I don't like to crate her, but she's been a touch destructive while we're gone and she's home alone. Everything you're about to say is advice I really need to hear."

Patrick, who'd gone back to studying Tess's home-made items that were still on the counter, brought over the puzzle and bottle and handed them to Tess. "Let's go through it twice. Once for practice. Let Orzo do what-ever he wants as you talk, but do your best to keep to your script."

Feeling considerably better, Tess nodded. "Yeah, okay. Tell me when, and I'll start."

—⁓—

There was no hint of the coming sunrise yet in the east as Mason parked in the nearest open spot across the street from Tess's grandma's house. It seemed like it had been more than a day and a half since he'd left the shelter, but he was in too deep to see her again before telling her everything, and he was dead set not just to tell her, but to show her.

And to do that, he'd needed her to have a day off.

The fact that she had two off in row made it even better. The trip could be done in a day, but it would make for a long one. He'd told Fabina, Tess's grandma, of his plan, and she'd agreed that he stretch it over two.

"I'll pack a bag for her," she'd said when he'd called to ask permission to do this. "And some food for the drive. And I'll expect you to give your gentleman's word that you'll be good to my granddaughter. I don't let her know, but she's been my favorite since she was born. I figure it has something to do with the fact that I've always rooted for the underdog. It's why I liked you the first time I watched you up at bat for the Red Birds and heard your story."

Mason wasn't sure when that had been, but he assumed the announcer had shared something about his lengthy recuperation from the lightning strike and how he'd overcome near paralysis in his left side to play again. What piqued his curiosity even more was what she said about Tess. When she didn't explain and moved on to something else, Mason decided it was something he was probably better off hearing from Tess.

He turned off the ignition and glanced back at John Ronald, who was staring out the window at the dark houses. Mason wondered how far John Ronald's range had been, if he'd ever roamed this far from downtown as a stray. "I won't be long, buddy."

He'd crossed the street and was jogging up the crooked concrete porch steps when the noisy wooden door pulled open. It was Fabina. She waved him up. "She's in the bathroom getting ready. Here's her bag. Get it packed away before she sees it. If she realizes it's an overnight trip, she'll want to repack everything I've sent for her."

Mason jogged back out with the small suitcase and tucked it behind the passenger seat, hoping John Ronald wouldn't start gnawing on it before he got back. Yesterday, he'd left the dog at home while he went out on a two-hour workout and grocery run and had come home to a million feathers on the floor, on the shelving, and some still floating in the air. Thankfully, it had just been one throw pillow that John Ronald had demolished and not the couch. In case the dog was considering taking his tension out on Tess's suitcase, Mason handed him the three-point deer antler he'd bought at a pet store a couple of days ago.

After a thorough sniff of the suitcase, John Ronald lifted the antler gently out of Mason's hand, locked it between his front paws, and began to gnaw away. By the time Mason was back at the house, Tess was in the family room giving her grandma a hug.

Mason felt his insides stir in appreciation at the sight of her. She was in dark-gray leggings that hugged her slender but curvy legs, suede boots that reached just below her knees, and a light-gray cashmere sweater. Tess's long hair was half pulled back in a clip, and she had a cream scarf tied around her neck.

And Mason was going to have a hard time not wanting to take it all off. His blood had been boiling hot ever since the other night. Long workouts at home and one at the gym had been the only thing to quell it.

"Morning," Tess said, grinning as she spotted him in the doorway. "Or close enough, anyway. Coffee? My grandma brewed a giant pot."

"Thanks. I'm good for now, but I thought we'd stop for breakfast later."

"Stop *what*?" Tess set her hands on her hips but smiled playfully. "Because I'm still in the dark about where we're going or what we're doing." She glanced out the window. "Literally and figuratively."

"I'm hoping you won't be disappointed."

"She won't." Fabina turned and disappeared behind

the kitchen wall before coming back with a worn canvas tote that seemed plenty full. "I packed you some food. Tess said you're learning to cook. Come for dinner soon. I'll show you some of my secrets."

"I'd like that."

Tess hugged her grandma goodbye a second time and grabbed a wool coat from the coat closet. After the door was shut behind them and they were headed down the stairs, Tess nudged him with her elbow. "Can I state for the record that it's a little weird my grandma knows where I'm going, and I don't."

Mason closed his hand over her lower back. "If you want me to tell you, I'll tell you. Though I suspect you'll figure it out soon enough. I've not yet met your father, but I can't imagine fearing evoking his wrath any more than I do your grandma's. I had to ask her permission. Something tells me she's good at holding a grudge."

Tess huffed in agreement. "You've no idea. I could seriously tell you some stories."

They'd crossed the darkened street, and Mason paused with his hand an inch above the handle of the front passenger door. In case Fabina was staring out the window, he didn't want the interior truck light turning on. Between the creamy-crisp scent of Tess's perfume and the warmth radiating off her in the chill fall air, his resolution was draining fast.

Tess shifted the tote bag of food from one hand into both, letting it rest against her shins, and looked up at him, her dark eyes lingering over his mouth before locking on it.

If he really let himself get started with what he wanted to do, he'd end up making a pit stop at his place. Instead, he jammed his hands into his jacket pockets and let his lips brush against hers for not long enough.

Suppressing a wave of guilt over the inadequacy of it, he pressed his lips against her forehead before pulling away. "I want to hear your stories. All of them. Your adventures in Europe. The misadventures that sent you there. The business you're trying to start. What else makes you tick...aside from dogs, because I've seen that. Things I should know about your family. Everything, Tess. I want to hear it all."

And if he could help it, today would mark the first day in an endless series in which he kept nothing from her either. At least, once they got where they were going, and he showed her all the things he needed her to see.

She smoothed her top lip over her bottom and studied him for longer than he'd spoken. He wanted to know what she was reading in his gaze but didn't ask. He hadn't felt like this about a girl since early college. A part of him had wondered if he'd be able to after all the messing around he'd done the last couple of years.

"Okay," she said. "But just a heads-up... Sometimes I ramble."

Chapter 22

WHENEVER TESS ATTEMPTED TO EXPLAIN THE complicated mess that was her family, a familiar swirl of frustration, hurt, and love swept through her. As they coasted northbound on I-55 in Mason's truck through vast, open fields, the sky was changing from a deep gray-blue to a pale silver-yellow in the east. Tess first dove into less-personal stuff, recapping the twenty-five-year silent war between two Hill families who'd both earned their livings for the better part of a century in the food industry. Competition between what was now Tess's uncle's sandwich shop and another Italian American family had turned sour in the late 1980s when it was discovered that one of Tess's great-aunts had added a can of store-bought pasta sauce to a family recipe in a sauce contest in which her family had beaten out all local competition.

In the rivalry that ensued, the Grasso family business had suffered for several years. Thankfully, aside from a few die-hards, customers had all but forgotten the indiscretion. Her uncle had taken over the business from her now-deceased great-grandfather twenty years ago, and thanks to his thoughtful changes, business was once again booming.

That ended the easy part. Confiding the reason why she'd fled to Europe stirred up a slew of painful memories she'd done her best to make peace with.

"I was an oops kid." Tess fiddled with the curve at the

rim of her boot, just below the bend of her knee. "Though figuring that part out didn't require any great thinking. My older brother and sister are twelve and thirteen years older than me. All my memories of them when I was little are of them busy with their friends. They left for college before I was old enough to really get to know them. Holidays with them now are like when you meet an old teacher and you want to talk, but there's really no connection anymore." She shrugged a shoulder and shifted in her seat. "I was okay with that. I was also good with the fact that my parents worked full-time and were always busy when they weren't working. My mom was really involved in the local theater, and when my dad wasn't at work, he was puttering around in the garage."

Tess considered her next words before letting them leave her lips. Whenever she chose them wrong, she ended up crying, and she wasn't about to do that. Not today.

"I don't think either of them were psyched about the work that goes into another kid, but a couple years ago, I found out how *not* psyched they really were. My mom at least. Who am I kidding? Probably my dad too. When I found out"—Tess swallowed—"I just sort of freaked. I love them, and I know they love me. But at one point, my mom was set on giving me up for adoption."

Mason reached over the wide console and squeezed her leg reassuringly. The warmth and strength of his hand were immeasurably comforting. "I'm sorry, Tess."

"It's okay. I'm okay with all of it now. And it's not that I wasn't loved. I was. I just had a different life from what most of my other family members had. I had no clue when I was little that I was raised differently, but I'd put the pieces together long before I had definitive proof."

"Definitive proof of what?"

"Of why my parents pretty much pawned me off on the rest of my family to raise me. I love my cousins, but there's this one. There's always one, isn't there?" She let out a small laugh and let her arm fall atop where his had come to rest on the wide console. "Well, *that* cousin and I have never gotten along, éven though we're just a year apart. She's the youngest of five, and she hated that I got to spend so much time alone with my grandparents growing up. After she told me, I figured out almost all my extended family already knew. So, anyway, one night there was a group of us playing bocce ball, and she was drunk and let it slip that I was nearly given up for adoption. The fact that one of my other cousins nearly knocked her out with a bocce ball was proof enough that it was true. Later, when I pressured her, my grandma confided everything."

Mason pulled her hand to his lips and pressed a kiss against it. His stubble tickled her skin. "I'm sorry, Tess."

"It's okay. Like I said, I've come to terms. So, I guess what happened was my mom hid her pregnancy from my dad and my brother and sister for the first five months that she was pregnant with me. Before she told my dad about me, she had already identified a family through an adoption agency who wanted to adopt me. That was how she told him. My dad met her at a coffee shop, and there was this random couple at the table with her. My dad flipped and went to his parents about it. That's when my nonna and nonno got involved. And if you want to talk about Nonna's grudge-holding, she mostly keeps quiet about it around me, but she thinks my mom is the devil."

"After meeting her and hearing this story, that doesn't surprise me one bit."

"I've made my peace with it. Mostly. It hurt at first. A lot. That's why I decided to leave for Europe. I'd already been thinking about it. Vet school was turning out to not be for me, and I had heard about the internship on that farm through a college friend. A part of me was screaming to go, but it felt like an impossible dream. Then that bomb was dropped and I just had to get away and Italy felt like the right place to be.

"After I'd been away a few months, I started seeing the whole thing in a different light. I'll never like that my whole family knew and no one told me. But on the other hand, all those sleepovers at my aunts' and uncles', vacations with my cousins, and so much amazing time with grandparents who doted on me... it's because *they* wanted me, even if my mom didn't. Not at first, at least."

"Tess," Mason said. "Shit. I don't know what to say. That's harsh. But kudos to you for looking at it the way you are. And you and your mom, how are you now?"

Tess shrugged a shoulder. "We talk, like, once a week. We were closer before I found out, but we were never close like some of my friends and their moms. We had a heart-to-heart when I came back for my grandpa's funeral. It helped, though we still hardly ever talk about personal stuff. I have Nonna though." She paused and pulled in a breath. There were still some heavy feelings about her mom trapped inside, hovering below the surface, but she was figuring out how not to let them rule her. And today wasn't about her mom. It was about her and Mason. "And since you wanted to know everything, remember a few weeks ago, when we first met at Citygarden and you told me about John Ronald?"

They both shot glances behind them at the sleeping dog, whose long legs splayed over the edge of the wide seat. His giant front paws twitched in the air as if he were chasing something. Tess hoped it was that—chasing and not being chased—he dreamed about.

"I couldn't forget that."

"Well, I read a lot as a kid. A lot. Everyone in my family thought it was weird because I was the only one who owned a library card, and I only pulled my head out of a book to look at a dog. For years, I had a thing for Tolkien and for the Harry Potter series. I used to pretend hobbits and wizards were my friends. I had a few other favorite books, but they changed over time. And they got more romantic the older I got. But that line from the poem—'Not all those who wander are lost'—I wrote it down and took it with me to Europe. Whenever I felt alone, I read it and it reminded me that my travel had purpose, even if I didn't know it yet, and it kept me going. I couldn't tell you any of that the day we met because it meant so much. I couldn't find the words. But I thought you should know."

His hand wrapped around her thigh again, his thumb stroking her atop her leggings. "I figured it was something like that. I could see the look on your face, and I knew it was more than a casual knowledge of the poem."

"And what about you? I take it you're a Lord of the Rings fan?"

"I hope this isn't where I disappoint you, but yes and no. I was when I read it the summer before eighth grade, and I've never forgotten it. I think it was the only complete series I ever read. My family wasn't big into reading either, and I hardly ever sat still enough to look at a book except when I was going to sleep, and even then, I was usually out in a matter of seconds.

"My mom picked the trilogy up at a neighbor's farm sale after I broke my wrist jumping out of the hayloft. It took me the whole time I was in a cast to finish the series, but I enjoyed it. A lot. I enjoyed the adventure in it. The worldbuilding. And that line is something I never forgot. I had a dog who wandered off around then, which probably has something to do with it too."

Tess leaned across the console, warring with her seat belt for more room, and pressed a kiss against Mason's temple, then his ear, then his neck. She opened her lips just enough for a taste of the clean, smooth skin of his neck.

Mason responded with what seemed like a reflexive murmur of appreciation. "You smell good."

"You taste good, so that makes us even."

"You know, when I was packing up this morning, it occurred to me that it's a good thing John Ronald is taking up the back seat. Otherwise, I'd be tempted to pull over somewhere secluded and drag you back there."

Tess giggled and trailed her kiss along the front of his neck just over his Adam's apple. She could feel the vibration from the moving truck in his body. "What makes you think it wouldn't be me dragging you? And besides, what do you mean, 'It's a good thing'?" She lifted her face even with his and gave an exaggerated bat of her eyes. "Are you implying this *isn't* a good thing?"

Mason looked away from the nearly empty highway long enough to press a solid kiss against her lips. "No. Not at all. But I gave your grandma my word that I'd behave like a gentleman. And besides, I don't want our first time to be in the back of a truck. You deserve better than that."

Tess considered his words as if she were trying on a new pair of shoes. He'd said *our first time* as if there was no question there'd be a first time—and a plethora more. "So, does that mean you've given thought to where you'd like it to be? Wait. Is that where we're going?"

"I can tell you emphatically that I'd like it *not* to be where we're headed today."

Mason's low chuckle reverberated through the truck's interior. John Ronald's head popped up at the sound. Catching the movement in her peripheral vision, Tess turned and met the dog's intense blue gaze. He studied Mason for several seconds before letting his head come to rest on the seat again. It wasn't the first glimpse she'd had of the dog's growing loyalty to his new owner.

Tess slid her tongue over the roof of her mouth as she considered Mason's answer. Suddenly, she sucked in a breath. She could think of only one place that would generate such a typical, emphatic no. "Oh my God. You're taking me home, aren't you? To your parents' farm." They were in Illinois, heading north, and if her internal map was accurate, his hometown was somewhere northwest of here. Only she was sure she remembered him telling her it was a five- or six-hour drive home.

No wonder they'd needed to leave so early.

His answering smile was wide and playful and made Tess want to kiss him again. "I couldn't think of another place where you might have more fun practicing driving again. Quiet, empty roads. Dirt roads. Back roads. Off-road. And there are a few things I want to show you while we're there."

Tess sat up straight in her seat. "Mason, you're a nut. A sweet, crazy nut. We're driving eleven hours in one day so that I can practice driving?"

His grin widened. "I think we'll have more fun if we do it in two, but if you want to come back tonight, we can."

"It's just… I didn't bring any clothes or a toothbrush or anything."

"That's where your grandma came in. She packed a bag for you. It's tucked on the floor behind your seat."

"*Nonna* packed a bag for me? You told my grandma we were staying somewhere overnight, and she packed a bag for me?" Tess clamped her fingers over her mouth and suppressed a horrified laugh. "Mason, you've no idea. It's going to be humiliating. I bet you a million dollars she packed the ugliest clothes in my closet and a pair of granny panties."

Mason laughed. "Really? I'm sorry. Maybe I should have told you, but I was going for the surprise factor. Though this is rural America. We'll pass a few dozen Walmarts along the way, if you want to make a pit stop. And besides, my parents would be fine if you were naked, Tess. Wait, that's me. They'd be fine if you were in a clown suit."

Tess's shoulders shook with a suppressed laugh. "I'll check out my stash when we stop to pee, which should probably be soon, by the way. And for the record, you're being forgiven for not giving me an adequate heads-up that I'm about to meet your parents."

Chapter 23

"ANYTIME YOU FEEL THE URGE TO TAKE THE WHEEL, LET me know. We shouldn't come across more than a few stray cars between here and the farm."

In summer and early fall, tourists drove these winding roads in flocks on nice weekends, taking in the lush countryside, picturesque farms, patchwork fields, and the slow-moving Mississippi River in the distance. In late fall, like now, the countryside had a subtler look. The endless array of greens and yellows and reds had faded into russet browns and amber golds, but Mason loved his hometown in all seasons.

It never failed to surprise him how after so many years away, he still remembered each curve of the road and the scenic views just over each turn. At one point, he'd been eager to move on, eager to leave the familiar. Now, he came back just often enough to remember it would always be a part of him.

"I think I can handle this. Only it's so pretty, I hate to miss anything with my eyes on the road."

"Trust me. You'll get your fill of cows and dead grass while we're here. Besides, in half a mile, we're turning onto a county road that's so seldom traveled, you'd think it was a private road. You can drive as slow as you'd like and take up the middle if you want."

"How long till we're at your parents'?"

"Not long. We're going in the back way. A half hour,

forty-five minutes tops, depending on how slow you take it."

They'd been on the road for five hours. Rather than stopping for breakfast, they'd loaded up on coffee at a gas station and enjoyed Fabina's array of sweet and savory pastries. He'd been refueling his truck when the thing Mason had feared could happen did. He'd been spotted by an older guy in a car at a nearby pump. But Tess had been inside in the bathroom and hadn't seen it. The man had asked for an autograph, and Mason had consented, signing a well-worn road map and doing his best to ward off further talk before Tess came out.

They'd stopped one other time, and Mason had parked off to the side of the gas station to let John Ronald stretch his legs. Although the dog had been uneasy at first, Mason would swear that the long-legged dog was growing to like truck rides.

There'd been opportunities in this morning's conversation, perfect segues for Mason to have jumped in, but his throat had locked up. He wasn't sure why, but he couldn't escape the feeling that once she saw where he came from, she'd digest it better.

Mason put on his blinker, even though there were no cars as far as the eye could see in either direction. "How 'bout it? Pull over?"

Tess shrugged. "Sure."

Mason pulled onto the shoulder, and John Ronald popped his head up as the truck slowed to a halt. The husky's mouth fell open in an easy pant. "Let's let him out to stretch those legs."

John Ronald's DNA test results had come back. Mason hadn't been surprised to find the dog was mostly husky with a few odd breeds tossed in, like Irish wolf-hound and Doberman, though they were harder to see.

There was a wide gravel shoulder at the intersection of the two roads. John Ronald scent marked on three scraggly mounds of grass and sniffed the chilly air. Tess, whose arms were locked over her chest, stepped close to Mason's side.

"It's colder up here. Like, a lot."

Mason pulled her in to his chest and pressed his lips against the top of her head. "Yeah, well, not only are we three hundred something miles farther north, but we're at a higher elevation too. You're hardly without snow in winter here starting in mid-December."

Tess lifted her mouth to his, and he let himself get lost in her kiss until his blood heated and the ache in his groin made it difficult to keep focused. He was almost disappointed when she was the first to pull away.

"Some part of me wants clarification, Mason, but I keep telling myself I don't need it. I lived for fourteen months in Europe with very little clarification at all, and it was the best time of my life. Until now, I guess."

It was all pressing against the tip of his tongue, but he had a plan, and they only had a little over twenty miles to go. Regripping John Ronald's leash, Mason lifted Tess into the air. Her arms locked around his neck, and her legs wrapped reflexively around his hips. He kissed her harder than he meant to and let his free hand slide under her sweater to experience the silky-smooth skin at the small of her back. "Give me till tonight. I'm hoping to give you all the clarification you could ever want, Tess."

Laughter bubbled up Tess's throat. "Mason. Seriously. There's a river flowing across the road. I'm supposed to drive through that? What if we get swept away? Did you see that IMPASSIBLE DURING HIGH WATER sign we passed?"

The lopsided smile that Tess adored lit Mason's face. "That there is what folks 'round here call a crick." He dropped his overkill of an accent and added, "And I hate to disappoint you, but it's not more than a couple inches deep. That's why the road goes over it in this spot. It's wide here, but not deep."

She'd been driving for nearly a half hour at her slower pace. About five minutes ago, they'd turned down a dirt road that ran along the back edge of Mason's family's farm. It was completely surreal that he'd grown up on a farm that was about as big as the square mile of land that held the tightly packed houses on the Hill. But here, land was abundant, and houses were few.

"Are you sure?" she asked.

"Yes. It's too shallow to even skip rocks here most of the time. There's good rock skipping a half mile up the road. We can head there on horseback later. Or tractor, if you prefer."

Tess temporarily lost focus on the dirt road in front of her. "There are horses here that we can ride?"

"They're practically as old as me, but yes. My mom has always kept a few around. Horses and cooking are her things."

"I can understand that. Horses probably would've been my thing too, if I'd ever had half a chance to be around them."

After readjusting her hands on the wheel, Tess hit the gas and the truck burst forward down the small slope and into the creek. She braced herself as the tires hit the water, but other than the sound of the water splashing under the bottom, she had just as much control as she did on dry gravel.

Driving the big, lumbering truck on empty country roads was surprisingly fun. And Mason had been right. Her confidence at being behind the wheel again was swelling. She intended to renew her license next week on her lunch hour.

As soon as she'd driven across the rocky creek and up a short hill, she needed to hit the brakes again. There was a wide gate blocking the road.

Mason unbuckled and hopped out. "Keeps the cows in." He shut the door, unhooked the gate, swung it open, and waved her through. There were thick wooden posts on either side, and Tess spent several seconds triple-checking the side mirrors, even though she could hear Mason through the closed windows telling her she'd fit through.

"You grew up very differently than me," she said once he hopped back in and she'd continued down the road. They were in a patch of sparse but pretty woods. Acres of fields were visible through the trees ahead.

"I won't argue that," he said. "When we were eating those spinach-and-ricotta pastries your grandma made, it hit me that we should arrange a cook-off one day. It might be impossible to tell who was better, since they're such different cooks, but I do know we'd come out the winners."

Tess laughed. "True. You know, I like your mom already."

"Because she cooks or because she has horses?"

Tess looked up from the dirt road long enough to

waggle an eyebrow Mason's way. "Because she raised you." John Ronald, who'd risen to his haunches and was looking out the window, started to whine. "I bet he'd love to run through these woods," she added.

"Yeah, I bet he would. I'm not so sure it'd be a good idea, as used to roaming as he is."

"You're probably right."

The road came to a V, and Mason pointed to the left. "Coming in the back way like this, we'll come to the barn first."

Fifty feet from the road, a dozen cows grazed on grass that had wilted brown from a deep freeze. Most of the cows were solid black, but a few had white faces. They lifted their heads to watch the truck pass but didn't seem afraid.

"I think I told you this land has been in my family for four generations, and the tide changed from a farm that was largely self-sufficient during my great-grandfather's time to specialization on a single crop—my grandfather's time—then on my dad's watch, back to rotating crops and keeping the land as healthy as the food that's produced on it. My dad never went to college, but he's working with the university agricultural department to get the land in shape, and if you ask me, he's doing a hell of a job."

"It looks beautiful to me." Tess spotted a tall, red barn around a bend in the road. She shifted her hands on the big steering wheel. "I think I'm starting to per-spire over the thought of meeting your parents, now that we're so close."

"They're great, Tess. And they're going to love you. Trust me."

After passing through one more gate, Mason directed her to park along the side of the barn rather than continuing several hundred yards and through another gate to a white two-story house that was nestled in a grove of tall trees.

"Wow." Tess parked, grabbed her jacket, and stepped down from the tall truck. It was too much to take in all at once. She'd never been on a real American farm except for once in kindergarten while on a field trip. The farms where she'd stayed in Europe had had a different look and feel. From inside the barn, there was a soft nicker. "Are the horses inside?"

"Usually just at night. Sounds like they are today." He reached into the back of the cab for John Ronald, who hopped out with his tail raised and ears perked in excitement. "Let's check it out."

Mason headed in through an open set of massive sliding doors with large *X*s on them. Inside, the barn was bigger than her uncle's sandwich shop. Five roomy horse stalls lined one side, and there was a wide, empty pen in the back that Tess guessed was for something like sheep or pigs. An impressive variety of tractors was parked on the other side.

From the front stalls, three inquisitive horses nickered and tossed their heads. Even from here, Tess could see the distinctive patterns of spots and colors on their coats. "They're beautiful."

John Ronald, who'd walked in nose to the ground as he sniffed deep enough to stir up dust, cocked his head at the nickering horses. The hair rose on the back of his neck, and he growled in their direction.

"It's okay, boy," Mason said. "I'll hang back with

him, and you can pet them. They're not biters, though they try to knock you off your feet with a good head nudging now and then."

"Are they all Appaloosas?" Tess asked.

"Yeah, all three. The two mares, Paula and Rose, are red roans. The beige-and-white spotted one is a gelding. Appy is his name. My mom usually lets them out after breakfast. I keep thinking it's later than it is, but she probably kept them in in case we want to go for a ride."

"It does feel later than quarter to eleven, that's for sure."

Tess stepped up to the first horse, Appy, petting his face the same direction his hair grew, like with dogs. He nuzzled her jacket with surprisingly dexterous lips and did a test chomp of her button. Behind her, from where Mason stood, John Ronald struggled to pull forward, not ceasing with a series of long, low growls that the horses seemed to care less about.

"From the sound of it, I don't think I'm the only one who hasn't gotten to spend enough time around horses."

"Yeah, something tells me we'll have to lock him in a bedroom if we go for a ride."

Tess headed farther in, giving the two mares quick pets as well, then turned toward the door again. As she did, a dusty poster tacked up on one of the barn walls caught her attention. It was a full-body shot of a baseball player for the Orioles while at bat. Dust-covered as it was, she could still make out the name Mason Redding across the top. The player's body partially covered an oversize number 47 that matched the number on his uniform. Even partially covered by dust, there was something about the player's stance and face shape that drew

Tess closer. She headed over, taking it in, becoming more certain the closer she got. She had to step around a tractor attachment of some sort, but she got close enough to swipe the dust off the player's face.

It didn't make sense, but Mason had posed for this picture.

From the front of the barn where he'd been squatting next to John Ronald, trying to calm him down, Mason noticed and stood up. "Tess…"

Tess looked from the poster to Mason as she wiped the dust from her fingertips. She could suddenly remember three distinct times she'd tried to ask Mason his last name, and they'd either gotten interrupted or the conversation had taken a different turn.

"Mason, did you pose for this at a carnival or something? Because it looks real. And I'm *so* not about to buy that you used to play baseball for the Orioles."

Mason dragged one hand through his hair. He looked from the poster to her and shook his head.

Tess swallowed, a weird sense of alarm dumping into her veins as she sensed the truth in his answer. Sporty and all-American: those had been her first thoughts on seeing him the first time. *Oh my God, the reason you noticed him in the first place was because of that man who was staring his way and talking baseball.*

"Are you telling me that you played professional baseball and you *never* bothered to tell me?" There was a pitch in her voice that only came out when something frightened her, and she didn't want to admit it. "How long? How long did you play for them?"

He shifted the leash from one hand to the other as John Ronald attempted to tug him toward the horses hard enough that Mason needed to lean back against the pull. "For the Orioles? For a year." He looked from her to the dog and back. "Let's get outside so we can talk."

Locking her arms across her chest, Tess followed him through the open doors and into the bright morning. She was spending the day on a farm in rural Iowa with a boyfriend who'd once played for the Orioles. Only he'd failed to mention it.

John Ronald was doing his best to drag Mason back in through the wide-open doors. He was barking, but Tess didn't wait for him to calm down. "Oh, by the way, I traveled to the moon a couple years ago. *Sorry if I forgot to mention it*."

"Tess, I was going to tell you today. I wanted you to see where I came from first. There's just so much hype around it."

Something in his words set off an alarm. *How* much hype? "Were you famous or something? Did you play for other teams?"

"Famous…no, not famous. But yes, I've played for other teams. I, uh, still do."

Something wasn't adding up, and an uncomfortable tension was curling around her ribs. "You *still* play? For what team?"

Mason grimaced as John Ronald did a full-circle tug in all directions in an attempt to drag him back into the barn. "A season with the Orioles. Another season with the Brewers. And for the last two, I've been with the Red Birds."

Tess thought of her grandma, a die-hard Red Birds fan who watched almost every televised game of each season. Her grandma had met him several times but hadn't recognized him. That could only mean he wasn't a starter or that big a player. Nonna would know all of them in her sleep.

Mason Redding. Mason Redding. Tess racked her brain to come up with something about him, but she hadn't followed baseball for a long time, and she'd been gone nearly as long as he'd played for the Red Birds.

Mason Redding.

Something came. She'd heard that name in casual conversation at her grandpa's wake and a few times since. She struggled to pull up the memory. Something had happened. An accident or something. Something about that player not being able to take part in the playoffs.

And something else about that player having been in the running for MVP.

How could Nonna not have recognized him?

That day in Citygarden, he'd had the remnants of a black eye and he'd had an arm in a sling. She'd asked what happened, and he'd been dismissive. Only he hadn't been dismissive. He'd been evasive.

"Let me see your phone."

Mason blinked. He looked tense, guilty, and this made the anticipation worse. "Can we put the dog away and talk first?"

"Can I please see your phone?"

With a sigh, Mason unlocked his phone and passed it her way. She pulled up the internet. Her fingers were shaking, but after three attempts, she managed to get *Mason Rredding ball payer* onto the screen and pressed Go.

The service was almost nonexistent here. Tess waited as the search image circled and circled. Finally, Google replied, *Did you mean: **Mason Redding ballplayer?*** She clicked on the bolded text and then selected Images.

Her hands were shaking, and tears were stinging her eyes. She turned her back and stepped away several feet. Slowly, images of Mason Redding, ballplayer, began filling the screen. Up at bat. Swinging and connecting with the ball. At press conferences. Catching pop flies. Pro shots. High-fiving other players. Being interviewed by sportscasters. Sliding into home base. Signing autographs. Surrounded by a posse of women ogling him at some sort of event. His arm around a gorgeous blond. His arm around a stunning redhead. Wearing a kilt and standing next to what looked like a supermodel in a leopard-print bikini. A crowd of media and emergency workers near an overturned white SUV.

Tess's stomach pitched. *Why* had no one noticed and told her?

Another wave of realization washed over her. Aside from Nonna and Georges, it had always just been just the two of them. At the park. In his truck. At his apartment. In the shelter.

She was so mad that she wanted to tackle him. She might have considered it if he wasn't struggling with the dog. Instead, she shoved his phone at him and kept walking, away from the house, the truck, the barn.

She crossed into the open field behind them and kept going. She'd nearly made it to the far side when Mason caught up with her.

John Ronald wasn't with him, so she could only assume the excited dog was currently scratching up his truck. Mason caught her arm and pulled her to a halt. "You have a right to be pissed, but please let me explain."

"*Pissed?*"

Tess whirled on him, her mind spinning a thousand different directions. Patrick had said they'd had a recent big donation from a baseball player. Had Mason Redding been the name he'd said? And what had Mason thought about the way she'd thrown herself at him? Even worse, how many times had she been the one to initiate the kissing? It had been her. Every time. Her face flushed hot with embarrassment and anger.

She shoved her hands hard against his chest, but it was like trying to shove a tree. "You *stupid head*! I'm so pissed I could just…just…" She clenched her fists tight. "In no way was that fair, Mason! You play flipping baseball for the St. Louis Red Birds, *and you didn't tell me*!"

Mason closed his eyes and drew in a calculated breath. "Tess," he said, opening them again. "I'm sorry. I truly am. Just please let me explain."

It was too much to process, the Mason Redding in the pictures she'd just seen and the Mason standing in front of her with the pleading look in his kind eyes. Tess looked away, anywhere but at him. That was when she noticed the two figures halfway between the house and the barn. A man and a woman, not walking anymore but looking their way.

She shook her head and swiped at the couple of stray tears that had rolled down her cheeks. "And this is how I get to meet your parents."

Chapter 24

FIXING FENCES. MASON WAS PRETTY SURE THIS WAS HOW his dad had worked through every problem of his life, and how the man must think everyone else could work through them as well. And on a farm as big as this one, there was always a section of fence that needed mending.

Lunch had been nothing less than awkward. Thank God for John Ronald's obsessiveness with trotting around the main floor of the house and staring out the windows as he whined at the cows in the distance. The excited dog had given Mason, Tess, and his parents something to talk about as they ate. Mason's dad wasn't much for bringing dogs inside the house unless it was too cold to keep them outdoors. And even though the high thirties of today were likely a refreshing welcome for the husky mix, his dad thankfully understood that John Ronald wasn't in the space to be left anywhere alone.

Before coming, Mason had asked his mom to put away any baseball pictures she might have up until after he'd had the chance to show Tess around the place. Even though he'd not put it into a concise statement, his parents seemed to understand that Tess meant a lot to him. So rather than dancing around the fact that, thanks to a long-forgotten poster in the barn, Tess now knew what he'd been dreading to tell her, Mason had brought it up while they assembled sandwiches on thick slices of his mom's homemade bread.

It was likely his parents had already figured this out, having witnessed her exodus across the field so soon after arriving, but they took the announcement in stride. Mason's dad had been quick to interject that at eleven years old, Mason had become the best kid in Dubuque County at doing his chores after his dad made a serious threat to pull him from his baseball team if he didn't find a way to get to them done. "Some things just run thick in your blood," his dad had said. "That was baseball for Mason. And he tells us it's dogs for you."

It was a simple effort to turn an awkward conversation into a less awkward one, and it had been from a man who'd never been that interested in chitchat. It had meant a lot to Mason.

Now, he and his dad were alone, three fields east of the barn, mending a downed section of fence in a field where his dad had grown kale this fall. His mom and Tess were out on horseback, and Mason had promised to catch up with them later.

Using a rope Mason had found in the garage, John Ronald was tied to a post thirty feet away. The long-legged dog seemed content enough as he trotted the line of the fence, marking it with more urine than Mason would've guessed he had in his body.

Mason had slipped into a comfortable pair of boots and a Carhartt jacket that his mom kept here for him and was halfway through driving in a new post. If his shoulder weren't still bothering him, he would've had it buried after a few hard slams of the post driver.

"Step aside, won't you?" his dad said. "I'll hit it for a few. The more you overuse that shoulder, the longer it'll be before you're back in the swing of things." His dad released a soft chuckle at his baseball reference as he grabbed the handle of the post driver.

Mason didn't object to letting him take over. He stepped back and rotated his shoulder in a slow arc, taking note of the positions in which he still felt a piercing burn. Afterward, he looked around, appreciating the open quiet of the country. The days were shorter now, and the sun was midway between high noon and sunset, basking the rolling hillside in a brush of gold.

"So, what do you think of Tess?" Mason asked. They'd been out here for a half hour and his dad hadn't asked a single question. It would be the opposite if he'd been working alone in the garden with his mom. He'd have been pelted with enough questions that he'd have been craving the quiet solitude of his father. Other than his dad's weathered skin and more slender frame, Mason had heard time and again that they'd been cut from the same mold.

"Cute kid. I see why you like her. Though the fact that you brought her home tells me it probably doesn't matter what I think. You've made up your mind."

"The only thing I'm sure of is that even though I've only known her a couple weeks, it feels longer."

"She's a hell of a lot better than the other one you brought home. The cheerleader. When was that? Eight, nine years ago now? I was happy to spot that one's taillights finally heading down the driveway."

"Ashley? If you remember, I didn't bring her. She showed up while I was home recovering from the lightning strike."

"Yeah, I remember now. Still, I suspect you've got enough of me in you that she'd have turned you plum crazy if you'd stuck with her too long. It was that voice of hers. Layered with more molasses than most maples can be tapped of. This Tess, on the other hand, she's got an ease about her I could see you never tiring of. The kind that'll help keep you calm when things heat up."

Mason crossed the ten feet to where John Ronald was standing at the full reach of his rope. He sank down, balancing on the balls of his feet as John Ronald pressed into him for a scratch.

"I won't disagree there."

His dad had never been much for asserting his take on things, so maybe that's why the few times he had stood out so starkly in Mason's mind. And over the years, Mason had given one of those bits of advice more thought than all the others.

His dad had offered that advice years ago at lunch when it was just the two of them at the table. His mom had gone somewhere; Mason couldn't remember where. He remembered the sting of his dad's comment as much as the words themselves. All these years later, even though Mason had dealt with so much since, that offhanded comment from his dad had morphed into one of his biggest fears.

"Back in my sophomore year of college, when we'd heard they were sending the big recruiters to my remaining games, you said something that stuck with me." Mason was surprised to find he was finally voicing his thoughts. He hadn't planned to. "You said if I played pro, it'd be harder to know when someone liked me for *me* and not for the hype."

Even though his back was to his dad as he petted John Ronald, Mason sensed the shift in his dad's posture.

"That so?" Mason's dad headed over, abandoning the post driver on top of the post.

Seeing his approach, John Ronald dashed away in the opposite direction as far as the rope would allow, reminding Mason that the dog had a way to go when it came to trusting strangers.

"If I did, I don't remember it." His dad came to a stop a foot or two away. He stretched his lower back, pressing his thumbs into the back of his hips as he did. "But as you've never been one to fabricate the truth, I won't argue it. Only don't tell me that's why you're having such a piss-poor time telling that girl what you do for a living."

Mason gave up attempting to beckon John Ronald their way again. "I guess there's some truth in it, that's all."

"I hate to break it to you, but you're even more like me on the inside than what everyone sees on the outside. You don't let people in easily, and when you do, it kills you when they leave. But listen to a wiser-from-his-years man rather than yourself. It's a risk, but you've got to trust the things you love." He pointed a dirt-streaked finger toward John Ronald. "That dog, for starters. You can't keep a dog like that tied to a leash or a rope his whole life. He's going stir-crazy. And the same goes for that girl. Show her who you are—all of it—and so long as she's no dummy, she'll realize you're a pretty damn good catch." He gave a swift nod as if to affirm his point and headed back to the half-driven-in post. "No pun intended on that last bit."

<hr>

When he'd planned this day, Mason had expected to have a few hours alone with Tess to show her some of the places that had been definitive in his first near two decades of life. Decades in which he'd pretty much lived and dreamed baseball. Like the spot in the low field where he'd been struck, for one thing. He'd gotten past the physical trauma the lightning strike had caused after many long months of struggle, but that struggle had come to define him. At the very least, it defined a huge part of his history. Then there were the various ball fields where his parents had driven him across the county for Little League and junior league baseball games. He'd also grown up thirty minutes from the *Field of Dreams* movie set. It was now a tourist attraction, and one he suspected Tess should see. Mason remembered touring the field where the movie had been filmed when he was a kid, thinking it'd be way cooler to play baseball than to act in movies.

But the flow of day hadn't progressed as he'd imagined. From fixing fences to horseback rides to a big family dinner with his sister and her husband and a few of Mason's cousins, there hadn't been a moment of downtime. There was tomorrow on the way out, at least.

The important thing, he'd determined, was that as the day progressed, he could sense Tess's anger ebbing. She was also great with his family. He'd known she would be. And he wasn't surprised when he was in the kitchen with his mom—during their one moment alone—and she applied one of her favorite labels, the salt of the earth, to Tess.

In answer, he'd said, "Yeah, but a different salt than you'd find around here. By the way, did you know they're selling salt gift sets now? I was thinking of getting you guys one. Salts of different colors and flavors mined from all around the world. Think Dad would appreciate it?"

"I think if you keep after him, he'll learn to appreciate more and more. We're settled in our ways, but not stuck. Not yet."

"That's good, because otherwise I don't think you'd appreciate what I'm giving you for Christmas." He was hoping the six-day spotlight tour of Europe would end up being a hit, but he suspected his dad would put up his fair share of grumbling about leaving his farm, even though Mason had arranged to leave it in the care of his more-than-capable cousin while they were away. At the time he'd made the purchase, Mason would have liked to have gone for a few weeks, but he'd suspected a longer trip could tip the scale to his dad deciding not to go. Now that John Ronald and Tess were so new in his life, Mason was glad he and his parents wouldn't be gone any longer either.

After the packed day, his mom's hearty dinner had been a hit. She'd served a meatless three-bean chili that his dad hadn't been able to find complaint with, corn bread, and green bean casserole, then brownie sundaes for dessert. After the food was cleared, they'd lingered around the dining room table for cards and a game of bingo.

It hadn't taken long for Tess to relax around his extended family, especially after his sister accidentally broke the ice as soon as she came through the door. While pulling him in for a hug, the whole room likely heard his sister's overly loud whisper of "So, does she know, or does she not know?" Tess's answer of

"I know, and I'm acclimating" was enough to start the laughter and a dozen good-natured jabs in Mason's direction from his family for having kept it from her.

"So, obviously you don't follow baseball," one of his cousins had added.

Tess's unapologetic reply of "No, but I've got a good reason to start" was enough that the last of Mason's unease over how she'd found out fell away. She was going to forgive him.

Tess continued to hold her own with his family throughout dinner and the games. Even though Mason knew she preferred wine, she joined in and had a few bottles of beer. When bingo was winding down, Tess closed her hand over his knee and asked to borrow his phone to call her grandma. She stepped outside without a jacket to make the call.

John Ronald, who'd finally settled down and was dozing in front of the fireplace on his back with his feet in the air, hopped to his feet and trotted to the side window to look out the door. He whined and stared after her.

Unsure if the dog simply wanted to be outdoors again or if he needed to pee and was finally giving a signal, Mason headed over to leash him. He took his time stepping into his boots and pulling on a coat, wanting to give Tess a few minutes of privacy. When he opened the door a few minutes after her and saw that it was starting to snow, he reached around to the coatrack and grabbed one of the extra flannels that his mom kept there for quick trips to the mailbox.

As soon as he was down the steps, John Ronald beelined to the nearest bush. He lifted his leg and peed. "Good boy." Mason was still praising him when John Ronald trotted back to the porch steps and peed again squarely on the middle of them. "Hey, not on the steps, buddy."

Thirty feet away, Tess was laughing and walking back toward the house. "Hopefully that'll slow down some once he's snipped."

"Yeah, let's hope." Mason met her halfway. John Ronald reached her first and jumped up, smacking his paws on Tess's chest as he gave her face a quick sniff. Stretched out like that, he was every bit as tall as Tess.

"That's a first," Tess said as he dropped back to all fours two seconds later.

"Yeah, I've got to get this reprimanding thing down better. When I correct him, he looks up at me like I'm hurting his feelings."

"You have a soft heart. I knew that before today, but it's easy to see here."

Mason held out the lined flannel jacket he'd grabbed. Tess was shivering in just a sweater. A thin blanket of clouds was passing over, spitting snow flurries.

"Think you'd be too cold to take a short walk? Just down the driveway."

"This will help," Tess said, slipping into the jacket.

Mason freed a thick lock of her hair that was trapped underneath the collar. The simple act set his blood to pulsing enough that he no longer felt the chill in the air.

She offered up his phone, and he slipped it into his jeans pocket. "Before I forget, I called Megan before I called my grandma. The puppies had another good day. And Dr. Washington was in. He gave Zoe the all clear to be kenneled with her siblings again. Her temp is right where it should be. She's still getting her formula from a syringe, but Dr. Washington thinks being with her brothers and sisters will help her strength continue to climb."

"That's amazing, Tess. I saw Patrick's Facebook post. They're crediting you with Zoe's recovery."

"I saw that too. Those fluids really helped, I'll say that."

"You're a talented woman, Tess. Don't forget it."

He watched her pull in a breath, which he was learning was her way not to shoot down a compliment.

"Thanks," she said finally.

"And how's your grandma?"

"Nonna? In the loop way more than me, it seems."

The way she said it, she didn't seem angry.

Mason offered an apologetic smile and savored the way her mouth seemed to turn up reflexively. He locked her hand in his as they fell into step alongside each other, heading toward the end of the long driveway. "I'm sorry, Tess. For everything. I loved how you were with me right from that first day in the park. I didn't want you to see me differently than you did."

Tess's shoulders sank as she released a breath. "I was thinking about that when I was out riding with your mom. I'd like to say I wouldn't have, but the truth is, I don't know. I just don't. A part of me wants to hang on to my anger, Mason, but I'm having a really hard time doing it. Nonna said she recognized you the day you brought over the laptop. She said she was due half the blame for you not telling me right away. But she's old-school Catholic, and they like to blame themselves. But just watch. Now that I know, all she needs to do is tell one person, and it'll be all over tomorrow. It's the sort of news that spreads in my neighborhood."

"So, uh, for the record, you'll see a grown man grovel

if you say you aren't, but do you think you're okay with the world knowing you're dating a baseball player?"

Tess leaned closer in to him as they walked. "It gives me the rumblies in my tummy, but yeah, I think so. But could you define it for me, please? Because everybody has a different idea of what dating means, and I'd like to make sure our ideas match up."

Mason cocked an eyebrow. "Certainly." He lifted her hand and pressed it against his chest as he talked. "Let's see, where to start… You can drive my truck whenever you'd like, for one thing. I'll give you a key and the codes to my place. If you're looking for drawer or closet space, you're welcome to whatever you'd like. There's plenty. Fridge space too, though I reserve the right to keep meat in it, so you'll have to get used to that."

Tess laughed and shoved against him. "You goof. I mean about seeing other people."

"Oh, that. Let's see. How would I define that? Well, for starters, I've got just about enough farm boy left in me to take anyone out who hits on you, inappropriately or not."

"Mason, seriously, I'm trying to get you to clarify whether you're okay committing to something exclusive."

They'd reached the end of the driveway, and patches of bright stars shone between the intermittent clouds. The narrow, winding road was empty in both directions. Other than the lights from the house, the only light was from the sky. Tess's skin took on a silky, radiant gleam, and her full lips had a magnetic pull.

"Am I okay committing to something exclusive?" He rocked back on his heels and looked up at the sky a few seconds. "Something exclusive," he repeated. He ran his thumb and forefinger along his chin in mock consideration.

"Mason, only one of us thinks you're funny, and it isn't me."

Rather than answering, he pulled her in for the kiss he'd been craving since the first rainy afternoon in his truck. Unlike before when she'd kissed him, he held nothing back. He locked one hand behind her back and drew her tight against him, savoring the way her delicate body pressed into him. Without losing a beat in the kiss, he tugged John Ronald closer, so he could lose his other hand in that silky mass of hair.

Her lips parted to greet his, beginning a slow dance of desire. He could taste the sundae and the hot chocolate she'd just been sipping. When he couldn't draw her close enough to satiate the desire building in him, he lifted her into the air, and her legs locked reflexively around his hips. He wanted to grind his body against hers and was debating where a good, tall tree was when he heard a small animal dart off through the thick grass directly across the road.

John Ronald bolted toward the sound, nearly knocking Mason off his feet and sending Tess tumbling into him.

"Shit. You okay?"

She landed on her feet but barely. "Yeah. What do you think that was?"

He shrugged. "A fox or rabbit, most likely." He leaned back against John Ronald's pull and whistled to get the dog's attention. As soon as he had it, he made John Ronald sit for one of the treats he'd been keeping in his pocket to promote impromptu training opportunities. "It was too fast to be a skunk or an opossum."

"Well, any of those are okay with me, because I was thinking of the movie *Signs* just now."

Mason laughed and locked hands with her again, leading her back toward the house. John Ronald was right, even if he didn't know it. There'd be a better time and place for all the things he was eager to do with Tess. "And by the way, I'm good with exclusive."

Chapter 25

TESS WAS ON THE BRINK OF DRIFTING OFF WHEN JOHN Ronald let out a single bark from across the hall where he was closed in with Mason in Mason's old bedroom. The charming, rustic bedroom that was Tess's for the night had once been his sister's but was now a guest room.

Yawning, Tess stretched her legs and arms. The plush double bed was a luxury compared to the thin, worn twin mattress she'd slept on at Nonna's the last month and a half.

Not only was she wired, but also thirsty, and her mind was starting to spin again. It didn't matter how early she'd woken up this morning, she wouldn't be falling asleep anytime soon. What a whirlwind of a day! Her boyfriend played for the St. Louis Red Birds. Maybe this fact was the single most daunting thing she'd experienced in years, but it didn't change all the wonderful things about him that she'd become crazy about.

And he was right across the hall. In a mostly quiet house. And that incredible kiss—the only one so far that had been one hundred percent his—still had her lips and body humming with energy.

Remembering his comment from this morning, a smile tugged at Tess's lips. Often, making a claim and sticking to it were two very different things.

Hopefully, tonight would prove to be one of them.

Downstairs, she could hear soft sounds emanating

from the TV. It was sweet that Mason's dad fell asleep on the couch most nights and halfway through the night went to the bed he'd shared with his wife for thirty-two years.

As quietly as possible, Tess got out of bed and sorted through her overnight bag again. As she'd suspected, Nonna hadn't packed anything more attractive than the baggy T-shirt she was already wearing. And worse, to leave the room, Tess would need to pair it with oversize gray sweatpants that not only didn't belong to her, but were three sizes too big.

After slipping them on and cinching them tight enough at the waist to keep them from sliding down as she walked, she dug through her purse, which thankfully she'd packed herself. After slipping her item of choice into her pocket, she tiptoed out and into the bathroom. She peed, finger-combed her hair, drank enough of the strange but clean-tasting well water straight from the faucet to quench her thirst, and rinsed out her mouth. Then, checking herself out in the mirror long enough to determine that if she gave it any more thought, she'd chicken out, she slipped back into the hall.

Mason's door wasn't locked, and she knew she couldn't knock without potentially drawing the attention of his dozing parents. Feeling as if she was about to commit breaking-and-entering, she slipped inside and closed the door as quietly as possible behind her.

The light was off, but there was enough light from outside not to need it. Mason was awake and sprawled across the top of his covers. He was sans shoes but still dressed from the day. The blue light of his phone lit his remarkably sculpted face.

John Ronald trotted over from the window as silently

as if he were walking on snow. He gave a determined sniff of her hands and her sweats, lingering for a second or two near the pocket where she'd slipped something that tested her confidence level simply by carrying it with her.

"Hey. So, are you busy?" She looked at Mason but gave John Ronald a determined scratch on his fuzzy cheek.

Mason dropped his phone and sat up. "Never for you. Just reading message boards about the trades that might be coming for the team this winter. I thought you'd be zonked out by now."

"I was. Almost. Then I woke up." She swallowed. "Do you think it might happen to you?"

"No. I have another two years on my contract, and I'm in a good position right now. I think I may lose a few buddies to other teams though."

"I'm sorry."

"Thanks, but it's part of the business." He motioned to the bed. "Have a seat."

She tiptoed across the floor and chose an empty spot at the foot of his bed. She faced him, folding her legs into a pretzel, and tucked her hands under her ankles. John Ronald lost interest and went back to the window.

"Has it changed much since you lived here?"

"A little. Mostly, it's the walls that are different. My mom painted a few years ago. She called to see if she could redecorate. Of course, I didn't care, but she kept more up than I would've guessed. Remind me to point some things out in the morning. They'll give you a laugh."

"Oh yeah? I will for sure."

Even at opposite ends and with both of them sitting up, there wasn't much extra space on the double bed.

Tess was hungry to lean in for more of that kiss. Aside from the fear and the insecurity and the hurt that had lingered most of the afternoon from the deceit, Tess realized something else had been boiling under her surface all day.

How completely sexy he'd looked in those online photos.

Fearing she'd lose her nerve, she jumped ahead. "So, um, so long as you're not busy, I have some questions. And some other things, like a demand actually. And some requests too. Since we're both awake and there's not much else to do, I figure now is as good a time as any."

A small smile parted his lips. "Any time you want to talk works for me. Want do you want to start with?"

His teeth gleamed in the moonlight, adding fuel to the want flaming up inside her. "I guess my biggest question is, do you have any other secrets? Big ones. I can wait for the little ones."

"You pretty much know my whole life story now, Tess. Since my mom told you about the lightning strike and just about everything else while you were on that ride, it seems." His tone was light and without a grudge.

"Yeah, that's crazy, Mason. I can't believe you were struck by lightning. Your mom told me about it, but I want to hear it all again from you. Tomorrow. If that's okay."

"Sure. It's one of the reasons I wanted to bring you here. There's a lot I want to show you tomorrow." He reached over and cupped a hand under one calf. "But right now, I'm suddenly a hell of a lot more curious about what's on the agenda for tonight."

Tess laughed and shook her head. "Sorry. It starts out heavy, and I'm hoping you don't get offended."

"It's okay. And I don't offend that easily."

"Then I'll just jump in. And I absolutely get it's hypocritical, but it still feels more pertinent to me to bring it up now than it did when I thought you just sold sports stuff."

His smile widened. "It's all fair game, Tess. Everything."

"Thanks. Okay, to start. I don't want to know about the girls you've been with before now. Not for ten minutes or ten days or ten months. I don't want to know *any* of it. The few pictures I saw when I Googled you today were enough. But I do want to know up front about any STDs or drug habits or porn addiction you might have. I'm not saying it's a game changer, but I want the truth, and I'm happy to tell you likewise."

Mason pressed his lips together and cleared his throat. "Okay. All fair questions. No drug habits, no STDs, and no porn addiction. None. I swear. I won't lie that I've partied hard at times, but I've always kept enough of my head on my shoulders to stay clean."

Tess nodded and felt a bit of the weight fall off her shoulders. She could tell by the look in his eyes that he was telling the truth. "Me too." When Mason raised one eyebrow, she added, "I never actually partied that hard. It's not my style, though I don't blame girls who do. I'm all for equality of the sexes. You should probably know that moving forward. I'm just agreeing that I'm clean." Tess held up one palm in the air. "No STDs. No drug habits. No porn addiction."

He chuckled. "Good. What else would you like to know?"

John Ronald, who'd been looking out the window on

one wall, trotted to the other wall to look out another window.

"A lot. I have a thousand questions. Literally a thousand. But we have the whole drive home tomorrow, and it's your turn to talk."

"It sounds like a good plan. I have a lot that I'm ready to share."

Tess gnawed her lower lip. "Good. I want to hear it all. In the meantime, you should know that I have anxiety. Ever since I was a kid. It's not crippling, and I've mostly figured out how to deal with it, but the idea of dating someone who a zillion girls would like to sleep with is going to be a big leap for me. Like I said, I'll do my best to avoid gossip columns and social media sites and all that other crap your mom mentioned is rife with lies and exaggeration about you, because I don't want to know about who you were with before unless there's someone you think you need to tell me about."

"I'll make that easy on you. There isn't. There's no one."

Tess pulled in a long breath and released it, feeling the rest of her tension ebb away. "So, this brings me to the next thing. I was lying across the hall thinking about the places that we have available for our first time and how most of them suck."

"Wait. We've moved to talking about our first time now?"

"Yes, unless you don't want to."

He shook his head and grinned. "I'm game. I just thought I was in for an inquisition the way this started."

"No, no inquisition. But it's late and we woke up early, so I figured I should get to the point. There's your place. Obviously. I can only imagine how nice it could be there—eventually—but I'm going to have to get over myself and some insecurities, Mason, and some place where you've likely partied hard is not where I want to consummate our relationship."

He nodded slowly. "Fair enough."

"There are new-to-us hotels, but it seems like that would feel a touch indifferent and maybe a bit cheap, so I'd rather not go that route. And I'm currently living with my grandma in a two-bedroom house with *really* thin walls and no TV playing in the middle of the night ever. And let's face it: you're big enough to overwhelm a twin bed without me even being on it. So…I was thinking that pretty much leaves us with here." She paused and let it sink in. "If you're good with it, that is. Though I should warn you before you answer, I was totally right about the granny panties."

Mason's mouth opened, but he didn't say anything for three solid seconds. "I'm game. I'm definitely game. And you had me at granny panties." He cocked an eyebrow. "On you, at least. But, Tess, I want our first time to be exactly what you want. And today's been half crap for you."

Tess shifted and stretched forward, bracing herself with her hands midway up the bed. She pressed her lips against Mason's ear, then his temple. "Not quite *half* crap. I rode a horse for the first time in my life, and my thighs hurt enough not to forget it. I met your parents and some of your family, and they're awesome. I got to see the amazing place where you grew up." She moved to his neck and let her lips trail to his Adam's apple. "And you're finally opening up to me. So, I'd say it was just a *touch* crap and a whole lot awesome. And this is exactly what I want."

He locked his hands around her waist and pulled her onto his lap. He swept her hair to one side and brushed his lips over her neck. She felt his body swell underneath her, pressing into her, melting the last of her anxiety. Melting everything but desire.

His hands slipped under her baggy T-shirt and over her body, and he released a soft murmur of appreciation when he realized they weren't impeded by a bra. He tugged the shirt up and off her body and brushed the palms of his hands over her breasts, then the tips of his fingers, then his lips. She tilted her head back and arched her spine, savoring the perfection of his movements.

His mouth was working his way to hers again when she pulled away and ran a finger over his lips. "Hold on. While I'm thinking about it, I brought along a three-pack of condoms. They're in my sweats."

He laughed and lost his hands in her hair. He brushed his lips over her earlobe and murmured in her ear. "That's good news, because I was thinking the same thing this morning but held out. I think I still have a few in the glove box of my truck, and I hope so, because I'm suddenly pretty damn sure we're going to need them too."

Chapter 26

THE SKY WAS A HINT LIGHTER IN THE EAST, PROMISING the coming sunrise. Mason pulled the spare pillow over his face, hoping to catch another hour of sleep now that Tess was gone.

Just after four, she'd woken him up to tell him she was headed to her room to crash another few hours. "I know we're adults and all, but it's my first time meeting your parents."

He'd stopped her from sliding back into her granny panties and T-shirt, and they'd made love one more time as quietly as possible. The TV had been turned off a few hours ago, and the house seemed to magnify all sound at this impossibly still point in the early morning.

Afterward, she'd slipped into her pajamas and was tiptoeing for the door when he'd gotten up and gone after her.

Hearing him behind her, she'd paused with her hand on the knob. "Did I forget something?"

"Two things, but you didn't forget them." The low, husky whisper he'd maintained seemed to give his words even more impact. "I know you said you didn't want to know about my past as far as this kind of stuff is concerned, but I wanted to tell you you're the only one I've ever been with in this room. And I was just lying there thinking how appropriate it is that it never happened here before, because I've also never been in love. Not until now."

She'd taken her hand off the doorknob, and her shoulders relaxed as she searched his face in the dim light.

"I wanted to tell you when we were outside last night, but it was easier to joke. Easier to play it cool. Only, I don't want to play it cool with you anymore. I love you, Tess."

She'd stepped in close and reached onto her tiptoes to press a kiss against his lips. "You don't have to." The kiss had deepened, stirring Mason's blood all over again. "And I love you too, Mason Redding. Every single inch of you."

After she left, Mason had done his best to fall back to sleep, but he was wired. And John Ronald was clearly finished with the confinement of the small room. Every time Mason so much as shifted, the dog was up and at the edge of the bed, ready to go. Finally, at five thirty, Mason threw off the covers and slipped into yesterday's clothes.

Rather than deal with locking John Ronald in the room while he stepped into the bathroom, Mason determined to get him outside as quickly as possible. It occurred to Mason that closed in the small room with him, the dog had made it through a full night without urinating on anything or tearing anything up. He was going to have to try that at home. Perhaps they could sleep in one of the smaller bedrooms on the main floor for a while.

The first time things had heated up between him and Tess, the taller-than-the-bed dog had stuck his cold, wet nose along the side of Mason's ass. It had been a cold jolt, and it hadn't been easy to get the inquisitive dog to stop paying attention to what was happening on the bed, but finally he'd gone back to the window and looked out into the night with a grunted sigh.

Downstairs, Mason threw on a jacket and stepped into his old boots, then leashed John Ronald. They headed out into the cold morning and down into the yard to urinate on a row of bushes together. "When in Dubuque…"

Back leg lifted as he peed a forever pee, John Ronald cocked his head in Mason's direction as if trying to understand his words. It was still an hour before the sun would be up, but the clear sky had lightened enough to make out the ground all around, and the stars were fading from east to west.

"You in the mood for a walk?"

John Ronald whined and looked toward the barn.

"Come on, not that way." Mason led him east, through two fields and out a back gate into a deep stretch of woods at one side of the property. His parents kept a well-maintained path through the woods, because his mom liked her daily walk through them, and his cousins liked to come over and ATV through them.

The woods were quiet and still, waiting for the sun.

Finally, Mason and the dog came to a different section of the creek that ran along the back edge of the property. The sky was getting lighter and lighter, and a thick blanket of steam rose off the water into the chilly morning air.

John Ronald lapped water forever, then looked up and whined.

"I know what you want. You're making your point just fine. But what if I let you go and you just keep going?"

John Ronald jumped up, pressing his front paws into Mason's chest and licking his chin.

"Easy, boy. All right, you win."

Mason asked him to sit, and once the dog did, with fear swirling in his stomach, Mason unhooked the leash.

John Ronald gave a shake of his head and darted into the middle of the creek. He dashed up and down it, then took off into the woods at a full run.

Mason closed his eyes and took in a slow, calculated breath. "Just come back, buddy."

———～～～———

There was power in his stride that the dog knew came from no longer being hungry. He ran and ran, stopping to sniff downed trees and boulders, underneath which animals had dug holes to hide. There were plants and wet, rotting leaves underfoot, and an endless array of rich, earthy smells. Some of them were so enticing that he paused for a deeper sniff.

Mostly, the dog ran and ran, savoring the new strength in his stride. He was built to run forever. He ran up hillsides and down them, along the creek, and on and on. He stopped, panting heavily, and spotted a small herd of deer watching him. He chased them deeper into the woods, on and on, until he was spent. Then he stopped, his breaths coming in giant heaves.

He returned to a new section of the creek and drank from it again, savoring the clean, sharp taste of it. He was still panting heavily when he thought of the man. Of Mason.

Even with his quicker, stronger stride than Donna's, Mason had not followed him. The dog sniffed the air, circling through the area until he caught Mason's scent on the breeze.

Mason was on the move, walking out of the woods.

The dog fell into a trot, cutting over the hillside, drawing closer and closer to Mason's scent.

Finally, the dog popped out on the trail immediately in front of him. Mason stopped walking and lifted his face toward the sky. The dog enjoyed hearing the deep rumble that meant Mason was happy.

Mason dropped low to the ground, and the dog moved in close to lick his face. He tasted the wet, salty drops that he'd tasted from time to time rolling down Donna's cheeks. But this was different. The dog understood that Mason was pleased with him, and he wanted to please him again.

He licked the drops away and remained still while Mason locked his arms tightly around his neck, trapping the dog in a new way. For a moment, the dog thought of a different man who'd long ago grabbed him by the neck and of all the things that had followed.

But that man and Mason were not the same, and today, the dog was not afraid.

Mason soon released the dog and stood tall again. John Ronald jumped up and boxed his paws on Mason's chest, then dashed in a circle. When Mason didn't follow, he ran back and did it again, boxing his paws on Mason's chest, then dashing around him in a circle.

"Okay, you want to run, let's run."

This time, when the dog took off into the woods, Mason ran along behind him. And this made the dog happy.

Chapter 27

IT ENDED UP BEING EASIER TO TELL THE SHELTER staff about Mason than Tess would have guessed. When she got back into work on Saturday, the final proof of the shelter's fall newsletter was waiting in her mailbox. Megan had paper-clipped a note on top asking Tess to proof it for errors before it went to print Monday.

On the third page was a picture of Mason taken at the beginning of October. He was standing in the front room of the shelter with Megan and Kelsey and Kurt. He'd donated money and supplies in response to the stories that had been running on the air about the dogs at the Sabrina Raven estate.

Seeing it, Tess's hair stood on end. What if she'd seen this picture before she met him? Would she have made the connection? If she'd known right from the start that Mason played for the Red Birds, would she have given him a fighting chance? And what about *him*? Would he have seen her any differently if she'd known he played for an MLB team?

Knowing her questions were no better than opening Pandora's box, Tess squelched the thoughts from her mind. There were no secrets between them now. And regardless of his high-profile profession, she'd never been so crazy about anyone.

"So, want to know something funny?" she asked

Patrick and Megan when she was done proofing the newsletter and had joined them.

They were moving the current round of cats out of the Cat-a-Climb. The Savannah cat was getting out of quarantine this morning, and since he was so full of energy, he was going to get some alone time in there to work some of it off. There was a line of volunteers and staff hoping to get a chance to play with him too. He was warming up around people a little, and Megan suspected than he wouldn't be able to resist a bout of play with anyone who walked in there with a feather duster.

"Always," Megan answered, hoisting a very overweight tabby-and-white male cat into her arms.

"It's kind of weird, but it turns out the Mason I'm dating is the Mason in this article on page three."

Patrick, who had a cat over each shoulder, stopped moving midstep. "The only Mason mentioned on page three is Mason Redding. He plays in the MLB for the Red Birds. He finished the regular season with a .340 batting average and 85 RBIs."

Tess pointed a finger. "Yep, that's the one."

Megan's jaw went slack. "Wow, Tess. I had no idea."

"Yeah, well, I didn't either. Not until the other day. I was mad at first that he didn't tell me, but I've forgiven him. He wanted me to get to know him first, and honestly, it was probably easier that way. By the time I found out, I knew him well enough not to be too intimidated by it."

"He's also number four on the list of most eligible bachelors in St. Louis this year," Patrick added, most likely having no clue that hearing it made Tess's stomach lurch.

Patrick slipped the cats into their cages and headed to the nearest computer behind the front counter. Tess was curious enough to follow him, even though she wasn't sure what he intended to do. Rather than pulling up something about Mason, Patrick pulled up the shelter's web page and scrolled down to Tess's first training video. They were going to shoot the second one early next week.

When Mason had played the video for his family at dinner two nights ago, it had had just over twenty likes and several positive comments. Tess was still getting used to seeing and hearing herself whenever it played, but she was happy that her advice seemed to be helping people.

"Sixty-three likes, and the comments seem to all be in line with the video." The line over Patrick's brow appeared as it did whenever he was working through something. Tess considered asking more but opted not to.

Megan joined them after putting the last cat away. She brushed cat hair from the cute V-necked maternity shirt that accented her boobs as much as her belly. "So, girl, that's a bit of a bomb to lay on someone. You sure you're taking it okay? What's he like in real life? He's the guy you found the puppies with? And the one who took in the stray dog?"

"Yeah, that's him. I'm adjusting. He's sweet. Really sweet. We drove up to his parents' farm in Iowa during my days off. They're good people too."

"That's good." Megan's tone was hopeful and light.

"He's coming by at the end of the day today. He wants to see the puppies since they're starting to open their eyes. Then afterward, I'm taking him by the Sabrina Raven estate to introduce him to some of the rescue dogs. His friend Georges is going to babysit John Ronald tonight since he's not good alone and Mason won't crate him. I called Kurt earlier. Mason and I are going out to dinner with him and Kelsey tonight. Since I'm closer to Kurt than to my real brother or sister, I figured I'd begin my family introductions with him. My nonna already knows him, and she's surprisingly good with us dating."

Megan leaned against the counter to stretch her back. She was due in just over a month, and Tess was excited to see whether it'd be a boy or girl. "It sounds like it's going well."

"When it's just us alone, it's easy. I'm not going to lie though. The thought of going out into the world with him makes me feel like I just swallowed a goldfish."

"Did you tell Kurt who he is?"

Tess shook her head, her ponytail swinging from side to side. "Nope. Just my boyfriend, Mason. I probably should've, I guess. Only, sometimes, jumping into the deep end of the pool is the best thing to do."

Megan smiled. "They'll adjust, though I wouldn't mind being a bird in the window at that restaurant tonight."

Chapter 28

THE NEXT WEEK AND A HALF WAS A WHIRLWIND OF WORK and play. Over lunch one day, Tess stepped out of work to renew her driver's license. She passed the driving test with nearly perfect marks. While she'd continue riding her bike when the weather was good, she'd drive Nonna's old car when it wasn't, or on days like today, Thanksgiving Day, when time was in short supply.

The shelter was closed to the public, and Tess and Patrick had come in for the morning shift. Two others would come in later for the evening shift.

Tess especially loved working with Patrick on days like today because he was great at both prioritizing and keeping on track. He'd taken on the bigger task of caring for the dogs in the kennels while she bottle-fed the now-thriving puppies and then took care of the cats.

Every Thanksgiving, Tess made sure to take time to write a long list of all the things she was thankful for. Zoe and her brothers and sisters were right near the top this year. So were Mason and John Ronald.

Since Thanksgiving with Tess's family was an all-day ordeal, starting with an early lunch and extending late into the evening, Tess hoped she and Patrick could wrap up in a few hours. Mason would be with her at Nonna's all afternoon and evening, and late tonight they were driving up to his parents' farm for a Friday Thanksgiving with his extended family.

She was more nervous about how all her cousins would act around Mason than she was about meeting the rest of his family.

While feeding and caring for the cats, Tess let the Savannah cat out of his cage to run around the front room. Now that he wasn't half-starving, his energy was over the top, and today was no different. He reminded her a bit of a Tasmanian devil in the way he played, dashing about, pouncing, arching his back, and attacking whatever was in sight. He pounced twice on curled-up, sleeping Trina. When Trina wasn't interested—she'd been play-attacked more than her fair share of times over the years—he took on Chance.

The Savannah cat couldn't hurt Chance. He was declawed in front, which was one reason he'd been so skinny when he was caught in the trap. It was difficult to impossible for a declawed cat to fend for himself in the wild. Chance, who was well into his senior years, woke up for a rough-and-tumble bout of play, and he and the Savannah cat chased each other in circles around the front room. And even though Chance couldn't see, he could find the long-legged cat immediately with his reliable sniffer wherever the cat tried to get stealthy.

Tess laughed as the exotic-looking cat hid, wriggling his hind end and tail, and pounced on Chance time and again, sending Chance into fresh scurries of his own. She couldn't wait until the naming contest underway for him wrapped up and he had a real name.

Once both cat and dog were tuckered out and Tess was finished caring for the rest of the kenneled cats, she put the Savannah cat away and headed into the back to help Patrick finish up with the dogs. Giving the dogs the care they needed was always a lengthier process. Tess had started the morning feeding the three-week-old puppies and would end it with a second feeding just before leaving. It still gave her the chills that seven puppies were alive because of John Ronald. They were full of vigor and health and had more than tripled in size since their first night here.

As she headed through the glass doors separating the dog kennels from the rest of the building, Tess found her gaze lingering on the empty kennel that until yesterday had belonged to Orzo, the short-legged corgi who was the first dog at the shelter she'd become really enamored with. Because of his gentle demeanor, Orzo had been the first dog introduced to some of the rehab dogs at the Sabrina Raven estate, and Tess had bonded with him even before starting work here.

After more than eight months at the shelter, it had begun to seem as if Orzo might be a permanent resident. Then yesterday, almost abruptly, he'd finally been adopted. Tess was happy to have been the staff member who got to oversee Orzo's adoption. During her time talking with Orzo's new family, she'd grown confident they'd be the perfect match for him.

The family who had adopted him was a family of five, an older couple and their three kids who'd been adopted from China in one fell swoop. A few months ago, the family had had to put their fifteen-year-old corgi to sleep due to her declining health. They came in not expecting to make any decisions, just to start what they expected to be an ongoing process of finding the right dog to fit into a gaping hole in their family.

However, when they'd come across Orzo, they'd

changed their minds. He was the right dog for them, and they didn't want to wait.

Tess was glad Orzo had found his forever home, one in which he'd be loved and well cared for, but she'd miss him. One of the kids had been begging her parents to hold her birthday party here, and if they agreed, the girl promised to bring Orzo back for it. Tess was hopeful it would happen.

"Who's left to go out?" she asked Patrick.

Patrick listed Fannie and six other dogs. Tess went for Fannie first, knowing the big Saint Bernard would need a good stretch of her legs and hips. Before stepping out the back door with her, Tess slipped on one of the spare jackets that hung by the door. Once outside, Fannie trotted straight for the Island of Many Smells, the gravel area at the back of the lot where dog after dog scent marked every day.

Tess zipped the jacket while Fannie sniffed and peed. The sun was shining overhead, but a cold snap had passed over the area. The high was only going to be a little above freezing today.

When Fannie was finished sniffing in the island, Tess led her along the back lot toward the edge of the building where Fannie liked to sniff the tall pines between the shelter and the jewelry store next door.

Tess had been told never to cross onto jewelry-store property, or the owner would likely call the police to complain. Apparently, the owner was a cranky old man and hadn't been on speaking terms with anyone at the shelter for years. Tess figured it was his loss, and from what she'd seen, she suspected the fact that he didn't seem to get much business was on him, not his proximity to an animal shelter as he claimed.

Fannie was midsniff on one of the tall pines when she perked her ears and looked sharply toward the front of the building. The hair on her scruff stood up, and her tail stuck up high.

"What is it, girl?" Tess craned her head, but she couldn't see beyond the side of the building. She wasn't positive, but she'd heard something coming from there that sounded like a sharp cough. She was switching the leash from one hand to the other when Fannie bolted off, tearing the leash out of Tess's fingers.

"Fannie!"

Tess ran after her, praying the excited dog didn't bolt into the street. Tess rounded the front of the building and spotted a man kneeling next to a parked car that hadn't been there a few minutes ago when she was cleaning out the cat kennels.

And Fannie was inundating his face with big, slobbery licks.

Tess stopped in her tracks. Fannie was a friendly, loving dog, but this was different. Fannie's whole body was wiggling in excitement. Tess couldn't see the man's face because it was buried in Fannie's fur and his arms were draped across her neck.

Tess's throat locked tight. Nearly four months had passed since Fannie had been found tied to a post out front. Ever since Tess had met the sweet, loving dog, she'd wondered who could've abandoned her like that.

She had a feeling she was about to find out.

Out of the corner of her eye, she saw Patrick heading around the side of the building, most likely having heard her yelling after Fannie. He was leading Circus, a two-year-old Dalmatian mix who had been surrendered last week. Tess was glad she wasn't going to have to face this man alone.

The man finally pulled his head up from Fannie's fur and saw that he had an audience. He stood up a bit unsteadily, swiping tears from his cheeks.

"I saw she was still available on your site. But I didn't let myself believe it until I got out of my car and she came running around the building. Guess you heard me, didn't you, Kona?"

Tess glanced at Patrick as he and Circus crossed the parking lot to join them. Fannie wasn't leaving the man's side. She walked around him in a circle, dragging her leash between her front legs and sniffing him as she wagged her tail. Her mouth was hanging open in a big, giant smile.

Dogs never hold a grudge. Even when they're tied to a pole and abandoned.

He was a thin, middle-aged man with salt-and-pepper hair. He had shaky hands and a pleading look on his face. "I hardly let myself hope."

"She was found almost four months ago, tied to that post. There was no note or anything."

He shook his head. "I'm sorry about that. Damn sorry. If you'll let me, I can explain."

His hand closed over top of Fannie's wide head, and she sat contentedly at his side.

Tess didn't know how to handle this, and Patrick wasn't jumping in. "Okay" was all she could think to say.

"You see, just short of two years ago, my wife of fourteen years died of cancer. It was a long, drawn-out battle and a hard one to watch. I turned to drink when I shouldn't have, and I ended up with two DUIs back to back. I thank God every day no one was hurt in the process of me coming to my senses. The ruling took a while to move through the courts, and while I was waiting, I sobered up. I haven't had a drink in seventeen months, and I'm bound and determined to never have one again. But I had a sentence to serve all the same." He stroked Fannie's ear as he talked.

"Kona's so big, it was hard to find someone who was willing to keep her. The man I left her with wasn't my first choice, but I trusted him to care for her until I got out all the same. Paid him well enough to do it too. When I got home two weeks ago, I learned he'd hightailed it out of town, and no one could say what he'd done with her. He stole some other things from me too, like my computer, but my only concern has been getting Kona back. The last few days, I've been going to the library searching online shelter adoption lists. I found her listed on your site yesterday, though it took me until today to work up the nerve to come here and see for myself. I wasn't entirely sure she'd still want me."

Any blame Tess might have wanted to place on this man had fled. "It looks like that needn't worry you anymore. She's a happy dog, but I don't think any of us have ever seen her this content." She looked over at Patrick. "What do we do?" she whispered.

"I'll pay you," the man said, having overheard. "For all the expenses you've had to face keeping her, and then some. I spent seventy-five days in jail, but I'm not destitute. I have a nice home and a big yard, and I can give her the care she needs. I always have. My wife and I, we never had kids. But Kona was as much a blessing as we ever asked for. And now it's Thanksgiving. I'd really like to spend it with my dog."

"In cases like this, we're supposed to receive proof of ownership," Patrick said, holding Circus back from Fannie and her owner.

"I have her papers in my car. I have paperwork to show you the truth of my story too, if you need it."

"We don't," Tess interjected. "Fannie... I mean, Kona's paperwork will be enough."

Patrick pulled out his keys and headed over to the front door of the shelter to unlock it. "We're closed today, but we can make the exception for you to have Thanksgiving with your dog."

Tess followed Patrick, but she stepped aside and held the door open for the man and Kona to follow them in.

"Thank you," the man said as he stepped through the door. "My name's Bill. I recognize you from the videos on your shelter's website. It's not every day a person gets this close to a practical celebrity, and I'm touched by your kindness."

Tess wasn't quite sure how to take the compliment. "Thanks, but I hardly think two dog training videos could make anyone famous."

"I was more referring to the fact that you're dating Mason Redding."

Tess's jaw went slack. How could he possibly know? "I don't...I don't understand."

"It was the number of comments on the videos that caught my attention. I figured anything that well-received was worth watching." He must have seen the astonishment she was feeling on her face because he added, "I'm sorry. I figured you knew."

Keeping Circus at his side, Patrick had headed straight for the computer and was pulling up the internet. Tess followed and peeked over his shoulder. She gasped when the videos were pulled up. The last time she'd looked, there'd been fewer than a hundred likes and a few dozen comments. Now there were several thousand likes, several hundred dislikes, and more than eight hundred comments.

Patrick frowned and drummed the fingers of one hand against the desk. "I suspected this would happen. Once the connection was made."

Tess attempted to read over Patrick's shoulder as he did a quick scroll down through the comments before abruptly shaking his head and shutting the browser window. She swallowed hard. She'd glimpsed the words *pinched face* and *beady eyes* in one, and in another, someone had called her a slut. *A slut*.

"I'll change the settings today. We can post the videos without comments enabled for a while."

"I'm sorry," Bill repeated. "My Lauren was always saying I don't know when to keep quiet. I just figured you knew."

Tess scratched the back of her neck. *Pinched face. Beady eyes. A slut.* "It's okay. I'm, uh, just glad to have the heads-up."

"I take it you know a lot about dogs," Bill said, most likely wanting to change the subject. He'd taken a seat and was running his hand down the length of Kona's back. She was leaning into it and nowhere close to leaving his side, even though he wasn't holding her to him. "I don't know much about them myself, but I've learned enough along the way to keep this girl happy. And I take my vet's advice. I figure that'll get us through."

"It should," Patrick said matter-of-factly. Without adding anything else, he headed through the doors in the back to take Circus back to his kennel.

In the sharply quiet room, Tess sorted through the adoption paperwork, only to realize her hands were shaking. *What did I ever do to get called a slut?*

Locating the correct forms, she headed over to the desk next to which Bill was sitting, doing her absolute best to put this news out of her mind. For the moment at least.

Chapter 29

CROWDED, LOUD, AND CHAOTIC. TESS HAD WARNED HIM, but Mason had figured it would be similar to the happy chaos that filled his parents' house every Thanksgiving. In a way, it was. But the commotion at Tess's grandma's house also reminded him of the press conferences he'd been to around trading day or the one after this year's All-Star game. Everyone was talking at once, and no one seemed to be paying attention to anyone else's answers.

Twenty-two adults and six kids were crowded into Fabina's thousand-square-foot house. And the noise level filling the inside proved it.

Tess had warned him not to eat a single thing before coming over. He'd listened, and when he saw the spread of food placed on the table for the first meal, he was glad he had. Tess's family practiced the two-meal Italian American Thanksgiving tradition. The first meal was Italian; the second, served four hours after the first, was the traditional American one, stuffed turkey and all.

The noon meal was a massive spread of homemade ravioli, pizza, antipasto, soup, lasagna, and stuffed artichokes. And wine. Bottomless glasses of wine. The bright, colorful food was served in even more colorful dishes and placed on a set of butter-yellow tablecloths covering a row of folding tables in the family room.

The meal began with a toast that ended in several shed tears since it was the family's first Thanksgiving without Tess's grandpa. The few minutes the big family spent sharing his stories were the only minutes of entirely audible conversation the whole meal.

During the rest of it, Mason did his best to follow one string of conversation at a time, especially when it was directed at him. Tess was crammed in at his side, and when the guys kept asking Mason his football predictions for the day, she interjected that just because he played baseball didn't mean they should be betting on his football predictions.

Throughout the meal, Tess was the brunt of a dozen vegetarian jokes, but she held her own, and Mason realized he never should have been prepared for anything else.

When it came to Tess's parents and what she'd already shared about them, Mason wasn't sure if he was reading more into it than the crowded day warranted, but although they were friendly, they also came across as particularly detached from their daughter. Fortunately, Mason also noticed the parental love shown toward Tess by several of her aunts, uncles, and cousins. And of course, there was Tess's grandma, who didn't even attempt to hide her bias for the granddaughter she'd had a large hand in raising. So, Tess hadn't been exaggerating. Rather than having a more typical mom and dad looking out for her, she had a big, massive family doing it.

Some semblance of quiet took over after the first meal was finished, and the TV was turned on to the current football game. The Kansas City Chiefs were playing the New England Patriots. Several of Tess's aunts headed into the kitchen, and a few family members stepped out to the porch to smoke.

Wine in one hand, Tess pulled Mason into her

bedroom. He'd been here a few times but had never been inside it. It was a small room, crowded with furniture loaded down with antiques, and the floor space was taken up by two well-worn twin beds covered by ancient-looking quilts.

Nothing about the room seemed to have Tess's touch. It troubled Mason that she didn't have a space of her own, but he decided to save that subject for another day.

She shut the door behind them and released a deep breath. "You survived. Other than my one cousin giving you an eye that you didn't even seem to notice, it wasn't like I feared."

"It was nice, Tess. And the food was incredible. Though I'm not sure I'll be able to eat a bite of meal number two in just a couple of hours."

She smiled. "This is my twenty-sixth Thanksgiving here. Everyone says that, and somehow everyone finds a bit more room in their stomachs. We girls just don't get on a scale for a few days."

She set her wineglass on a nightstand and stepped close, wrapping her arms around him and burying her face in his chest. Her voice was muffled, but he was still able to discern her words. "Mason, I know I came on to you first, but you don't think I'm a slut, do you?"

"Hey," he said, pulling back and lifting her chin so he could see her face. "Hell no. What's this about?"

She dug her top teeth into her lower lip and shook her head. Tears brimmed in her eyes. "It's stupid. Sticks and stones, that's all."

"Tess, someone hurt your feelings, and I'd like to know who."

She was shaking her head when her phone rang. Last

week, he'd given her a replacement for the one that had been stolen, which she'd accepted after making him promise not to buy her anything else for a long time. Mason figured that was also a conversation for another time.

"Hang on. It's Kurt. He's called twice, and I haven't picked up."

Mason waited, tension suddenly lining every muscle as Tess warded off whatever Kurt was offering. "No, Kurt, absolutely not. Thanks, but no thanks. That's the last thing the shelter needs. Besides, it's fixed now. Patrick turned off all comments. It won't happen anymore. At least not on the shelter's site. Look, I gotta go. I'll call you later."

"Oh shit, Tess," Mason said, mentally linking the dots. "We've been connected on social media, haven't we? I was hoping that by lying low, we could keep out of the spotlight."

She shrugged, slipping her phone back into her pocket. "Kurt thinks barking back at the world will shut everyone up. But I'm pretty sure all it would do is stir the pot."

"When did you find this out? And I'm doing my best not to get jealous that you confided in him before me."

"This morning, and it's not like that. This is the first second we've had alone all day, and honestly, I didn't want to unleash this on you before you stepped into the lion's den that's my family. But that guy I was talking about in there, the one who came in for Fannie today? Well, what I didn't share out there was that he said he felt like he was in the presence of a celebrity or something. I thought he was talking about the videos, but then he clarified that it was because I'm dating you."

"Oh shit, Tess. I'm sorry."

"It's not your fault, Mason. Patrick disabled the comments linked to the videos. When I left to come here, Patrick was headed to Kelsey's parents. He has Thanksgiving with them every year. I guess they're all together right now. You're getting to know Kurt, so you'll believe me when I say he's kind of like my big brother and Mr. T rolled into one."

"I won't disagree there. So, how bad is it?" He yanked out his phone and pulled up the shelter's website. Tess's two training videos were there, but the comments and likes had been disabled. Next, he went to Instagram and pulled up Tess's profile page. He'd liked a few of the pictures she'd posted of Zoe and her brothers and sisters earlier this week. Had that been enough to connect them? Or had it happened some other way?

Regardless, Tess's Instagram photos were getting thousands of likes, dislikes, and comments. He scrolled down for a few seconds. Some of the ones he read were supportive. Others were heartlessly cruel and untrue.

"Tess, can I have your Instagram password? We should freeze your account for a few weeks. And I'll clean it up before you look at it again."

She blinked. "I didn't know they'd found that too."

He pulled her in again, locking his arms around her. "It's just the transition, Tess. Things are always rocky when they're in transition."

"I know. I know that, and I'm okay. It just came as a surprise, that's all."

He pressed a kiss against her forehead. "They'll move on to someone or something else soon enough. I promise. I've seen it happen with some of my teammates when they've gotten serious about someone. Once it's obvious they're committed, the comments die down. Though if you'd be interested in jump-starting things, we could always elope."

She laughed, and he felt her shoulders relax. "No eloping, but if you're game, I have an idea that I think could help settle things down in a different way."

"Anything. Just name it."

"Thanks. It'll take a few days to get it together. But so long as you're free Sunday afternoon, come by the shelter and bring John Ronald. Whether it works, or it doesn't, at least we'll give them something more productive to talk about."

Chapter 30

WHEN THE IDEA CAME TO HER, TESS HAD PICTURED herself, Patrick, Mason, and John Ronald alone in the front room for the filming. However, as Sunday progressed, she realized that wouldn't be the case at all.

The mean jabs Tess had taken through the comments on her training videos had riled up several people. Seeing the way they were ready to rise to defend and support her, it hit Tess how perfectly she'd found her place at the High Grove Animal Shelter.

She'd come home from Europe determined to work for herself doing essentially the same thing she was doing here at the shelter. Only working here, she was part of a team. And that team was making it clear they had her back.

Megan and her stepdaughter, Sophie, one of the shelter's junior protectors, would be in the audience. Megan's husband and stepson were hoping to be able to catch the filming as well, but they'd be joining later. Also intent on showing their support were several of the volunteers, including Marv, one of the senior volunteers who worked in the gift shop several days a week, and Mia, the artist who'd helped Tess feel at ease during the first filming.

Twenty minutes before Mason was due to arrive, Kurt and Kelsey showed up from the Sabrina Raven estate to be part of the audience also. Tomorrow, the sale of the shelter's off-site property to Kurt would be official, but Tess suspected even after he owned it, people—including Kurt and Kelsey—would continue to call it by Sabrina's name for a long time to come. He and Kelsey were living there together and would continue to use the house as a training base until the last dogs were ready to come through the shelter's main doors and enter the adoption program.

"If you'd like me to get up there and say a few words, I will," Kurt said, closing a strong hand over Tess's shoulder.

Tess shook her head, laughing. "Thanks, but I've got this." To Kelsey, she added, "You can take the boy out of the military, but you can't take the military out of the boy."

Kelsey laughed along with her. "I won't argue with you there. If we have kids someday and one of them gets bullied, at least I know what's coming."

Since both Mason and John Ronald were going to be a part of this video session, Patrick thought it would be best to film them on the small training stage by the gift shop that was used for evening training classes and birthday parties.

Determining that her nerves would get the best of her if she didn't stay busy, Tess used the remaining time to set up the stage with the activities she'd prepared for John Ronald. During the video session, she intended to present ways to keep dogs like him busy when they were alone, as well as offering potty-training advice for dogs who loved to scent mark.

Suspecting the new video was going to get more views than she'd ever anticipated when she started this process, Tess had considered wearing something nicer than the basic shelter uniform—jeans and a purple shelter logo T-shirt with a long-sleeved white shirt underneath—but decided against it. She didn't add any more makeup than for the first two tapings when the world had no clue she was dating a guy high up on the list of St. Louis's most eligible bachelors.

The truth was, the people who were determined not to like her wouldn't care whether she was dolled up. And Tess wasn't doing this to win a popularity contest. This video was about a dog. A remarkable dog who'd not only brought her and Mason together, but who'd also saved the lives of seven remarkable puppies. He was stubborn and willful too, and Mason had his hands full getting the free-roaming stray to adjust to the life of a domesticated dog. This made John Ronald the perfect candidate for her training series.

And if people were going to talk about her and Mason anyway, they might as well see a larger slice of the truth and hopefully become inspired.

Tess had just finished placing items on and behind the stage when she spotted Mason's big, red truck pulling into the lot. To her surprise, he wasn't alone. And it wasn't Georges who was with him.

She studied the passenger as he got out, wondering if he was one of Mason's teammates, and if she'd recognize him if he was.

"I didn't know they knew each other," Megan said, meeting Tess halfway across the room. Mason was getting John Ronald out of the back, and the guy was walking around to join them. "What a connected world."

"Who is he?"

"That's Ben, the architect who designed some of our renovations. The one everyone talks about because he summited Everest this spring." Megan looked around the room, finally nodding toward Mia, who was unwrapping a new shipment of ceramic paw-print frames in the gift shop. "Mia made the introduction. He and her, uh, husband are friends."

Tess nodded, understanding Megan's hesitation. Tess had heard Mia was separated and filing for divorce, though she seemed to be taking it okay.

Just before Mason reached for the door, Sophie, the junior protector who was walking around with a purring Trina draped over her neck, let out a gasp that penetrated the room. "Oh, wow. He looks just like he does in the poster on my brother's wall."

Tess's belly flipped. These sorts of comments would take some getting used to. So would people stopping them on the street to ask for an autograph when they were just walking a couple blocks for a cup of coffee.

It wasn't that these events made her see Mason differently. It was that she'd never imagined loving anyone who had to deal with being placed on a pedestal by the masses. It made her worry about things like bad seasons and off days and injuries. The Mason that Sophie was seeing belonged to St. Louis culture. And for good or bad, Tess was determined to be there for the real man underneath all the hype and help him through it whenever he needed it.

As soon as the two guys and John Ronald were through the door, John Ronald spotted Trina draped across Sophie's neck and began to lunge and bark, taking the attention off the fact that a Red Birds player was walking into the shelter.

Typically unfazed by overexcitable dogs, Trina

hissed and twitched her tail from atop her perch, and John Ronald growled back. Trina jumped down from Sophie's neck and up onto a counter where she arched her back and hissed a second time.

John Ronald let out a single high-pitched bark before turning his attention to the small crowd of people filling the shelter's front room at five o'clock on a Sunday. Tess introduced Mason to the volunteers and staff that he'd not yet met and shook Ben's hand a minute later.

Ben was a few inches shorter than Mason—but then again, almost everyone was shorter than Mason—and had short, dark hair and dark eyes framed by thick lashes. While he was friendly enough, Ben seemed to have a reserved, quiet air about him that didn't match up with Mason's almost always playful one. Tess wondered what they had in common but figured she'd learn soon enough.

Patrick, with GoPro in hand, was the first of the group to get to business. "I'll shoot from a few different angles, but mostly from the tripod. When Tess's training session is over, we're going to film John Ronald being reintroduced to the puppies in the new playroom. We'll use that footage in more than just this video series. And I'm hoping to get a shot with all of them together that's good enough for the cover of our next calendar. The cover picture is as much about the story as it is the photo, and John Ronald's story is cover-worthy."

John Ronald, who'd been growing more and more attached to Tess, pulled toward her and jumped up to lick her chin, which was an easy reach on legs as long as his. Tess buried her face in his muzzle and scratched behind his ears. When she pulled away, she batted at the loose fur she'd sent flying in the air. "You know,

Patrick, if I've ever met a dog with a more cover-worthy story, I can't recall it."

After a blur of last-minute activity as her friends took their seats and Patrick flipped on a giant, soft light box he'd just purchased for filming the ongoing series, Tess smoothed the front of her shirt, reaffirming it was still tucked evenly into the waist of her jeans. One hand bumped against the buckeye in her pocket as she did. She pulled it out and ran her thumb across the smooth, shiny nut.

It's just a nut. And you know full well luck is what you make of it.

Without drawing anyone's attention, Tess jogged over to where Trina was perched. A bit uncharacteristically, the cat was still eyeing John Ronald and twitching her tail. Tess plopped the nut in front of her and gave her a quick scratch on the silky fur along her cheek.

"I bet you'll have some fun with this. I don't need it anymore."

A few minutes later, Tess found herself onstage facing an intimate audience, a camera, and a bright light. Seated on a stool next to her was a strapping celebrity that presumably a whole city of people wanted to cheer for, or sleep with, or hang pictures of on their walls.

She swallowed hard and pushed away a fleeting fear that she wouldn't remember a single thing she wanted to say. But then Mason gave her a small, discreet wink, and John Ronald barked at Trina as the cat swatted the buckeye across the counter, and Tess's fear fell away.

She started with basics, sticking to the same script used to begin the previous two videos, introducing herself and reviewing the purpose of the video series. Then she introduced Mason, saying his first and last name, but opting not to mention what he did for a living. People would either know or they wouldn't, and that wasn't Tess's business.

Right before Tess was ready to introduce him, John Ronald, who'd been sitting at attention at Mason's side, pawed the treat-dispensing dog puzzle on the floor in front of him. He also let out a gigantic woof that resounded through the building, as if declaring he was ready for his part.

After that, all Tess really needed to say was that she and Mason had gotten together because of a dog. And ever since then, things had been falling into place. For all three of them.

Mason's Vegetarian Meat Loaf

Ingredients

- 1 cup (dry) brown lentils (about 3 cups cooked)
- 8 ounces baby portabella mushrooms, diced
- 1 large yellow onion, diced
- 1 green bell pepper, diced
- 4 garlic cloves, minced
- 2 carrots, shredded
- 2 tablespoons olive oil
- Salt and pepper
- ¾ cup walnuts, finely chopped
- 1 cup flour
- 1 cup panko bread crumbs
- 2 tablespoons dried oregano
- 2 tablespoons dried thyme
- 1 tablespoon dried parsley
- 2 eggs, beaten
- 4 tablespoons tomato paste
- 3 tablespoons vegan Worcestershire sauce (or substitute with your own preference for Worcestershire)

Balsamic Glaze

- ⅓ cup ketchup
- 4 tablespoons balsamic vinegar
- 1 tablespoon maple syrup

Directions

Preheat the oven to 375°F, and line two regular or one long loaf pan(s) with parchment paper.

Cook the dry lentils per package directions; using vegetable broth instead of water will boost flavor. When they're cooked, strain the lentils and place them in a large bowl.

Finely chop the mushrooms, onion, green pepper, and garlic (preferably with a food processor) and shred the carrots, keeping the vegetables separated. Heat the olive oil in a large skillet on medium and add the onion and garlic. Sprinkle with salt and pepper, then cook for 2 to 3 minutes. Add the mushrooms, carrots, and green pepper, then cook until soft. Remove from heat and set aside.

Mash half of the lentils, then add them back into the bowl along with the remaining lentils and the sautéed vegetables. Process the walnuts to very finely chopped, then add to the bowl along with the flour, bread crumbs, oregano, thyme, and parsley.

In a small bowl, mix together the eggs, tomato paste, and Worcestershire sauce, and then add to the lentil mixture. Stir together, and pour the mixture evenly into the loaf pan(s), then smooth the top(s) with a spatula.

Combine ketchup, balsamic vinegar, and maple syrup in a small bowl and mix well. Spread the mixture evenly over the loaf or loaves, then bake for 40 to 45 minutes. Allow to cool for 10 minutes before serving. Great with mushroom gravy and mashed potatoes.

Tess's Pumpkin Peanut Butter Dog Treats

Ingredients

- 2 cups flour (stoneground wheat or choice of flour)
- ½ cup rolled oats
- 2 eggs, beaten
- 1 cup canned pumpkin
- 4 tablespoons peanut butter
- ½ teaspoon ground cinnamon
- ½ teaspoon salt

Directions

Preheat oven to 350°F.

Mix all ingredients together a bowl. The dough should be dry and thick. Roll the dough out until it is ½ inch thick. Cut into treats using dog- or bone-shaped cookie cutters.

Bake on an ungreased cookie sheet in the preheated oven until the treats are hard, 15 to 40 minutes depending on the size of the treats. Allow them to cool and further harden before giving them to a dog.

If you love heart-warming, animal-friendly contemporary romance like Debbie Burns's My Forever Home, *you'll love the world of Laurel Kerr's* Where the Wild Hearts Are *series.*

Read on for a look at Book 1:

Wild on my Mind

The increasingly insistent squeaks broke through Katie Underwood's intense concentration. Cocking her head to the side, she paused in her drawing. The chirping grew more and more demanding, the sound bouncing off the sandstone rocks surrounding her. At first, Katie thought a flock of birds was scolding her for invading their sanctuary, but she didn't spot any flying overhead in the waning light.

She started to turn back to her sketchbook, intent on taking advantage of the last rays before the sun dipped below the horizon, but something stopped her. The squeaking had the plaintive quality of an animal calling for help, and Katie had never been able to resist a wounded critter. Shoving her art supplies in her backpack, she followed the direction of the sound. Climbing a few feet above the ledge where she'd been sketching, she realized the cries originated from a cave that she remembered from childhood games with her four brothers.

Dropping to her hands and knees, Katie peered inside the crevice, wishing she had a flashlight. The pearly glow of twilight barely reached the back of the small alcove. She would have crawled inside, but both cougars and wolves haunted this sandstone promontory. As much as Katie loved wild creatures, she did not wish to encounter a wounded predator in a tight space.

Once her eyes finally adjusted to the gloom, Katie's heart simply melted. Tucked into a corner lay three squirming cougar cubs. One of the disgruntled fluffs chose that exact moment to howl its displeasure. A tiny pink mouth, framed by delicate whiskers, opened wide as the kit mewed in frustration. Katie could just barely make out the black spots peppering its grayish-brown fur.

She started to crawl forward and then stopped. Katie didn't know what would happen if she got her scent on the little guys. Resting on her haunches, she debated her next step. The mother might return, but Katie couldn't shake the feeling that the kits were either orphaned or abandoned. A neighboring rancher had recently been complaining about attacks on his livestock by pumas, which is what he called cougars or mountain lions, and he'd been known to shoot them in the past.

Katie reached for her cell phone. No signal. She would need to climb down to the old homestead and use the landline. Before she left, Katie stared back into the crevice where the cubs clumsily toddled in search of milk. "Don't worry, babies," she promised. "I'll be back with help."

As Bowie Wilson made the sharp turn onto the old Hallister spread, the suspension of his ancient pickup groaned loudly. He had a hell of a time keeping the vehicle running. The zoo sorely needed a new truck, but funds were tight and getting worse. They'd barely staved off foreclosure this past winter, and attendance hadn't picked up this spring. They were down to just a handful of volunteers and staff—a far cry from the animal park's heyday.

Pulling up to the old homestead, Bowie cut the engine and turned to wake his passenger, the former owner of the zoo. The eighty-year-old had fallen asleep on the twenty-minute drive to the ranch. Bowie had debated whether to bring Lou, since the older man generally headed to bed about now. But, unlike Bowie, Lou was a trained vet, and he could immediately start treatment on the cubs if they were seriously dehydrated or malnourished.

As Bowie waited for Lou to descend from the pickup, the front door to the old ranch house banged open. A woman, backlit by the porch light, waved. Although Bowie couldn't make out her features, he could easily spot the flash of her fiery-red hair. As she stepped out of the brightness and moved closer, the moonlight washed over her and gently illuminated her face. Her brown eyes widened at the sight of him.

Bowie couldn't quite read her emotion. Shock? Dismay? Recognition? Considering the size of their town, the latter was likely, but despite the fact that she seemed vaguely familiar, he couldn't place her. And he was pretty certain he'd remember a woman like her: all curly auburn hair, curves in the right places, and expressive chocolate-brown eyes. She exuded an earthy sexiness that appealed to him, awakening sensations that had lain dormant for far too long. Between his responsibilities as a single dad with an eleven-year-old daughter and his duties at the zoo, Bowie hadn't been with a woman in years.

Unfortunately, he had no time to appreciate this one. At least not now. Not with abandoned cougar cubs to rescue.

The woman focused her attention on Lou. "My parents are inside if you want to wait with them. It's a pretty difficult climb to the cubs."

Lou thanked her and headed to the homestead. The woman waited until he had disappeared into the house before she whirled back to Bowie. She thrust a head-lamp in his direction, smacking his chest in the process.

"Here, take this. You'll need it to see," she bit out before she turned and strode gracefully toward the rock promontory silhouetted against the starry sky. Something about her gait reminded him of an Amazon warrior. An irate one. Although he'd spent most of his youth with adults angry at him—some with cause, some without—Bowie wasn't accustomed to facing a hot blast of fury anymore. He lived a quiet life now, and he had no idea what he could've done to upset this particular woman. It would be his crappy luck that the one female who attracted him also instinctually hated his guts.

When the woman reached the base of the rock forma-tion, she bounded up the lower boulders with the sure-footedness of a mountain goat. Even if she had taken an immediate dislike to him, Bowie found his eyes follow-ing her lithe shape in the dim light. She moved with a combination of fluidity and unbound energy that made him wonder what she'd be like in bed.

Forcing those unprofessional thoughts from his mind, he concentrated on finding footholds. It wasn't easy keep-ing pace. His reluctant guide clambered up the cliff almost as quickly as she walked. Bowie figured she must know the land pretty well, since only moonlight illuminated the landscape, and she hadn't turned on her headlamp.

"I guess you've climbed here before," he said.

She nodded, but she still didn't seem too happy.

"Yes. My mom's folks, the Hallisters, lived out here, so I grew up playing on these rocks with my brothers. My parents moved out here after my dad's retirement."

That could explain why she looked vaguely familiar,

but not her anger toward him. Perhaps he'd seen her around as a kid when she'd visited her relatives. She looked close to Bowie's age, and in his early teens, he'd worked on a ranch nearby. That was until he'd broken his leg and the rancher, who'd been his foster parent, had thrown him right back into the system. Bowie had never known a real home before Lou and his late wife, Gretchen, had taken him in after yet another guardian had kicked him out on his eighteenth birthday when the reimbursement checks stopped.

Deciding to try one more time to befriend the woman, Bowie asked, "So did you come to Sagebrush Flats a lot as a kid?"

She gave a snort of patent disgust. Even though the climb had just become more difficult, the woman picked up speed. Confused as hell, Bowie had no choice but to follow her up the cliff.

———

If the lives of baby cougars hadn't hung in balance, Katie would have left Bowie Wilson stranded on the rocks until morning. After all, he'd done a lot worse to her back in high school. And despite all his horrible pranks, he'd apparently forgotten that she had ever existed. That angered Katie more than anything. With all that Bowie had made her endure, she deserved at least a sliver of room in his memory. Even after high school graduation, she would wake up in her dorm, dreaming of her old classmates laughing at her. Because of Bowie.

Oh, she knew Bowie was the mastermind behind all the awful tricks. His high school girlfriend, Sawyer Johnson, might have taunted Katie since elementary school, but it had never amounted to more than snide and not very clever remarks before Sawyer had started dating Bowie. Sure, some of Sawyer's comments had hurt, but they hadn't scarred and certainly hadn't caused the all-consuming humiliation that Bowie's pranks had.

And what horrible thing had Katie done to Bowie to warrant such malicious attention?

She'd had the temerity to form an innocent, school-girl crush on him. That was all.

Katie had never even acted on her feelings. She doubted that Bowie would ever have noticed her if Sawyer hadn't pointed out Katie's secret infatuation. Through the years, Katie had never been able to figure out exactly why Bowie had decided to target her so viciously. Sawyer had never liked Katie, and Bowie might have just enjoyed making other people suffer. Either way, she'd become his favorite mark. And it had all started in the worst way possible.

Bowie had duped Katie into believing that he returned her feelings. For two weeks, Katie had lived in euphoric bliss, oblivious to the fact that Bowie was dating Sawyer. In retrospect, Katie should have realized that the cute bad boy would have had no interest in the nerdy girl. However, teen TV shows told a different story, and she'd stupidly believed the fantasy they peddled.

Which was how Bowie had managed to trick Katie into kissing a pig in the janitor's closet. Even worse, Sawyer had filmed the entire horrifying episode and slipped a clip of Katie puckering up to the hog into the student-run morning announcement program that ran on the televisions anchored at the front of each homeroom. For the rest of her high school career, she'd become known as "Katie the Pig-Kisser." That is, if they weren't calling her the oh-so-creative "Katie Underwear," a name Sawyer had coined in the first grade.

When Katie had left Sagebrush for college twelve years ago, she'd been more than happy to leave high school behind. Unfortunately, her escape hadn't turned out quite as she'd dreamed. She'd planned to become an artist, maybe in New York, LA, or even Tokyo. Instead, she'd traded a small town with tumbleweed for one with trees. Worse, she'd found herself the oddball out again in the male-dominated mulch plant in Minnesota where she'd worked designing packaging and performing the secretarial tasks that her boss assigned to her instead of her more junior male counterpart.

All told, it hadn't been hard to quit her job when her father, a retired police officer, was shot by an ex-con, Eddie Driver. Even if Sagebrush didn't offer many career opportunities, Katie's family had needed her. Her mother had never handled crises well, despite being the wife of a former chief of police, and Katie's four brothers couldn't handle their mother in a crisis.

Unfortunately, Katie hadn't counted on running into Bowie again. As wild as he'd been as a teenager, she'd figured he would have left their dusty hometown long ago. But it appeared that he hadn't. She knew one thing for certain, though. After publicly humiliating her and effectively ending any chance of her dating anyone else in high school, Bowie Wilson had simply and utterly forgotten her.

"Uh, ma'am? Where exactly are we headed?"

Ma'am? Really? Although she supposed it was better than Katie Underwear.

"Up."

"I see that, but where did the mother cougar leave her cubs?" The patience in Bowie's tone irritated Katie even more. How dare he act like he was the rational one?

She whipped around to glare at him. Even in the harsh light of the LED lantern, Bowie was a handsome man.

"We're headed to a cave," she bit out.

Twelve years ago, Bowie could have doubled for a teenage heartthrob with the shock of jet-black hair that had always dangled over his piercing gray eyes. Now, with that hair neatly trimmed and a five-o'clock stubble dusting his jaw, he looked like a model posing for an outdoor magazine. As an immature youth, he'd possessed a bad boy prettiness that appealed to girls—even self-proclaimed geeks like her. The years had toughened his features, hardening his male beauty into something more alluring and dangerous, even to a woman who should have known better.

Much better. Darn the man if he still didn't have the capacity to make Katie's hormones dance a happy little jig.

She steamed. If time hadn't mattered, she might have taken them on a more difficult path. Even then, she doubted that it would have fazed Bowie. Despite never climbing on this particular rock face before, the man moved like a machine. She could just imagine his muscular forearm extending as he reached for the next hold. His bicep would flex as he hoisted his body…

Katie cursed at herself. Sometimes she found her vivid imagination more of a burden than a gift. It had certainly brought her more difficulties than successes.

Thankfully, they quickly arrived at the small cave.

Katie started inside, but a warm hand rested on her shoulder. Even through the fabric of her T-shirt, she could feel Bowie's heat and the strength of his fingers. An unbidden shiver slid through her.

"Let me go first." Bowie's breath caressed the sensitive skin on the back of Katie's neck, and she had to fight to suppress another shudder. "The mother cougar may have returned."

Bowie dropped to his knees and used the light from his headlamp to scan the cave before crawling inside. With his larger frame, it took him a few seconds to wiggle through the narrow passage. As soon as Bowie moved far enough into the alcove for Katie to enter, she crawled over to the cubs. They moved clumsily about, searching for milk and their mother's warmth. One yawned. Its tiny whiskers flexed as it emitted a long squeak. The others followed suit. Katie's heart squeezed. She resisted the urge to gather the little fluffs against her chest. She still didn't know the protocol on handling kits this small, and she didn't want to harm one inadvertently.

"Their eyes aren't even open yet!" she said.

Bowie nodded. "Nor are their ears at this stage. They must be less than ten days old." The awe in his voice caused Katie to turn sharply in his direction. He appeared just as infatuated with the cubs as she was. Was this the same man who'd once tied granny panties to the undercarriage of her car along with the sign HONK IF YOU SEE MY UNDERWEAR?

Bowie reached for one of the mewling cubs and cradled it against his muscular chest. The little guy burrowed against him, and Katie's hormones went crazy again. Just when she thought the scene couldn't get any sweeter, the kit yawned, showing its miniature pink tongue. Then with one more nuzzle against Bowie's pecs, it heaved a surprisingly large sigh as it fell asleep. Bowie's handsome features softened into a gentle smile as he stroked the baby cougar's spotted fur with one callused finger.

If Katie hadn't suffered years of Bowie's cruel teasing, she would have found herself halfway in love with him. He'd appeared to be the ideal boyfriend once before, but it had all been a veneer, the perfect trap for a geeky girl with silly dreams of romance. And Katie, the woman, would not fall prey to his outward charms again.

"Can I pick up one of the cougars too?" The cuteness of the cub would serve as a nice distraction from her unwanted feelings.

Bowie nodded. "They'll need to be hand-reared, so they're going to end up imprinting on humans anyway. Unfortunately, we won't be able to reintroduce them to the wild, but we can save them."

Katie lifted one of the furry bundles, marveling at the softness of its fur. The little guy emitted a small, contented sound and immediately snuggled against Katie's warmth. She could feel a cold, teeny nose against her skin as the cub rested its head in the crook of her arm. And right then and there, Katie fell in love. With the tiny kit. Definitely not with the man.

Although she hated putting the baby puma down, she knew the little trio needed more than just a warm cuddle. "Did you bring something to carry the cubs back down the mountain with?"

Bowie grimaced and shook his head. "I didn't know the climb would be so steep."

And, Katie realized, she hadn't given him time to grab something from his truck either. To her surprise, Bowie was too polite to point that out.

"Do you want me to run back to the house to get a backpack?" she asked.

Bowie shook his head. "We'll have to improvise. I'm not sure how long the cubs have been without milk, and we need to get them out of this cave as soon as possible."

Katie scanned the dirt floor of the alcove and saw nothing—not even a twig. She turned back to ask Bowie what he planned on using and stopped. He was halfway out of his shirt. Normally, Katie wouldn't blatantly ogle a man, but…those abs. And pecs. His biceps flexed as he ripped his shirt down the middle so it made one thick band. Bowie Wilson might be just as bad for Katie as an entire carton of rocky road ice cream, but he looked just as temptingly scrumptious.

Bowie froze as he lifted his head and found the auburn-haired woman watching him as if she wanted to lick him all over. Something equally hot and elemental whipped through him. He'd never had this much of a visceral response to any woman. If it weren't for the baby mountain lions, he might have been crazy enough to accept her unspoken offer…even if he didn't know whether she'd jump him or push him down the cliff.

The lady—who he'd mentally taken to calling Red—might be showing an attraction to his body, but she didn't appear to like him. At all. She reminded him a bit of the zoo's honey badger, Fluffy—all snarls, bad temper, and teeth. In the wild, Fluffy's relatives were known to take

down king cobras, and Bowie couldn't shake the feeling
that Red viewed him as one giant snake.

Still, Red had looked soft, sweet even, while cud-
dling the runt of the litter against her breasts. Sugar
and spice—that was Red. And damn if the combination
didn't intrigue him.

As a single father, Bowie should know better than
to lust after a woman who was all fire one moment and
pure honey the next. If he ever started dating seriously,
he'd need an even-tempered partner who could handle
the ups and downs of parenthood. He'd already dated
one female chimera and learned a lesson about falling
for someone with a dual personality. His high school
girlfriend, Sawyer, had been classy and elegant with an
outward poise that had impressed and intimidated the
hell out of his teenage self. But inside, she had a childish
mean streak that could strike at any time. She had never
wanted anything to do with their daughter, and for that,
Bowie was actually grateful. He loved his baby girl and
wanted to protect her from the Sawyers of the world for
as long as possible.

"Is that going to work?" Red asked, jerking her head
toward his ruined T-shirt. She still snuggled the kit to
her breasts as she peered at him.

"It should," Bowie said, withdrawing his Leatherman
from his pocket. He cut two slices near the bottom of
his shirt and then tore them off to use as bindings.
With the zoo's piss-poor budget, he'd learned to find
creative solutions with the supplies on hand. Within
a few moments, he had jerry-rigged a semblance of
a bag. He tested it with a few rocks first. Satisfied it
would hold three pounds' worth of wiggling cubs, he

carefully placed the babies inside, including the one in Red's arms.

"You always were smart."

Bowie glanced up at Red. That hadn't sounded like a compliment, but it wasn't the only thing that confused him. She certainly acted like she knew him, but he still couldn't place her.

"How do we know each other?" he finally asked. She glared, looking every inch like an irate Fluffy during one of his particularly bad moods.

"Think a little harder."

Somewhere, a memory flickered. A fleeting glimpse of red hair. But then the recollection floated away, out of reach. Bowie shook his head. "Sorry, ma'am. You seem familiar, I promise, but I just can't remember from where."

Rather than mollify Red, his words only fanned the flames shooting from her eyes. Still on her haunches, she spun around and then scrambled out of the cave. Sighing, he gathered his bundle of cubs and followed.

Acknowledgments

Two years ago, when I began the Rescue Me series, I was already an owner of two adopted shelter dogs. The everyday stories I've encountered while researching the lives of shelter dogs and cats for this series have made me an even stronger proponent of the remarkable work done by shelters and foster agencies across the country. St. Louis, like most cities, has its share of stray cats and dogs, many of whom have stories similar to the animals in this series.

Although John Ronald is fictional, the rough times he encounters are faced by many city-dwelling strays. Every week, dedicated rescue workers comb streets and abandoned buildings with the intent of capturing free-roaming strays, healing them, and helping connect them with caring new owners. Remarkable work is accomplished by organizations like Stray Rescue of St. Louis, Gateway Pet Guardians, and St. Louis Feral Cat Outreach, and I am donating a portion of my proceeds from *My Forever Home* to St. Louis–based shelters.

I want to thank Deb Werksman, my editor at Sourcebooks Casablanca, for helping to make this series ever stronger with her guidance. Deb, your insight has been invaluable, and it means a lot that you love John Ronald, Tess, and Mason as much as I do. In addition to Deb, there's an entire team at Sourcebooks and Sourcebooks Casablanca who played a part in shaping

My Forever Home into a book ready for readers' hands, and they have my gratitude. I also thank my agent, Jess Watterson, at Sandra Dijkstra Literary Agency, for her constant support.

On a local level, I have several people to thank for helping me "keep it real." Thanks to Ann Holmes, baseball and Cardinals guru, for her baseball stats. Thanks to Sandy Thal and Theresa Schmidt for insightful beta reads of *My Forever Home*. My thanks also goes out to my family for their tireless support and cheerleading along the busy and sometimes daunting road of writing for publication. I especially thank my teens, Emily and Ryan. Emily, who learned the city streets surrounding Ballpark Village while driving carriages, helped me connect with real places in which I imagined Mason living and John Ronald roaming. Ryan deserves credit for all things car in my books and for helping me find the best little sandwich shop in the Hill.

Finally, I'd like to thank Rescue Me series readers for the rescue stories of their own that they've shared. Together, we're making a difference.

About the Author

Debbie Burns lives in St. Louis with her family, two phenomenal rescue dogs, and a somewhat tetchy Maine coon cat who everyone loves anyway. Her hobbies include hiking, gardening, and daydreaming, which, of course, always lead to new story ideas.

Debbie's writing commendations include a Starred Review from *Publishers Weekly* and a Top Pick from *RT Book Reviews* for *A New Leash on Love*, as well as first-place awards for short stories, flash fiction, and longer selections.

You can find her on Twitter @_debbieburns, on Facebook at facebook.com/authordebbieburns, on Instagram at _debbieburns, and at authordebbieburns.com.

Also by Debbie Burns

RESCUE ME
A New Leash on Love
Sit, Stay, Love